THE WIZARD FROM NOWHERE

As he looked at the abandoned cabin, Rudy thought the sunlight was playing tricks on him. Then, as he shaded his eyes, he couldn't tell what it was. A line of brightness widened in front of him. He had the impression that air, cabin, and California hills were being folded aside to reveal piercing light, blinding darkness, and swirling colors beyond.

Through the gap, a dark form stumbled. Then the blazing vision was gone. There remained only an old man in a brown robe, holding a gleaming, smoking sword in one hand and a wailing baby in the other arm.

Rudy blinked. "Who in hell are you? And where—?"

The old man sheathed the sword in one smooth, competent gesture. "I came through the Void and am called Ingold Inglorion. This is Altir Endorion, last Prince of the House of Dare."

By Barbara Hambly
Published by Ballantine Books:

DRAGONSBANE

THE LADIES OF MANDRIGYN
THE WITCHES OF WENSHAR

THE SILENT TOWER
THE SILICON MAGE*

The Darwath Trilogy
THE TIME OF THE DARK
THE WALLS OF AIR
THE ARMIES OF DAYLIGHT

SEARCH THE SEVEN HILLS

*Forthcoming

The Time Of The Dark

Barbara Hambly

A Del Rey Book

BALLANTINE BOOKS • NEW YORK

For Laurie

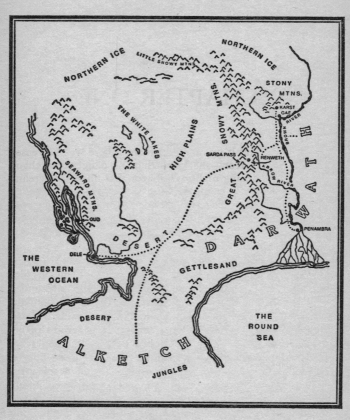

The Reaches of the Dark

CHAPTER ONE

Gil knew that it was only a dream. There was no reason for her to feel fear—she knew that the danger, the chaos, the blind, sickening nightmare terror that filled the screaming night were not real; this city with its dark, unfamiliar architecture, these fleeing crowds of panic-stricken men and women who shoved her aside, unseeing, were only the vivid dregs of an overloaded subconscious, wraiths that would melt with daylight.

She knew all this; nevertheless, she was afraid.

She seemed to be standing at the foot of a flight of green marble stairs, facing into a square courtyard surrounded by tall peak-roofed buildings. Fleeing people were shoving past her, jostling her back against the gigantic pedestal of a malachite statue, without seeming to be aware of her presence at all; gasping, wild-eyed people, terrified faces bleached to corpses by the brilliance of the cold quarter moon. They were pouring out of the gabled houses, the men clutching chests or bags of money, the women jewels, lap-dogs, or children crying in uncomprehending terror. Their hair was wild from sleep, for it was deep night; some of them were dressed but many were naked, or tripping over bedclothes hastily snatched, and Gil could smell the rank terror-sweat of their bodies as they brushed against her. None of them saw her, none of them stopped; they stumbled frantically up those vast steps of moonlit marble, through the dark arch of the gates at the top, and out into the clamoring streets of the stricken city beyond.

What city? Gil wondered confusedly. *And why am I afraid? This is only a dream.*

But she knew. In her heart she knew, as things are known in dreams, that this scene of frenzied escape was even now being repeated, like the hundredfold reflections in a doubled mirror, everywhere in the city around her. The knowledge and the horror created a chill that crept along her skin, crawled wormlike through her guts.

They all felt it, too. For not a man would stop to lean on the pillar behind her, nor a woman stumble on the steps at her feet. They looked back with the blank, wide eyes of madness, their frenzied gaze drawn as if against their will to the cyclopean doors of ancient time-greened bronze that dominated the wall opposite. It was from these that they fled. It was behind this monstrous trapezoidal gateway that the horror was building, as water builds behind a weakening dam a soft, shifting, bodiless evil, an unspeakable eruption into the land of the living from out of black abysses of space and time.

There was motion, and voices, in the cavern of the arched gateway behind her, muffled footfalls and the thin, ringing whine of a sword as it was drawn. Gil turned, her thick hair tangling in her eyes. The wild, jumping dance of wind-bent torches silhouetted crowding forms, flickering across a face, a blade-edge, the dull pebbled gleam of chain mail. Against the thinning tide of desperate civilians, the Guards stepped into the cool pewter monochrome of the moonlight—black-uniformed, lightly mailed, booted, men and women both, the honed blades of their weapons shining thinly against the play of the shadows. Gil could catch a glimpse of a nervous rabble of hastily armed civilians massing up behind them, whispering in dread and fumbling with unpracticed hands at the hilts of borrowed armament, grim fear fighting terrified bewilderment in their half-seen faces. And striding down ahead of them all was an old man in a brown robe, an old wizard, hawk-eyed and bearded and bearing a sword of flame.

It was he who stopped on the top step, scanning the court before him like a hunting eagle while the last of the fleeing, half-naked populace streamed raggedly up the stairs past Gil, brushing against her, unseeing, past the wizard, past the Guards, bare feet slapping hollowly in the black passage of the gates. She saw him fix his gaze on the doors,

2

knowing the nature of that eldritch unseen horror, knowing from whence it would come. The battered, nondescript face was serene behind the tangled chaparral of beard. Then his gaze shifted, judging his battleground, and his eyes met hers.

He could see her. She knew it instantly, even before his eyes widened in startled surprise. The Guards and volunteers, hesitating behind the old man, unwilling to go where he was not ahead of them, were looking around and through and past her, dubiously seeking the wizard's vision in the suddenly still moonlight of the empty court. But he could see her, and she wondered confusedly why.

Across the court, from the cracks and hinges of those timeless doors, a thin, directionless wind had begun to blow, stirring and whispering over the silver-washed circles of the pavement, tugging at Gil's coarse black hair. It carried on it the dank, cold scent of evil, of acid and stone and things that should never see light, of blood and darkness. But the wizard sheathed the gleaming blade he held and came cautiously down the steps toward her, as if he feared to frighten her.

But that, Gil thought, would not be possible—and anyway she was only dreaming. He looked like a gentle old man, she thought. His eyes, blue and bright and very fierce, held in them neither pride nor cruelty, and if he were afraid of the shifting, sightless thing welling in darkness behind the doors, he did not show it. He advanced to within a few feet of where she stood shivering in the green shadows of the monstrous statue, those blue eyes puzzled and wary, as if trying to understand what he saw. Then he held out his hand and made as if to speak.

Abruptly, Gil woke up—but not in her bed.

For a moment she didn't know where she was. She threw out her hand awkwardly, startled and disoriented, as those suddenly wakened are, and the cold fluted marble of the pedestal's edge bit savagely into her palm. The night's damp cold knifed her bare legs, froze her naked feet on the pavement. The cries of fear from the night-gripped city came to her suddenly clearer on the wind, and with them the elusive scent of water. For an instant, the shrieking horror of what lay behind the doors was like a gripping hand at her throat, and then it sank, whirled

3

away like leaves in the face of shock and confusion and even greater horror.

She had waked up.

She was no longer dreaming.

She was still there.

All the eyes were on her now; startled, uncertain, even afraid. The warriors, still gathered at the top of the broad polished steps, stared in surprise at this thin young woman, dark-haired and scantily clad in the green polka-dot cowboy shirt that she habitually wore to bed, who had so suddenly appeared in their midst. Gil stared back, clutching for support the sharp edge of the marble behind her, weak with shock and frantic with bewilderment and dread, her legs shaking and her breath strangling in her throat.

But the wizard was still there, and she realized that it was impossible to be truly afraid when she was with him.

Quietly, he asked her, "Who are you?"

To her own surprise she found the voice to answer. "Gil," she said. "Gil Patterson."

"How did you come here?"

Around them the black wind blew stronger from the doors, rank and cold and vibrant with brooding abhuman lusts. The Guards murmured among themselves, tension spreading along the line, visible as the humming quiver of a tautened wire—they, too, were afraid. But the wizard didn't stir, and the mellow, scratchy warmth of his voice was unshaken.

"I—I was dreaming," Gil stammered. "But—this—I—it isn't a dream anymore, is it?"

"No," the old man said kindly. "But don't be afraid." He raised his scarred fingers and made some movement in the air with them that she could not clearly see. "Go back to your dreams."

The night's cold faded as the cloying haziness of sleep blurred sound and smell and fear. Gil saw the Guards peer with startled eyes at the blue, flickering shadows that she knew were all they could now see. Then the wizard spoke to them, and they followed him as he strode across the deserted pavement of the court, facing into the black winds and the nameless menace of the doors. He raised his sword, a long two-handed blade, and it sparked in the darkness like summer lightning. Then, as if an explosion had rocked the vaults below the building, the doors burst open, and blackness poured forth over them like smoke.

Gil saw what was in the darkness, and her own screams of terror woke her.

Her hands shook so badly she could barely switch on the bedside lamp. The clock on the table beside her bed said two-thirty. Drenched in sweat and colder than death, Gil fell back against the pillow, whispering frantically to herself that it was only a dream—only a dream. *I am twenty-four years old and a graduate student in medieval history and I will have my Ph.D. in a year and it's stupid to be afraid of a dream. And it was only a dream. It's all over now and none of it was real. It was only a dream.*

She told herself this, staring out from the fortress of worn sheets and cheap blankets at the convincing familiarity of her own apartment—the Levi's lolling out of the half-closed dresser drawer, Rooster Cogburn glowering down from a poster on the wall, the absent-minded litter of textbooks, tissues, pennies, and dog-eared paperbacks that strewed the threadbare shag of the rug. She thought about the early hour of today's seminar, glanced again at the clock and the lamp, and considered seeking sleep and darkness. But though she was, as she had said, twenty-four years old and almost a Ph.D., far too old to be troubled by the fears felt in a dream, she rolled over after a short time and groped *Wayfaring Life in the Middle Ages* from the floor beside her bed. She found her place in it, and by act of will forced herself to become fascinated by the legal status of the King's Highway in fifteenth-century England.

She did not trust herself to sleep again until it was almost dawn.

Oddly enough, Gil remembered nothing of the dream until nearly a week later. And what she did remember, driving home from the university in the tawny-golden brilliance of a California September afternoon, was the wizard's voice, wondering where she had heard it, the warm timbre of it and the characteristic break in tone, the velvet smoothness sliding into roughness and then abruptly back.

Then she remembered the eyes, the city, the shadows, and the fear. And she realized, turning her red VW down

5

Clarke Street toward her apartment building, that it wasn't the first time she'd dreamed about that city.

The odd thing about the first dream, Gil recalled, maneuvering into a narrow parking space on the perennially crowded cul-de-sac, was that, though there had been nothing at all in it to cause her fear, she had been afraid and had waked up chilled with a lingering sense of dread.

She had dreamed of wandering alone in a vaulted chamber, so huge that the lines of shadow-curtained arches supporting the low, groined ceiling had vanished into darkness all about her. Dust had stirred mustily beneath her bare feet, had coated the disused junk and dilapidated boxes piled between and among the pillars, and had fogged the distant glow of a yellow flame that she was following to its source, a little tallow-dip lamp burning beside the dark sweep of a red porphyry Stair. All around her, as cloaking as the dust, as ubiquitous as the shadows, was that sense of lurking fear, of being watched from the darkness by things that had no eyes.

The pallid flame had gleamed dully on the broad red steps and had thrown back the half-seen shape of monumental bronze doors at their top, but had drawn no reflection from the leaden blackness of the basalt floor, in spite of the fact that the floor was as smooth as glass, polished by the passage of countless feet; how this could be in the deeps of the vaults she did not know, and it was clear from the dust that few if any came here now. The floor was old, far older than the walls, though how she knew this Gil was not sure—older, she thought, than the city over her head, or any city of mankind. In the midst of that dark pavement, right before the lamplit steps, one single slab of the floor was new, hewn of pale gray granite, its surface rough against the worn, silken smoothness of the rest of the floor, though it, too, was covered with that agelong mantle of dust.

In the darkness above her a door creaked, and light wavered across the many arches. Gil slipped back into the shadow of a pillar, though she knew it was only a dream, and knew that people here could not see her because they did not exist. A woman, a servant by her dress, came padding down the steps with a basket on her arm, holding a lamp up above her head; at her heels lumbered a hunchbacked slave, peering around him at the darkness

6

out of shadowed, wary eyes. The woman led the way unconcernedly down the Stair, across the smooth dark floor,
turning aside to avoid walking on the odd granite slab,
although her goal—a bin of dried apples—lay directly
opposite the foot of the stairs, and the odd slab was in no
way raised above the level of the rest of the floor. The
hunchback made an even wider circuit, moving from pillar
to pillar, woofing and clucking quietly to himself and
never taking those sharp, fear-filled eyes from the pale
stone.

The woman loaded her basket and handed it to the
hunchback to carry. She started back toward the steps
and paused, irresolute, clearly telling herself not to be a
silly, superstitious goose, that there was no reason to be
afraid, not of the darkness that pressed so close around
her, and certainly not of six feet by twelve of pavement
that was gray instead of black, granite instead of basalt.
But in the end, she took the long way around, to avoid
walking on that odd slab.

*That's why it's rough, when the rest of the floor is so
weirdly smooth,* Gil thought. *No one walks on it. No one
has ever walked on it.*

Why?

But even the sense that the two dreams were somehow
connected held only a kind of passing curiosity for her,
until the third dream. They did nothing to disturb the fabric
of her daily existence. She continued to spend hours in the
university library, searching scholarly articles and moldering Middle English town records, jotting information on
index cards that she later sorted out at the kitchen table
back in the Clarke Street apartment, trying to make sense
of what she knew. She graded undergraduate papers,
sweated over her grant proposal, and had her dealings
with friends and lovers—the routine of her life—until she
dreamed of that beleaguered city again.

She knew it was the same city, though she looked down
on it now from above. She found herself standing in the
embrasure of a tall window, in a tower, she thought. So
bright was the moonlight that she could discern the patterns
of the courtyard pavement far below, see the designs
worked into the wrought-iron lace of the gates, and make
out even the shadows of the fallen leaves, like a furring of

7

dust on the ground. Raising her eyes, she could catch, across the peaked maze of rooftrees, the glimpse of distant water. In the other direction, the black shoulders of mountains loomed against the hem of a star-blazing sky.

In the room behind her a solitary tongue of flame stood above the polished silver of the lamp on the table, and by its small, unwavering glow she could distinguish the furnishings, few and simple, each exquisitely wrought out of dark wood and ivory. Though the design and motifs were alien to her eyes, she could recognize in them the creative height of a well-founded tradition, the product of a sophisticated and tasteful culture.

And she saw that she was not alone.

Against the chamber's far wall stood the room's largest piece of furniture, a massive ebony crib, its scrolled railings veined in mother-of-pearl that caught the dim lamplight. Above it, all but hidden in the massed shadows, a tall canopy loomed, with an emblem picked out in gold: a stylized eagle striking, beneath a tiny crown. This emblem was repeated, stitched in pinfire glints of bullion, on the black surcoat of the man who stood beside that crib, head bent and silent as a statue, looking down at its sleeping occupant.

He was a tall man, handsome in an austere way. Some silver showed in his shoulder-length brown hair, though Gil would not have put his age much above thirty-five. From the soles of his soft leather boots to the folds of the billowing robe that covered surcoat and tunic, the man's clothing was rich, of a piece with the subdued grandeur of the room, dark, plain, flawlessly tailored of the most expensive fabric. The gems in the hilt of his sword flickered like stars in the lamplight with the small movement of his breath.

A sound in the corridor beyond made him raise his head, and Gil saw his face, haunted with the expectation of terrible news. Then the door beside him opened.

"I thought I should find you here," the wizard said. For one moment Gil had the absurd notion that he was speaking to her. But the man in black nodded, his face setting into lines worn by grim concentration on a problem beyond solving, and his long, slender hand continued to stroke the inward-curling circles of the rail of the crib.

"I was on my way down," he apologized, his voice

muffled, his face turned half away. "I only wanted to see him."

The wizard closed the door. The movement of the air made the single lampflame shudder, the flickering color briefly gilding sunbursts of wrinkles around his eyes, showing that same expression of weariness and strain. Gil saw that he, too, wore a sword, belted over the pale homespun of his robe. The hilt of it was not jeweled, but was worn silky with years of use. He said, "There is no need. I doubt they will attack again tonight."

"Tonight," the man in black repeated somberly. His bitter eyes were a hard smoke-gray, like steel in the dense shadows of the little room. "What about tomorrow night, Ingold? And the night after? Yes, we pushed them back tonight, back down under the earth where they belong. We won—here. What about in the other cities of the Realm? What have you seen in that crystal of yours, Ingold? What has been happening elsewhere tonight? In Penambra in the south, where it seems now even my governor has been slain, and the Dark Ones haunt his palace like foul ghosts? In the provinces along the valley of the Yellow River to the east, where you tell me they hold such sway that not a man will leave his house after the sun goes in? In Gettlesand across the mountains, where the fear of the Dark Ones is so great that men will stay within their doors while the White Raiders ride down off the plains to burn and loot among them at will?

"The Army cannot be everywhere. They're scattered in the four corners of the Realm, most of them still at Penambra. We here in Gae cannot hold out forever. We may not even be able to hold the Palace, should they come again tomorrow night."

"That is tomorrow," the wizard replied quietly. "We can only do what we must—and hope."

"Hope." He said it without scorn or irony, only as if it were a word long unfamiliar, whose very sound was awkward upon his tongue. "Hope for what, Ingold? That the Council of Wizards will break this silence of theirs and come out of hiding in their city at Quo? Or that, if and when they do, they will have an answer?"

"You narrow hope when you define it, Eldor."

"God knows it's narrow enough as it is." Eldor turned away, to pace like a restless lion to the window and back,

9

taking the room in three of his long strides. He passed within a foot of Gil without seeing her, but Ingold the wizard looked up, and his eyes rested briefly, curiously, on her. Eldor swung around, his sleeve brushing Gil's hand on the windowsill. "It's the helplessness I can't stand," he burst out angrily. "They are my people, Ingold. The Realm—and all of civilization, if what you tell me is true—is falling to pieces around me, and you and I together cannot so much as offer it a shield to hide behind. You can tell me what the Dark Ones are, and where they come from, but all your powers cannot touch them. You can't tell us what we can do to defeat them. You can only fight them, as we all must, with a sword."

"It may be there is nothing we can do," Ingold said, settling back in his chair. He folded his hands, but his eyes were alert.

"I won't accept that."

"You may have to."

"It's not true. You know it's not true."

"Humankind did defeat the Dark, all those thousands of years ago," the wizard said quietly, the flickering of the light doing curious things to the scar-seamed contours of his weathered face. "As to how they did it—perhaps they themselves were not certain how it came about; in any case, we have found no record of it. My power cannot touch the Dark Ones because I do not know them, do not understand either their being or their nature. They have a power of their own, Eldor, very different from mine—beyond the comprehension of any human wizard, except, perhaps, Lohiro, the Master of the Council of Quo. Of what happened in the Time of the Dark, three thousand years ago, when they rose for the first time to devastate the earth— you know it all as well as I."

"Know it?" The King laughed bitterly, facing the wizard like a beast brought to bay, his eyes dark with the memory of ancient outrage. "I remember it. I remember it as clearly as if it had happened to me, instead of to my however-many-times-great-grandfather." He strode to stand over the wizard, shadowing him like a blighted tree, the single lamp flinging the great distorted shape of him to blend with the crowding dimness of the room. "And *he* remembers, too." His hand moved toward the crib, the vast shadow-hand on the wall its dark echo, toward the

10

child asleep within. "Deep in his baby mind those memories are buried. He's barely six months old—six months, yet he'll wake up screaming, rigid with fear. What can a child that young dream of, Ingold? He dreams of the Dark. I know."

"Yes," the wizard agreed, "you dreamed of it, too. Your father never did—in fact, I doubt your father ever feared or imagined anything in his life. Those memories were buried too deep in him—or perhaps there was simply no need for him to remember. But you dreamed of them and feared them, although you did not know what they were."

Standing in the cool draft of the window, Gil felt that bond between them, palpable as a word or a touch: the memory of a gawky, dark-haired boy waked screaming from nameless nightmares, and the comfort given him by a vagabond wizard. Some of the harshness left Eldor's face, and the grimness faded from his voice, leaving it only sad.

"Would I had remained ignorant," he said. "We of our line are never entirely young, you know. The memories that we carry are the curse of our race."

"They may be the saving of it," Ingold replied. "And of us all."

Eldor sighed and moved back to the crib in reflective silence, his slim, strong hands clasped lightly behind his back. But he was not now looking down at the child asleep. His eyes, brooding away into the shadows, lost their sharpness, focusing on times beyond his lifetime, on experience beyond his own.

After a while he said, "Will you do me one last service, Ingold?"

The old man's eyes slid sharply over to him. "There is no *last*."

The lines of Eldor's face creased briefly deeper with his tired smile. He was evidently long familiar with the wizard's stubbornness. "In the end," he said, "there is always a last. I know," he went on, "that your power cannot touch the Dark Ones. But it can elude them. I've seen you do it. When the night comes that they rise again, your power will allow you to escape, when the rest of us must die fighting. No—" He raised his hand to forestall the wizard's next words. "I know what you're going to say. But I want you to leave. If it comes to that, as your

11

King, I order you to. When they come—and they will—I want you to take my son Altir. Take him and flee."

The wizard sat silent, but his beard bristled with the set of his jaw. At last he said, "For one thing, you are not my King."

"Then as your friend, I ask it," the King said, and his voice was very low. "You couldn't save us. Not all of us. You're a great swordsman, Ingold, perhaps the greatest alive, but the touch of the Dark is death, to a wizard as well as to any other. Our doom is surely upon us here, for they will come again, as sure as the ice in the north, and there can be no escape. But you can save Tir. He's the last of my line, the last of Dare of Renweth's line— the last of the lineage of the Kings of Darwath. He's the only one in the Realm now who will remember the Time of the Dark. History itself has all but forgotten; no record at all exists of that time, bar a mention in the oldest of chronicles. My father remembered nothing of it—my own memories are sketchy. But the need is greater now. Maybe that has something to do with it—I don't know.

"But I know, and you know, that three thousand years ago the Dark Ones came and virtually wiped humankind from the face of the earth. *And they departed away again.* Why, Ingold, did they depart?"

The wizard shook his head.

"He knows," Eldor said softly. "He knows. My memories are incomplete. You know that; I've told you a dozen times. He's a promise, Ingold. I'm only a failed hope, a guttered candle. Somewhere in his memory, the heritage of the line of Dare, is the clue that all the rest of us have forgotten, that will lead to the undoing of the Dark. If I ever had it, it's buried too deeply; and he's the only other one. Him you must save."

The wizard said nothing. The quiet flame of the lamp, pure and small as a gold coin, reflected in his thinking eyes. In the stillness of the room, that tiny gleam was unmoving, the pool of waxy gold that lay around the lamp on the polished surface of the table as steady and sharply defined as a spotlight. At length he said, "And what about you?"

"A King has the right," Eldor replied, "to die with his kingdom. I will not leave the final battle. Indeed, I do not see how I could. But for all the love you have ever

12

borne me, do this thing for me now. Take him, and see him to a place of safety. I charge you with it—it is in your hands."

Ingold sighed and bent his head, as if to receive a yoke, the gold of the lamplight limning his silver hair. "I will save him," he said. "That I promise you. But I will not desert you until the cause is hopeless."

"Do not trouble yourself," the King said harshly. "The cause is hopeless already."

Deep below the dark foundations of the Palace a hollow booming resounded, like the stroke of a gigantic drum, and Gil felt the sound vibrate through the marble of the floor. Eldor's head jerked up and around, his long mouth hardening in the smooth gold and shadows, his hand flinching automatically to the hilt of his jeweled sword, but Ingold only sat, a statue of stone and darkness. A second booming shivered the weight of the Palace on its deep-found piers, as if struck by a great fist. Breathless in the closeness of that peaceful room, three people waited for the third stroke. But no third stroke fell; only a cold, creeping horror that prickled Gil's hair seemed to seep into the silence from below, the wordless threat of unknown peril.

Finally Ingold said, "They will not come tonight." Through his weariness, his tone was certain. "Go to the Queen and comfort her."

Eldor sighed; like a man released from a spell that had turned him to stone, he shifted broad, rawboned shoulders to relax the tension from his back. "The landchiefs of the Realm meet in an hour," he excused himself tiredly, and rubbed at his eyes, his fingers grinding the dark smudges that ringed them. "And I should speak with the Guards before then about moving provisions out of the old vaults under the Prefecture, in case our supply lines are cut. But you're right, I should go to see her . . . though first I should speak with the Bishop about bringing Church troops into the city." He began to pace again, the restless movement of an active man whose mind forever outran his body. Ingold remained seated in the carved ivory chair with its little gilded deer-hoof feet, and the flame before him moved with Eldor's motion, as if it, too, were drawn by the restless vitality of the man. "Will you be at the council?"

13

"I have given all the help and advice I can," Ingold replied. "I shall remain here, I think, and try again to get in touch with the wizards at Quo. Tir may not be our only answer. There are records in the Library at Quo, and traditions handed down from master to pupil over millennia; knowledge and the search for knowledge are the key and the heart of wizardry. Tir is an infant. By the time he learns to speak, it may be too late for what he has to tell us."

"It may already be too late." The flame bowed with the soft closing of the door behind Eldor.

Ingold sat for a time after he had gone, brooding silently on that pure small slip of fire. The glow of it played across his shadowed eyes, touched the knuckles of his folded hands—blunt-fingered, powerful hands, nicked all over with the scars of old sword cuts and marked on one heavy wrist with an age-whitened shackle gall. Then he rubbed his eyes tiredly and looked straight into the deep hollow of shadow where Gil stood, framed by the intricately screened filigree of the pillars beside the window. He beckoned to her. "Come here," he said gently, "and tell me about yourself. Don't be afraid."

"I'm not afraid." But as she took a hesitating step forward, the lamplight darkened, and the whole room was lost to her sight in the foggy mazes of sleep.

Gil told no one about the third dream. She had spoken of the second one to a woman friend who had listened sympathetically but hadn't, she felt, understood. Indeed, she didn't understand it herself. But the third dream she mentioned to no one, because she knew that it had been no dream. The certainty troubled her. Maybe, she told herself, she would tell her friend about it one day, when enough time had passed so that it was no longer important. But for now she locked it away, with several other irrelevant matters, in her secret heart.

Then one night she woke from a sound sleep standing up. She saw, as her eyes cleared, that she was in a sunken courtyard in that deserted city. The great houses surrounded her like lightless cliffs, and moonlight drenched the square, throwing her shadow clearly on muddy and unwashed flagstones under her bare feet. The place was deserted, like a courtyard of the dead. Where the ghastly silver light blanched the facade of the east-facing house, she saw that its great doors had been blown off their hinges from within and lay in scattered pieces about her feet.

From out of that empty doorway, a sudden little wind stirred, restless and without direction, turning back on itself in a small scritching eddy of fallen leaves. She sensed beyond the blind windows and vacant doors of that house a sound, a fumbling movement, as if dark shifted through dark, bumbling eyelessly at the inner walls, seeking a way out. She swallowed hard, her breath quickening in fear, and she glanced behind her at the arched gateway that led out into the deserted street beyond. But the gate was dark, and she felt a clammy, unreasoning terror of walking beneath the clustered shadows in the high vault of the enclosed passage.

The wind from the house increased, chilling her. She edged her way back toward the dark gate, feeling herself beginning to shiver, her feet icy on the marble pavement. The silence of the place was terrible; even the screaming flight of that first night would have been more welcome. Then she had been in a crowd, though unseen; then she had not been alone. Silent and terrible, the lurker waited on the threshold of that dark house, and she knew that she must flee for her life. She would not be able to waken out of this dream; she knew that she was already awake.

Then, out of the corner of her eye, she had the brief impression of something moving, low to the ground, in the shadows by the wall. Swinging around, she saw nothing. But she thought that the darkness itself was reaching out toward her, damping even the moonlight.

Turning, she fled, her black shadow running on the ground before her in the ivory moonlight. Broken stone and iron gashed her bare feet as she plunged into the black arch of the gate, but the pain was swallowed in icy fear as thin, aimless winds tugged at her—as she sensed, rather than saw, something move in the utter blackness over her head. She stumbled into the street outside, her bleeding feet leaving red blotches on the wet slime of the cobbles, running, running in heart-bursting panic through the empty boulevards of the city that she now saw lay half in ruins, the silent pavements cluttered with rubble and new-stripped human bones. Shadows, black and as staring as walls of stone, confronted her with new horrors at every turn; gargoyle shapes of terror lurked under every eave and fallen rooftree. The only sounds in all that empty city of freezing night were the moist, pattering slap of her bare feet on stone and the gasp of her laboring breath, the only movements her own frenzied flight and that of her jerking, leaping shadow, and, behind her, the drifting movement of wind and darkness pouring after her like smoke. She fled blindly down black canyons, feet numb, legs numb, stumbling over she knew not what, knowing by instinct in which direction the Palace lay, knowing that Ingold the wizard was there and that Ingold would save her.

She ran until she woke, sobbing, clutching her pillow in the dark, soaked with cold terror-sweat, her body aching with exhaustion. Only gradually did the filtered moonlight register the familiar things of the Clarke Street apartment, alien to her wondering eyes, as if both worlds were now equally hers. She forced her gasping breath to slow, forced her mind to think; her legs smarted; her feet were like ice beneath the covers. In a confused clutching at the straws of sanity she thought, *That's why I dreamed of having cold feet; because my feet* are *cold.* She groped for the light with trembling fingers, turned it on, and lay there shivering, repeating to herself the desperate, unbelieving litany: *It was only a dream, it was only a dream. Please, God, let it be only a dream.*

But even as she whispered, she felt the sticky wetness matting her numb toes. Reaching down, unwillingly, to warm them, she brought her fingers back streaked with fresh blood, from where she had cut her feet on the broken stone in the gateway.

Five nights later, the moon was full.

Its light woke Gil, startling her out of sleep into a split-second convulsion of fear, until she recognized the night-muted patterns of familiar things and realized she was in her place on Clarke Street. Waking suddenly in the night, she was seldom sure anymore. She lay still for a time, listening open-eyed in the darkness, waiting for the quick flood of panic to subside from her veins. White moonlight lay on the blanket beside her, palpable as a sheet of paper.

Then she thought, *Dammit, I forgot to put the chain on the door.*

16

This was purely a formality, a bedtime ritual; the apartment had a regular lock and, moreover, the neighborhood was a quiet one. She almost decided to forget the whole thing, roll over, and go back to sleep; but after a minute, she crawled out of bed, shivering in the cold, and groped her peacock kimono from its accustomed place on the floor. Wrapping it about her, she padded silently into the dark kitchen, her feet finding their way easily. Her hand found the light switch by touch in the darkness and flicked it up.

The wizard Ingold was sitting at the kitchen table.

Absurdly, Gil's first thought was that this was the only time she'd seen him in decent lighting. He looked older, wearier, the brown and white of his homespun robes faded and stained and shabby, but he was essentially the same fierce, gentlemanly old man she knew from her dreams: the advisor of the dark King; the man whose face she'd seen reflected in the foxfire glow of his sword, striding down to meet the darkness.

This is stupid, she thought. *This is crazy*. Not because she was seeing him again—for she'd known all along that she would—but because it was in her apartment, her world. What the hell was he doing here if it wasn't a dream? And she knew it wasn't. She glanced automatically around the kitchen. The supper dishes—and the previous night's supper dishes—were piled unwashed on the counter, the table top invisible under a litter of apple cores and index cards, cups of moldering coffee and sheets of scribbled notebook paper. Two of her old T-shirts were dumped over the back of the chair on which Ingold sat. The seedy electric clock behind his head read just past three. It was all too squalidly depressing to be anything but real—she was definitely neither asleep nor dreaming.

"What are you doing here?" she asked.

The wizard raised shaggy eyebrows in surprise. "I came to talk to you," he replied. She knew the voice. She felt that she had always known it.

"I mean—how did you get here?"

"I could give you a technical explanation, of course," he said, and the smile that briefly illuminated his face turned it suddenly very young. "But would it matter? I crossed the Void to find you, because I need your help."

"Hunh?"

It was not the kind of response best suited to what she'd

17

read of dealing with wizards, but Ingold's eyes twinkled with fleeting amusement. "I would not have sought you out," he told her gently, "if I didn't."

"Uh—" Gil said profoundly. "I don't understand." She started to sit down opposite him, which involved clearing two textbooks and the calendar section of the *Times* off the chair, then paused in a tardy outburst of hospitality. "Would you like a beer?"

"Thank you." He smiled, and gravely studied the opening instructions inscribed on the top of the can. For a first time, he didn't do badly.

"How could you see me?" she asked, sliding into her chair as he shook the foam off his fingers. "Even when it was a dream, even when no one else could—King Eldor and the Guards at the gate—you could. Why was that?"

"It's because I understand the nature of the Void," the wizard said gravely. He folded his hands on the table, the blunt, scarred fingers idly caressing the gaudy aluminum of the can, as if memorizing its shape and feel. "You understand, Gil, that there exists an infinite number of parallel universes, meshed in the matrix of the Void. In my world, in my time, I am the only one who understands the nature of the Void—one of a bare handful who even suspects its existence."

"And how did you learn about it, much less how to cross it, if no one else in your world knows?" Gil asked curiously.

The wizard smiled again. "That, Gil, is a story that would take all night to do justice to, without advancing the present situation. Suffice it to say that I am the only man in perhaps five hundred years who has been able to cross the curtain that separates universe from universe—and having done so, I was able to recognize the imprint of your thoughts, your personality, that had been drawn across the Void by the mass vibration of worldwide panic and terror. I believe there are a very few others in your world who, for whatever reason, be it psychic or physical or purest coincidence, have felt, from across the Void, the coming of the Dark. Of them all, you are the only one with whom I have been able to establish contact. It was seeing you, speaking to you, and then having you materialize not only in thought but in body, that made me understand what is happening with regard to the Void."

18

Outside, a truck rumbled by on Clarke Street, its sound muffled with distance and the night. Somewhere in the apartment building, a toilet flushed, a faint echoing gurgle along the pipes. Gil stared down at the table for a time, her eye automatically noting her own jagged black handwriting spelling out cryptic notes with regard to the upkeep of fourteenth-century bridges, then looked up again at the wizard calmly drinking beer across from her, his staff leaned against the wall at his side.

She asked, "What is happening with the Void?"

"When I spoke with you in Gae," Ingold went on, "I realized that our worlds must lie in very close conjunction at this time—so close that, because of the psychic crisis, a dreamer could literally walk the line between them and see from one into the next. This is both a rare and a temporary occurrence, a one-in-a-million chance for two worlds to drift so close. But it is a situation that I can use to my advantage in this emergency."

"But why did it happen now, at the time of crisis?" Gil asked, the harsh electric glare rippling in the embroidery of her gaudy sleeves as she leaned forward across the table. "And why did it happen to me?"

He must have caught the suppressed slivers of uneasiness and fear of being singled out in her voice; when he replied he spoke gently. "Nothing is fortuitous. There are no random events. But we cannot know all the reasons."

She barely hid a smile. "That's a wizard's answer if I ever heard one."

"Meaning that mages deal in double talk?" His grin was impish. "That's one of our two occupational hazards."

"And what's the other one?"

He laughed. "A deplorable tendency to meddle."

She joined him in laughter. Then after a moment she grew quiet and asked, "But if you're a wizard, how could you need my help? What help could I possibly give you that you couldn't find for yourself? How could I help you against—against the Dark? Who is, or what is, the Dark?"

He regarded her in silence for a moment, judging her, testing her, watching her out of blue eyes whose surface brightness masked a depth and pull like the ocean's. His face had grown grave again, settled into its sun-scorched lines. He said, "You know."

She looked away, seeing in her unwilling mind mono-

19

lithic bronze doors exploding off their hinges; seeing shadows that ran behind her, inescapable as ghostly wolves. She spoke without meeting his eyes. "I don't know what they are."

"Nor does anyone," he said, "unless it's Lohiro, the Master of Quo. It's a question whose answer I wish I had never been set to seek, a riddle I'm sorry I have to unravel.

"What can I say of the Dark Gil? What can I say that you don't know already? That they are the sharks of night? That they pull the flesh from the bones, or the blood from the flesh, or the soul and spirit from the living body and let it stumble mindlessly to an eventual death from starvation? That they ride the air in darkness, hunt in darkness, and that fire or light or even a good bright moon will keep them away? Would that tell you what they are?"

She shook her head, hypnotized by the warm roughness of his voice, caught by the intensity of his eyes and by the horror and the memory of even more appalling horrors that she saw there. "But you know," she whispered.

"Would to God I did not." Then he sighed and looked away; when he turned his head again, there was only that matter-of-fact self-assurance in his face, without the doubt, or the fear, or the loathing of what he knew.

"I—I dreamed of them." Gil stumbled on the words, finding it unexpectedly more difficult to speak of that first forerunning dream to one who understood than to one who did not. "Before I ever saw them, before I ever knew what they were. I dreamed about a—a vault, a cellar—with arches going in all directions. The floor was black and smooth, like glass; and in the middle of that black floor was a slab of granite that was new and rough, because nobody ever walked on it. You said they came from—from beneath the ground."

"Indeed," the wizard said, looking at her with an alert, speculative curiosity. "You seem to have sensed their coming far ahead of its time. That may mean something, though at the moment I'm not sure . . . Yes, that was the Dark, or, rather, the blocked-up entrance to one of their Nests. Under that granite slab—and I know the one you're talking about—is a stairway, a stairway going downward incalculable depths into the earth. It was with the stairways, I believe, that it all began.

"For the stairways were always there. You find representations of them in the most ancient prehistoric petroglyphs: vast pavements of black stone and, in the midst of them, stairs descending to the deepest heart of the earth. No one ever went down them—at least, no one who came back up again—and no one knew who built them. Some said it was the titans of old, or the earth-gods; old records speak of the places as being awesome, full of magic. For a long time they were considered to be lucky, favored by the gods—the old religion built temples over them, temples which became the centers of the first cities of humankind.

"All this was millennia ago. Villages grew to towns and then to great cities. The cities united; states and realms spread along the rich valleys of the Brown River, on the shores of the Round Sea and the Western Ocean, and in the jungles and deserts of Alketch. Civilization flowered and bore its fruits: wizardry, art, money, learning, war. Records of that time are so scarce as to be almost nonexistent. Only beguiling fragments of chronicles remain, mostly in the Library at Quo, a teasing sliver of a civilization of great depth and richness, of sublime beauty and wisdom and truly foul decadence, a society that parented first wizardry and then the Church and the great codes of civil law.

"I am virtually certain that some kind of tradition existed then regarding the Dark Ones, simply because the word for them was in the language. *Sueg*—dark—*isueg*—an archaic, personalized form of the same word. But they were only a vague rumor of shadow on the edges of the oldest legends—the misty memory of hidden fear. And if there was such a tradition, it did not connect them with the stairways themselves. So they remained, rooted in the abysses of time, an ancient mystery buried in the heart of civilization.

"Of the destruction of the ancient world we have no coherent account. We know that it happened within a matter of weeks. That what struck, struck worldwide, we also know—a simultaneous siege of horror. But the horror and the confusion were so overwhelming that virtually no record was preserved; and since defense against the Dark generally entailed uncontrolled use of fire as a weapon, we lost what little information we might have had about their coming. We know that they came—but we do not know why.

21

"Unable to fight, humankind fled and retreated to fortified Keeps, behind whose massive walls they led a windowless existence, creeping forth by day to till their fields and hiding when the sun went down. For three hundred years, absolute chaos and terror held sway on the earth, because there was no knowing where or when the Dark would come. Civilization crumbled, fading to a few glowing embers of the great beacon light that it had once been.

"And then—" Ingold spread his hands, showing them empty, like a sideshow magician. "The Dark no longer came. Whether the cessation was sudden or gradual, we cannot be sure, for by that time few people were literate enough to be keeping accurate records. Little villages had grown up outside the Keeps; in time, new little villages appeared on the crumbling ruins of the ancient cities whose very names had been forgotten through the intervening years. There were wars and change and long spaces of time. Old traditions faded; the very language changed. Old songs and stories were forgotten.

"Three thousand years is a long time, Gil. You're an historian—can you tell me, with any accuracy, what happened three thousand years ago?"

"Uh—" Gil cast a hasty scan over her memories of *Ancient Civilizations 1A*. Marathon? Stonehenge? Hyksos' invasions of Egypt? As a medievalist, she had only the foggiest impressions of anything prior to Constantine. What must it be like, she wondered, for the average Joe Doakes who hadn't been to college and didn't like history much anyway? Even something as hideous as the Black Death, an event which had grossly and permanently impacted western civilization, was only a name to eighty percent of the population—and that was only six hundred years ago.

Ingold nodded, his point made. It occurred to Gil to wonder how he had known that her subject was history, but he went on, as she was beginning to find was his habit, without explaining. "For many years I was the only one who knew anything about even the old tales of the Dark. I knew—I learned—that the Dark Ones were not utterly gone. Eventually I learned that they were not even much diminished in numbers. And I heard things that made me believe that they would return. Eldor's father had me banished for speaking of it, which I thought small-minded of him, since sending me away could not reduce the danger—

but perhaps he thought that I was lying. Eldor believed me. Without his preparations, I think we would all have perished the first night of their rising."

"And now?" Gil asked softly.

"Now?" The night was far spent; the lines of weariness etched into his scarred face seemed to settle a little deeper. "We are holding out in the Palace at Gae. The main body of the Army under the command of the Chancellor of the Realm, Alwir, the Queen's brother, has been in Penambra, where the raids were the worst. They should return to the city within days; but without a miracle they will be too late to prevent catastrophe. I have tried vainly to get in touch with the Council of Wizards in the Hidden City of Quo, but I fear they, too, may be besieged. They have retreated behind their defenses of power and illusion. Though I still have hopes that we can hold out long enough for Lohiro to send us aid of some kind, I would not want to wager the lives of my friends on that hope. The defenders at the Palace need me, Gil. Though I cannot do much, I will not leave them until it is beyond doubt that no effort of mine can save them.

"And that," he said, "is where I need your help."

She only looked at him, uncomprehending.

"You understand," Ingold went on in that same quiet tone, "that by leaving it that late, I shall be cutting my escape very fine. In the last extremity, my only course will be to flee across the Void into some other world—this world. I can cross back and forth at will with relative impunity. Normally such a crossing is a shocking enough physical trauma for an adult. For an infant of six months, even under my protection, it can be injurious, and two such crossings in a short span of time could do the child real harm. I will therefore have to remain a day in this world, with the child, before I can return to some safer spot in my own."

The light dawned. Gil smiled. "You need a place to hole up."

"As you say. I need an isolated spot and a few creature comforts—a place to pass that time in obscurity. Do you know of such a place?"

"You could come here," Gil offered.

Ingold shook his head. "No," he said decidedly.

"Why not?"

23

The wizard hesitated before answering. "It's too dangerous," he said at last. He rose from his chair, moved restlessly to the flat rectangle of the window, and pushed the curtain aside, looking out, down into the apartment courtyard below. The greenish reflections of the courtyard lights in the waters of the swimming pool rippled over the old marks of alien battles on his face. "Too many things could happen. I have a great mistrust of fate, Gil. My powers are severely limited in your world. If something were to go wrong, I have no desire to try to explain my presence or that of the child to the local authorities."

Gil had a brief, disturbing picture of Ingold, like some bearded refugee from the Society for the Preservation of Dungeons and Dragons in his shabby robes and killing sword, having a close encounter with the local police or the Highway Patrol. Despite her impression that the Highway Patrol would come off second best, she realized such a confrontation could not be risked. Not with so much at stake.

"There's a place we used to go past on trail rides," she said, after a moment's thought.

"Yes?" He turned back from the window, letting the curtain swish shut.

"A girl I used to go to school with lives out near Barstow—it's in the desert, way the hell east of here. I spent a couple weeks out there two summers ago. She had horses, and we used to ride all over the back-hills country. I remember there was a cabin, kind of a little house, out in the middle of some abandoned orange groves in the hills. We holed up there one afternoon during a thunderstorm. It isn't much, but there's running water and a kerosene stove, and it's as isolated as you could want."

Ingold nodded. "Yes," he murmured, half to himself. "Yes, it should do."

"I can bring you food and blankets," she went on. "Just tell me when you'll be there."

"I don't know that yet," the wizard said quietly. "But you'll know, at the time."

"All right." Though Gil was normally a suspicious person, it never occurred to her to question him, and this did not even surprise her about herself. She trusted him, she found, as if she had known him for years.

Ingold reached across the table and took her hand.

24

"Thank you," he said. "You are a stranger to our world and you owe us nothing—it is good of you to help."

"Hey," Gil protested softly. "I'm not a stranger. I've been in your world, and I've seen the Dark. I just about met King Eldor, as a matter of fact." Then she paused, confused at her blunder, for she remembered that the King and the wizard were friends, and that Eldor was almost certainly going to die before the week was out.

But Ingold passed over her error like the gentleman he was. "I know Eldor would have been pleased to make your acquaintance," he said. "And you shall always have his gratitude, and mine, for . . ."

Some sound in the night made him suddenly alert, and he broke off, raising his head to listen.

"What is it?" Gil whispered.

Ingold turned back to her. "I'm afraid I must go," he said politely. His voice seldom betrayed worry or fear—he might have been making his excuses because of a prior engagement for tea with the Queen of Numenor. But Gil knew that something was happening, across the Void, in the embattled Palace at Gae.

He rose to go, the straight dark line of his mantle breaking over the sword at his hip. Gil thought of the danger and of the Dark waiting on the other side of the Void. She caught at his sleeve. In a voice smaller than she meant, she said, "Hey, take care."

His smile was like the coming of the sun. "Thank you, my dear. I always do." Then he walked a few paces to the center of the kitchen and put out his hand to push the fabric of the universe aside like a curtain. As he did so, he drew his sword, and Gil could see the cold light that burned up off the blade as he stepped into the mist and fire beyond.

CHAPTER TWO

It was the goddam motherless fuel pump!

Rudy Solis ident'fied immediately the gasp and drag of the old Chevy's engine, automatically checked his rear-vision mirror, and scanned the dark, straight, two-lane highway ahead, though he knew there was nothing resembling a light in fifty miles. With all of Southern California to choose from, naturally the thing would decide to give up the ghost in the dead, endless stretch of desert and hill country that lay between Barstow and San Bernardino, miles from anywhere in the middle of Sunday night.

Rudy wondered if he could make it back to the party.

Be a lot of sorrow and tears if I can't, he thought to himself, glancing over his shoulder at the ten cases of beer stacked amid the shredded foam, old newspapers, and greasy articles of unidentifiable clothing heaped in the sagging back seat. The engine faltered, coughed apologetically, and chugged on. Rudy cursed the owner of the car, the seventh-magnitude rock-and-roll star at whose party he'd been drinking and sunburning himself into a stupor all weekend, and the buddies who'd volunteered him to make the beer run, thirty miles down the hills to Barstow; cursed them impersonally, and threw in a few curses at himself as well for being euchred into going.

Well, serves 'em right. Next time they want somebody to buy their beer for 'em, they can damn well lend me a decent car.

But the fact was that most people had arrived at Tarot's party on motorcycles, as Rudy himself had. And Tarot—

26

who had started out life as James Carrow and was still known as Jim when not wearing his flameout stage make-up—wasn't about to lend his custom Eldorado to anybody, no matter how few cases of beer were left.

Well, what the hell. Rudy shook back the long hair from his eyes and risked another glance at the unrelieved blackness of empty desert reflected in his rear-view mirror. Everybody up at that hundred-thousand-dollar hideaway in the canyons was so drunk by this time that it was impossible to see what difference ten more cases of beer could make. If worst came to worst—which it looked like it was going to, from the sound of that engine—he could always find someplace in the hills to hole up in until morning and try to hitch a ride to the nearest phone then. There was a service road about ten miles farther on that he knew of, which would take him to a dilapidated shack in what remained of an old orange grove. Half-plastered as he was, he didn't relish the idea of trying to do anything about the engine tonight, nor was the thought of sleeping by the road real appealing. Rudy took a drink from the half-empty bottle of wine propped on the seat beside him and drove on.

Rudy had been driving and dealing with cars and motorcycles half his life—not always with legal sanctions —but it took all his expertise to nurse the failing Chevy the mile or two from the last lighted billboard to the rutted track of the service road. The lag and jerk of the big V-8 engine as he maneuvered through potholes, gravel slides, and the ruinous washes of old stream beds made him wonder if the problem wasn't simply a blocked line. He itched to climb out, raise the hood, and check—except that he had nothing resembling a light with him, and the odds were that, once stopped, nothing short of total rebuilding would get the stupid car started again. The feeble glare of the headlights picked out landmarks he knew from his motorcycle trips back this way: an oak tree twisted into the shape of a disapproving monk, gloomily damning the couples who came out here to park; a rock like a sleeping buffalo, silhouetted against the star-luminous sky. Rudy's hobby of hunting with bow and arrow had given him a familiarity with half the wild country left in Southern California, a knowledge of these silent desert hills as casual as his knowledge of the inner workings of a V-8 engine or of the floor plan of his own sparsely furnished apartment. He was as much at home here as he was anywhere else.

Sometimes more so. Maybe the hunting was the reason, or maybe only the excuse. There were times when he simply took pleasure in being alone, a different pleasure from what was to be had from partying and raising hell, from horsing around with the guys at the body shop, from rat-pack weekends in the desert. Never self-analytical, Rudy only understood that he needed the solitude, needed the touch of the empty land and the demand for slow skill and perfect accuracy. Perhaps it was this that had kept him on the edge of the biker crowd; he'd become acquainted with them at the body shop but never of them. Or perhaps it was simple cowardice.

Whatever his reasons, he was accepted for what he was; and though not part of any motorcycle gang, as an airbrush painter and pinstriper at Wild David's body shop in Fontana, he was part of that world. Hence, he understood his inclusion in Tarot's party—not that anybody in Southern California was excluded from Tarot's party. Tarot's local reputation included an apocryphal story about being a former member of the Hell's Angels. But, thinking the matter over as he guided the thrombotic car deeper and deeper into the blackness of the hills, Rudy couldn't imagine any gang admitting a member as essentially chickenhearted as Jim Carrow.

The car's front wheels dropped suddenly into a twelve-inch water-cut in the road with a heart-rending scrape of oil pan against rock. Rudy tried the engine twice and got only a tired whirring in response. He opened the door and climbed cautiously out, boots slipping on the round stones of the dry stream bed. Two days of continuous partying didn't help his footing much. He ascertained at once that pushing wouldn't help matters, for the car was nose-down with its front bumper inches from the far bank of the gully. It might, he decided, kneeling in the soft sand, be possible to back out if the engine could be started, but it wasn't something he'd want to try at one-thirty in the morning.

Disgusted, he straightened up.

Starlight showed him the shape and roll of the hills, the shallow valley opening out to his right, with a dark clustering of dry, black-leaved citrus trees. The shack—a cabin, really—would be over there in the dense shadow of the hill, a hundred yards farther on.

Made it, he thought. *Thank God for small favors.*

It was surprising how silent the night was. There was little silence in the world; even away from people, there was usually street noise, airplanes, air conditioning. The cooling metal of the car's engine ticked softly in the darkness; now and then, dried grass sighed at the memory of wind. Rudy's eyes, adjusting to the wan glow of the Milky Way, slowly made out the edges of the cabin's roof line, the shapes of long grass and twisted trees. His footfalls seemed very loud in that world of darkness.

Walking carefully, if not precisely staggering, he collected two six-packs of beer from the back seat and the remainder of his bottle of muscatel from the front. His head was beginning to ache. *Just what I need. A busted fuel pump and a hangover to fix it with. They'll probably figure I took the beer money and headed for Mexico.*

He made his way up to the shack.

It stood solitary against the dark of the hills, the long grass around its peeling walls concealing the fossilized remains of dead farm equipment and broken bottles, the shabby asphalt tile of the roof sagging under the weight of accumulated leaves. He mounted the crazy front steps and set down his burdens on the narrow front porch, the mild chill of the sweet-scented night making him shiver as he stripped off his greasy denim jacket, wrapped it around his hand, and punched out a pane of the window beside the door to let himself in.

The lights worked, surprisingly. *Hookup to the power lines in the grove,* he decided, taking a quick look around the dingy kitchen. So did the sink, giving cold water but not hot. *Well, you can't have everything.* In the cupboard under the sink he found three cans of pork and beans with prices stamped on them that were at least four years old, and a kerosene stove with half a can of kerosene.

Not bad, he reflected, *if I had anything to cook.* Further exploration revealed a minuscule bathroom and a cell-like bedroom at the end of a narrow hall, with a sagging cot whose threadbare mattress would have been thrown out of any jail in the state as cruel and unusual.

Nothing to write home about, he thought, returning to the kitchen and thence to the star-limned silence of the front porch. He donned his jacket, on which the faded blue denim was rather gaudily illuminated with a flaming skull with roses in its eyes, and settled back against the doorjamb to polish off the muscatel and watch the night in peace. As the dark quiet of the hills soaked into his soul, he decided that there was, after all, something to be said for the place, a perfection of solitude in many ways superior to all the beer busts thrown by all the rock stars of California.

After a long time of silence he returned inside to sleep.

He woke up wondering what he'd done to annoy the little man with the sledgehammer who lived inside his head. He rolled over, to his instant regret, and wondered if he was going to die.

The room was barely light. He lay for a time staring at the shadows of the dry, cobwebby rafters, memories of yesterday and last night leaking back to his protesting consciousness: Tarot's party; the fact that it was Monday and he was supposed to be back at work in the body shop, painting flaming sunsets on custom vans; last night's beer run to Barstow; and that pig of a Chevy. *It might be just the fuel lines,* he told himself, his mind backtracking creakily through the obstacle course of a splitting headache and assorted other symptoms of the immoderate consumption of muscatel. If that was the case, he could be under way in a few hours. If it was the pump, he was in for a long walk.

Rudy made his way out of the house and down the steps, blinking in the pallid light of dawn. He was soon cursing the owner of the car. There wasn't anything resembling a tool in all the bushels of trash in the trunk or on the back seat.

There was a shed half-buried in the weeds farther back in the groves behind the cottage, and he spent ten grimy minutes picking through spider-infested debris there in search of tools. The result was hardly satisfactory: a rusted Phillips screwdriver with a dog-chewed handle; a couple of blades with the business ends twisted; and an adjustable end wrench so corroded that he doubted it could be used.

The sun was just clearing the hills as he stepped out again, wiping his hands on his jeans; all around him the clear magic colors of day were emerging from the dawn's grayed pastels. The house, formerly a nameless bulk of shadow, ripened into warm russets and weathered sepias, its windows blazing with the sun's reflected glory like the dazzle of molten electrum. As Rudy stood there in the shadow of the shed, he thought for a moment that it was this burning glare that was playing tricks on his eyes.

Then he saw that this was not so, but for a moment he didn't know what it was. He shaded his eyes against the blinding silvery shimmer that hung in the air like a twisting slit of fire, blinking in the almost painful brilliance that stabbed forth as the slit, or line of brightness, widened scarcely a dozen yards in front of him. He had the momentary impression that space and reality were splitting apart, that the three dimensions of this world were merely painted on a curtain, and that air and ground and cabin and hills were being folded aside, to reveal a more piercing light, blinding darkness, and swirling nameless colors beyond. Then, through that gap, a dark form stumbled, robed and hooded in brown, a drawn sword gleaming in one hand and a trailing bundle of black velvet gripped tightly in the crook of the other arm. The sword blade was bright, as if it reflected searing light, and it smoked.

Blinded by the intensity of the light, Rudy turned his face away, confused, disoriented, and shocked. When he turned back, the blazing vision was gone. There remained only an old man in a brown robe, an old man who held a sword in one hand and a wailing baby in the other arm.

Rudy blinked. "What in hell was I drinking last night?" he asked aloud. "And who the hell are you?"

The old man sheathed the sword in one smooth, competent gesture, and Rudy found himself thinking that whoever this was, he must be very quick on the draw with that thing. It looked real, too, balanced and razor-sharp. The old man replied, in a scratchy baritone, "I am called Ingold Inglorion. This is Prince Altir Endorion, last Prince of the House of Dare."

"Hunh?"

The old man drew back the hood from his face, revealing a countenance wholly nondescript except for the remarkable blueness of the heavy-lidded eyes and for its expression of awesome serenity. Rudy had never seen a face like that, gentle, charming, and supremely in command. It was the face of a saint, a wizard, or a nut.

Rudy rubbed his aching eyes. "How'd you get here?"

31

"I came through the Void that separates your universe from mine," Ingold explained reasonably. "You could hardly have missed it."

He's a nut.

Curious, Rudy walked slowly around him, keeping his distance. The guy was armed, after all, and something in the way he'd handled the sword made Rudy sure he knew how to use it. He looked like a harmless old buffer, except for the Francis of Assisi get-up, but years of association with the brotherhood of the road had given Rudy an instinctive caution of anybody who was armed, no matter how harmless he looked. Besides, anybody running around dressed like that was obviously certifiable.

The old man watched him in return, looking rather amused, one thick-muscled hand absently caressing the child he held into muffled whimpers, then silence. Rudy noticed that the old man's dark robes and the child's blankets were rank with smoke. He supposed they could have come out of the shadows around the corner of the house in the moment the reflected sunlight had blinded him, giving the impression they'd stepped out of a kind of flaming aura, but that explanation still didn't tell him where they'd come from, or how the old man had happened to acquire the kid.

After a long moment's silence Rudy asked, "Are you for real?"

The old man smiled, a leaping webwork of lines springing into being among the tangle of white beard. "Are you?"

"I mean, are you supposed to be some kind of wizard or something?"

"Not in this universe." Ingold surveyed the young man before him for a moment, then smiled again. "It's a long story," he explained, turned, and strolled back toward the house as if he owned the place, with Rudy tagging along in his wake. "Would it be possible for me to remain here until my contact in this world can reach me? It shouldn't be long."

What the hell? "Yeah, sure, go ahead." Rudy sighed. "I'm only here myself because my car died on me—I mean, it's not really my car—and I have to check out the pump and see if I can get it running again." Seeing Ingold's puzzled frown, he remembered the guy was supposed to be from another universe where, since they used swords—

32

and he'd still like to know where the old man had picked that one up—the internal combustion engine hadn't been invented. "You do know what a car is?"

"I'm familiar with the concept. We don't have them in my world, of course."

"Of course."

Ingold led the way calmly up the steps and into the house. He proceeded straight on down the hall to the bedroom, where he placed the child on the stained, lumpy mattress of the cot. The baby immediately began working himself free of his blankets, with the apparently fixed intention of rolling off and braining himself on the cement floor.

"But who *are* you?" Rudy persisted, leaning in the doorway.

"I told you, my name is Ingold. Here, enough of that . . ." He reached down and stopped Prince Tir from worming himself over the edge. Then he glanced back over his shoulder. "You haven't told me your name," he added.

"Uh—Rudy Solis. Where'd you get the kid?"

"I'm rescuing him from enemies," Ingold stated matter-of-factly.

Wonderful, Rudy thought. *First the fuel pump and now this.*

Untangled, the kid was revealed to be a crawler of six months or so, with a pink rosebud of a face, fuzzy black hair, and eyes that were the deep unearthly blue of the heart of a morning glory. Ingold set the kid back in the middle of the bed, where he promptly started for the edge again. The old man removed his dark, smoke-smelling mantle and spread it out like a groundcloth on the floor. Under it he wore a white wool robe, much patched and stained, a worn leather belt, and a low-slung sword belt that supported the sword and a short dagger in beat-up scabbards. The whole setup looked authentic as hell.

Ingold picked up the child again and put him down on the mantle on the floor. "There," he said. "Now will you stay where you are put and fall asleep like a sensible person?"

Prince Altir Endorion made a definite but unintelligible reply.

"Good," Ingold said, and turned toward the door.

"Whose kid is he?" Rudy asked, folding his arms and watching the old man and the child.

For the first time that look of self-command broke, and grief, or the concealment of grief, tightened into the muscles of the old man's face. His voice remained perfectly steady. "He is the child of a friend of mine." he replied quietly, "who is now dead." There was a moment's silence, the old man concentrating on turning back the cuffs of his faded robe, revealing a road map of old scars striping the hard, heavy muscle of his forearms. When he looked up again, that expression of gentle amusement was back in his eyes. "Not that you believe me, of course."

"Well, now that you mention it, I don't."

"Good." Ingold smiled, stepping past Rudy into the narrow hall. "It's better that you shouldn't. Close the door behind you, would you, please?"

"Because, for one thing," Rudy said, following him down the hall to the kitchen, "if you're from a whole other universe, like you say, how come you are speaking English?"

"Oh, I'm not." Ingold located one of the six-packs of beer on the kitchen counter and extricated a can for himself and one for Rudy. "Speaking English, that is. You only hear it as English in your mind. If you were to come to my world, I could arrange the same spell to cover you."

Oh, yeah? Rudy thought cynically. *And I suppose you figured out how to operate push-tab beer cans the same way?*

"Unfortunately, there's no way I can prove this to you," Ingold went on placidly, seating himself on the corner of the grimy formica table top, the butter-colored morning sunlight gilding the worn hilt of his sword with an edge like fire. "Different universes obey different physical laws, and yours, despite its present close conjunction with my own, is very far from the heart and source of Power. The laws of physics here are very heavy, very certain and irreversible, and unaffected by . . . certain other considerations." He glanced out the window to his right, scanning the fall of the land beyond, judging the angle of the sun, the time of day. The expression of calculation in his eyes, adding up pieces of information that had nothing to do with Rudy or with maintaining a role, troubled Rudy with a disquieting sense that the old man was too calm about it, too matter-of-fact. He'd met masqueraders before; living in Southern California, you could hardly help it. And, young or old, all those would-be Brothers of Atlantis had the same air of being in costume, no matter how cool they were about it. They all knew you were noticing them.

This old croaker didn't seem to be thinking about Rudy at all, except as a man to be dealt with in the course of something else.

Rudy found himself thinking, *He's either what he says he is, or so far out in left field he's never coming back.*

And his indignant outrage at being beguiled into admitting two possibilities at all was almost immediately superimposed on the uneasy memory of that gap of light and the colors he'd thought he'd seen beyond.

Watch it, kiddo, he told himself. *The old guy's not hitting on all his cylinders. If you're not careful, he'll have you doing it next.* So he asked, "But you are a wizard in your own world?" Because the outfit couldn't be for anything else.

Ingold hesitated, his attention returning to Rudy; then he nodded. "Yes," he said slowly.

Rudy leaned back against the counter and took a pull at his beer. "You pretty good?"

Ingold shrugged and seemed to relax, as if reassured by the disbelief in Rudy's tone. "I'm said to be."

"But you can't do any magic here." A foregone conclusion—the ersatz Merlins of the world did not often operate outside a friendly environment.

But the ersatz Merlins of the world didn't usually smile, then hide the smile, at the suggestion of fraud. "No. That isn't possible."

Rudy simply couldn't figure the guy. But something in that serene self-assurance prompted him to ask, "Yeah, but how can you be a wizard without magic?" He finished his beer, crumpled the aluminum with one hand, and tossed it into the corner of the bare room.

"Oh, wizardry has really very little to do with magic."

Taken off-balance, Rudy paused, the old man's voice and words touching some feeling in his soul that echoed, like the distant note of a long-forgotten guitar. "Yeah, but—" he began, and stopped again. "What is wizardry?" he asked quietly. "What is magic?"

"What isn't?"

There was silence for the space of about two long-drawn breaths, Rudy fighting the sudden, illogical, and overwhelming notion that that was the reply of a man who understood magic. Then he shook his head, as if to clear it of the webs of the old man's crazy fantasies. "I don't understand you."

Ingold's voice was soft. "I think you do."

He really did step out of that light.

In another minute you'll be as crazy as he is.

Confusion made Rudy's voice rough. "All I understand is that you're crazier than a loon . . ."

"Am I really?" The white eyebrows lifted in mock offense. "And just how do you define crazy?"

"Crazy is somebody who doesn't know the difference between what's real and what's just in his imagination."

"Ah," Ingold said, all things made clear. "You mean if I disbelieved something that I saw with my own eyes, just because I imagined it to be impossible, I would be crazy?"

"I did not either see it!" Rudy yelled.

"You know you did," the wizard said reasonably. "Come now, Rudy, you believe in thousands of things you've never seen with your own eyes."

"I do not!"

"You believe in the ruler of your country."

"Well, I've seen him! I've seen him on television."

"And have you not also seen people materializing out of showers of silver light on this television?" Ingold asked.

"Dammit, don't argue that way! You know as well as I do . . ."

"But I don't, Rudy. If you choose deliberately to disregard the evidence of your own senses, it's your problem, not mine. I am what I am . . ."

"You are not!"

Slowly, in an absent-minded imitation of Rudy's can-squashing ritual, Ingold crushed his empty beer can into a wad slightly smaller than his own fist. "Really, you're one of the most prejudiced young men I've ever met," he declared. "For an artist you have singularly little scope."

Rudy drew in his breath to reply to that one, then let it out again. "How did you know I'm an artist?"

Amused blue eyes challenged him. "A wild guess." In his heart Rudy knew it had been nothing of the kind. "You are, aren't you?"

36

"Uh—well, I paint airbrush pictures on the sides of custom vans, and pinstripe motorcycle fuel tanks, that kind of stuff." Seeing Ingold's puzzled frown, he conceded, "Yeah, I guess you could call it art."

There was another silence, the old man looking down at his scarred hands in the sunlight on the table top, the isolated cabin utterly silent but for the faint creaking insect noises in the long grasses outside. Then he looked up and smiled. "And is it beneath your dignity to have friends with, I think you call it, nonstandard reality?"

Rudy thought about some of the people who hung around Wild David's bike shop. Nonstandard was one way of putting it. He laughed. "Hell, if I felt that way I'd have maybe about two friends. Okay, you win."

The old man looked startled and just a little worried. "You mean you believe me?"

"No—but it doesn't bother me if it doesn't bother you."

If he's schizo, Rudy found himself thinking later in the morning, *he's got it all down.* Wizardry, the mythical Realm of Darwath, the Hidden City of Quo on the Western Ocean where the garnered learning of a hundred generations of mages was stored in the dark labyrinths of Forn's Tower—Ingold had it all, seemed to know it as intimately as Rudy knew his own world of bars and bikes and body shops, of smog and steel. Through the long, warm morning, Rudy messed with the Chevy's engine, Ingold lending a hand occasionally when one was needed and staying out of the way when it wasn't, and their talk drifted over magic, the Void, engines, and painting. Ingold never slipped up.

Not only was he totally familiar with his own fantasy world, but Rudy noticed he had the lapses of knowledge that a man imperfectly acquainted with this world would have. He seemed totally fascinated with Rudy's world, with the wonders of radio and television, the complexities of the welfare system, and the mysteries of the internal combustion engine. He had the insatiable curiosity that, he had said, was the hallmark of wizards: the lust for knowledge, almost any kind of knowledge, that superseded even the most elementary considerations of physical comfort or safety.

If it wasn't for the kid, Rudy thought, glancing from

37

the tangled shadows of the car toward the wizard, who was seated in the long grass, thoughtfully dissecting and examining a seed pod, *I wouldn't care. Hell, the guy could claim to be Napoleon and it'd be no business of mine. But he's got no business with a kid that young, wandering around a million miles from noplace.*

And his hangover hallucination of their stepping out of the burning air returned to him, the absolute reality of the vision, far clearer than anything muscatel or anything else had ever done for him, something about it troubled him, something he could not yet define.

Then the rusted nut he was working on gave way, and other matters claimed his attention. Ten minutes later he crawled out from under the car, grease-smudged, hot, and disgusted. Ingold set aside the seed pod and raised his eyebrows inquiringly.

Rudy flung the wrench he was holding violently into the dirt. "Goddam fuel pump," he sighed, and dropped cross-legged to the ground at the wizard's side.

"It is the pump, then, and not the line?" Rudy had briefed him on the problem.

"Yeah." He cursed, and elaborated on the car, its owner, and things in general. He finished with, "So I guess the only thing to do is walk to the highway and hitch."

"Well," Ingold said comfortably, "my contact in this world should be here very shortly. You could always get a ride back to civilization with her."

Rudy paused in wiping his oily hands on a rag he'd fished out of the back seat. "Your what?"

"My contact in this world." Seeing Rudy's surprise, Ingold explained. "I shall be stranded the night in your world and, though on occasion I've starved, I see no reason to do it if it can be avoided."

"So you're just passing through, is that it?" Rudy wondered if there was, in fact, such a contact, or if this was yet one more strange figment of the old man's peculiar imagination.

"In a manner of speaking," Ingold said slowly.

"But if you're a wizard in your own world, how come you'd starve?" Rudy asked, more out of lazy curiosity than anything else. "How come you can't just make food appear if you're hungry?"

"Because it doesn't work that way," Ingold said simply.

"Creating the illusion of food is relatively simple. To make a piece of grass like this one convincingly resemble bread requires only that in taste, texture, and appearance, I convince you that you are eating bread. But if you ate it, it would provide you no more nourishment than the grass, and on a steady diet of such things you would quickly starve. But literally to transform the inner nature of the grass would be to alter reality itself, to tamper with the fabric of the entire universe."

"Lot of trouble to go through for a crummy piece of bread."

"Well, more than that, it's potentially dangerous. Any tampering, no matter how small, with the fabric of the universe is perilous. That is why shape-changing is seldom done. Most high-ranking wizards understand the principle behind turning oneself into a beast—with the mind and heart of a beast—but very, very few would dare to put it into practice. An archmage might do it, in peril of his life. But . . ." He raised his head suddenly, and Rudy caught the far-off chugging of an engine in the still, pale air of afternoon.

"My friend," Ingold explained. He got up, brushing dry grass and twigs off his robe. Rudy scrambled likewise to his feet as a dusty red Volkswagen beetle crept into view around the shoulder of the hill.

"This I gotta see."

The bug's tires surrounded it in a light cloud of dust as it made its slow approach, bumping cautiously over every rut and pothole of the treacherous road. It came to a stop a few yards away, the door opened, and a girl got out.

She took one look at Rudy and stopped, her eyes filled with suspicion and distrust. Then Ingold stepped down the bank toward her, both hands held out in welcome. "Gil," he said. "This is Rudy Solis. He thinks I'm crazy. Rudy— Gil Patterson. My contact in this world."

They regarded each other in silent animosity.

Gil would almost have preferred the Highway Patrol. This character had "biker" writen on him in letters a foot tall: greasy jeans, grubby white T-shirt, scarred boots. Dark hair faintly tinged with red fell loosely on either side of a long widow's peak almost to his shoulders; cocky dark-blue eyes under sharply backslanted black brows gave her an arrogant once-over and dismissed her. She noted the bump of an old break on his nose. RUDY was tattooed on a banner across a flaming torch on his left wrist. *A real prize.*

Kind of tall and scrawny, but not bad-looking, Rudy decided, checking her out. *Bitchy, though, I bet. A real spook.* Beyond that he noted the worn jeans, blue checkered shirt, lack of make-up, unworked hands and bitten nails, and cool, pale, forbidding eyes. *Where'd Ingold dig her up?*

Ingold went on, "Rudy's been stranded here with car trouble. Could you take him back with you as far as he needs to go when you leave, Gil, as a favor to me?"

Her eyes went warily from Ingold to Rudy, then back to the wizard's face. Ingold rested a hand briefly on her shoulder and said quietly, "It's all right. He doesn't have to believe me, Gil."

She sighed and forced herself to relax. "All right," she agreed.

Rudy had watched all this with curiosity bordering on annoyance. "Well, don't do me any favors."

Those pale gray eyes grew colder. But Ingold's hand tightened almost imperceptibly on Gil's bony shoulder, and she said, in a more natural voice, "No, it's all right."

Rudy, in turn, relaxed and meant it when he said, "Thank you. Uh—can I give you a hand with that?" for Gil had turned back to the car and was fetching out assorted provisions, including canned beef stew and diapers, from the back seat. He dropped back a pace to walk beside her as they followed Ingold up to the cabin, however, and as soon as the old man was out of earshot Rudy asked softly, "Who is he?"

She regarded him with those pale schoolmarm eyes— old-maid eyes in the face of a girl his own age. "What did he tell you?"

"That he was some kind of a wizard from another universe."

When Gil was embarrassed, she became brusque. "That's his story."

Rudy refused to be put off. "Where'd you meet him?"

Gil sighed. "It's a long story," she said, falling back on Ingold's usual explanation. "And it doesn't matter, not really."

"It matters to me," Rudy said, and glanced up ahead of

40

them to where Ingold was just vanishing into the shadows of the little house. "You see, I like the old guy, I really do, even if he isn't playing with a full deck. I'm just worried some kind of harm will come to the kid."

They stopped at the foot of the rickety steps, and Gil looked carefully for the first time at the young man's face. It was sun-bronzed and sensual, but not a crass face, nor a stupid one. "Do you think he'd let any harm come to Tir?"

Rudy remembered the old man and the child together, Ingold's gentle competence and the protectiveness in his voice when he spoke to the baby. "No," he said slowly. "No—but what are they doing out here? And what's gonna happen when he goes wandering back to civilization like that?"

There was genuine concern in his voice, which Gil found rather touching. *Besides,* she thought, *if I hadn't had the dreams, I'd probably think the same.*

She shifted her burden from one hand to the other. "It will be okay," she assured him quietly.

"You know what's going on?"

She nodded.

Rudy looked down at her doubtfully, not quite satisfied and sensing something amiss. Still, in one real sense this girl *was* Ingold's contact with reality, which in spite of his obvious shrewdness and charm the old man sorely needed. And yet—and yet— Troubled visions of the old man stumbling out of a blazing aura of silver light returned to him as he started up the steps, Gil climbing at his heels. He swung around on her abruptly, to ask, "Do you believe him?"

But before Gil could answer, the cabin door opened again, and Ingold re-emerged onto the narrow porch, a flushed, sleepy infant in his arms. "This is Prince Altir Endorion," he introduced.

Gil and Rudy came up the last few steps to join him, the question left unanswered. On the whole, Gil disliked children, but, like most hard-hearted women, she had a soft spot for the very young and helpless. She touched the round pink cheek with gingerly reverence, as if afraid the child would shatter on contact. "He's very beautiful," she whispered.

"And very wet," Ingold replied, and led the way back into the house.

It was Rudy who ended up doing the changing as the only one with experience in the task, while Gil made a lunch of beef stew and coffee on the kerosene stove, and Ingold investigated the light switches to see how electricity worked. Rudy noticed that, among other things, Gil had brought an extra can of kerosene; though, if he recalled, the little stove had been out of sight beneath a counter when he'd first come in, and there had been no signs that the house had been entered in years.

How had Ingold known?

Gil came over to him and set a styrofoam cup of steaming black liquid on the floor at his side. She watched Rudy playing tickle-me with Tir for some moments, smiling, then said, "You know, you're probably the first man I've ever seen who'd volunteer for diaper duty."

"Hell," Rudy told her, grinning. "With six younger brothers and sisters, you get used to it."

"I suppose so." She tested one of the wobbly chairs, then sat in it, her arm resting over the back. "I only had the one sister, and she's just two years younger than I am, so I never knew."

Rudy glanced up at her. "Is she like you?" he asked.

Gil shook her head ruefully. "No. She's pretty. She's twenty-two and already getting her second divorce."

"Yeah, my next-next younger sister's like that," Rudy said thoughtfully, fishing in the pocket of his discarded jacket for his motorcycle keys, which Tir received with blissful fascination and proceeded to try to eat. "She's seventeen years old, and she's been around more than I have." He caught Gil's raised eyebrow and askance look, and followed her eye to the decoration on the back of his jacket—skulls, roses, black flames, and all. "Aah, that," he said, a little embarrassed at it. "Picasso had a Blue Period. I had my Pachuco Period."

"Oh," Gil said distastefully, not believing him. "Are you in a gang?"

Rudy sat back on his heels, hearing the tone in her voice. "What the hell do you think I do, live in Fontana and go out on raids?"

Since that was exactly what she thought he did, she said, "No. I mean—" She broke off in confusion. "You mean you painted that yourself?"

"Sure," Rudy said, reaching over to spread out the

offending garment with its elaborate symbology and multiple grease stains. "I'd do it better now—I'd have different lettering, and no fire; the fire makes it look kind of trashy. That is, if I did it at all. It's kind of tacky," he admitted. "But it's good advertising."

"You mean you make your living at that?"

"Oh, yeah. For now, anyway. I work at Wild David Wilde's Paint and Body Shop in Berdoo, and painting's a hell of a lot easier than body work, let me tell you."

Gil contemplated the jacket for a moment longer, her chin resting on her folded hands on the back of the chair. Though morbid, violent, and weird, the design was well-executed and argued a certain ability and sensitivity of style. "Then you're not a biker yourself?"

"I ride a motorcycle," Rudy said. "I like bikes, work on them. I'm not in a gang, though. You can run yourself into real trouble that way." He shrugged. "Those guys are really heavy-duty. I couldn't do it."

Ingold came back in, having traced the power cables to their sources and explored the land around the little house as if seeking something in the dusty silence of the groves. Gil dished up canned beef stew and bread. As they ate, Rudy listened to the girl and the wizard talk and wondered again how much this thin, spooky-looking woman believed the old man, and how much of her conversation was tactful humoring of an old, well-loved, and totally crazy friend.

It was impossible to tell. That she was fond of him was obvious; her guarded stiffness relaxed, and with liveliness her face was almost pretty. But it was Ingold who dominated and led, she who followed, and there were times when Rudy wondered if she was as crazy as the old man.

"I never understood that about the memories," Gil was saying, blowing on her coffee to cool it. "You and Eldor talked about it, but I don't understand."

"No one really understands it," Ingold said. "It's a rare phenomenon, far rarer than wizardry. To my knowledge, in all the history of the Realm it has appeared in only three noble houses and two peasant ones. We don't know what it is or why it works, why a son will suddenly recall events that happened to his grandfather, when the grandfather never exhibited such a talent in his life, why it seems to descend only in the male line, why it skips one

43

generation, or two, or five, why some sons will remember certain events and be ignorant of others that their brothers recall with exacting clarity."

"I could be like a double-recessive gene," Gil began thoughtfully.

"A what?"

"A genetic trait . . ." She stopped. "Jeez, you people don't understand genetics, do you?"

"As in horse breeding?" Ingold asked with a smile.

She nodded. "Sort of. It's how you breed for a trait, how you get throwbacks, the more you inbreed. I'll explain it sometime."

"You mean," Rudy said, drawn into the conversation in spite of himself, "Pugsley here is supposed to remember stuff that happened to his dad and his grandpa and stuff like that?" He jiggled the baby sitting in his lap.

"He should," Ingold said. "But it's a gamble, for we do not know for certain if—and what—he will remember. His father remembers—remembered—" There was a slight shift, almost a crack, in the wizard's rusty voice as he changed the tense. "—things that happened at the time of their most remote ancestor, Dare of Renweth. And, Gil, it was Dare of Renweth who was King at the time of the rising of the Dark Ones."

"The who?" Rudy asked.

"The Dark Ones." The touch of that heavy-lidded, blue gaze gave Rudy the uncomfortable feeling of having his mind read. "The enemy whom we flee." His eyes shifted back to Gil, the light from the western window slanting strong and yellow on the sharp bones of her face. "Unfortunately, I fear the Dark Ones know it. They know many things—their power is different from mine, of a different nature, as if from a different source. I believe their attacks were concentrated on the Palace at Gae because they knew that Eldor and Tir were dangerous to them, that the memories the King and Prince held were the clue to their ultimate defeat. They have—eliminated—Eldor. Now only Tir is left."

Gil cocked her head and glanced across at the pink-cheeked baby, gravely manipulating a bunch of motorcycle keys in Rudy's lap, then at the wizard, profiled against the cracked and grimy glass of the window through which the hills could be seen, desolate, isolated, dyed gold by the deep slant of the light. Her voice was quiet. "Could they have followed you here?"

Ingold looked up at her quickly, his azure-crystal eyes meeting hers, then shifting away. "Oh, I don't think so," he said mildly. "They have no notion that the Void exists, much less how to cross it."

"How do you know?" she insisted. "You said yourself you don't understand their powers, or their knowledge. You have no power at all in this world. If they crossed the Void, would they have power?"

He shook his head. "I doubt they could even exist in this world," he told her. "The material laws here are very different. Which, incidentally, is what makes magic possible—a change in the ways the laws of physics operate . . ."

As the conversation turned to a discussion of theoretical magic and its relation to the martial arts, Rudy listened, puzzled; if Ingold had his end of the script down pat, Gil sure as hell had hers.

After a time, Ingold took charge of Tir to feed him, and Gil made her way quietly out onto the porch, seeking the silence of the last of the westering sunlight. She sat on the edge of the high platform, her booted feet dangling in space, leaning her arms along the bottom rail of the crazy old banister and watching the hills go from tawny gold to crystal, like champagne in the changing slant of the light, the air luminous with sunlit dust one moment, then suddenly overlaid with the cool of the hills' shadow. The evening wind slurred softly through the lion-colored grass of the wastelands all around. Each rock and stunted tree was imbued by the light with a unique and private beauty. The light even lent something resembling distinction to the sunken wreck of the blue Impala and the nondescript VW, half-hidden by the screen of whispering weeds.

She heard the door open and shut behind her then and smelled the dark scent of tallow and wool permeated with smoke as Ingold settled down beside her, once more wearing his dark mantle over the pale homespun of his robe. For some minutes they didn't speak at all, only watched the sunset in warm and companionable silence, and she was content.

45

Finally he said, "Thank you for coming, Gil. Your help has been invaluable."

She shook her head. "No trouble."

"Do you mind very much taking Rudy back?" She could tell by his voice he'd sensed her dislike and was troubled by it.

"I don't mind." She turned her head, her cheek resting on her arm on the rail. "He's okay. If I didn't know you, I probably wouldn't believe a word of it myself." She noticed in the golden haze of the light that, though his hair was white, his eyelashes were still the same fairish gingery red that must have been his whole coloring at one time. She went on. "But I'm going to drop him off at the main highway and come back. I don't like leaving you here alone."

"I shall be quite all right," the wizard said gently.

"I don't care," she replied.

He glanced sideways at her. "You couldn't possibly help, you know, if anything did happen."

"You have no magic here," she said softly, "and your back's to the wall. I'm not going to leave you."

Ingold folded his arms along the rail, his chin on his crossed wrists, seeming for a time only to contemplate the rippling tracks of the wind in the long grass below the porch, the rime of sun-fire like a halo on the distant hills. "I appreciate your loyalty," he said at last, "misguided though it is. But the situation will not arise. You see, I have decided to risk going back tonight, before it grows fully dark."

Gil was startled, both relieved and uneasy. "Will Tir be okay?"

"I can put a spell of protection over us both that should shield him from the worst of the shock." The sun had touched the edges of the hills already; the evening breeze wore the thin chill of coming night. "There should be a good two hours of daylight left in my own world when Tir and I return—there seems to be a disjunction of time involved in the Void, your world and mine not quite in synch. We should be able to come to cover before dark."

"Won't that be an awful risk?"

"Maybe." He turned his head a little to meet her eyes, and in the dimming evening light she thought he looked tired, the shadows of the porch railings barring his face

46

but unable to hide the deepened lines around his mouth and eyes. His fingers idled with the splinters of the wood, casually, as if he were not speaking of danger into which he would walk. "But I would rather take that risk than imperil your world, your civilization, should the Dark prove able to follow me through the Void."

Then he sighed and stood up, as if dismissing the whole subject from his mind. He helped her to her feet, his hand rough and warm and powerful, but as light and deft as a jeweler's. The last glow of the day surrounded them, silhouetted against the burning windows. "I am entitled to risk my own life, Gil," he said. "But whenever I can, I draw the line at risking the lives of others, especially those who are loyal to me, as you are. So don't be concerned. We shall be quite safe."

CHAPTER THREE

"Where you headed?" Gil carefully guided the VW in a small circle, bumping slowly over stones and uneven ground, and eased it back onto the road again. The road, the hills, the dark trees of the grove had turned gray-blue and colorless in the twilight. In her rear-view mirror, Gil saw Ingold's sword blade held high in salute. She could see him on the cabin porch, straight and sturdy in his billowing dark mantle, and her heart ached with fear at the sight. Rudy, chewing on a grass blade, one sunburned arm hanging out of the open window, was about as comforting as reruns of *The Crawling Eye* on a dark and stormy night.

"San Bernardino," Rudy said, glancing back also at the dark form of the wizard in the shadows of the house.

"I can take you there," Gil said, negotiating a gravel slide and the deep-cut spoor of last winter's rains. "I'm heading on into Los Angeles so it's not out of my way."

"Thank you" Rudy said. "It's harder than hell to get rides at night."

Gil grinned in spite of herself. "In that jacket it would be."

Rudy laughed. "You from L.A.?"

"Not originally. I go to UCLA; I'm in the Ph.D. program in medieval history there." Out of the corner of her eye she glimpsed his start of surprise, a typical reaction in men, she had found. "Originally I'm from San Marino."

"Ah," Rudy said wisely, recognizing the name of that wealthy suburb. "Rich kid."

"Not really." Gil objected more to the label than to the

48

facts. "Well—I guess you could say that. My father's a doctor."

"Specialist?" Rudy inquired, half-teasing.

"Child psychiatrist," Gil said, with a faint grin at how well the label fitted her.

"Yow."

"They've disowned me," she added with a shrug. "So it doesn't matter." Her voice was offhand, almost apologetic. She turned on the headlights and dust plumed whitely in their feeble glare. By their reflection Rudy could see that her face wore the shut, wary look again, a fortress defended against all comers.

"Why the hell would they disown you?" He was indignant in spite of himself for her sake. "Christ, my mother would forgive any one of my sisters for murder if she'd just finish high school."

Gil chuckled bitterly. "It's the Ph.D. mine objects to," she told him. "What up-and-coming young doctor or dentist is going to marry a research scholar in medieval history? She doesn't say that, but that's what she means." And Gil drove on for a time in silence.

The dark shapes of the hills loomed closer around the little car, the stars emerging in the luminous blue of the evening sky, small and bright with distance. Staring out into the milky darkness, Rudy identified the landmarks of his trip into the hills, rock and tree and the round, smooth shapes of the land. The green eyes of some tiny animal flashed briefly in the gloom, then vanished as a furry shape whipped across the dark surface of the road.

"So they kicked you out just because you want to get a Ph.D.?"

She shrugged. "They didn't really kick me out. I just don't go home anymore. I don't miss it," she added truthfully.

"Really? I'd miss it like hell." Rudy slouched back against the door, one arm draped out the window, the wind cool against wrist and throat. "I mean, yeah, my mom's house is like a bus stop, with the younger kids all over the place, and the cats, and her sisters, and dirty dishes all over the house, and my sisters' boyfriends hanging out in the back yard—but it's someplace to go, you know? Someplace I'll always be welcome, even if I do

49

have to shout to make myself heard. I'd go crazy if I had to live there, but it's nice to go back."

Gil grinned at the picture he painted, mentally contrasting it with the frigid good taste of her mother's home.

"And you left your family just to go to school?" He sounded wondering, unbelieving that she could have done such a thing.

"There was nothing there for me," Gil said. "And I want to be a scholar. They can't understand that I've never wanted to do or be or have anything else."

Another long silence. Up ahead, yellow headlights flickered in the dark. Long and low, the cement bridge of the freeway overpass bulked against the paler background of the hills; like a glittering fortress of red and amber flame, a semi roared by, the rumble of its engine like distant thunder. The VW whined up the overpass; Rudy settled back in his seat, considering her sharp-boned, rather delicate face, the generosity belying the tautness of the mouth, the sentimentalism lurking in the depths of those hard, intelligent eyes. "That's funny," he said at last.

"That anybody would like school that much?" Her voice held a trace of sarcasm, but he let it go by.

"That you'd want anything that much," he said quietly. "Me, I've never really wanted to have or do or be anything. I mean, not so much that I'd dump everything else for it. Sounds rough."

"It is," Gil said, and returned her attention to the road.

"Was that where you ran into Ingold?"

She shook her head. Though it hadn't seemed to bother the wizard that Rudy thought him a candidate for the soft room, she didn't want to discuss Ingold with Rudy.

Rudy, however, persisted. "Can you tell me what the hell that was all about? Is he really as cracked as he seems?"

"No," Gil said evasively. She tried to think up a reasonable explanation for the whole thing that she could palm off on Rudy to keep him from asking further questions. At the moment a queer uneasiness haunted her, and she didn't feel much in the mood for questions, let alone obvious disbelief. In spite of the occasional lights on the highway, she was conscious as she had never been before of the weight and depth of the night, of darkness pressing down all around them. She found herself wishing vaguely

50

that Rudy would roll up his window instead of leaning against the frame, letting the night-scented desert winds brush through the car.

Billboards fleeted garishly by them, primitive colors brilliant in the darkness; now and then a car would swoosh past, with yellow eyes staring wildly into the night. Her mind traced the long road home, the road she'd seen in last night's aching dream of restlessness that had told her where she must come, then had framed awkwardly the next chapter of her thesis, which had to be worked on tonight if she were going to make her seminar deadline. But her mind moved uncontrolledly from thing to thing, returning again and again to that silent, isolated cabin, the salute from the blade of an upraised sword . . .

"You believe him."

She turned, startled, and met Rudy's eyes.

"You believe him," he repeated quietly, not as an accusation, but as a statement.

"Yes," Gil said. "Yes, I do."

Rudy looked away from her and stared out the window. "Fantastic."

"It sounds crazy . . ." she began.

He turned back to her. "Not when he says it," he contradicted, pointing his finger accusingly, as if she would deny it. "He's the most goddam believable man I've ever met."

"You've never seen him step through the Void," Gil said simply. "I have."

That stopped Rudy. He couldn't bring himself to say, *I have, too.*

Because he knew it had just been a hallucination, born of bright sunlight and a killing hangover. But the image of it returned disturbingly—the glaring gap of light, the folding air. *But I didn't see it*, he protested; *it was all in my head.*

And, like an echo, he heard Ingold's voice saying, *You know you did.*

I know I did.

But if it was all a hangover hallucination, how did he know it?

Rudy sighed, feeling exhausted beyond words. "I don't know what the hell to believe."

"Believe what you choose," Gil said. "It doesn't matter.

He's crossing back to his own world tonight, he and Tir. So they'll be gone."

"That's fairy-tale stuff!" Rudy insisted. "Why would a— a wizard be toting a kidnapped Prince through this world on the way to someplace else anyway?"

Gil shrugged, keeping her eyes on the highway.

Annoyed, he went on. "And besides, if he was going back tonight to some world where he's got magical powers, why would he need to bum my matches off me? He wouldn't need them there."

"No, he wouldn't," Gil agreed mildly. Then the sense of what Rudy had said sank in, and she looked quickly across at him. "You mean, he did?"

"Just before we left," Rudy told her, a little smug at having caught the pair of them out. "Why would he need matches?"

Gil felt as if the blood in her veins had turned suddenly to ice. "Oh, my God," she whispered.

I am entitled to risk my own life . . . but I draw the line at risking the lives of others . . .

As if a door had opened, showing her the room beyond, she knew that Ingold had lied. And she knew why he had lied.

She swerved the Volkswagen to the side of the highway, suspicion passing instantaneously to certainty as the threadbare tires jolted on the stones of the unpaved shoulder. There was only one reason for the wizard to need matches, the wizard who, in his own world, could bring fire at his bidding.

There was only one reason, in this world, that the wizard would need fire tonight.

He hadn't spoken of going back until she'd offered to remain with him, until she'd spoken of the possibility of the Dark following him through the Void. He had refused to flee Gae until all those who needed him were utterly past help. So he would take his own chances, alone in the isolated cabin, rather than risk involving anyone else.

"Climb out," she said. "I'm going back."

"What the hell?" Rudy was staring at her as if she'd gone crazy.

"He lied," Gil said, her low voice suddenly trembling with urgency. "He lied about crossing the Void tonight.

He wanted to get rid of us both, get us out of there, before the Dark Ones come."

"What?"

"I don't care what you think," she went on rapidly, "but I'm going back. He was afraid from the beginning that they'd come after him across the Void . . ."

"Now, wait a minute," Rudy began, alarmed.

"No. You can hitch your way to where you're going. I'm not leaving him to face them alone."

Her face was white in the glare of the headlights, her pale eyes burning with an intensity that was almost frightening. *Crazy,* Rudy thought. *Both of them, totally schizoid. Why does this have to happen to me?*

"I'll go with you," he said. It was a statement, not an offer.

She drew back, instantly suspicious.

"Not that I believe you," Rudy went on, slouching against the tattered upholstery. "But you two gotta have one sane person there to look after that kid. Now turn this thing around."

With scarcely a glance at the road behind her, Gil jammed the accelerator, smoking across the center divider in a hailstorm of gravel, and roaring like a tin-pan thunderbolt into the night.

"There," Rudy said, half an hour later, as the car skidded to a bone-jarring stop on the service road below the groves. Ahead of them on its little rise, the cabin was clearly visible, every window showing a dingy yellow electric glare. Gil was out of the car before the choking cloud of dust had settled, striding quickly over the rough ground toward the porch steps. Rudy followed more slowly, picking his way carefully through the weeds, wondering how in hell he was going to get out of this situation and what he was going to say to his boss back at the body shop. *Dave, I didn't make it to work Monday because I was helping a wizard rescue a baby Prince out someplace between Barstow and San Bernardino?* Not to mention explaining why he never made it back to Tarot's party from the beer run.

He looked around him at the dark landscape, distorted by starlight, and shivered at the utter desolation of it. Cold, aimless wind stirred his long hair, bearing a scent that was not of dusty grass or hot sunlight—a scent he'd never smelled before. He hurried to catch up with Gil, his boot-heels thumping hollowly on the board stairs.

She pounded on the door. "Ingold!" she called out. "Ingold, let me in!"

Rudy slipped past her and reached through the pane of glass he'd broken last night to unlock the door from the inside. They stepped into the bare and brightly lighted kitchen as Ingold came striding down the hallway, his drawn sword in his hand and clearly in a towering rage.

"Get out of here!" he ordered them furiously.

"The hell I will," Gil said.

"You can't possibly be of any help to me . . ."

"I'm not going to leave you alone."

Rudy looked from the one to the other: the girl in her faded jeans and denim jacket, with those pale, wild eyes; the old man in his dark, billowing mantle, the sword gripped, poised, in one scarred hand. *Loonies,* he thought. *What the hell have I walked into?* He headed down the hall.

Tir lay wrapped in his dark velvet blankets on the bed, blue eyes wide with fear. The only other thing in the bare room was a pile of kindling in one corner, looking as if every piece of wooden furniture in the little cabin had been broken up; next to it stood the can of kerosene. Steps sounded behind him in the hall, and Ingold's voice, taut as wire, said, "Don't you understand?"

"I understand," Gil said quietly. "That's why I came back."

"Rudy," Ingold said, and the tone in his voice was one of a man utterly used to command. "I want you to take Gil, get her in the car, and get her out of here. Now. Instantly."

Rudy swung around. "Oh, I'm gonna get out of here all right," he said grimly. "But I'm taking the kid with me. I don't know what you guys think you're doing, but I'm not leaving a six-month-old kid to be mixed up in it."

"Don't be a fool," Ingold snapped.

"Look who's talking!"

Then, as Rudy bent to pick up the child from the bed, the lights went out.

In one swift movement, Ingold turned and kicked the door shut, the sword gleaming like foxfire in his hand.

The little starlight leaking through the room's single window showed his face beaded with sweat.

Rudy set the whimpering baby down again, muttering,
"Goddam fuses." He started for the door.

Gil gasped. "Rudy, no!"

Ingold caught her arm as she moved to stop him. There
was deceptive mildness in his voice as it came from the
darkness. "You think it's the fuse?"

"Either that or a short someplace in the box," Rudy
said. He glanced over his shoulder at them as he opened
the hall door, seeing their indistinct outlines in the near-
total blackness; the faint touch of filtered starlight haloed
Ingold's white hair and picked out random corners of Gil's
angular frame. The edge of Ingold's drawn sword glim-
mered, as if with a pallid light of its own.

The hall was black, pitch, utterly black, and Rudy
groped his way blindly along it, telling himself that his
nervousness came from being trapped in a house in the
middle of nowhere with a deluded scholar and a charming
and totally insane old geezer armed with a razor-sharp
sword, a book of matches, and a can and a half of kerosene. After that stygian gloom, the dark kitchen seemed
almost bright; he could make out the indistinct forms of the
table, the counter; the thread-silver gleam on the hooked
neck of the faucet; the pale, distinct glow of the windows
by the door; the single one in the left with the broken pane.

Then he saw what was coming in through the broken
pane.

He never knew how he got back to the bedroom,
though later he found bruises on his body where he'd
blundered against the walls in his flight. It seemed that
one instant he was standing in the darkness of the tiny
kitchen, seeing that hideous shape crawling through the
window, and that next he was falling against the bedroom
door to slam it shut, sobbing. "It's out there! It's out
there!"

Ingold, standing over him in the gloom, scarred face outlined in the misty gleam of his sword blade, said softly,
"What did you expect, Rudy? Humans?"

Firelight flared. Gil had made a kind of campfire out of
splintered kindling in the middle of the cement floor and
was coughing in the rank smoke. Lying on the sagging
mattress, Tir was staring at the darkness with eyes huge

with terror, whimpering like a beaten puppy afraid to bark. Another child would have been screaming; but, whatever atavistic memories crowded his infant brain, they warned him that to cry aloud was death.

Rudy got slowly to his feet, shaking in every limb with shock. "What are we gonna do?" he whispered. "We could get out the back, make it down to the car . . ."

"You think the car would start?" In the smoldery orange glare, the old man's eyes never left the door. Even as he was speaking, Rudy could see that both his hands were on the long hilt of the sword, poised to strike. "I doubt we would make it to the car in any case. And—the house limits its size."

Rudy gulped, cold with shock, seeing that thing again, small and hideous and yet rife with unspeakable terror. "You mean—it can change its size?"

"Oh, yes." Sword in hand, Ingold moved cat-footedly to the door. "The Dark are not material, as we understand material. They are only incompletely visible, and not always of the same—composition. I have seen them go from the size of your two hands to larger than this house in a matter of seconds."

Rudy wiped sweating palms on his jeans, sickened with horror and totally disoriented. "But if—if they're not material," he stammered, "what can we do? How can we fight?"

"There are ways." Firelight played redly over Ingold's patched mantle as he stood, one hand resting on the door-knob, the other holding ready the gleaming witchfire of the blade, his head bowed, listening for some sound. After a moment he spoke again, his voice barely a whisper. "Gil," he said, "I want you to take Tir and get between the bed and the wall. Rudy, how much of a fire do we have left?"

"Not much. That wood was dry as grass. It's going quick."

Ingold stepped back from the door, though he never took his attention from it. The little room was filled with smoke, the flaring fire already sinking, feebly holding at bay the encroaching ring of shadows. Without looking back, he held out his hand. "Give me the kerosene, Rudy."

Wordlessly, Rudy obeyed.

Moving swiftly now, Ingold sheathed his sword in a single fluid gesture, took the can, and set to work, un-

56

screwing the filler-cap and throwing a great swatch of the clear liquid over the dry wood of the door. It glittered in the yellow firelight, its throat-catching smell mixing with the gritty foulness of the smoke, nearly choking Gil, who stood with her back pressed to the icy concrete of the wall, the muffled baby motionless in her arms. The fire's light had gone from yellow to murky orange, the brown shadows of the wizard's quick, sure movements wavering, vast and distorted, over the imprisoning walls. Ingold came back toward her and saturated the mattress with the last of the kerosene, its stink nearly suffocating her at close range. Then he set the empty can down softly, turned and drew his sword again, all in one smooth move; all told, he had had his sword sheathed for less than forty seconds.

He returned to the center of the room, a few feet in front of the dying fire, which had fallen in on itself to a fading heap of ash and crawling embers. As the darkness grew around him, the pallid light that seemed to burn up off the blade grew brighter, bright enough to highlight his scarred face. He said softly, "Don't be afraid." Whether it was a spell he cast, or merely the strength of his personality alone, Gil did not know, but she felt her apprehension lessen, her fear give place to a queer, cold numbness. Rudy moved out of his frozen immobility, took the last stick of unburned kindling, and lit it from the remains of the blaze.

Darkness seemed to fill the room and, heavier than the darkness, a silence that breathed. In that silence Gil heard the faint blundering sounds in the hall, a kind of chitinous scratching, as if dark fumbled eyelessly through dark. Against her own heart, she could feel the baby's heart hammering with small violence, and a chill wind began to seep through the cracks in the door, touching her sweating face with feathers of cold. She could smell it, the harsh, acid blood-smell of the Dark.

Ingold's rusty voice came very calmly out of the shadows. "Rudy," he said, "take that torch and stand next to the door. Don't be afraid, but when the creature comes in, I want you to close the door behind it and light the kerosene. Will you do that?"

Empty, cold, keyed up long past the point of feeling anything, Rudy whispered, "Yeah, sure." He sidled cautiously past the wizard, the flaming wood flickering in his hand. As he took his post by the door, he could feel the presence of the thing, a nightmare aura of fear. He felt it bump the door, softly, a testing tap, far above his own eye level, and his flesh crawled at the touch. The thing would pass him—if it did pass him and didn't turn on the nearest person to it as it came through the door—within touching distance. But on the other hand, the thought crossed his mind that if it did pass him, there was nothing to prevent him from slipping out that open door and making a run for the car.

If the car would start. If, having polished off Ingold and Gil, the Dark didn't come after him anyway. No! The need was to finish it now—the Dark One, the Enemy, the thing from across the Void, the obscene intruder into the warm, soft world of the California night . . .

Groping for the shattered ends of his world-view, Rudy could only stand in darkness beside the door, torch in hand, and wait.

The last glow of the embers was fading, the only light in the room now Rudy's smoldering torch and the gleaming challenge of the blade that Ingold held upright before him, his eyes glittering in the reflected witchlight like the eyes of an old wolf. There was a sibilant rustle of robes as he stirred, bracing himself, a whispering sigh as the dying ashes collapsed and scattered. The wind that ruffled so coldly through the cracks in the door seemed to drop and fail.

In the same instant that the door exploded inward, Ingold was striding forward, blade flashing down in an arc of fire to meet the bursting tidal wave of darkness. Rudy got a hideous glimpse of the fanning canopy of shadow and the endless, engulfing mouth, fringed in sloppy tentacles whose writhings splattered the floor with smoking slime. As if released from a spell, Tir began to scream, the high, thin, terrified sound going through Rudy's brain like a needle. The sword flashed, scattering fire; the creature drew back, unbelievably agile for that soft floating bulk, the slack of its serpentlike tail brushing Rudy's shoulders as it uncoiled in a whip of darkness. The thing filled the room like a cloud, its darkness covering them, seeming to swell and pulse as if its whole bloated, obscene body were a single slimy organ. The whip-tail slashed out,

58

cutting at Ingold's throat, and the wizard ducked and shifted inward for position with the split-second reflexes of a far younger man. In his dark robes, he was barely to be seen in the darkness; mesmerized, Rudy watched, hypnotized by the burning arc of the wizard's blade and the thing that snatched at him like a giant hand of shadow.

Gil was screaming, "The fire! The fire!" The sound was meaningless to his ears; it was the heat of his touchlight burning down almost to his hands that made him remember. As if awakened from a dream, he started, kicked the door shut, and hit the greasy smear of the kerosene with the last burning stump. The door exploded into fire, scorching Rudy as he leaped back.

The Dark One, thrown into crimson visibility, writhed and twisted as if in pain, changing size again and shooting up toward the ceiling. But streaks of fire were already rushing up the walls to the tinder-dry rafters. Sparks stung Rudy's exposed hands and face as he ducked across the open space of the floor and threw himself over the bed to crash against the wall at Gil's side. More sparks rained, sizzling, on the wet, twisting shadow of the Dark.

The room was a furnace, blinding and smothering. Bleeding light silhouetted the creature, which fled this way and that, seeking a way out. Trapped by the fire, it turned like a cat and fell on Ingold, the whiplike tail elongating into spiny wire, slashing at his hands, his eyes, its claws catching at his body. The blade carved smoking slivers from the soft tissue, but the thing loomed too big, moved too swiftly in the cramped space, for Ingold to get in for a killing blow. Flattened against the wall, suffocating in the heat, and burned by the rain of falling sparks, Gil and Rudy both could see that Ingold was being pushed steadily back toward the corner where they crouched behind the filthy bed, hampered fatally by his need to remain at all costs between the creature and the Prince. He fell back, a step at a time, until Gil could have stretched her arms across the bed and touched his shoulder. Now, along with the sparks, they were burned by the flying droplets of acid that scattered like sweat from the creature's twisting body.

Then the Dark One feinted with claws and tail, eluding the slash of the blade by fractions of an inch and throwing itself past the wizard with a rush. In the same split second Ingold flung himself over the mattress to the wall, between

59

Gil and Rudy. As he did so, whether by accident or by design, the kerosene-saturated cotton went up in a wall of fire that singed the hem of his cloak and engulfed the Dark One in a roaring wave of scarlet heat. For one second Gil was conscious only of the wild, terrified screaming of the child in her arms, of the howling inferno only feet from her body, and of the heat of the holcaust that swallowed her. Then the wall of fire bulged inward, and the black shape appeared, distorted and buckling, blazing as it hurled itself, burning and dying, upon them all. Gil screamed as hot wind and darkness covered her.

Then all things vanished in a sudden, blinding firefall of light and color and cold.

CHAPTER FOUR

There was only wind, and darkness. Gil stirred, her body one undifferentiated ache, frozen to the bone. The motion brought her stomach up into her throat. She felt as if she had swum a long way in rough cold water after a heavy meal, sickened and exhausted and weak. There seemed to be a weight of warm velvet clutched in her tired arms, a taste of earth and grass in her mouth, and the rankness of smoke in her jacket and hair.

All around her, there was no sound but the wind.

Painfully, she sat up. The child in her arms was silent. Under wispy starlight, she could make out bleak, rounded foothills stretching away in all directions around her, stony and forsaken, and combed incessantly by the ice-winds out of the north. Close beside her lay Ingold, face down, all but invisible in the darkness save for the faint edge of starlight on his drawn sword. A little farther away Rudy was sitting, curled in a semifetal position with his head clasped between his hands.

She asked, "You okay?"

His voice was muffled. "Okay? I'm still trying to figure out if I'm alive." He raised his head, his dark, slanting eyebrows black in the starlight against the whiteness of his face. "Did you—were you—?"

She nodded.

He dropped his head back to his hands. "Christ, I was hoping it was all a hallucination. Are we—wherever Ingold comes from?"

He still won't say it out loud, Gil thought. She looked

around her at the ghostly pewter landscape, indistinct under the starlight, and said, "We're sure not in California."

Rudy got up, stumbling as he came over to collapse beside her. "The kid okay?"

"I don't know. I can't wake him. He's breathing—" She pressed her fingers to the child's waxy cheek, brought her lips close to the little rosebud mouth, and felt the thin trickle of breath. "Ingold said two crossings in twenty-four hours could do him a lot of harm."

"The way I feel now, I don't think I could survive another one no matter when I did it. Let's see." He took the child from her, joggled him gently, and felt how cold his face was. "We'd better wake Ingold. Does this place have a moon?"

"It should," Gil said. "Look, the constellations are the same. There's the Big Dipper. That's Orion there."

"Weird," Rudy said, and brushed the long hair back from his face. He turned to scan the barren landscape. Shoulder upon shoulder, the hills massed up to a low range of mountains in the north, a black wall of rock edged with a starlit knife blade of snow. Southward, the rolling land closed them in, except for a dark gap through which could be glimpsed the remote glimmer of a distant river. "Wherever the hell we are, we'd better get someplace fast. If any more of those things show up, we're in deep yoghurt. Hey!" he called to Ingold, who stirred and flung out one groping hand to catch the hilt of his sword. "Stay with us, man."

"I'll be all right," Ingold said quietly.

Lying, Gil thought. She touched his shoulder, found his mantle splotched all over with great patches of charred slime that brushed off in a kind of flaky, blackish dust. Her own right sleeve was covered with it, the back of her hand and wrist smarting and scorched. The Dark One, in dying, had come very close to taking them all.

Ingold half-rolled over, brought his hand up, and rubbed his eyes. "Is the Prince all right?"

"I don't know. He's out cold," Gil said worriedly.

The wizard sighed, dragged himself to a sitting position, and reached out to take the baby from Rudy's arms. He listened to Tir's breath and stroked the tiny face gently with one scarred hand. Then he closed his eyes; for a long time he seemed to be meditating. Only the thin moaning of the wind broke the silence, but all around them the night was alive with danger. Gil and Rudy were both aware of the depth of the darkness as they had never been, back in the world of Southern California, where there was always a glow in the sky from somewhere, competing with moon and star. Here the stars seemed huge, intent, staring down with great, watchful eyes from the void of night. Darkness covered the land, and their one brief contact with the Dark was all Rudy and Gil had needed to make them conscious of how unprotected they were, how uneasy with the ancient fear of being in open ground at night.

At length Tir gave a little sob and began to cry, the weak, persistent cry of an exhausted baby. Ingold rocked him against his chest and murmured unintelligible words to him until he grew silent again, then held him, looking for a moment into the dark distance, idly stroking the fuzzy black hair. For a moment Gil saw, not a wizard rescuing the Prince and heir of the Realm, but only an old man cradling the child of his dead friend.

Finally he looked up. "Come. We had best move on."

Rudy got stiffly to his feet and gave first Gil, then Ingold, a hand up. "Yeah, I wanted to ask you about that," he said as the wizard handed Gil the child and proceeded to wipe his sword blade on the corner of his mantle and sheathe it. "Just where can we go to, clear the hell out here?"

"I think," the wizard said slowly, "that we had best make for Karst, the old summer capital of the Realm, some fifteen miles from here in the hills. Refugees from Gae have gone there; we can get shelter, and food, and news, if nothing else."

Rudy objected uneasily. "That's a helluva long way to go truckin' around in the middle of the night."

"Well, you may stay here, of course," the old man agreed magnanimously.

"Thanks a lot."

The rising moon edged the hills in a thin flame of silver as they moved off, the shadows of the rolling land profound and terrible in the icy night. Ingold's dark mantle whispered like a ghost across the silver grass.

"Uh, Ingold?" Rudy said hesitantly as they started down

the long slope of the land. "I'm sorry I said you were a nut."

Ingold glanced back at him, a glint of the old mischief in his eyes. Gravely, he said, "Apology accepted, Rudy. I'm only pleased we were able to convince you—"

"Hey—" Rudy bristled, and the wizard laughed softly.

"I admit it was not a very likely story. Another time I shall do better."

Rudy picked his way down the stony trail after him, dusting black crud off the gaudy sleeves of his patched jacket. "I hope you don't plan to do much of this," he said. "It's too damn hard on your friends."

They were on the move until just before dawn. Though the night was profoundly silent and cold, nothing worse was seen or heard. If the Dark Ones hunted, they did not hunt these hills.

After several miles Ingold left the wind-combed silver slopes of the foothills, and they began working their way up a steep wooded valley that seemed to lead straight back into the heart of the mountains, with the scent of the crackling mat of autumn leaves under their feet and from somewhere the far-off trickling sounds of water. Only once in the woods did Ingold break the silence, to say, "I'm avoiding the main road up from the plains and leading you into Karst by the back way. The road would make walking easier, but it will be crowded with refugees and consequently in greater danger from the Dark Ones. I personally have no desire for further swordplay tonight."

Gil, weary already from stumbling over broken ground with fifteen pounds of sleeping infant in her arms, wondered how Ingold had managed this far, after the original battle at the Palace of Gae, no sleep, and the fight with the Dark in the isolated shack in the orange groves. Did all wizards have that kind of reserve strength to draw on, she wondered, or was Ingold simply incredibly tough and enduring? In the shadows of his hood, his face was white and tired, his eyes circled by dark smudges of weariness. Red welts marked where the thing's whiplike tail had cut his face, and the shoulders of his mantle were scattered with spark-holes; dappled with the wan starlight, he moved through the darkness of the woods as straight and serene as some old gentleman out for an afternoon promenade in the park.

They stepped from the dark beneath the trees into the clearer area of second growth along the stream, and the music of the water grew suddenly louder to their ears. After the darkness of the woods, even the shifting moonlight seemed bright. It illuminated a ghostly dreamscape of black and pewter, of deep patches of river sand and water-smoothed rocks. Before them, up the stream bed, loomed the black wall of the mountain's flank, featureless against the muted glow of the sky, save for one spot of orange, a distant glimmer of fire in the night.

"There," Ingold said, pointing. "That will be Karst. There we should find what is left of the government of the Realm of Darwath."

Karst, when they reached the town, reminded Gil of every wealthy mountain resort town she had ever seen, beautiful with a self-consciously rustic elegance of roomy, splendid houses mingled with ancient trees. As they passed the dark mansions, locked up tight in leafy shadows, she could make out variations of the architecture which she had never before seen, but which were eerily familiar to her—the clusters of smooth, narrow pilasters, the twining plant motifs of the capitals, and, here and there, pierced stone molding in an elaborate geometrical design. As they came toward the center of town she saw sheep and cows tethered or in folds close around some of the buildings, their staring eyes gleaming in fright in the darkness. As they passed out of the woods, the path they walked turned to cobblestones, the mossy pavement down the center of the lane sporting a thin, silver trickle of water. For a moment, walls enclosed them in sinister shadow; then they emerged into firelight as brilliant as day.

The town square was deserted. Huge bonfires had been kindled there, the flames reaching fifteen feet toward the cool, watching stars, the light gleaming redly on the black waters of the great town fountain with its wide lichen-rimmed bowl and dark, obscure statuary. In the flickering shadows surrounding the square, Gil could distinguish the walls and turrets of several opulent villas, the fortresslike towers of what she guessed was a church, and the massive foursquare bulk of what was undoubtedly the Grand Market and Town Hall, three and a half storeys of gemlike half-timbering, like black and white lace in the dark. It was for this edifice that Ingold made.

The double doors of the hall were ten feet high and wide enough to admit a cart and team, with a little man-size postern door cut in one corner. Ingold tested it; it was bolted from within. Since his body interposed between them and the door, Gil didn't see what he did, but a moment later he pushed it open and slipped through into the light and the clamoring noise beyond.

The entire lower floor of the building, one immense pillared market hall, was jammed to bursting with people. It was deafening with the unceasing chaos of voices, rank with grease and urine and unwashed bodies, smelly clothes and fried fish. A blue fog of woodsmoke hid the groined ceiling, stung the eyes, and limited visibility to a few yards in any direction. It must have been close to five in the morning, but people wandered around, talking, arguing, fetching water from a couple of half-empty butts over in one corner of the room. Children dashed aimlessly between the serried pillars and endless jumbled mounds of personal belongings; men stood in clusters, gesturing, cursing, sharpening swords. Mothers called to children; grandmothers and grandfathers huddled next to pitiful bundles of possessions, elbow to elbow with one another in hopeless confusion. Some people had brought crated ducks, chickens, and geese; the gabble of fowl and stink of guano mingled with the rest of the sensory onslaught. Gil glimpsed a girl of about ten in the homespun dress of a peasant, sitting on a pile of bedding, cradling a sleek brown cat in her arms; somewhere else, a woman in yellow satin, her elaborately coiffed hair falling in haglike disarray around her face, rocked back and forth on her heels next to a chicken crate and prayed at the top of her voice. The firelight threw a glaring orange cast over everything, turning the crowd and enclosure into a scene from the anteroom of Hell.

Smoke stung Gil's eyes and made them water as she picked her way in Ingold's wake through the close-packed ranks of people, sidestepping pots, pans, water buckets, bundles of clothes and bedding, small children and men's feet, heading toward the massive stairway that curved upward from the room's center to the floor above, and the table at the foot of those stairs.

Someone recognized Ingold and called out in surprise. His name was repeated, back and back, washing like ripples of meaningless sound to the far corners of that shadow-muffled room. And that sound was of awe and wonder and fear. People edged away from the wizard's feet to let him pass by. Someone snatched a sleeping child back; someone else raked a bundle of clothes and a money-bag out of his path. Magically, an aisle opened before him, an aisle lined with obscure forms and the glitter of watching eyes, a path to the table at the foot of the stairs and the small group of people assembed about it.

Except for the soft clucking of some chickens and one infant crying, the hall had fallen silent. Expectant eyes pinned them, the hooded form of the wizard in his singed brown robe, the man and woman, strangers in outlandish garb of scuffed blue denim, the bundle of dirty black blankets the woman carried in her arms. Gil had never felt so conspicuous in her life.

"Ingold!" A big man in the black uniform Gil recognized at once from her dreams came striding from the group to meet them, caught Ingold, and crushed him in a bear-hug that could easily have broken ribs. "We gave you up for dead, man!"

"Giving me up for dead is always unwise, Janus," Ingold replied a little breathlessly. "Especially when . . ."

But the big man's eyes had already shifted past him, taking in Rudy, Gil, and the grimy bundle in Gil's arms, the grubby gold of the emblems embroidered there. His expression changed from delight and relief to a kind of awe-struck wonder, and he released the wizard numbly, as if he had half-forgotten him. "You saved him," he whispered. "You saved him after all."

Ingold nodded. Janus looked from the child back to the sturdy old man at his side, as if he expected Ingold to vanish or change shape before his eyes. The murmuring voices of the multitude swelled again, like the swell of the sea, and washed to the far corners of the crowded room. But around the table, there was still that island of silence.

Into that silence Ingold said, perfectly calmly, "This is Gil, and this is Rudy. They were kind enough to aid me in the Prince's rescue. They are strangers from another land and know nothing of the Realm or its customs, but they are both loyal and valiant."

Rudy ducked his head, embarrassed at the description. Gil, for her part, had subconsciously avoided thinking anything positive about herself for the last fifteen years and blushed hotly. Undisturbed, Ingold continued. "Gil, Rudy—Janus of Weg, Commander of the City Guards of Gae." His gesture included the two still seated at the table. "Bektis, Court Wizard of the House of Dare; Govannin Narmenlion, Bishop of Gae."

Startled that Ingold did not hold the title, Gil looked at Bektis, a self-consciously haughty man with the signs of the Zodiac worked into the borders of his gray velvet cloak. Because of the shaven head that gave the Bishop of Gae the look of some ancient Egyptian scribe, and because of the voluminous scarlet robes that hid the thin, straight body, it took Gil a moment to realize that this was a woman, but there was not a second of doubt that she was a Bishop. That harsh ascetic face would tolerate nothing less than spiritual command and would trust no one else to guard sufficiently the honor of her God.

As proper acknowledgments were made and the Bishop extended her dark amethyst ring to be kissed, Gil heard behind her the low murmur of Janus' deep voice speaking to Ingold. ". . . fight in the hall," he was saying. "Alwir's set up refugee camps here . . . sent patrols into the city . . . convoying food . . . bringing people to safety here . . ."

"My lord Alwir has taken command, then?" Ingold asked sharply.

Janus nodded. "He is the Chancellor of the Realm, and the Queen's brother."

"And Eldor?"

Janus sighed and shook his head. "Ingold, it was like a slaughterhouse. We reached Gae just before dawn. The ashes were still hot—parts of the Palace were still in flames. It was burned—"

"I know," Ingold said quietly.

"I'm sorry. I forgot you were there. The roof of the hall had caved in. The place was like a furnace. Bones and bodies were buried under the rubble. It was too hot to do much searching. But we found this, back by the door of that little retiring room behind the throne. It was in the hand of a skeleton, buried under the fallen rafters." He pointed to something on the table.

With the practiced grip of one long accustomed to

handling such things, the Bishop picked up the long, straight, two-handed sword and offered it hilt-first to Ingold. Though it was badly fire-blackened, Gil could recognize the pattern of rubies on the hilt. Once in a dream, she'd seen those gems gleam in lamplight with the movement of the breath of the man who'd worn them. Ingold sighed, and bowed his head.

"I'm sorry," Janus said again. His tough, square face was marked with weariness and grief under the reddish stubble of beard; he had lost a friend he valued, as well as a King. Gil remembered a lamplit room, a tall man in black saying, ". . . as your friend, I ask you . . ." She grieved with the old man's grief.

"And the Queen?" The tone of his voice indicated that Ingold knew what answer to expect.

"Oh," Janus said, startled, raising his head. "She was taken prisoner."

Ingold started, shocked. *"Prisoner?"* Shaggy eyebrows drew down over his nose. "Then I was right."

Janus nodded. "We finally caught them at it. They can carry weight; those tails of theirs are like cable. The Ice-falcon and a dozen of the boys were trapped in the main vault. They'd been guarding the Stair since the slab was broken—"

"Yes, yes," Ingold said impatiently. "I thought they were killed in the first rush. I discounted them. It doesn't do," he added, with the quick ghost of a grin, "to discount the Icefalcon—but go on."

"Well, the fire in the hall spread throughout the Palace— anyone who was trapped anywhere started burning things for the light. The Dark Ones came back down to the vaults like a river of night, dragging what must have been half a hundred captives, mostly women and some of the dooic slaves, yammering and screaming like beasts. The Icefalcon and the boys had the sense not to fire the vault and they put up a hell of a fight. In the end, half the pris-oners got left aboveground, and the Dark fled back down the Stair. Five of the women and some of the dooic died, of shock, we think—"

"And the Queen?"

Janus shifted from foot to foot uncomfortably, his eyes troubled. "She was—badly shocked."

The wizard regarded him narrowly for a moment, sifting

the sound of his voice, the evasion of his stance. "Has she spoken?"

Bektis the Court Wizard broke in officiously, his voice low. "It is my own fear that the Dark Ones devoured her mind, as so often happens to their victims. She has lain raving in a kind of madness, and with all the arts at my command I have been unable to summon her back."

"Has she spoken?" Ingold repeated, glancing from Janus to Bektis, seeking something; Gil could not tell what.

"She called for her brother," Janus said quietly. "He arrived with his men and a great part of the Army a few hours after daylight."

Ingold nodded, and seemed satisfied. "And this?" He gestured around him, at the silent sea of people crowded in the smoky hall.

Janus shook his head wearily. "They've been coming up the mountain all day," he said. "A great train of them formed around us when we left the Palace. They've been pouring up the road ever since. And three-quarters of them are without food. It isn't entirely fear of the Dark that makes them leave Gae—even with all the Guards and Alwir's regiments, Gae is broken. There's a madness in the town, even by daylight. All law is gone. We rode in just after dawn, to the relief of the Palace, and people were already looting it. Every farm within ten miles of the city has been abandoned—harvests rotting in the fields while refugees starve on the roads. Karst's a small town, and they're fighting over food here already, and over water, and for space in every building. We may be safe here from the Dark, but by tomorrow I'll wager we're not safe from one another."

"And what," Ingold asked quietly, "makes you think you're safe here from the Dark?"

Shocked, the big man started to protest, then fell silent. The Bishop slid her eyes sideways at Ingold, like a cat, and purred, "And what, my lord Ingold, know you of the Dark?"

"Only what we all know," a new voice said. Such was the quality of it, deep and regal, like a fine-tuned woodwind played by a master, that all eyes turned toward the speaker, the man who stood like a dark king, gilded by the glare of the torches. His shadow rippled down before him like water as he descended; like a second shadow, the wings of his black velvet cloak belled behind him. His pale face was coldly handsome, the regular fleshly features marked with thought and wisdom as with a carefully wielded graving tool. The wavy raven-black hair that framed his face half-obscured the chain of gold and sapphires that glittered over his shoulders and breast like a ring of cold blue eyes. "There is a certain amount of profit and prestige attendant upon warnings of disaster, as we all have seen."

"There is profit only for those who will heed them, my lord Alwir," Ingold replied mildly, and his gesture took in the smoke-fouled shadows of the room behind them, the grubby mob that had for the most part gone back to chattering among themselves, chasing children, arguing over space and water. "And sometimes even that is not enough."

"As my lord Eldor found." The Chancellor Alwir stood for a moment, his height and elegance dominating the small, shabby form of the wizard. His face, naturally rather sensual, was controlled into a cool mask of immobility, but Gil sensed in the posture of his big, powerful body the tension and distrust between the two men that looked to be of long standing. Alwir was annoyed, Ingold wary. "Indeed," the Chancellor went on, "his warning was the first; the stirring of the memories of the House of Dare long buried in his family. Yet that did not save him. We surmised that you had taken the Prince and fled the battle, when we did not find your sword in the rubble of the hall —though indeed there were enough of the fighters, toward the end, who snatched up the weapons of the fallen to make that not a sure clue. Was it possible, then, for you to assume the form of the Dark and so escape their notice?"

"No," Ingold replied, without elaboration. But a murmuring went through those nearest the table—for the hall was crowded to the bursting-point, and the conference between wizard and Chancellor, though conducted in low tones, had at least two hundred onlookers besides the five who stood closest to them. Gil, standing half-forgotten with the sleeping child in her arms and her back to the monstrous newel post of the granite stair, could see the glances men gave to Ingold. Fear, awe, and distrust; he was uncanny, an alien even in the Realm. A maverick-wizard, she realized suddenly, and subject to neither king nor law. People could believe of him, and evidently did, that he could take the form of the Dark.

"And yet you contrived it somehow," Alwir went on. "And for that we thank you. Will you be remaining in Karst?"

"Why did you leave Gae?"

Dark, graceful brows lifted, startled and amused at the question. "My dear Ingold, had you been there—"

"I was there," Ingold said quietly. "In Gae at least there was water, food, and buildings in which to hide sufficient for all. At least there one could be reasonably safe from one's fellow man."

"Karst is certainly smaller," Alwir conceded, glancing deprecatingly about him at the jammed, airless cavern of the smoky hall. "But my men and the City Guards under the able leadership of Commander Janus can control the people more easily than in that crazy half-burned labyrinth that is all that remains of the most beautiful city in the West of the World. The Dark haunt the river valleys," he went on, "like the marsh sickness of the south; but, like the marsh sickness, they shun the high ground. It may be possible to make a pact with them, such as the mountain sheep make with the lions of the plain. To avoid the lion, one stays clear of his runs."

"To avoid the hunter," Ingold replied in that same quiet tone, "the deer shun the towns of men, but men seek them in the forest. The Dark never stalked the high country because there was no profit in it. When their prey flee there, thither they will come, to take them in open ground, scattered broadcast halfway to Gettlesand, without wall or fire, believing themselves safe."

The sapphires flashed in the torchlight as the Chancellor shifted his weight, and his cornflower-blue eyes were as hard as the jewels. "Two days ago there was a King at Gae," he said. "And now there is none. This situation is temporary. Believe me, Ingold Inglorion, a city of people cannot come and go as lightly as you do yourself. We obviously could not remain in Gae . . ."

"Why not?" the wizard bit at him.

The slipping temper showed in the steel that suddenly edged his voice. "It was chaos there. We . . ."

"That will be as nothing," Ingold said slowly, "to the chaos you will find when the Dark Ones come here."

In the silence that followed, Gil was conscious of the rustling presence of the onlookers and eavesdroppers, chance-camped around the parchment-littered table that was all the headquarters the Realm of Gae now had—men and women, with their children or bereft of them, sitting or curled uncomfortably on their blankets, drawn against their will into the vortex around the tall, elegant Chancellor and this shabby pilgrim whose only possession seemed to be the killing sword at his hip. Though all around them in the obscure, pillared fastnesses of the hot, murky hall there was subdued talk and movement, here there was none. The duel was fought perforce in the presence of witnesses.

Alwir seemed to remember them, for the tension in him eased perceptibly, and his voice was lighter, with just a trace of amusement, as he said, "You run ahead of yourself, my lord wizard. The Dark have not come to Karst— of all the cities in this part of the Realm, it is without trace of their Nests. As I have said, this state of affairs is temporary; it takes time to relocate and reorganize. Those who have refugeed here have nothing to fear. We shall make of Karst the new heart of the Realm, away from the danger of the Dark; it is here that we shall assemble an army of the allies of mankind. We have sent already to Quo, to the Archmage Lohiro, for his advice and aid, and south for help, to the Empire of Alketch."

"You've *what?*" It was Ingold's turn to be shocked and as angry as Gil had ever seen him.

"My dear Ingold," Alwir said patronizingly, "surely you don't expect us to sit on our hands. With the aid of the armies of the Empire of Alketch, we can carry the fight into the Nests of the Dark. With such aid and that of the Council of Wizards, we can attack the Dark in their own territory, burn them out, and rid the earth once and for all of that foul pestilence."

"That's nonsense!"

Alwir hooked his thumbs in his jeweled belt, clearly satisfied that he had taken the wizard off his usual balance. "And what would you propose, my lord wizard?" he asked silkily. "Returning to Gae, to be devoured by the Dark?"

Ingold recovered himself, but Gil could see, from her post by the stairs, how shaken he had been by the Chancellor's suggestion. When he spoke, his voice was very quiet. "I propose that we go to ground," he said, "at Renweth."

"Renweth?" Alwir threw back his head, as if uncertain whether to explode into rage or laughter. *"Renweth?* That

73

frozen hellhole? It's ten days' journey from the end of the world, the jumping-off place of Hell. We might as well dig our graves and bury ourselves in them. Renweth! You aren't serious!"

The Bishop shifted her black, lizard's gaze to Ingold curiously and spoke for the first time. "The monastery there closed twenty years ago, during the Bad Winter. I doubt there's even a village there anymore." Her voice was a dry, thin whisper, like the wind whistling through bleached bones in the desert. "Surely it is too isolated from the heart of the Realm to establish as its capital?"

"Isolated!" Alwir barked. "That's like saying Hell has an unseasonable climate. A backwater pit in the heart of the mountains!"

"I am not concerned with the Realm," Ingold said, his scratchy voice uninflected now, but his eyes glittering in the murky torchlight. "There is no Realm anymore, only people in danger. You deceive yourself to think political power will hold together when every man's thoughts are on refuge alone." The Chancellor made no reply to this, but along his cheekbones Gil saw the flush of anger redden the white skin. Ingold went on. "Renweth Vale is the site of the old Keep of Dare. From the Keep, whatever else you choose to do, you can hold off the Dark."

"Oh, I suppose we could, if the Keep's still standing," the Chancellor admitted brusquely. "We could also hold them off if we lived in the wilds like the dooic, hiding in caves and living on bugs and snails, if you wanted to go that far. But you're not going to fit the entire population of the Realm into the Keep of Dare, for all your vaunted magic."

"There are other Keeps," the Bishop put in suddenly, and Alwir shot her a look black with anger. She ignored it, re-folding her long, bony fingers, her parchment-dry whisper of a voice thoughtful. "There is a Keep in Gettlesand that they still use as a fortress against the incursions of the White Raiders; there are others in the north . . ."

"That they've been using to cure hides in for the last three thousand years," Alwir snapped, really angry now. "The Church might not suffer much, my lady Bishop, in the breakup of human civilization; your organization was made to hold sway in scattered places. And you, my lord wizard, think your own kind wouldn't be hurt—wanderers and brothers to the birds. But it's a long trek to Renweth." He jerked his head at all those watching eyes, that blur of faces in the blue fog of smoke—the girl with the cat, the old man with his crates of chickens, the fat woman in her nest of sleeping children. "How many of these would survive a half-month of nights in the open, journeying through the river valleys where the road runs down to Renweth Vale? We are safe here, I tell you—safer than we'd be on the way."

There was a murmuring among them, a shoal-whisper of agreement and fear. They had fled once from comfortable homes and pleasant lives in a city now deteriorating into lawlessness by day and nightmare terror by dark—a weary climb up muddy roads, burdened by all they could carry away with them. Frightened and confused, they had no desire to flee farther, and there was not one of them who, by hope of Heaven or fear of Hell, could have been induced to spend the night in the open.

Alwir went on, his voice dropping to exclude all but those closest in the smoky glare that surrounded the foot of the stairs. "My lord Ingold," he said quietly, "you held a great deal of power under King Eldor, power based on the trust he had in you from the time he was a child under your tutelage. How you used that power was your own affair and his; for you had your secrets that even those of Eldor's family were not privy to. But Eldor is dead; his Queen lies raving. Someone must command, else the Realm will destroy itself, like a horse running mad over a cliff. Your magic cannot touch the Dark—your power in the Realm is over."

Their gazes met and locked, like sword blades held immobile by the matched strength of their wielders. The tension between them concentrated to a core of silence unbroken save by the sound of their breathing; blue eyes looking into blue, framed in darkness and the smoldery glare of jumping torchlight.

Without taking his eyes from Alwir's, Ingold said, "King Eldor is dead. But I swore to see his son to a place of safety, and that place is not Karst."

Alwir smiled, a thin change of his lips that neither touched nor shifted his eyes. "It will have to be, won't it,

75

my lord wizard? For I am his Regent now. He is under my care, not yours." Only then did his eyes move, the entire stance of his body changing, and his voice lightened, like that of an actor stepping out of a role—or into one. His smile was genuine then, and deprecating. "Come, my lord," he said pleasantly. "You must understand that there are conditions under which life is definitely not worth preserving, and I'm afraid you've named one of them. Now—" He held up his hand against the wizard's next words. "I'm sure we will get off with less drastic consequences than the complete dismantling of civilization. I admit we are hard-pressed for certain things here, and I do not doubt that there are more refugees from Gae and the surrounding countryside coming up the mountain tomorrow. We're sending a convoy of the Guards down to the storehouses under the Prefecture Building at the Palace of Gae as soon as it grows light. As for getting in touch with the Archmage Lohiro, I'm afraid your colleagues seem to be in hiding, and it is beyond even Bektis' powers to get through to them."

"There is a glamour thrown over the City of Quo," Bektis said stiffly, looking down his high, hooked nose at Ingold. "With all my spells and the magic of fire and jewel, I have been unable to pierce it."

"I'm not surprised," Ingold said mildly.

The Bishop's flat black gaze rested briefly upon them both. "The Devil guards his own."

Ingold inclined his head toward her politely. "As does the Straight God, my lady. But we wizards are of neither world and so must protect ourselves as best we can. As the stronghold of the teachings of wizardry, Quo has always been guarded against invasion and destruction. I doubt that any wizard, however skilled, could pierce the town's defenses now."

"But that is what you propose to do?" Alwir asked, a note of genuine curiosity stealing into his trained melodious voice. He had won his battle—or at least this particular gambit. He could afford now to drop pose and ploy that Gil sensed were habitual with him.

"It is what I propose to try. As soon, as I said, as I have seen the Prince to a place of safety. But first, my lord Alwir, I need rest, for myself and my two young friends.

They have journeyed far from their homes, and will set out on their return before today's sun sets. And, by your leave, I would like to see the Queen."

There was a stirring in the hall beyond; someone opened the postern door, and the sudden, sharp draft of fresh, biting air threw smoke over them, making the Bishop cough, a dry, rasping sound. Beyond the door, the darkness was stained with paler gray.

As if the opening of that small door had let in an unfelt wind that stirred the crowded multitude like leaves, ripples of movement eddied restlessly throughout the dim, smoky chamber. Some people settled down to sleep at last, secure for the first time in the long night; others got up and began to move about, the rise in their talk like the voice of the sea when the tide turns. The draft from the door caused the torchlight to flicker jerkily over stone arches and haggard faces. Men and women who had hitherto kept their distance from the red-lit circle of power and danger surrounding the great of the Realm edged stealthily closer, and Gil could hear the murmuring whisper in the shadows behind her as she stood against the banister with the flushed, sleeping child in her arms. "That's his Little Majesty himself? . . . That's his little lordship, and a sweeter child there never was . . . Praise God he be safe . . . They say old Ingold stole him clean away from the Dark—he's a caution, ain't he? . . . Tricky old bastard, I say. Mirror of Satan, like all them wizards . . . He has his uses, and he did save the Prince that would have been dead, sure as the ice in the north . . . King, now; Lord Eldor's only child . . ."

The great unwashed, Gil thought, and straightened her cricked back against hours of standing and the accumulated weight of the sleeping child in her arms. People came as near as they dared—for she, too, was an outworlder and uncanny. She could smell on them the stench of old sweat and the grime of travel. At her movement Tir woke, grasped at a handful of her hair, and began to whimper fretfully.

Rudy, who had been slumped, dozing, on the granite steps at her feet, glanced up at her, then stood up stiffly and held out his arms. "Here," he said, "I'll hold him for a while. Poor little bugger's probably starving."

Gil started to hand him over, then stopped in mid-motion

77

as Alwir turned toward them. The close-crowding people fell back. "I shall take the child," he said, speaking to Gil and Rudy as if they had been servants, "and give him to his nurse."

"Let the Queen see him first," Ingold said, materializing quietly at his elbow. "That, I think, will help her more than any medicine."

Alwir nodded absently. "It may be that you are right. Come." He turned away and moved up the stairs into the shadows, the child beginning to fret and cry weakly in his arms. Ingold started to follow him, but Janus caught the sleeve of his brown mantle and held him back.

"Ingold—can I ask a favor of you?" His voice was pitched low to exclude all but those nearest him—Govannin had already gone to speak to a couple of shaven-headed monks in scarlet, and Bektis was ascending the stairs in Alwir's wake, his long hands tucked in his fur-lined sleeves and a look of pious despair on his narrow face. Ordinarily, Gil thought, the Commander of the Guards would be a big, roaring man, like an Irish cop; but strain and worry had quieted him, aging his square pug face. "We're riding for Gae in half an hour. The Icefalcon's already rounding up the troops. We've got as many of the Guards as we can spare and Alwir's private soldiers. The woods are full of bandits, refugees, people who'd kill for food, now it's so short, and in Gae it will be worse. The law's destroyed, whatever Alwir says about holding the Realm together— you know that, and so do I, and so does he, I think."

Ingold nodded, folding his arms against the cold that was blowing in from outside. With that cold came the growing murmur of voices, the rattle of cart wheels on cobblestones, and the far-off creaking of leather.

"I know it's hell to ask you," Janus went on, "after all you've done. God knows, whatever Alwir says, you've done a hero's part. But will you ride with us to Gae? The storage vaults are underground, and we may need you, Ingold, to get the food clear safely. You can't touch the Dark but you can call the light and you're the finest swordsman in the West of the World besides. We need every sword we can get. I asked Bektis to come, as a wizard, but he won't." The Commander chuckled wryly. "He says he won't risk leaving the Realm without a wizard to council its rulers."

78

Ingold snorted with laughter or indignation, then was silent. Outside could be heard the voices of Guards and the sound of people coming into the square, new refugees already arriving in the town. In the corners of the smoky hall could be heard the muted rattle of cook pots, a man's complaining voice, young children crying.

The wizard sighed deeply, but nodded. "All right. I can sleep in one of the carts on the way down—I must see the Queen first, though. Get as many carts and as many swords as you can." He turned toward the stairs, his white hair matching the gold of the torchlight as he moved. Gil took a step after him, uncertain whether to call his name, and he stopped, as if he had heard her speak. He came back down to her. "I shall be back before night falls," he said quietly. "By day you two should be safe enough, but don't wander about alone. As Janus says, the town isn't safe. Before sunset I'll return to send you back through the Void."

"Isn't that a little soon?" Rudy asked doubtfully. "I mean, you were right about the Void crossing being rough, and that will be only—" He calculated on his fingers. "—fifteen or sixteen hours."

"I understand the risk," Ingold said. "You're both young and strong and should take no permanent harm from it. And consider the alternative. By daylight, you're safe in Karst; so far Alwir seems to be right, and the Dark do not haunt these hills. But I have no surety what another night will bring. Our worlds lie very close; the Dark followed me across the Void once, and it would be too easy for one to do so again. I said once that I was the only one who understands the Void, and as such I have a responsibility. I cannot let them contaminate other worlds. Surely not one as populous and as undefended as yours. Another night could trap you here," he finished bluntly. "For if the Dark are anywhere near, I will not send you back."

"So you don't believe Alwir," Rudy said, folding his arms and slouching against the great granite newel post.

"No. It's only a matter of time until the Dark Ones come to Karst, and I want you well away from here before it happens."

"Hey, affirmative, man. When you get back to town, I'm gonna be right here on the front steps waiting for you."

Ingold smiled. "You're wise," he said. "You two alone have the option to leave this world. With what will come, believe me, you are to be envied." And he was gone, moving up the long stairway as lightly as if he hadn't been without sleep for two nights, and was swallowed by the shadows at the top.

CHAPTER FIVE

The first sensation in Gil's mind, as she stepped from the dark slot of the postern door into soft pearl daylight and bone-chilling morning cold, was relief. She had made it, somehow, through the bizarre terrors of the night; she had lived to see dawn. She could not remember when she had ever taken such conscious pleasure in simple daylight.

The second sensation was dismay. As she came out on the top step, the noise and stink hit her like a wall. People were quarreling, arguing, yelling at the tops of their voices, demanding where food could be found, squabbling over the possession of ragged and frightened animals, and clustering in an arm-waving group around the doorways of buildings already jammed to the rafters with refugees demanding admittance; others were milling around the half-drained town fountain, bickering over water in voices sharp with the anger bred of fear. The growing light showed Gil faces pale and taut, wary eyes shifting like those of rats. They were physically and mentally angling for a toehold of position in this slipping world. The ice-breeze of the mountains bore on its cold breath the drifting stench of untended waste.

Jesus, Gil thought, appalled, *they're setting themselves up for cholera, plague . . . you name it. How much do these people know about sanitation and disease anyway?*

And her third sensation, as she stood shivering at the top of the steps in the biting cold, was ravenous hunger. She gave the matter some thought. The Commander of the Guards seemed to be on Ingold's side, and could probably be talked into giving her something to eat on the basis of her connection with the wizard. She made her way down the steps, having to pick her path around a middle-aged man in soiled broadcloth who seemed to have set up camp on the lowest step with every intention of staying there, to where half a dozen men and women in the black uniform of the City Guards were readying the transport carts to join the convoy to Gae. They were evidently under the command of a tall young man with ivory-blond braids that hung to his waist, who was currently engaged in a heated argument with a knot of civilians in dirty homespun. The chief of the civilians was shaking his head emphatically, the Guard gesturing to the mob in the square. As she came close, he dismissed the men in disgust and swung around to face her, regarding her from under colorless brows with eyes as light and cold as polar ice.

"Can you drive?" he demanded.

"A horse?" Gil asked, startled, her mind going to cars.

"I don't mean geese. If you can't drive, will you lead on foot? Or ride the bloody thing. I don't care."

"I can ride," Gil told him, suddenly aware of why she was being asked. "And I don't fear the Dark."

"You're a fool, then." The captain stared down at her, those haughty white-blond brows drawing slightly together as he took in her alien clothes. But he said nothing of it, only turned to call to a grizzle-haired woman in a shabby black uniform. "Seya! Get this one a cart with riding reins." He turned back to Gil. "She'll take care of you." Then, as Gil started to go with Seya, he asked, "Can you fight?"

Gil stopped. "I've never used a sword."

"Then if we're ambushed, for God's sake stay out of the way of those who can." He turned away, calling out orders to someone else, as concise and cold as a hunting cat. The woman Seya came up to Gil, wry amusement on her deep-lined face, her sword slapping at her soft booted feet.

"Don't let him fret you," she said, glancing after his slim, retreating figure. "He'd put the High King himself to driving a cart if we were short, with never a by-your-leave. There, look."

Gil followed the gesture of the woman's hand and saw Janus and Ingold standing in the middle of the ruckus at the foot of the steps, surrounded by quarreling drivers, gesturing Guards, and rickety carts. The tall captain was talking to them, gazing down the length of his aristocratic nose. Janus looked shocked, Ingold amused. The wizard swung himself up into the nearest cart, settled down on the driver's seat, and gathered the reins into his hands as deftly as a coachman.

The sun cleared the spiky peaks in the east as they were leaving the last houses of Karst behind them, brightening the scene without dispersing the white mist lying so thickly among the trees. Gil was mounted uncomfortably on the narrow harness-saddle of a fat roan, drawing a cart close to the head of the convoy. She could see that most of the vehicles in town had been commandeered, far more than could be provided with civilian drivers who were willing to return to the haunted city of Gae. Many were driven by Guards, and a thin, straggling line of them walked on either side of the train—men and women both, she saw, mostly young, though there were gray or balding heads visible up and down the line as well. They moved restlessly, and she could see the marks of strain and exhaustion clearly on their faces. These were the fighters who had borne the brunt of the defense of Gae.

As the light grew, Gil could make out little camps of refugees in the woods, straggling out along the road and far back among the trees. There were refugees on the road, too, men and women in wrinkled and dirty clothes, carrying awkward bundles of blankets and cooking pots on their backs, pushing makeshift wheelbarrows, or dragging crude travois. Now and then a man would be leading a donkey, or a woman drawing an unwilling cow at the end of a rope. Mostly they did not stop and gave only scant attention to the winding file of carts and their ragged line of escorts. They were too weary with flight and fear to have any thought but for the refuge ahead.

Eventually, the road dipped and bent. Beyond the thin screen of brown-leaved trees, Gil felt the wind freshen and change. She looked up to see the land fall away on one side of the road, to show her the city of Gae.

Recognition caught at her heart. It lay in the distance, surrounded by its many walls, held in the crook of the river's arm, facing out across a plain turned tawny gold with autumn and latticed with the white of the city roads. It was almost as if she had lived there, walked those close-angled streets, and known from childhood that skyline of turrets and branches. Against the morning sky, six spires of stone rose up, flying buttresses bereft of the walls they had supported, stretching like the bony fingers of a skeleton hand into the whiteness of the air.

"The trees are bare," a man's light, breathless voice said beside her. "In summer it was a garden."

She looked down. By her knee, pacing with the jogging of the cart, walked the pale-haired captain, his eyes reflecting the flat white light of the sky. She said, "I know."

The light eyes shifted back to her face. "You're Ingold's far traveler."

She nodded. "But I've been in Gae."

Again there were no questions, only a docketing of information in his mind. He was spare and loose-boned; in the mingling shadows of the trees, she saw that he was younger than she'd first supposed—in his early twenties, possibly a few years younger than she was. It was the toughness, the sheath of self-sufficiency, that aged him—that and the long wrinkles scored by weather around his pale eyes. After a moment he said, "I am called the Icefalcon of the Guards."

"My name is Gil," she said, ducking as they passed beneath the overhanging branches of a huge oak. Gae was lost to them once more behind the woods of rust and silver and opal mist. The sound of the cart wheels mingled with the crackle of the dead leaves underfoot.

"In the old language of the Wath, *gil* means ice," he said absently. "*Gil-shalos*—a spear of ice, an icicle. I had a hunting hawk by that name once."

Gil looked down at him curiously. "Then your own name would be—Gil-something-or-other."

He shook his head. "In the language of my people, we call the icefalcon *Nyagchilios,* Pilgrim of the Sky. Why did you come with us?"

"Because you ordered me to," Gil replied.

The Icefalcon raised colorless eyebrows. But he did not ask further, and she could not have answered if he had done so. She only knew that she had felt drawn to these calm and competent warriors; asked to join them, she could not have stayed away.

They broke from the woods and came down out of the foothills, riding through the lion-colored grasses of the plain as if swimming in a lake of soft, blown gold, the sun small and remote in a colorless morning sky. They passed more refugees, straggling family or neighborhood groups, wretched single men and women carrying the last of their possessions on their backs, confused gangs of children, the older herding the younger like geese. The edges of the road were scattered with the flotsam of flight—books, bedding, and in one place a silver bird cage, dainty as lace, on whose open door-frame a pink, ornamental finch sat chirping fearfully in the sky-wide freedom of the winds. The Ice-falcon pointed out Trad's Hill, the round promontory in the middle of the golden plain, crowned with its lichened cross, but Gil's eyes went past it to the walls of Gae. She saw towers mounting spire on shattered spire, arch and corbel and crenelations as fine as hand-tooled miniatures, with woven trellises of bare branches, and above it all, the broken, arching ribs of the buttresses that were all that remained of the Palace.

And as surely as she knew her name, Gil knew that somewhere in that city there was a square whose steps were guarded by statues of malachite, where bronze doors lay broken among the rubble. Somewhere was a vault with the red porphyry Stair, an odd slab in the smooth basalt of the floor, and a shadow-crowded archway into an empty and ruined street. Cold wind stung her chapped hands on the dirty leather of the riding reins; the jog of the slow-moving cob between her knees and the squeal of cart wheels came like elements of waking into an uncertain world of dreams; and with them came the mellow, rusty voice that floated back along the line of march, like a breath of mist on the wind, talking with the Commander of the Guards.

Gae stank of death. Gil had not been prepared for it, and it took her by the throat like a strangler's hand. Her otherworld life had encompassed enough bus stations, rock concerts, and weekends in the desert to have in some measure inured her to the stench of Karst, but the fetor that hung like a cloud over the ruined city was the miasma of rot, dead rot that her world was wont to hide or incinerate.

The streets lay empty to the sunlight, the echoes of hooves and booted feet and the creaking wheels of the carts ringing back off bare walls. House after house bore signs of burning—caved-in upper storeys, charred timbers jutting like the broken ribs of picked carcasses, barricaded doors and windows with the telltale crawling of soot reaching halfway up the walls above them. Gil saw how some of the walls had been broken inward; in other places, little slides of rubble spewed down into the street, mixed with stripped, rat-chewed bones. The hollow shadows rustled with the suggestion of a rodent population released from its old war with man and gorged on the spoils of victory. From the tops of broken walls, wild scrawny cats watched them with mad eyes. Gil held the short riding reins of her fat carthorse and tried not to be sick.

"Three days ago it was going," a man's soft voice said beside her, and she almost jumped. "And now it is gone." Ingold had drawn up his cart next to her, blinking in the sharp changes of the barred and broken sunlight.

Something unwholesome rustled and flicked out of sight behind a garden wall. Gil shivered, feeling unclean. "You mean the city?"

"In a sense." A branch cracked under the wheels. The Icefalcon, scouting alongside, turned sharply at the sound. Gil could see they all felt it, all sensed the foulness of those buzzing, crawling streets. What must it be, she wondered, to be coming back now, after having known it, grown up with it, as it was?

Her eye traveled slowly down the broken lines of a graceful colonnade that bordered the street, picking out sophisticated motifs of mathematics and flowers, the gaiety and balance of its multiple interwoven friezes. She remembered again the furnishings of Tir's nursery, museum pieces of inlaid ivory and ebony. All that was rich and beautiful of this civilization, all the good things that could be had, could once have been found here. She turned her horse's head a little to avoid the black ruin of a doorway in which the body of a woman lay sprawled in shadow, one gnawed white arm trailing limply in the sun, diamonds sparkling on the wrist among crawling flies.

Even for those who had survived, there was no going back. She wondered if the people up at Karst had realized this yet.

Ingold did. She saw it in the hard set of his mouth, in the line of pain that had appeared between his brows. Janus did. The Commander of the Guards looked white and ill; but beyond that, strange on a pug face that would

86

look more at home above a Coors T-shirt and a six-pack of beer, was a look of a deep, quiet, and aching regret. His expression was that of a man who looked on tragedy and understood the meaning of what he saw. The Icefalcon— It was hard to tell. That enigmatic young man picked his fastidious way through the ruins of human civilization with the single-minded wariness of an animal, uncaring for anything beyond his personal safety and the accomplishment of his job.

Under her, the horse let out a sudden, frightened squeal and threw up its head with white, rolling eyes. Almost beneath their hooves, two shambling, misshappen things broke cover from a ruined doorway and fled down the lane at a scrambling run. Gil had a horrified glimpse of flat, semi-human faces under snarling manes of reddish hair, of hunched bodies and trailing, apelike arms. She stared after them, shocked and breathless, until she heard Ingold say softly, "No, let them go." Turning, she saw that the Icefalcon had taken bow and arrow from one of the carts, preparatory to shooting the creatures down. At Ingold's command he paused, one pale eyebrow raised inquiringly, and in those few instants the creatures, whatever they were, had vanished down the lane.

The Icefalcon shrugged and replaced his weapons. "They're only dooic," he stated, as a self-evident fact.

Ingold's face was expressionless. "So they are."

"We'll have them all around the carts, once we get the food." He might have been speaking of rats.

The wizard turned back to his own business and flicked the reins of his mismated team. "We can deal with them then." The convoy started forward again, jostling in the cold shadows of the narrow streets. After a moment the Icefalcon shrugged again and slipped back, catlike, to his place in the Guard line.

"What are they?" Gil asked of the Guard nearest her, a fair-haired young man with the shining face of an apprentice Galahad, walking at her other side. "Are they— people?"

He glanced up at her, shading his eyes against the sunlight that fell through the breaks in the buildings. "No, they're only dooic," he repeated the Icefalcon's excuse. "Don't you have dooic in your land?"

Gil shook her head.

"They do look like people," the Guard went on casually. "But no, they're beasts. They run wild in most of the wastelands of the West—the plains beyond the mountains are crawling with them."

"Your people might call them Neanderthal," Ingold's soft voice said at her side. "If they're caught they're put to work in the south cutting cane, or in the silver-mines of Gettlesand, but many people train them for household tasks as well. They're said to make useful slaves, but evidently no one considered them worth taking when their owners fled."

The dry distaste in his voice wasn't lost on the young Guard. "We could never afford to feed them," he protested. "Food's short enough in Karst." And he added to Gil, as if excusing himself, "I never liked them myself."

The grain stores were in the vaults of the City Prefecture Building, a low, solid structure that formed one side of the great Palace square. As the convoy drew up before it, Gil saw that it had been little touched by fire, though clearly there had been looting going on—a trail of muddy tracks, torn grain sacks, and spilled corn led like a stream up the steps from the sunken doorway, to be dispersed among the general garbage of the square. The square itself she recognized, though she had last seen it from the window of a tower that had now fallen to flaming ruin: a broad expanse of patterned marble; wide gates of intricately worked iron; and trees whose bare gray branches were scorched from the inferno that had swallowed the last battle. The monumental shadow of the Palace reared to her left, storey upon storey of sliding ruin, the gutted belly that had been the Throne Hall of the Realm laid open to the day, half-buried under rubble and ash.

This, then, was the Palace of Gae, she thought, viewing it dispassionately, sane and awake and by daylight, from the back of a fat, jittery carthorse, with her hands blistered from the reins and her eyes aching from lack of sleep. This was what she had come to see, the place where Eldor had died, the place she had known in dreams. This was where humankind had fought—and lost—its last organized battle against the Dark.

By the look of those blackened ruins, it was very clear that the place had been looted before the ashes were cold.

More voices, angry this time, rang against the stone

walls of the square in faint derisive echoes. Turning from her silent contemplation, Gil saw that a little group of carters and Guards had formed before the wide, shallow steps that led down to the broken doors of the Prefecture, centering on Commander Janus and a big, brawny man in homespun whom Gil remembered vaguely as having driven the lead cart. The man was saying, "Well, *this* driver's not going down to fetch no grain. If the top level of the vaults has been cleared out like you say, that means going down the subcellar, and that's death, sure as the ice in the north."

Someone else chimed in over the general din of agreement. "The vaults is haunted, haunted by the Dark. I said I'd drive a cart, but going against the Dark ain't in it."

A Guard shouted back, "Well, who in hell did you think was going down for the stuff?"

Janus, red-faced with anger, spoke quietly, his brown eyes cold. "Every man knows the value of his own courage. Those drivers brave enough to do so can help us fetch the food out. I have no use for cowards. Icefalcon, I'm leaving you in charge on top. Pick twelve Guards and shoot anyone or anything that comes near the food once we get it up here. Get it loaded and be ready to move out."

From the back of the cart he had been driving, Ingold handed down a bundle of cold pitch torches, then stepped down himself, bringing with him a six-foot walking staff on which he leaned tiredly.

The Commander disengaged a torch from the bundle and went on. "Gae isn't empty, by any means. It's dead, but every corpse has its maggots. There's danger above the ground as well as below." He turned and walked, torch in hand, toward the steps. Without a glance at him, Ingold made a slight gesture with his fingers; the cold torch in the Commander's hand burst into flame with a loud *whoof!* The other Guards, and over half the drivers, clustered around to get their own torches and light them from his.

As Gil was picking up a torch from the bundle on the ground, Ingold stepped over to her and laid a hand on her shoulder. "That didn't apply to you, Gil. This is none of your affair."

She looked up at him, then straightened to bring her eyes level with his. "You don't have to look after me specially," she said. "I'll stay with the Guards."

He glanced back over his shoulder at the small group

already descending to the vaults, then at the long train of empty carts that would have to be filled by afternoon. "I brought you here against your will," he said quietly. "You are in my charge. I won't demand that you put yourself in danger of death in another universe, when you're going back to your own tonight. This is no dream, Gil. To die here is to die."

The ice-winds from the north pierced her thin jacket like a knife, and the heatless sun glared in her eyes without power to warm her. From the steps a woman's voice—Seya's, she thought—called out. "*Gil-shalos!* You staying or coming?"

She yelled back, "Coming!" Ingold caught her arm as she started to move off. To him she said, "I won't get in your hair, I promise."

He smiled, the weary lines of his face lightening with a brief illusion of youth. "Like a bat, eh? As you will. But as you love your life, stay close to the others." And he walked with her to join the Guards.

They worked swiftly in the darkness of the vaults, soundlessly, with drawn swords, their efficiency impaired by the need to keep together. Following the bobbing chain of weak yellow lights, Gil found herself almost afraid to breathe, straining every nerve for the glimpse of some anomalous motion in the blackness, the breath of alien wind. In the deeper vaults where the food was stored, the endless darkness was all a whisper of tiny pattering feet and a sea of glaring little red eyes, gray bodies swarming soundlessly away from the light of the torches; but beside the fear of the Dark, that was of no more moment than a cockroach on the wall might have been. They carried burden after burden back toward the light, sacks of grain, cured meats, great waxed wheels of cheese, treading the swiftest path they could under their loads, with Ingold flitting beside them like a will-o'-the-wisp, sword in one hand, the tip of his upraised staff throwing clear white light that dispelled the crowding shadows.

It was hard labor, and they kept it up all the forenoon. Gil's arms ached; her blistered hands were smarting, her nerves humming like a plucked bowstring every time she dumped a burden of corn or dried fruit or an unwieldy slab of cheese onto the pile at the top of the steps and turned back down to the waiting darkness. Her head throbbed with hunger and fatigue. Toward afternoon she was trembling uncontrollably, the stairs, the vaults, and the men and women around her blurring before her eyes. She stopped, leaning against the carved pilasters of the great doorway, trying to get her breath; someone passed her in a black uniform, bearing a torch, and laid a light, companionable hand briefly on her shoulder. Blindly, she followed him back into the vaults.

It was well into afternoon when the job was done after a last, sweating hour of loading the carts. Lightheaded and sick with weariness, Gil wondered if it were only a hallucination on her part or if they were really watched from every black window by unseen eyes—if the prickling on the back of her neck were some premonition of real danger or only the result of fatigue whose like she had never before known. That last hour she had noticed no one and nothing, only the pain that throbbed with every movement of her tired arms.

When someone said that Ingold was gone, she could not remember when she had seen him last.

"He was with us on the final trip out of the vaults, I think," Seya was saying to the Icefalcon, wiping sweat from her brow with the sleeve of her damp undertunic.

"But not after?"

The woman shook her head. "I really don't remember."

"Did anyone see him above the ground?"

Glances were exchanged, heads were shaken. No one could recall. The fat carter in brown said, "Well, he's a wizard, and he's got his tricks, to be sure. Likely he'll meet us halfway up the mountains. Let's go, I say, if we're to make Karst in the daylight."

The remark evidently didn't merit reply—Guards were already picking up the smoldered ends of doused torches and rekindling them from a little fire someone had lit in a corner of the court for warmth. Gil joined them as a matter of course, though she knew that there was no question of staying together for this search. Janus saw her as she was going down the steps and called out. *"Gil-shalos!"* But before he could go to her, the fat carter caught him by the arm and started a long expostulation about reaching Karst before night. Quietly, Gil slipped into the shadows.

It was different, entering the vaults alone. Her single

91

torch called forth leaping, distorted shapes on the low groinings of the ceiling, her own footfalls multiplied eerily in the darkness, as if she were being stalked by a legion of goblins. The red gleams of wicked little eyes blinked momentarily from the impenetrable gloom around her, then were gone. All the stillness seemed to breathe. Some instinct warned her not to call out, and she continued alone in silence, scanning the maze of dark pillars for some sign of that bobbing white light or the soft tread of booted feet—though now that she thought of it, Ingold was a man who could move as noiselessly as a shadow. She left the trampled way the salvagers had taken and turned toward the deeper vaults, wandering down identical aisles of dark stone pillars, granite trees in a symmetrical forest, her torchlight calling no reflection from the smooth black basalt of the floor.

She felt it grow upon her gradually, imperceptibly; a sense of having passed this way before, a lingering sense of unnamed dread, an uneasy feeling of being watched from the dark by things that had no eyes.

How she could have helped Ingold she could not have said, for she was unarmed and less familiar than he with the haunts of the Dark. But she knew he had to be found and she knew that he was exhausted, pushed far past the limits of his endurance; she knew that, wizard or not, in such a state mistakes were fatally easy to make.

She had almost given up the hope of finding him when she saw the faint reflection of white light against the dark granite of the pillars. She hurried toward the light, coming at last to a cleared space in that stone forest, where her torchlight gleamed on the dark sweep of the red porphyry Stair that curved upward to the blown-out ruin of cyclopean bronze doors, with nothing but darkness beyond them. Among the rubble of disused furniture and dusty old boxes, she could make out the shapes of skeletons, bones scattered among the pillars, stripped of their flesh by the Dark. Almost at her feet, a sword-split box had disgorged its contents, and dried apples lay strewn among the skulls.

She knew the place; the familiarity of it made her heart pound and the blood din in her ears. But no granite slab broke the ancient regularity of the smooth basalt of the floor. Only a great rectangular hole gaped where it had lain, black and yawning, the blasphemous gate of the abyss. And down from the pavement black stairs led, unspeakably ancient, cold with the ruinous horror of uncounted millennia, looking as she knew they would look, even in her dreams—as they had looked since the beginning of time. The damp chill that breathed out of that darkness brushed her cheek like the echo of primordial chaos, an evil beyond comprehension by humankind.

And up from that unspeakable chasm, like the distant glow of a far-off lamp, shone the soft white light she had been seeking. It picked out the curves of the ceiling arches, echoed in the lines of a skull and the delicate roundness of the bone over the eye socket. Hands shaking, Gil stooped and picked up a long sword that lay on the floor amid a tumble of acid-eaten handbones. With the balanced weight of the hilt in her hand she felt better, steadier, and less afraid. She held the torch aloft and walked to the edge of the abyss.

Far down the stairs, outlined by the soft brightness of his staff's white radiance, she could see Ingold. He stood as unmoving as a statue some fifty steps below her, just at the point where the stairs curved and were lost to sight in the black throat of the earth. His face was intent, as if listening for some sound which Gil could not hear. He had sheathed his sword, and his right hand hung empty at his side. As she watched, he moved with the slow hesitance of one hypnotized, down one step, and then another, like a man in a trance following enchanted music. She knew that after another step or two she would lose sight of him utterly, unless she chose to follow him down. He took the next step, the shadows closing him around.

"Ingold!" she called out in despair.

He turned and looked inquiringly up at her. "Yes, my dear?" His voice echoed softly, ringing against the darkness of the overarching walls. He stared around him, at the stairway and the walls, and frowned, as if a little surprised to find he had come that far down. Then he turned thoughtfully to look at the deeper chasm below him again, and Gil remembered with a shiver that he had once told her that curiosity was the leading characteristic of any wizard, and that a mage would pursue a riddle to the brink of his own grave. For a moment she had the terrible impression that he was toying with the notion of descending

93

that eldritch stairs, of walking willingly into the trap to see of what it consisted.

But he turned away and came up toward her, the darkness seeming to fall back at the advent of his light. He emerged to stand beside her on the top step and asked quite calmly, "Do you hear it?"

Gil shook her head, mute and frightened. "Hear what?"

His blue gaze rested on her face for a moment, then moved away, back toward that endless dark. There was a slight frown between his white brows, as if his mind worried at a riddle, oblivious to the danger in which they stood. She sensed that danger all around them, watching and waiting in the shadows, pressing behind them as if it would drive them into the accursed pit. But when he spoke, his rusty voice was calm. "You don't hear anything?"

"No," Gil said softly. "What do you hear?"

He hesitated, then shook his head. "Nothing," he lied. "I must be more tired than I thought. I—I thought—I didn't think I had descended the stairs quite that far. I hadn't meant to."

That, more than anything else, shocked her—the note of exhaustion in his voice, the admission of how close he had come to being trapped. He frowned again, looking down at the darkness that gaped below his feet, puzzling at some new knowledge, disconcerted, not by the darkness, but by something else.

Then he sighed and let the matter go. "You came alone?" he asked.

She nodded, a curiously forlorn figure in her grubby jeans, with her guttering torch and the borrowed sword heavy in her hand. "The others are searching, too," she explained—no explanation, really, as to why she had come alone.

"Thank you," he said quietly, and laid a hand on her shoulder. "It's extremely likely that you just saved my life. I—I feel as if I have been under a spell, as if—" He broke off, and shook his head as if to clear it. "Come," he said at last. "This way out is quicker. Keep the sword," he added as she moved to lay it down where she had found it. "You may need it. Its owner never will again."

*   *   *

By the time the convoy reached Karst the air was cold, and the late, weary day was drawing down to evening. They traveled slowly, for the underfed horses were dead-beat and the road steep and foully muddy. The closer they got to the town, the more often they were stopped by men and women who had been camping in the woods and who came hurrying down the steep banks to them, begging for something to eat. Only a little—it was always only a little.

Janus, riding in the lead, shook his head. "There'll be shares given out at Karst."

"Bah!" A woman in a torn purple gown spat. "Karst—if you can get into the town! And them as are there'll be sure they get first pickings!"

The Commander only looked down with stony eyes. "Move aside." He kneed his sweat-darkened horse forward, past her. The wagons had not even stopped.

"Pig!" the woman yelled at him, and bent to pick up a stone from the roadway. It struck his back hard enough to raise dust. He didn't turn. "All of you, pigs!!"

It wasn't what Gil had expected. Walking beside her horse's head, hanging grimly onto the cheekpiece of the bridle to keep from staggering, she'd half-expected to be cheered into town. *But,* she thought cynically, *people are people—nobody cheers the lunchwagon unless he gets first dibs on the food.* She looked back along the line of the convoy and saw none of her own feeling reflected in the strained and dusty faces of the other Guards. *It's a hell of a thing,* she thought, *to risk your life to feed someone and have him pelt you with mud on your way into town.* But she supposed the Guards had seen too much of human nature in this crisis ever to be surprised by anything again.

They walked quietly along the blue evening road with a tirelessness and an endurance she bitterly envied. The civilians moved dully with fatigue, leading the over-burdened horses in silence. The sun had already vanished behind the tips of the surrounding mountains, and the evening grew cold. It would soon be night. Someone had scrounged a heavy, hooded cloak for her from the ruins of the Palace, and it flapped awkwardly around her ankles, the folds of it catching on her sword; the rhythmic slap of the scabbarded weapon against her calf was curious,

95

but somehow comforting. She would take the sword back to California with her along with the memory of this strange and terrifying place.

Where in hell are all these people coming from? she wondered, as a dozen or more came scrambling down the ferns of the roadside and into the way of the carts. She straightened up and scanned the woods, picking out the hundreds of trashy little campsites that strewed the slopes all around Karst. *Sweet Mother of God, do they think there's a magic force-field around the place? Did they really buy that line of Alwir's about how safe they all are?* The refugees tacked themselves onto the train, keeping pace with exhausted horses and their Guards, tagging them through the blue rivers of shadow between the first outlying buildings. Some of the Guards drew their swords, but no move was made against them; the people simply followed, crowding one another but not the warriors, only making sure of being at the distribution point when shareouts began. Gil heard the murmur of voices thrown back by the moss-grown walls, a restless tension and discontent. So many people, so few wagons, so little food!

And then they moved into the twilit square. Gil paused in shock, stiffening as if against a physical blow, and cold apprehension fisted in her chest. The square was nearly solid with people, all ages, both sexes, dirty, in rags or clothes soiled enough to be rags, and watchful as wolves. The great bonfires of last night had been kindled at the four corners of the square, and the leaping scarlet light repeated itself a millionfold in their glittering eyes, like the eyes of the rats in the vaults. The ugly tension was palpable; even Gil's horse, drooping with weariness, sensed it and threw up its head with a snort of fear.

At the head of the convoy, Janus moved his horse toward the mob that was headed for the villa across the square where the food was to be stored. There was a slight movement, an uneasy convection current in the dark mass of eyes and faces, but no one stepped aside. The Commander's war horse fidgeted and sidestepped from that wall of hatred. Janus drew his sword.

Then Gil felt the cart she was leading creak with a sudden motion, and Ingold, who had been dozing in the back, swung himself up onto the driver's seat. In the firelight, he was visible to everyone in the square, the hood falling back from his head to reveal his craggy face with its rough chaparral of white beard and his eyes as cold and hard as the storm sky. He said nothing, did nothing, only stood leaning on his staff, looking down at the mob in the square.

After a long moment of silence, men shifted away from the doors of the villa. A pathway widened before the Guards, their convoy, and the wizard.

Janus' voice was crisp on the chilly air. "Start unloading. Get the stuff indoors, under triple guard." But he himself did not dismount. Other Guards emerged from the villa, mixed with Alwir's red-liveried private troops and the warrior-monks of the Church, also in red, the blood-troops of God. Gil leaned against the shoulder of the carthorse, feeling the sweat cold on her face, the warmth of the beast through cloak and jacket and shirt against her arm, tired and glad it was over. The mob in the square had fallen back, crowding one another around the bonfires, but they watched the moving lines of armed men stowing the food, and that restless murmuring never ceased.

Gil heard someone call out. "My lord Ingold!" Turning, she saw someone beckoning urgently from the Town Hall steps. She saw the wizard scan the crowd, judging it, but few of the people were watching him now; all eyes were riveted, as by enchantment, on the food. He swung himself lightly down from the cart, and the crowd rippled back from where he landed on his feet. They moved, not in dread or fear, exactly, but in awe of something they did not and could not comprehend. He did not have to push his way through them to the steps.

If Gil hadn't been watching him, following his path with her eyes, she would have completely missed what happened next. A man, cloaked and hooded in red, stood waiting for him on the steps of the Town Hall, holding a rolled parchment in one hand, flat and colorless in the deep shadows thrown by the fires. He handed Ingold the parchment and drew his sword.

Gil saw Ingold read what was written there and look up. She could feel, even at that distance, the fury and indignation that tautened every line of his body, the wrath that smoked off him. A dozen men in red emerged quietly from the shadows and surrounded him. They all carried drawn swords.

For one instant, she thought he would fight. And she thought, *Oh, my God, there'll be a riot,* and queer, cold fury put fire-ice into her veins. Several of the red troops evidently thought so, too, for they flinched back from him. Gil remembered that, in addition to being a wizard, Ingold was supposed to be one hell of a swordsman. Then he held his hands up to show that they were empty, and the men closed him in. One of them took his staff, another his sword, and they all vanished into the shadows of the Town Hall doors.

Stunned, Gil turned to see if Janus had witnessed this, but the Commander's back was to her, his attention held by the mob. The Guards were still working, carrying grain, sides of bacon, and sacks of potatoes and corn up the steps of the villa and through the guarded darkness of the doors. She doubted anyone besides herself had seen the arrest. *They timed that,* she thought suddenly. *And they counted on his going quietly, rather than triggering a riot by resistance.*

Rage swept her then, leaving no room for fear. She looked back at the steps, splotched by shadow and fire-light. They were empty, as if nothing had happened. The wizard might simply have disappeared.

CHAPTER SIX

A dying civilization. A land locked in fear. A world going down in a welter of hopeless chaos before an enemy that could not be fought. And, Rudy thought, strolling down the mossy cobbled streets of Karst through the cool sunshine of that mellow afternoon, *one hell of a lot of people standing nose-deep in the sewer, with the tide coming in.*

If it weren't jammed to the ceilings with people, Karst would be a pretty town, he reflected. *That is, if you had indoor plumbing and some kind of central heating and streets you weren't likely to break your ankle on.* This lane was relatively uncrowded and quiet, winding away from the town square to lose itself in the woods; it was paved in lumpy, fist-size cobbles that were high and dry along the walls on both sides and heavily upholstered with bright green moss down the center, through which a thread of silver water reflected the sky. Rudy had slept—badly—in a stuffy and flea-infested closet on the third floor of the Town Hall, and had spent what was left of the morning and most of the afternoon poking around Karst, trying to scrounge food and water, scraping acquaintance with refugees and Guards and some of the Bishop's people, and checking out the town. He'd come to the conclusion that if Alwir didn't get his act together fast, they'd all be dead in short order.

There were simply too many people. Gil and Ingold were right, whatever the Chancellor liked to say. Contrary to the assertions of most of his teachers in public school,

Rudy was not stupid, merely lacking in appreciation for the public school system. He'd listened to the council last night—with as little room as there was in the hall, it would have been hard to help eavesdropping—and had seen today what was happening in Karst. He'd walked through the camps in the woods, trashy, filthy, lawless. He'd witnessed seven fights—three over allegations of food theft, two over water, and two for no discernible reason at all. He'd heard the stump preachers and soapbox orators propounding different solutions to the problem, from suicide to salvation, and had seen one ugly old man stoned by a pack of children and several of their elders because he was supposed to be in league with the Dark— as if anyone could get anywhere near the Dark Ones to be in league with them. Mostly Rudy sensed the tension that underlay the town like a drawn wire and had felt, with an uneasy shock, that closeness to that line that divided a land of law from a land without it. He'd seen the handful of Guards left in town trying to keep some kind of order among far too many people. Though it was a new sensation for him to have sympathy for the fuzz, he found he did. He wouldn't have wanted to play cop to that madhouse.

The smoke of cook fires turned the air into a stage-three smog alert, wherever he wandered in the town or in the woods. Now, as he headed back toward the square, shadows began to move up the rock walls of the little lane, and the distant clamor of voices in the square was muffled by the walls, muted to a meaningless murmur like the far-off sounding of church bells. In spite of hunger, the crowds, the threat of plague, and the fear of the Dark, Rudy found himself oddly at peace with the world and with his own soul.

Beyond the wall to his right he heard voices, a woman's and a girl's. The woman was saying, "And don't you go let him be putting things in his little mouth."

The girl's voice, gentle and demure, replied, "No, ma'am."

"And don't you be letting him wander away and hurt hisself; you keep a sharp eye on him, my girl."

Rudy recognized the emblem on the half-open grille of rusty iron at the gap in the wall, the three black stars that someone had said belonged to the House of Bes, the House ruled by Chancellor Alwir. Rudy paused in the gate. If this was Alwir's villa, then the women were probably talking about Tir.

Beyond the gap in the wall he could see the sloping garden, brown with cold and coming frost, and beyond that the rock wall of a terrace that backed the massive, gray shape of a splendid mansion. He was right; two women stood in the huge arched door of the house, spreading out, of all things, a bearskin rug in the last of the pale golden sun. The fat woman in red was doing this, with much bustle and huffing, while the slender girl in white stood, in the classic pose of women everywhere, with the baby riding her hip.

The fat woman continued to scold. "You see he doesn't get chilled."

"Yes, Medda."

"And don't you get chilled, neither!" The fat woman's voice was fierce and commanding. Then she went bustling back into the dark shadows of the door and was gone.

Rudy ducked through the gateway and made his way up silent paths fringed with sere brown hedges. Overhead, arthritic yellow leaves trembled in the watery blue of the air. Even moribund with autumn, the garden was immaculate. Rudy, pausing in its mazes to orient himself toward the haughty bulk of the villa, wondered whom they got to trim the hedges every day.

The baby sitter had settled herself down on the corner of the bearskin next to the Prince. She looked up, startled, as Rudy swung himself over the balustrade to join them. "Hello," she said, a little timidly.

Rudy gave her his most charming smile. "Hi," he said. "I'm glad to see you've got him out here—I was afraid I'd have to ask permission from every Guard in the house to see how he is."

The girl relaxed and returned his smile. "I should be taking him in before long," she apologized, "but it's probably one of the last warm days we'll have." She had a low voice and an air of shyness; Rudy put her age at somewhere between eighteen and twenty. Her crow-black hair was braided down past her hips.

"Warm?" Like most Californians, Rudy was thin-blooded. "I've been freezing to death all afternoon. What do you people consider cold?"

Startled, she raised her eyes to his; hers were dark,

101

luminous blue, like Crater Lake on a midsummer afternoon. "Oh!" She smiled. "You're the companion of Ingold, one who helped him rescue Tir."

And, indeed, Tir was making his way purposefully over to Rudy across the bearskin, tangling himself in the black and white silk of his gown. Rudy folded up to sit cross-legged beside the girl and gathered the child into his lap. "Well—" he said, a little embarrassed by that awe and gratitude in her eyes. "I just kind of stumbled into that. I mean, it was either come with him or die, I guess—we didn't have much choice."

"But still, you had the choice to be with him in the first place, didn't you?" she reminded him.

"Well—yeah," he agreed. "But believe me, if I'd known what it was all about, I'd *still* be running."

The girl laughed. "Betrayed into heroism," she mocked his assertion gently.

"Honey, you don't even know." Rudy extricated Tir's exploring hands from his collar and dug in his pocket for his key ring, which the child, in blissful fascination, proceeded to try to eat. "You know," he went on after a few minutes, "what floors me about this whole thing is that the kid's fine. After all he's been through from the time Ingold got him out of Gae until we got him back here, you'd think he'd be in shock. Is he? Hardly! Babies are so little, you'd think they'd break in your hands, like—like kittens, or flowers."

"They're tough." The girl smiled. "The human race would have perished long ago if babies were as fragile as they look. Often they're tougher than their parents." Her fingers made absent-minded ringlets of the black, downy hair on Tir's tiny pink neck.

Rudy remembered things said in the hall and other talk throughout the day. "How's his mom?" he asked. "I heard she—the Queen—was sick. Will she be okay?"

The girl hesitated, an expression of—what? Almost grief—altering the delicate line of her cheek. "They say the Queen will recover," she answered him slowly. "But I don't know. I doubt she will ever be as she was." The girl shifted her position on the rug and put the long braid of her hair back over her shoulder. Rudy stopped, another question unspoken on his lips, wondering suddenly how and under what circumstances this girl had made her own escape from Gae.

"And your friend?" The girl made an effort, and withdrew her mind from something within her that she would rather not have looked at. "Ingold's other companion?"

"Gil?" Rudy asked. "I guess she went with the Guards to Gae this morning. That's what they tell me, anyway. You wouldn't get me within a hundred miles of that place."

"You're within ten," the girl said quietly.

Rudy shivered. "Well, I can tell you I'll be farther away before sundown. Food or no food, you'd have to be crazy to go back there."

"I don't know," the girl said, toying with the end of her braid. "They say the Guards are crazy, that you have to be crazy, to be a Guard. And I believe that. I would never go back, not for anything, but the Guards—they're a rare breed. They're the best, the finest corps in the West of the World. It's their life, fighting and training to fight. The Guards say it's like nothing else, and for them there *is* nothing else. I don't understand it. But then, nobody does. Only other Guards."

Pro ballplayers would, Rudy thought. *Heavy-duty martial artists would.* He remembered some of the karate black belts he knew back home. Aloud, he said, "God help anyone or anything that takes on a bunch of people like that. Ingold's with them, too."

"Oh," the girl said quietly.

"Do you know Ingold?"

"Not—not really. I—I've met him, of course." She frowned slightly. "I've always been a little bit afraid of him. He's said to be tricky and dangerous, all the more so because he appears so—so harmless. And, of course, wizards—there are those who believe that wizards are the agents of evil."

"Evil? Ingold?" Rudy was startled and a little shocked. A more harmless old man he could never hope to find.

"Well—" She hesitated, twining the end of her braid through her fingers. Tir, having misplaced or forgotten the keys, caught at the soft black rope with tiny hands. "The Church teaches us that the Devil is the Lord of Illusion, the Prince of Mirrors. Illusion is the wizards' stock in trade; they trade their souls for the Power, when they go to that school in Quo. The Council of Wizards owes allegiance to no one. There is no check on what they might do."

So that explained the Bishop, Rudy thought, *and her watchful dark gaze that slid so disapprovingly over the wizard at that hurried council last night. A witch hunter, no error.*

The girl went on. "Of course he was a friend and counselor of—of the King—"

There was something, some catch, in her voice that made Rudy look over at her quickly, and it occurred to him to wonder what the late, great King Eldor had had to do with his son's nanny on the sly. Not that he blamed Eldor, he thought.

"But Ingold had his—purposes," she continued quietly. "If he saved Tir, it was because of the—the inherited memories of the Kings of Darwath, the store of knowledge within him that may one day be used against the Dark. Not because Tir was only a child, helpless and in danger." Her eyes were down, considering the bent head of the child nuzzling around on the bearskin before her. Her voice was shaky.

She really cares for Pugsley, Rudy thought suddenly. *Hell, since Queens*—at least in his muzzy democratic understanding of the matter—*don't take care of their own babies, she probably raised the little rug-rat.* She wouldn't see him as a Prince—or even as King of Darwath, since Eldor had died—but only as a child she loved, as Rudy loved his baby brother. It changed her in his eyes.

"You really believe that?" he asked softly. She didn't answer, nor did she look at him. "Hell, when you come right down to it, it's his job. If he's the resident wizard, he's got to do stuff like that. But I think you're wrong."

For a time she didn't speak, and the silence came over the garden again, a contented silence, bred of the long afternoon light and what might be the last golden day of autumn. The sun had already slipped through a milky film of cloud on the western peaks; the blue shadow of the villa marked off the cracks in the terrace pavement like a sundial, creeping steadily up on the bearskin and its three occupants. Looking out over the austere brown and pewter patchwork of the frost-rusted garden beds, Rudy felt the peace of the place stealing over his spirit, an archaic, heartbreaking beauty, a silence of old stone and sunlight, of something seen long ago and far away, like a lost memory of what had never been, something as distant as the reflections in still water, yet clear, clear as crystal. Every pale stone of the terrace, every silken grass blade thrust between them and turned gold now with the year's turning, contained and preserved that magic light like the final echo of dying music. It was a world that yesterday he had never known and, after tomorrow, would never see again, but the present moment seemed to have been waiting for him since the day of his birth.

"Alde!" A sharp voice cut that silver peace, and the girl whirled, startled and guilty as a child with her hand in the cookies. The fat woman in red stood in the doorway, hands on her broad hips fisted and face lumpy and red with annoyance. Rudy scrambled to his feet as she bawled out, "Sitting on the cold pavement! You'll catch your death! And his Little Majesty, to be sure!" She came bustling out, clucking and scolding like a mother hen with one chick. "Take him inside, child, and yourself—the air's grown nippy . . ."

But for all that she flustered around him as if he weren't there, Rudy knew the real problem was that Alde wasn't supposed to be wasting her time talking with some stranger instead of watching the baby as she was supposed to. The girl gave him a helpless, half-amused shrug of her eyebrows, and Rudy gallantly stooped to gather the bearskin in his arms. The thing weighed a ton.

"What's she think I'm gonna do, kidnap him?" he asked in a whisper as the older nurse waddled back into the house, baby in arms.

Alde smiled ruefully. "She worries," she explained unnecessarily. She bent to retrieve the motorcycle keys, which had fallen from the folds of the rug. She wiped the slobber off them with a corner of her skirt and tucked them back in his pocket for him.

"She boss you around like that all the time?" he asked. "I thought for a minute she was gonna spank you."

Alde's smile widened, and she ducked her head. She was laughing. "Medda just thinks of Tir as her baby. Nobody can look after him the way she can, not even his own mother."

Rudy had to smile, too. "Yeah, my aunt Felice is like

that. To hear her carry on with my mother, you'd never think Mom had raised seven kids all by herself. But you just got to let them do it."

"Well, you certainly can't change them," Alde agreed. "Here—I can take that rug. Medda would faint if you came inside. She knows what's due to the House of Bes . . . No, it's all right, I've got it."

They paused, arms mutually entwined in the moth-eaten red fur. "Your name's Alde?" he asked.

She nodded. "Short for Minalde," she explained. "Someone told me yours. If . . ."

"Alde!" Medda's shout came from within the villa.

"Take care of yourself," Rudy whispered. "And Pugsley."

She smiled at the nickname and ducked her head again as if to hide the smile. "You also." Then she turned and hurried through the great doors, the claws of the bearskin clinking softly on the polished floor.

The sky overhead had lost the paleness of day. The sun was long gone past the mountain's rim, and swift twilight had come down. All that afternoon's peace and beauty notwithstanding, Rudy had no intention of spending another night in this world. Besides which, he realized he was painfully hungry, and food was notoriously hard to come by. He made his way down the dead garden and through the rusted gate. He found the lane beyond almost totally dark, though the sky above still held a little of the day, like the sky above a canyon. As the shadows moved up the mountain toward Karst, he began his hunt for the wizard and the way home.

"Rudy!" He turned, startled to see Gil materialize out of the gloom, striding quickly toward him, followed by a tall young man with white Viking braids who wore the already-familiar uniform of the City Guards. He noticed that Gil had scrounged a cloak from somewhere and wore a sword belted over her Levi's. The outfit made him grin. This was a long way from the lady and scholar of yesterday afternoon . . .

"Where's Ingold?" he asked as they drew near.

Gil answered shortly. "He's been busted."

"Busted?" For a minute he couldn't take it in. "You mean *arrested?*"

"I saw it," Gil said tightly.

106

Close up now, Rudy saw that she looked exhausted, drawn, those cold gray-blue eyes sunk in purple smudges in a face that had gotten pointy and white. It didn't do much for her looks, he thought. But there was a hardness in her eyes now that he wouldn't have wanted to tangle with.

She went on. "A bunch of troops came and got him on the Town Hall steps while the Guards were busy unloading the supplies."

"And he just went with them?" Rudy asked, aghast and disbelieving.

The tall Guard nodded. "He knew that it was go or fight. The fight would trigger a riot."

The light, spare voice was uninflected, unexplaining, but the scenario sprang to Rudy's mind. The Guards backed Ingold and would have rushed to help; the people in the square would go after the food; all the pent-up violence of the day would condense in rage and fear and terror of the night. The town would go up like gunpowder. He'd been in enough small-scale riots at the Shamrock Bar in Fontana to know how that went. But what was all right in the safety of a steel-mill town on Friday night would be death and worse than death on a large scale, played for keeps out of hunger and fury and frustration. Bitterly, he remarked, "They sure knew their man. Who nailed him, do you know?"

"Church troops, from Gil's description," the Icefalcon said. "The Red Monks. The Bishop's men, but they could have acted on anyone's orders."

"Which anyone?" Rudy demanded, his glance shifting from Gil to the Icefalcon in the dimness of the shadowy lane. "Alwir? When he couldn't push him out at the council last night?"

"Alwir always feared Ingold's power over the King," the Guard said thoughtfully.

"His men wear red, too," Gil added.

The Icefalcon shrugged. "And the Bishop certainly doesn't relish the thought of an agent of Satan that close to the throne."

"A what?" Gil demanded angrily, and Rudy briefed her on the local Church stand on wizardry. Gil's comment was neither scholarly nor ladylike.

"The Bishop is very strong in her faith," the Icefalcon said in his soft neutral voice, the tone as colorless as his eyes. "Or—the Queen could have put out the order for his arrest. From all accounts she has never trusted Ingold, either."

"Yeah, but the Queen's out on a Section Eight these days," Rudy said unkindly. "And whoever popped him, we've got to find where they're keeping him, if we don't want to end up spending another night here."

"Not to mention the next fifty years, if they decide to wall him up in some dungeon and forget about him," Gil added, her voice sharp with fear.

"Yeah," Rudy agreed. "Though I personally wouldn't want to be the one in charge of putting that old duffer out of the way permanently."

"Look," the Icefalcon said, "Karst isn't that big a town. They will have put him in the Town Hall jail, in the vaults below Alwir's villa, or in the Bishop's summer palace somewhere. Divided, we can find him within the hour. Then you can do—whatever you will do."

The shift in inflection of that soft, breathless voice made Rudy's nerves prickle with the sudden premonition of disaster, but the inscrutable frost-white eyes challenged him to read meaning into the words. Alde had said that the Guards were all crazy. Crazy enough to jailbreak a wizard out from under the noses of the Powers That Be? They were Ingold's—and now, by the look of it, Gil's—allies. Rudy wondered if he wanted to mess with the whole thing.

On the other hand, he realized he didn't have much choice. It was a jailbreak in the dark or spending the night and God alone knew how many other nights besides in this world. Even standing in the quiet of the dark lane, Rudy had begun to feel nervous. "Okay," he said, with as much cheerfulness as he could muster under the circumstances. "Meet you back at the Town Hall in an hour."

They parted, Rudy hurrying back toward Alwir's garden gate, running over in his mind how he'd go about getting on the right side of Alde and, more importantly, Medda, in order to get in and search the villa.

Gil and the Icefalcon headed in the other direction, instinctively hugging the wall for protection, guided by the reddish reflection of the fires in the town square. It was fully dark, a bitter overcast night, and Gil shivered, feeling the trap of the lane, aware of how restricted it was on the sides and how open from above. Cloak and sword tangled around her feet, and she had to hurry her steps to catch up with the long strides of the young man before her.

They were within sight of the firelit crowds in the square when the Icefalcon stopped and raised his head to listen like a startled beast. "Do you hear it?" His voice was a whisper in the darkness, his face and pale hair a blur edged in the rosy reflection of the bonfires. Gil stopped also, listening to the cool quiet of the night. Pine-scented winds blew the sounds from beyond the town, far-off sounds changed by the darkness, but unmistakable. From the dark woods that ringed the town, the wind carried up the sounds of screaming.

The Dark Ones had come to Karst!

There was no battle at Karst—only a thousand rear-guard actions fought in the haunted woods by companies of Guards, of Church troops, and of the private troops of the households of noble and landchief. Patrols made sorties from the blazing central fortress of the red-lit town square and brought in huddled clusters of terrified refugees, the scattered stragglers who had survived that first onslaught.

Gil, who found herself, sword in hand, hunting with the Icefalcon's company, remembered that first chaotic nightmare in Gae and wondered that she had thought it frightening. At least then she had known where the danger lay; in Gae there had been torchlight and walls and people. But here the nightmare drifted silently through wind-touched woods, appearing, killing, and departing with a kind of hideous leisure. Here there was no warning, only a vast floating darkness that fell upon the torches between one eyeblink and the next; soft mouths gaping wide, like canopies of acid-fringed parachutes; claws reaching to tear and to hold. Here there were the victims; a pile of stripped, bloody bones among the sticks of a half-built campfire or the blood-dewed shrunken mummy of a man sucked dry while a yard away his wife knelt screaming in helpless horror at the sight.

Naturally coldhearted, Gil was made neither helpless nor, after the first few victims, sick. Rather, she was filled with a kind of cool and lightheaded rage, like a cat that kills with neither fear nor remorse.

In those first chaotic minutes, she and the Icefalcon doubled back to the Guards' Court at a run. There they found a wild confusion of men arming, companies forming, Janus' deep booming voice cutting through the holocaust of sound, demanding volunteers. Since she was wearing a sword, somebody shoved her into a company—they were halfway out of town, armed with torches and pitifully few to meet the Dark, when she fought her way up to the front of the patrol and yelled to the Icefalcon, "But I don't know how to use a sword!"

He gave her a cold stare. "Then you shouldn't wear one," he retorted.

Someone else caught her by the shoulder—the woman Seya she'd met that morning by the carts—and drew her back. "Aim at the midline of the body," she instructed Gil hastily. "Cut straight down, or straight sideways. There's a snap to the wrists, see? Hilt in both hands—not like that, you'll break both thumbs. You have to go in close to kill, if they're bigger than you are, which they will be, outside like this. Got that? You can pick up the rest later. Stay in the center of the group and don't take on anything you can't handle."

Watchword for the night, Gil thought wryly. But it was surprising, the first time those dark, silent bulks materialized out of the misty darkness between the trees, how much of that hasty lesson she could put into practice. And she learned the first principle of any martial art—that surviving or not surviving an encounter is the ultimate test of any system, lesson, or technique.

In one sense it was easy, for those nebulous bodies offered little resistance to the razor-sharp metal. Precision and speed counted rather than strength; for all their soft bulk, the Dark Ones moved fast. But Seya had not mentioned that the Dark Ones stank of rotting blood, nor had she described the way the cut pieces folded and trailed and spattered everything with human blood and blackish liquid as they disintegrated. This Gil found out in that crimson pandemonium of fire and dark trees, death and flight and war. And she found out, too, that there was less fear in the attack than in the defense and that, no

110

matter how little sleep or food you have had in the last forty-eight hours, you could always fight for your life. She fought shoulder to shoulder with the black-uniformed Guards of Gae and ragged volunteers in homespun. She ran in the wake of the fighters as they moved through the woods like a wolfpack, gathering lost and terrified fugitives and shepherding them back toward Karst. The cold electricity of battle-lust filled her like fire and drove out weariness or fear.

In time, the dozen or so warriors of the Icefalcon's company rounded up some fifty refugees. They circled them in a loose cordon and gave torches to as many of them as were capable of carrying such things; most persisted in holding to possessions, money, and food, and a good thirty were women carrying children in their arms. For the third time that night, they started back for Karst. Woods and sky were utterly black, the dark trees threshing in the wind. All around them could be heard screaming and wailing. It was a Dantean scene, lit by the jerky glare of torches.

Someone behind her cried out. Looking up, Gil saw the Dark materializing in the inky air, with a sudden drop of slobbering wings and the slash of a thorned wire tail. She stepped into it, sword whining as she swung, aware of Seya on her right, someone else on her left. Then she was engulfed in darkness, wind, and fire, cutting blindly. The fugitives behind her were packing closer and closer together like sheep, the children shrieking, the men crying out. Shredded veils of disintegrating protoplasm slithered to the ground all around her. She saw the man on her left buckle awkwardly to his knees, dry and white and dewed all over with blood as the Dark One rose off him like some giant, flopping, airborne blob. Wave after wave of darkness came pouring from the woods.

The Icefalcon raised his light voice to a harsh rasp. "This will be the last trip, my sisters and brothers. There are more now than there were. We'll have to hold the town."

In the momentary lull, as the Dark Ones gathered like a lightless roof of storm overhead, a Guard's voice cried bitterly, "Hold *that* town? That collection of wall-less chicken-runs?"

"It's the only town we have. Now, run!"

And they ran, through the black nightmare of alien pursuit, with the winds stirring after them like the breath of some unspeakable abyss. It was a nightmare of woods, darkness, sinuous half-seen forms, flame, and stumbling terror. They ran toward the refuge of Karst, and the Dark Ones followed.

CHAPTER SEVEN

Hell of a joke on Alwir! Rudy slumped back against the
clustered pilasters framing the open archway from the
villa's main reception-hall out to its entryway and shut his
eyes. But nothing could block out the wild glare of the
torches, the screaming that went through his head like a
hacksaw, and the dizzy sickness of fatigue. *That whole
sales pitch about everything being hunky-dory and let's
make Karst capital of the new Realm had gone down the
tubes. And Ingold, whatever the hell they did with him,
was right all along.*

He opened his eyes again, the sensory burn-out of the
hall stabbing body and brain like crimson knives. It was
like the waiting room of Judgment Day. The hall and
entryway on either side of the fluted arch were mobbed
wall to wall with people, refugees driven in from the woods
and the town square who had taken shelter here when the
defense lines around the town had caved in. People were
weeping, praying, cursing, all at the tops of their lungs;
they were milling like panic-stricken sheep when the wolf
was in the fold. The jackhammer din was like the final set
of a rock concert, so deafening that no single sound was
audible, and the faces illuminated by the bleeding torchlight seemed to mouth senselessly. The packed heat of the
room was smothering, the air foul with smoke and human
fear. Detachedly, Rudy wondered if he were involved in
one of Gil's nightmares. But he was too hungry to be
asleep for one thing; and for another, it looked as if he'd
started at the wrong end of the dream and couldn't remem-

ber going to bed. He wondered if the end of the world was going to be this noisy. He hoped not.

Like Satan in the chaos of the fire, Alwir stood in the middle of the room, blood from his cut cheek making a red track in the sweaty slime of his face. One hand rested on the pommel of his sword, the other gestured, black and eloquent—he was speaking with Commander Janus and Bishop Govannin, who stood leaning on her drawn sword, her robe girded up for fighting. Under the marks of battle, that thin skull-face of hers was calm. Rudy reflected dryly to himself that it looked as if everybody in town knew how to handle a sword except him. Alwir suggested something, and the Bishop shook her head in somber denial. The angry, insistent sweep of the Chancellor's gesture took in all the room. Rudy had a bad feeling that he knew what the problem was.

The villa was indefensible.

It was obvious. They'd been driven there when the defenses around the square had crumbled, when darkness like a fog had sapped the light of the fires. One minute, it seemed, Rudy had been standing in the line of armed men, awkwardly gripping the hilt of a sword somebody had shoved into his hands, backed by the wind-whipped, flaring blaze of dozens of bonfires and the yammering cries of the unarmed civilians who were crowding in the square for protection and watching with uneasy terror the restless stirrings in the darkness beyond the light. Then the darkness had begun to draw closer, the shifting suggestion of nebulous bodies growing increasingly clear. Looking behind him, Rudy had seen the bonfires pale and weaken, the flames robbed of their light. And then he'd been caught in the blind stampede for walls to hide behind, for any shelter against that encroaching terror. He'd been one of the lucky ones. The square and the streets outside were littered with the unlucky.

And the irony of it was, Rudy thought, surveying the scarlet confusion before him, that this place which they'd trampled over each other to reach was about as defensible as a bird cage.

It was a summer palace. A man didn't have to study architecture to guess that one. The whole place was designed to let in light and air and summer breezes. Colonnades joined to open galleries; dainty, trefoiled arches

114

opened into long vistas of wide-windowed rooms; and the long double stairway rising from the entry-hall to his left terminated in a balcony gallery that communicated with the rest of the villa by a series of airy, unwalled breezeways. The whole thing would be as much use as a lace table-cloth in a hurricane. If he hadn't been half-blind with exhaustion and within kissing distance of a horrible death, Rudy could have laughed.

Janus offered some other plan. Alwir shook his head. *Nix on anything that means going outside,* Rudy thought. Blackness seemed to press like a bodiless entity against the long windows that ran the length of one wall. A few minutes ago, the orange reflection of firelight had been visible through them. Now there was only darkness. The multi-voiced baying of the fugitives had begun to fade, men and women making little forays into the murky dimness of the entry-hall beyond the arch, as if seeking a safer room for their hiding, but unwilling to leave the main crowd to do so. Alwir pointed downward, to the floor or, Rudy guessed, to the cellars of the villa. The Bishop asked him something that made his eyes flash with anger.

But before he could reply, a rending crash sounded from somewhere in the deeps of the house, the violence of it shaking the stone walls on their foundations.

In the hush that followed, Janus' voice could be heard to the far corners of the hall. "East gallery," he said briefly.

A woman began to scream, a steady, unwavering note. A few feet from him, Rudy saw a young woman of about his own age tighten her clutch on a gaggle of smaller children who clung to her skirts for courage.. A fat man with a garden rake for a weapon hopped to his feet and began to glare around, as if expecting the Dark to come rushing down from the throbbing air. The mob in the room packed tighter, as if they could conceal themselves from the Dark by doing so.

Their voices climbed to a crescendo of wild terror through which Alwir's trained bass battle voice cut like a cleaver. "With me! We can defend the vaults!"

Someone began howling. "Not the vaults! Not underground!"

Rudy scrambled to his feet, cursing, narrowly missing cutting off his own fingers with the sword he still held. He personally didn't care where they holed up, as long as it had nice thick walls and only one door. People were yelling, swaying, surging after Alwir through the arched doorway at the far end of the hall. Torches were being pulled down from the walls, the flailing red light throwing the room into a maelstrom of jerking shadow.

Someone shoved against Rudy in the mob, fighting against the current to go the other way, and he caught at a familiar arm.

"Where the hell are you going?"

Minalde's hair had come unbraided and hung against her torn and dirty white gown. "Tir's up there," she said fiercely. "I thought Medda had brought him down." Shoulders jostled them, throwing them close together. In the whiteness of her face, her eyes were iris-colored in the torchlight.

"Well, you can't go up there now!" As she pulled angrily at his grip, Rudy added, "Look, if the door's locked and there's some kind of light in the room, they'll miss him, he'll be fine. There's a zillion people down here for them to get."

"They know who he is," she whispered desperately. "It's him they want." With a swift jerk she freed her arm and plunged toward the stairs, slipping between the crowding bodies like an eel.

"You crazy female, you're gonna get killed!" Rudy shoved his way after her, his larger size hampering him, the crowd dragging him inexorably along. He saw Alde stop by the foot of the stairs and take a torch from its holder. Elbowing and struggling frantically, he reached the place moments later, snatched another torch, and dashed up after her into the darkness. He caught her at the top and grabbed her arm in a grip that would leave bruises.

"You let me go!"

"The hell I will!" he yelled back at her. "Now you listen . . ."

With an inarticulate sob of fury she thrust her torch into his face. He leaped back, barely catching himself from going backward down the stairs, and she was gone, a flicker of white fluttering down the wind-searched gallery, her torch streaming in her wake like a banner. Rudy followed profanely.

In spite of the Dark, she left the nursery door open for him. He stumbled through and slammed it shut behind him, gasping with exertion and terror and rage.

116

"You're insane, do you know that?" he shouted at her. "You could get the both of us killed! You didn't even know if the kid was still alive—"

She wasn't listening. She bent over the gilded cradle and gathered the child in her arms. Tir was awake, but silent, as he had been in that dilapidated shack in the orange groves of California, dark-blue eyes wide with understanding fear. The girl shook back the waves of hair from her face and smoothed the child's round cheek with her fingers. Rudy could see that her hands were shaking.

"Here," he said roughly, and pulled a shawl from the table beside the crib. "Make a sling and tie the kid to you. You're gonna need your hands free to carry the torches." She obeyed silently, not meeting his eyes. "I don't know whether I shouldn't brain you myself. It might knock some sense into your head."

She took her torch from the wall holder where she'd placed it and turned back to him, her eyes defiant. Rudy grunted in an unwilling and inarticulate concession to her courage, if not to her brains. "You're gonna have to tell me how to find these vaults they're talking about."

"Down the stairs, through the arch at the end of the big hall, down the steps to the right," she said in a small voice. "It will be the main vault, where they store the wine. That's the only room large enough."

He took up his own torch again and glanced briefly around that small octagonal room with its dull gold hangings and filigreed ebony fixtures. Then he looked back at the girl, her face as white as her gown in the flickering shadows. "Yeah, well, if we get killed . . ." he began to threaten, then stopped. "Aah," he growled. "I still think you're crazy." He handed her his torch and edged to the door of the room, gripping the sword hilt in both hands, as he had seen Ingold do. Alde stood back from him without a word.

"You ready?"

"Yes," she said softly.

He muttered, "Here goes nuthin', sweetheart," and took a step forward. In one quick movement, he kicked the door open and slashed. The Dark One that dropped through like an inky storm of protoplasm split itself on the brightness of the blade, splattering the three of them with stinking liquid; the second, immediately following the first, withdrew almost instantly on an aimless swirl of wind. No shapes were visible in the dark corridor stretching before them—only a restless sense of movement down at the far end. He caught Alde by the arm and ran.

Fluttering shadows pursued them down the hall, monster shapes of himself, the girl, and the child. The torchlight briefly illuminated the open arches to their left; but beyond, sight failed in an endless abyss of blasphemous night. Rudy could sense the Dark all around them, watching them with a queer, horrible intelligence, waiting only for the unguarded moment to pounce. From the top of the stairs they looked down at the chasm of the hall, where a dropped torch, burning itself out on the floor, revealed a ruin of filth, torn clothes, discarded shoes, and smashed furniture trampled in the flight. Around the far archway and dimly visible in the hall beyond, a straggle of bones and bloodless, crumpled bodies showed what had happened moments after he'd followed Alde up the stairs; and beyond that archway, slipping over the bodies, a gliding shifting darkness seemed to flow.

Rudy's breath strangled in his throat. Exposed as they were at the top of the stairs, nothing could have induced him to descend to that hall, to try to cross that floor. Beside him Alde gasped, and he looked where she pointed. Four or five things like black snail shells clung to the great arched ceiling of the room, long tails hanging down, wavering in the moving air. The dim torchlight played over the chitinous gleam of their shiny backs, and picked out claws and spines and the glittering drool of acid that ran from their tucked mouths down the stone ribbing of the wall. Then, one by one, they released their hold, dropping down into the air, changing shape—changing size—melting into the shadows. Though he'd watched them as they let go, Rudy had no idea where they'd gone.

Alde whispered, "There's another way into the vaults. It's back this way. Hurry!"

Needless waste of words, Rudy thought, striding beside her down the gallery, the soft evil winds stirring in his long hair. How many of the things did it take to kill the light of a fire? A dozen? Half a dozen? Four? His T-shirt and denim jacket were clammy with sweat; his hand ached on the hilt of the sword. The shadows all around them seemed to be moving, pressing closer upon them. The torchlight reflected darkly in Tir's watching eyes. A doorway opened on a corridor, wind-searched and smelling of the Dark. There was a sense of something that followed, soft-breathing and always out of sight. Alde's breath came like a swift-breaking series of sobs; his own footsteps seemed eerily loud. A small black doorway led to the sudden, twisting spiral of a lightless corkscrew stair, down and down, steep as a ladder and perilously slippery; the amber flicker of the torches gilded stone walls barely a yard apart.

Then they reached the bottom and smelled all around them the damp, nitrous odor of underground.

"Where the hell are we?" Rudy whispered. "The dungeons?" Dampness gleamed like phosphorus on the rough walls and pooled among the lumpy stones of the floor.

Alde nodded and pointed down the corridor. "That way."

Rudy took one of the torches from her and held it low, so as not to brush the stone ceiling with the flame. "These were really the dungeons?"

"Oh, yes," the girl said softly. "Well, way back in former days, of course. Every great House of the Realm kept its own troops and had law over its own people. The High Kings, the Kings at Gae, changed all that; any man can appeal from a landchief's or a lord's court to the King's now. That's for civil crimes, of course; the Church still judges its own." She hesitated at a branching of the ways. The dungeons were a black labyrinth of cramped wet passageways; Rudy wondered how she could be so confident. "Down here, I think."

They passed along the narrow way, the light of their torches touching briefly on shut doors, hewn heavy oak strapped in bronze and iron, sometimes on a level with the crude flagstones of the passage, sometimes sunk several moss-slippery steps below it. Most of the doors were bolted, a few sealed with ribbon and lead. One or two were bricked up, with a hideous finality of judgment that made Rudy's palms clammy. It was brought back to him that he was in another universe, a world totally alien to his own, with its own society, its own justice, and its own summary ways of dealing with those who tried to buck the system.

Alde stumbled, catching at his arm for support. Stopping to let her steady herself, Rudy felt the shifting, the movement of the air, the smell that breathed on his face. He could see nothing in the corridor ahead. The close-hemmed walls narrowed to a rectangle of darkness that the torchlight seemed unable to pierce, a darkness stirred by wind and filled with a terrible waiting. Wind licked at the flames of his torch, and he became suddenly aware of the darkness filling the passage at his unprotected back. It might have been only the overstretched tension of his nerves, the strain of keeping his senses at fever-pitch for endless nightmare hours—but he thought that he could see movement in the darkness before him.

Half-paralyzed, he was surprised he could even whisper. "We've got no business here, Alde," he murmured. "See if you can find one of those doors that isn't locked."

He never took his eyes from the shadows. By the change in the torchlight behind him, he knew she was edging backward, checking door after door. The light of his own torch seemed pitifully feeble against the pressing weight of the darkness all around him. Then he heard her whisper, "This one's bolted, not locked," and he moved back slowly to join her.

The door stood at the bottom of three worn steps, narrow and forbidding, its massive bolts imbedded in six inches of stone. Rudy handed Alde his torch and stepped down to it, his soul shrinking from the trap of that narrow niche, and used his sword to cut the ribbons that bound the great lead seals to the iron. The metal was disused and stiff, scraping in shrill, rusty protest as he worked back the bolt; the hinges of the narrow door screaked horribly as he pushed it ajar.

From what he could see in the diffuse glow from Alde's torches, the place was empty, little more than a round hole of darkness with a black, empty-eyed niche let into the far wall and a small pile of moldy straw and bare, dusty bones. The queer, sterile smell of the air repelled him, and he stepped inside cautiously, straining his eyes to pierce the intense gloom.

But even half-ready as he was, the rush of darkness struck too swiftly for him to make a sound. Between one heartbeat and the next, he was seized by the throat, and a weight like the arm of death hurled him against the wall, driving the breath from his body. His head hit the stone, his yell of warning strangling under the crushing pressure of a powerful forearm; he felt the sword wrenched from his hand and the point of it prick his jugular. From the darkness that closed him in, a voice whispered, "Don't make a sound."

He knew that voice. He managed to croak, "Ingold?"

The strangling arm lessened its force against his windpipe. He could see nothing in the darkness, but the texture of the robe that brushed his hand was familiar. He swallowed, trying to get his breath. "What are you doing here, man?"

The wizard snorted. "At the risk of belaboring the obvious, I am breaking jail, as your friends would so vulgarly put it," the rusty, incisive voice snapped. "Is Gil with you?"

"Gil?" He couldn't remember when he'd last seen Gil. "No, I—Jesus, Ingold," Rudy whispered, feeling suddenly very lost and alone.

Strengthening light shifted in the dark arch of the door, shadows fleeing crazily over the uneven stone of the walls. Minalde stepped through the door and stopped, her eyes widening with surprise at the sight of the wizard. Then she lowered her gaze, and a slow flush of shame scalded her face, turning it pink to the hairline. She wavered, as if she would flee into the corridor again, though she obviously could not. In her confusion, she looked about to drop one or both torches and plunge them all in darkness.

Rudy was still recovering from his surprise at this reaction when the old man crossed the room to her and gently took one of the flares from her hand. "My child," he said to her softly, "a gentleman never remembers anything a lady says to him in the heat of anger—or any other passion, for that matter. Consider it forgotten."

This only served to make her blush redder. She tried to turn away from him, but he caught her arm gently and brushed aside the black cloak of her hair that half-hid the silent infant slung at her breast. He touched the child's head tenderly and looked back into the girl's eyes. There was no tone of question in his voice when he said, "So they have come, after all."

She nodded, and Ingold's lips tightened under the scrubby forest of unkempt beard. As if reminded of their danger, Alde slipped from his grasp, her hand going to the door to close it.

Ingold said sharply, "Don't."

Her eyes went from him to Rudy, questioning, seeking confirmation.

Ingold went on. "If you close that door it will disappear, and we may all be locked in here forever." He gestured toward the foot of the little wall-niche, where a skull stared mournfully from the shadows. "There are spells laid on this cell that even I could not work through."

"But the Dark are out there, Ingold," Rudy whispered. "There must be hundreds of people dead in the villa upstairs—thousands in the square, in the woods. They're everywhere, like ghosts. It's hopeless, we'll never . . ."

"There is always hope," the wizard said quietly. "With the seals on the door of this cell, there was no way I could have left it—but I knew that someone would come whom I could overpower, if necessary. And someone did."

"Yeah, but that was just a—" Rudy hesitated over the word. "A coincidence."

Ingold's eyes glinted with an echo of their old impish light. "Don't tell me you still believe in coincidence, Rudy." He handed back the sword. "You'll find a seal of some kind hung over the bolts of the door. Remove it and place it there in the niche for the time being. I'll shut you in when I leave. Here, at least, in all the town of Karst, you will be safe until I can return for you or send someone to get you out. It's drastic," he went on, seeing Minalde's eyes widen with fear, "but at least I can be sure the Dark will not come here. Will you stay?"

Rudy glanced uneasily at Alde and at the skull in the dark niche. "You mean," he asked warily, "once that door is shut, we can't get out?"

"Precisely. The door is invisible from the inside."

Open, the door looked perfectly ordinary; it was the shadow-haunted darkness of the corridor beyond that worried Rudy. The dim yellow torchlight edged the massive iron of its bindings and revealed the roughness of the ancient smoke-stained oak slabs. Wind stirring down the corridor made the lead seal hanging from the bolts move, as if with a restless life of its own. Rudy noticed that, though Ingold stood close to the door, his torch upraised in one hand, he would not touch it.

"Quickly," the wizard said. "We haven't much time."

"Rudy." Alde's voice was timid, her eyes huge in the torchlight. "If I will be safe here—as safe as anywhere in

122

this town tonight—I would rather you went with Ingold. In case something—happened—I'd feel better if two people knew where we were, instead of only one."

Rudy shivered at the implications of that thought. "You won't be afraid here alone?"

"Not any more afraid than I've been."

"Get the seal, then," Ingold said, "and let us go."

Rudy stepped gingerly to the door, the smoldering yellow light from within the cell illuminating the narrow slot of the opening and no farther. The seal still dangled from its cut black ribbons, a round plaque of dull lead that seemed to absorb, rather than reflect, the light. It was marked on either side with a letter of the Darwath alphabet; as he reached to touch it, he found himself repelled by a loathing he could put no name to. There was something deeply frightening about the thing. "Can't we just leave it here?"

"I cannot pass it," Ingold said simply.

The horror, the irrational vileness, concentrated in that small gray bulla were such that Rudy never thought to question him. He simply lifted the thing by its black ribbons and carried it at arm's length to throw deep into the shadows of the niche. He noticed Alde had stepped back as he'd passed with it, as if the aura radiated from it was like the smell of evil.

Alde fitted the end of her torch into a crack in the stonework of the wall and turned back to him, cradling the child in both arms.

"We'll send someone back for you," Rudy promised softly. "Don't worry."

She shook her head and evaded Ingold's glance; the last Rudy saw of her was a slender white figure cloaked in her tangled hair, the child in her arms. The darkness of the doorway framed them like a gilded votive in a shrine. Then he shut the door and worked home the rusty iron of the bolts.

"What was that thing?" he whispered, finding himself unwilling even to touch the bolts where it had hung.

"It is the Rune of the Chain," Ingold said quietly, standing on the top of the worn steps to scan the corridor beyond. "The cell itself has Power worked into its walls, so that no one within may find or open the door. With the Rune of the Chain spelled against me, even if I could have found the door, I could not have gone through. Presumably I would have been left here until I could be formally banished—or, just possibly, until I starved."

"They—couldn't do that, could they?" Rudy asked queasily.

Ingold shrugged. "Who would have stopped them? Ordinarily, the wizards look out for their own, but the Archmage has vanished, and the City of Wizards lies sunk in the rings of its own enchantments. I am very much on my own." Seeing the look on Rudy's face, compounded of horror and shocked proprieties, Ingold smiled, and some of the grimness left his eyes. "But, as you see, I would have gotten out, magic or no magic. I am glad that you brought Alde and the baby with you. It was by far the best thing you could have done. Here, at least, they will be safe from the Dark."

He raised his torch, the sickly glow of it barely penetrating the obscurity of the passage. "This way," he decided, indicating the direction in which Rudy and Alde had been headed before.

"Hey," Rudy said softly as they started down that dark and wind-stirred corridor. The wizard glanced back over his shoulder. "What was that all about with her?"

Ingold shrugged. "At our last meeting the young lady threatened to kill me—the reason isn't important. She may repent the sentiments or merely the social gaffe. If one is going to . . ."

And then a sound rocked the vaults, a deep, hollow booming, like the blow of a monster fist, and the shock of it shivered in the very walls. Ingold paused in his stride, his eyes narrowing to a burning glitter of concentration as he listened; then he was striding down the corridor, Rudy following behind with drawn sword. As they turned the corner, Rudy saw the wizard shift the torch in his hands, and the rough wood seemed to elongate into a six-foot staff, the fire at its tip swelling and whitening to the diamond brilliance of a magnesium torch, searing like a crystal vibration into every crack of those stained and ancient walls. Holding the blazing staff half like a lamp, half like a weapon, the wizard moved ahead of him, shabby cloak billowing in his wake like wings. Rudy hurried after, the darkness falling back all around them and closing in behind.

Somewhere very close to them, a second blow resounded,

shaking the stone under their feet like the smash of a piston driven by an insanely giant machine. Cold and hollow with hunger and fatigue, Rudy wondered shakily if they'd be killed, but the thought of it was strangely impersonal. Corridors converged, widening the darkness where they trod; he could now smell water and mold, and all around them the stone-acid stink of the dark. Somewhere, all that was left of the mob who had taken refuge in Alwir's villa—the handful of Guards and the scarlet Church troops, the fat man with his garden rake and the young woman with her attendant mob of children, and all the other faces that had swum in the glaring maelstrom abovestairs—were cowering in the dark, jumping shadows of the vaults, watching with horrified eyes the might of the Dark Ones hammering the barred iron doors, the only line of defense, from their massive hinges.

The might of the Dark! Rudy felt it, like a blow in the face, as the third explosion rocked the foundations of the villa; he felt the contraction of the air, and the evil intelligence watching them as they passed. The winds had begun to whip through the passageways like the rising forerunners of a gale, fluttering in Ingold's mantle and twisting at his own long hair. The light from the staff in the wizard's hand broadened to a blaze like hot noon, scorching out the secrets of the darkness, and in its blinding glare they turned a corner into a major thoroughfare and saw through the heavy shadows that blotted the air like smoke the great doors that lay at the end.

Though Rudy could see no single form, no shape in the darkness, he sensed the malevolence that beat the air with the movement of a thousand threshing wings. Their power seemed to stretch across the corridor like a wall; beyond it, barely visible in the clotted shadows, he could see the broad line of torchlight under the barred doors. There were no sounds from the people behind those doors. Those who had made it to that last covert in the vaults faced the Dark in silence.

He felt the change in the Dark, the sudden surge of that terrible alien power, and the thunder of that explosive sound roared in his ears as he saw the doors buckle and collapse, breaking inward in a flying hurricane of splintering wood. Sickly failing torchlight showed him faces beyond the broken doors and silhouetted smoky forms taking sudden shape in the darkness.

Into that darkness Ingold flung himself without so much as breaking stride, the cold light hurling around him like the explosion of a bursting star. Rudy followed, clinging to the light as to a mantle, and for one brief, terrible instant it seemed that the darkness streamed back on them, covering and smothering that brilliant burning light.

Whether it was exhaustion playing tricks on his mind or some magic of the Dark, Rudy did not know. He did not think he had shifted or closed his eyes and knew he hadn't looked away. But for one instant, there was the darkness, pouring down over the light. And the next moment, there was only light, white and chill, surrounding the strong, shabby form of the old man who stalked down that empty corridor. Streaming through the broken doors, the white light fell on waxy, pinched faces, was reflected from terrified eyes, and edged the steel in the hands of the thin line of troops stretched between the packed mob of surviving refugees and the doors. Then the light faded, shrinking naturally from the blinding glow to the yellow splotch of simple torch flame.

Rudy knew that the Dark were gone. He sensed it in some way he could not be sure of. There were none in the vaults, none left in the villa over their heads. Following Ingold down toward the doors, their footfalls echoing hollowly in the empty shadows of the corridor, he could feel the emptiness stretching around and behind him into the darkness. Whether the Dark had drawn off before the wizard's wrath or simply faded away, sated with their night's kill, he didn't know. In a way it didn't matter. All that mattered was that they were gone. He was safe. He had survived the night.

At the realization of it, a weariness came over him, as if all strength had been suddenly drained from his body. He stumbled and caught the wall for support. Ingold moved on to the broken threshold, where three figures had detached themselves from the line of Guards and stood framed in the ruin of wood and iron. Under the filth and slime of battle, Rudy recognized Alwir, Janus, and Bishop Govannin.

Without a word, the Commander of the Guards of Gae stepped forward, dropped to one knee before the wizard, and kissed his scarred hand. At this gesture of fealty the Chancellor and the Bishop exchanged a glance of enigmatic distrust and disapproval over the Guard's bowed back. The echoes of the empty corridor murmured back the Commander's words: "We thought you'd gone."

Ingold touched the man's bent red head, then raised him, his eyes on Alwir's. "I swore I would see Tir to a place of safety," he replied calmly, "and so I will. No, I had not gone. I was merely—imprisoned."

"Imprisoned?" Janus' thick brows met over russet, animal eyes. "On whose orders?"

"The detention order was unsigned," the wizard said in his mildest voice. "Merely sealed with the King's mark. Anyone who had access to it could have done so." The light of the guttered torch in his hand flared in the hollows of exhaustion-shadowed eyes. "The cell was sealed with the Rune of the Chain."

"The use of such things is illegal," Govannin commented, folding thin arms like a skeleton's, her black, lizard eyes expressionless. "And it would have been a fool's act to order such a thing at such a time."

Alwir shook his head. "I certainly sealed no such order," he said in a puzzled voice. "As for the Rune— There was said to be one somewhere in the treasuries of the Palace at Gae, but I always thought it merely a legend. I am only thankful that you seem to have effected your escape in time to come to our aid. Your arrest was obviously a mistake on someone's part."

The wizard's gaze went from the Chancellor's face to the Bishop's, but all he said was, "Obviously."

Much later in the morning, Rudy backtracked their steps to the doorless cell, empty now and standing open, with the intention of taking that dark seal and dropping it quietly down a well. But, though he found the place all right, and searched through the dusty bones of the niche, someone else had clearly been there before him, for he could find no trace of it anywhere.

CHAPTER EIGHT

"Will she be all right?"

"If the arm doesn't fester."

The voices came distinctly to Gil, like something heard in a dream; as in a dream, she could identify them without being clearly able to say why. As if she lay at the bottom of a well, she could look up and see, a long way away, the tall shape of Alwir, blotting the sun like a cloud; beside him was the Icefalcon, light and cool as wind. But the water of the well she lay in was pain; crystal-clear, shimmering, acid pain.

Alwir's melodious voice went on. "If it festers she'll lose it."

And the Icefalcon asked, "Where's Ingold?"

"Who knows? His talent is for timely disappearances."

Curse him, Gil thought blindly. *Curse him, curse him, curse him* . . . Alwir moved away, and a bar of sunlight fell on her eyes, like the stab of a knife. She twisted her head convulsively aside, and the movement wrenched at the sodden mass of pain wrapped around the bones of her left arm. She wept in agony and despair.

In her delirium she dreamed, and in her dream she saw him. From the dark place where she stood, she could look into her lighted kitchen, back in the apartment on Clarke Street; a stale litter of old coffee cups and papers was on the table, and the half-finished research was strewn about the room like blown leaves in autumn. It seemed as if she had only to step down to reach it, as if a few strides would take her from this place to home, to the university, to the quiet life of scholarship and the friends and security of her own time and place. Dimly she heard the phone ringing there and knew it was one of her women friends calling, as they had been calling for two days now. They would be worried—soon they would begin to search. The thought of their pain and fear for her hurt Gil almost as much as her injured arm, and she tried to go into the kitchen to answer the phone, but she found that Ingold stood in her way. Hooded, his sword gleaming like foxfire, he rose before her, a dark shape blown and wavering on the wind. No matter how she turned and shifted, he was always in her way, always turning her back. She began to cry, "Let me go! Let me go!" in helpless fury. Then wind caught at him, swirling his brown mantle into a black cloud of shadow, and in his place a Dark One rode the twisting air. She tried to run, and it was upon her; she tried to fight with the sword she suddenly found in her hands, but as she cut at it, its huge, slobbering mouth snatched at her, leaving a trail of acid down her arm that seared into the flesh until she cried out in pain.

She saw her arm, bone and torn flesh, then. She saw the hand that touched it, molding and kneading at the ripped ruin of muscle. In her dreaming, she was reminded of a man molding putty or seaming together colored clays. It was Ingold's hand, nicked and marked with old scars, and calloused from the grip of a sword—and there he was, tired and shabby, eyes bright in circles of black exhaustion. She struck at him with her good hand, sobbing weak obscenities at him because he wouldn't let her go back, because he had trapped her here, cursing him and fighting against his strong, sure touch. Then that part of the dream faded also, and utter darkness took her.

From the Town Hall steps, Rudy watched what remained of the powers in the Realm coming to council. It was early afternoon now, and bleak clouds had begun to gray the light of the day, piling heavily over the mountains like the threat of doom. He had eaten, slept, and helped the Guards and those survivors of last night's horrors who were still capable of directed action in the gruesome task of cleaning the bloodless corpses and stripped bones out of the gory mud of the square. Now he was cold, weary, and sickened in his soul. Even with the worst of the

129

mess—the hopeless, twisted wrecks that had once been living people—out of the way, the square wore a look of absolute desolation. Strewn and trampled in the mud were the pitiful remains of flight—clothes, cook pots, books torn and sodden with mud, salvage from Gae whose owners would have no further use for it. During burial detail that morning, Rudy had found what he judged to be a small fortune in jewels, mixed with the churned slush in the square—precious things dropped unheeded in last night's desperate, futile scramble for refuge.

Karst was a town of the dead. People moved about its streets blindly, stumbling with weariness or shock or grief. Half-heard through the town, the muffled wailing of sobs was as prevalent today as the woodsmoke and stench had been yesterday. The places that had been so crowded were three-quarters empty. People passed in the streets on their blind errands and looked at one another, but did not ask, because they did not dare, *What now?*

Good question, Rudy thought dryly.

What now, when the Dark Ones were everywhere, when he was an exile in an alien universe, hiding and dodging until something—the Dark, the cold, starvation, the plague, or whatever—got him before he could make it back to the safety of his own? And who knew how long that was going to be? Maybe even Ingold didn't. Anyway, what if somebody jailed Ingold again, and this time nobody came? Or what if somebody jailed *him?* It was possible—he was a stranger, unfamiliar wtih the customs, ignorant of the laws that could get him dumped into one of those bricked-up slammers he'd passed last night. Hell, he didn't even know the language, if anyone wanted to get technical about it.

Rudy was well aware that he hadn't spoken a word of English since he'd been here. How he understood, let alone spoke, the Wathe, the common tongue of the Realm, he wasn't even prepared to guess. But Ingold had said something about arranging it, back in California when he'd still regarded the old man as a harmless lunatic. Rudy guessed that was damn big medicine for somebody Alwir talked about as a kind of conjuring tramp.

He saw Ingold and Alwir crossing the square together, an uneasy partnership for sure. The Chancellor was striding amid the swirl of his flame-cut crimson cloak, rubies glittering like blood on the doeskin of his gloves; Ingold walked beside him, leaning on his staff like a tired old man. God knew how, but the wizard had reacquired both staff and sword.

His voice, strong and raspy with that characteristic velvet break in its tone, drifted to Rudy as the two men mounted the steps. ". . . staring us in the face, all of us. Our way of life, our entire world, is changed, and we would be fools to deny it. All the structures of power are altered, and by no kind of machinations, magic, might, or faith can we keep what we have held."

Alwir's deep, mellow tones replied. "And you, my friend. Wizardry has failed, too. Where is your Archmage now? And the Council of Quo? That boasted magic . . ."

They passed within, the crimson shape and the brown. *He's got a point there,* Rudy thought tiredly. *I may be ignorant, but I'm not dumb. As a refugee camp or a rally-ing-point for civilization, this burg has had it.* He surveyed the silent square. Yesterday real estate could have been sold here at fifty dollars a square foot. It was a bust market now, the mud compounded of earth, rain and spent blood.

He recognized some of the others coming across the square, making for the council meeting. They were the nobles or notables of the Realm whom people had pointed out to him—Christ, was it only yesterday?—as he'd bummed around Karst, not a care in the world, checking out the lay of the land. He recognized a couple of the landchiefs of the Realm who'd ridden up to Gae to aid the late King and subsequently refugeed to Karst—a young blond surfer-type and a big, scarred old buffer who looked like John Wayne playing the Sheriff of Nottingham—Janus of the Guards, in a clean black uniform but beat-up as an Irish cop after a Friday night donnybrook, with a black eye and a red welt down the side of his face; the Bishop Govannin, leaning on the arm of an attendant priest; and a couple of depressed-looking local merchants who'd been trading off a black market in food and water while there was still a shortage to kick up the prices.

Rudy glanced at the angle of the shadow cast by the fountain. The council could last most of the afternoon—they had to figure out their next course of action before night fell again. Rudy wondered if he could catch up with Ingold after it was over, maybe see if there were some way

131

he could get back without letting all the Dark Ones in the world through the Void after him. Maybe the Archmage, Lohiro of Quo, would have some ideas on that—he was, after all, Ingold's superior—if they could find the guy, that is.

But then he caught sight of a familiar face across the square, and the thought dropped from his mind. She wore black velvet now instead of the plain white gown of yesterday; with her hair braided and coiled in elaborate gleaming loops, she looked a few years older. She reminded him of a young apple tree in its first blossom, delicate and poised and graceful as a dancer.

He got to his feet and came down the steps to her. "I see you're all right," he said. "I'm sorry I didn't come back for you myself, but at that point all I wanted to do was find some quiet corner and fall asleep in it."

She smiled shyly at him. "It's all right. The men Alwir sent had no trouble finding the place. And after all you'd done last night, I think I would have been ashamed of myself if you'd lost sleep to come after me and make sure I didn't get into any more trouble." She looked tired and strained, more fragile than she had last night; Rudy felt he could have picked her up in one hand. She went on. "I owe you my life, and Tir's twice over."

"Yeah, well, I still say it was a crazy stunt to pull in the first place. I ought to have my head examined for going after you."

"I said once before you were brave." She smiled, teasing. "You can't deny it now."

"Like hell." Rudy grinned.

The corners of the girl's blue-violet eyes crinkled with laughing skepticism. "Even when you followed me up the stairs?"

"Oh, hell, I couldn't let you go by yourself." He looked down at her gravely for a moment, remembering the terror of that wind-searched open gallery and the stygian mazes of the vaults. "You must care a lot for the kid, to go back for him that way."

She took his hand, her fingers slim and warm in the brief touch. "I do," she said simply. "Tir is my son. If I alone had died last night, it might have made no difference to anyone, anymore. But I shall always thank you for saving him."

She turned and mounted the steps, moving with a dancer's quicksilver lightness. The Guards at the door bowed to her in an elaborate salute as she passed between them, and she vanished into the shadows of the great doors, leaving Rudy standing open-mouthed with astonishment in the mud of the square.

The Guards' Court at the back of the town had once been the stableyard of some great villa. To Gil's trained eye, the overly intricate coats of arms over gatehouse and window-embrasure whispered of new money and the vast inferiority complex of the parvenu. In the cold afternoon light, most of the court was visible from where she lay on a scratchy bed of hay and borrowed cloaks, aching with weariness and the aftermath of pain, looking out from the dim blue shadows of the makeshift barracks.

Daylight wasn't kind to the place. The lean-to that ran around three sides of the stone courtyard wall had been roughly converted into barracks, and the mail, weapons, and bedrolls of some seventy Guards were heaped haphazardly among the bales of fodder. The mud in the center of the court was slippery and rank. In a corner by a fountain, someone was cooking oatmeal, and the drift of smoke on the wind cut at Gil's eyes. In the mucky space of open ground, thirty or so Guards were engaged in practice, muddy to the eyebrows.

But they were good. Even to Gil's inexperienced eye, their quickness and balance were obvious; they were professional warriors, an elite corps. Lying here, as she had lain most of the day, she had seen them come in from duty; she knew that all of them had fought last night and, like her, bore the wounds of it. She had noticed in the confusion of last night that very few of the dead were Guards, and now she saw why; the speed, stamina, and unthinking reactions were trained into them until the downward slash-duck-parry motion of attack and defense was as automatic as jerking a burned finger from flame. They trained with split wood blades like the Japanese *shinai*, weapons that would neither cut nor maim but which left appalling bruises—nobody was armored and there wasn't a shield in the place. Gil watched them with an awe that came from the glimmerings of understanding.

"What do you think?" a cool voice asked. Looking up,

she saw the Icefalcon standing beside her, indistinct in the murky shade.

"About that?" She gestured toward the moving figures and the distant clacking of wooden blade on blade. He nodded, pale eyes aloof. "You need it, don't you, to be perfect," she said, watching the quick grace of the warriors that was almost a dance. "And that's what it is. Perfect."

The Icefalcon shrugged, but his eyes had a speculative gleam in their silvery depths. "If you have only one blow," he remarked, "it had better be perfect. How's your arm?"

She shook her head wearily, not wanting to think about the pain. "It was stupid," she said. The bandages showed a kind of grubby brown through the torn, ruined sleeve of the shirt that had been part of a corpse's gown. "I was tired; it shouldn't have happened."

The tall young man leaned against the wall and hooked his thumbs in his swordbelt in a gesture common to the Guards. "You didn't do badly," he told her. "You have a knack, a talent that way. I personally didn't think you'd make it past the first fight. Novices don't. You have the instinct to kill."

"What?" she exclaimed, more startled than horrified, though on reflection she supposed she should have been more horrified than she was.

"I mean it," the Icefalcon said in that colorless, breathy voice. "Among my people that is a compliment. To kill is to survive the fight. To kill is to want very much to live." He glanced out into the gray afternoon, his long, thin hands folding over his propped knee. "In the Realm they consider that such ideas are crazy. Perhaps your people do, too. So they say that the Guards are crazy; and by their lights, perhaps they are right."

Perhaps, Gil thought. *Perhaps.*

It would look that way from the outside, certainly. That striving, that need, was seldom understood, any more than Rudy had understood why she would turn away from her home and family for the sake of the terrible and abstract joys of scholarship. In its way, it was the same kind of craziness.

A little, bald-headed man was moving through the mazes of the combatants, watching everything with beady, elf-bright brown eyes. He stopped just behind Seya, scratching his close-clipped brown beard and observing her efforts against another Guard of about her size and weight. She cut and parried; as she moved forward for another blow, he stepped in lightly and hooked both her legs from under her, dumping her unceremoniously in the mud. "Stronger stance," he cautioned her, then turned and walked away. Seya climbed slowly to her feet, wiped the goop from her face, and went back to her bout.

"There are very few," the Icefalcon's soft voice went on, "who understand this. Very few who have this instinct for life, this understanding for the fire of perfection. Perhaps that is why there have always been very few Guards." He glanced down at her, the light shifting across the narrow bones of his face. "Would you be a Guard?"

Gil felt the slow flush of blood rise to her face and the quickening of her pulse. She waited a long time before she answered him. "You mean, stay here and be a Guard?"

"We are very short of Guards."

She was silent again, though a kind of eager tension wired its way into her muscles and a confusion into her heart. She watched the little, bearded, bald man in the square step unconcernedly between swinging blades to double up a tall Guard with a blow in mid-stroke, step lightly back with almost preternatural timing, and go on to correct his next victim. Finally she said, "I can't."

"Indeed," was all the Icefalcon said.

"I'm going back. To my own land."

He looked down at her and raised one colorless brow.

"I'm sorry," she muttered.

"Gnift will also be sorry, to hear that," the Icefalcon said.

"Gnift?"

He gestured toward the bald man in the square. "He is the instructor of the Guards. He watched you in the vaults at Gae and last night. He says you could be good."

She shook her head. "If I stayed," she said, "it would only be a matter of time until I died."

"It is always," the Icefalcon remarked, "only a matter of time. But you are right." He looked up as another shadow loomed beneath the low, shingled roof.

"Hey, Gil." Rudy took a seat on the hay bale beside her. "They said you were hurt. Are you okay?"

She shrugged, the movement making her wince in spite of herself. "I'll live." In the dimness Rudy looked shabby and seedy, his painted jacket a ruin of mud and charred slime, his long hair grubby with sweat, though he'd managed to come up with a razor from someplace and was no longer as unshaven as he'd been yesterday. Still, she reflected, she couldn't look much better.

"Their council meeting's broken up," he informed her, scanning the wet, dreary court before him with interested eyes. "I figure Ingold should be around someplace, and it's high time we talked to him about going back."

Across the court a small group emerged from the shadows of the tall gatehouse. Alwir, Govannin of Gae, Janus of the Guards, and the big, scarred landchief someone had said was Tomec Tirkenson, landchief of Gettlesand in the southwest. The Chancellor's cloak made a great bloody smear of crimson against the grayness of the murky day, and his rich voice carried clearly to the three in the shadows of the barracks: ". . . woman will believe anything, rather than that she left her own child to die. I am not saying that he *did* substitute another child for the Prince, if the Prince were killed by the Dark—only that he could have done so easily."

"To what end?" the Bishop asked, in that voice like the bones of some animal, bleached by desert sun. Under the white of the bandage, Janus' face reddened. Even at that distance, Gil could catch the dangerous gleam in that rufous bear-man's eyes.

Alwir shrugged. "What end indeed?" he said casually. "But the man who saved the Prince would have far greater prestige than the man who failed to save him, especially since it is becoming obvious that his magic has little effect upon the Dark. A Queen's gratitude can go far in establishing a man's position in a new goverment. Counselor of the Realm is quite a step for a man who started life as a slave in Alketch."

Anger flaring clearly in his face, Janus began to speak, but at that instant the Icefalcon, who had detached himself from the shed and made his way unhurriedly over to the group, touched the Commander's sleeve and turned his attention from what could have been a dangerous moment. They spoke quietly, Alwir and Govannin listening with mild curiosity. Gil saw the Icefalcon's long, thin hand move in her direction.

Alwir raised graceful eyebrows. "Going back?" he asked,

surprised, his deep, melodious voice carrying clearly across the open court. "This is not what I have been told."

There was no need to ask of whom they spoke. Gil felt herself grow cold with shock. She threw off the cloaks under which she lay and got to her feet, crossing the court to them stiffly, her arm throbbing at every step. Alwir saw her and waited, a look of thoughtful calculation in the cornflower depths of his eyes.

"What have you been told?" Gil asked.

The eyebrows lifted again, and the cool gaze took her in, shabby and dirty and bedraggled beside his immaculate height, wordlessly expressing regret at the type of people Ingold chose as friends. "That Ingold cannot, or will not, let you return to your own land. Surely he spoke to you of it."

"Why not?" Rudy demanded. He had come hurrying, unnoticed, in Gil's wake.

Alwir shrugged. "Ask him. If he is still in Karst, that is—sudden arrivals and departures are his specialty. I have seen nothing of him since he left the meeting, quite some time ago."

"Where is he?" Gil asked quietly. It was the first time she had spoken with Alwir, the first time, in fact, that she could remember the tall Chancellor taking even a passing notice of her, though there was an uneasiness in her mind associated with him, quite apart from her suspicions about who had ordered Ingold's arrest.

"My child, I haven't the slightest idea."

"He's been staying in the gatehouse," landchief Tirkenson grunted, his big, grimy hand gesturing toward the narrow fortification that overspanned the court gate. "I haven't heard he's left town yet."

Gil turned on her heel, making for the tiny door of the gatehouse stair without a word.

"Gil-shalos!" Alwir's voice called her back. In spite of herself, she stopped, compelled by the command in his tone. She found she was breathing fast, as if she had been running. Wind stirred the tall man's cloak, and the blood rubies glittered on his hands. "No doubt he will have good reasons for what he does—he always does, my child. But beware of him. What he does, he does for his own purposes."

Gil met Alwir's eyes for the first time, as if she had never before seen his face clearly, studying the proud, sensual features as if she would memorize them, the droop of the carved lips that showed his disdain for those beneath him, the arrogance in the set of the jaw, and the ruthless selfishness in the glint of the eyes. She found herself shivering with a pent-up rage, and her hands remembered their grip on the hilt of a sword. "All men have their purposes, my lord Alwir," she said quietly. She swung about and left him, with Rudy following.

Alwir watched them go, vanishing into the black slit of the gatehouse door. He recognized Gil's hatred for what it was, but he was used to the hatred of his inferiors. He shook his head sadly and dismissed her from his mind.

Neither Gil nor Rudy spoke as they climbed the black, twisting stair. It led them to a room, hardly wider than a hallway, situated over the gate itself; warped windows of bull's-eye glass admitted only the cool whiteness of the light and blurred swimming impressions of color and shape. The place had been built as the quarters for the gate porter, but was now used for the storage of the Guards' food. Sacks of flour and oatmeal lined the walls like sandbags on a levee, alternating with wax-covered wheels of scarlet cheese. Over a low pile of such provisions at the far end of the room a blanket and a fur rug had been thrown; a small bundle of oddments, including a clean robe, a book, and a pair of knitted blue mittens, was rolled up at the foot of this crude bed. Ingold sat in the room's single chair next to the south window, as unmoving as stone. The cold white windowlight made him look like a black and white photograph, etched mercilessly the deep lines of age and wear that ran back from the corners of his heavy-lidded eyes to his shaggy temples, and marked with little nicks of shadow the scars on his hands.

Gil started to speak, then saw that he was looking into a jewel that he had set down on the windowsill, staring into the gem's central facet as if seeking some image in the heart of the crystal.

He looked up at them and smiled. "Come in," he invited.

They picked their way cautiously through the clutter of the room to the small patch of clear floor space by the wizard's bed. They found seats on sacks and firkins.

Gil said, "Alwir tells me you're not sending us back."

138

' Ingold sighed but did not look away from the bitter challenge in her face. "I'm afraid he's right."

She drew in a deep breath, pain, fear, and dread twisting together within her. Crushing emotion under an inner silence that she could not afford to break, she asked quietly, "Ever?"

"Not for some months," the wizard said.

Her breath leaked out again, the slow release of it easing nothing. "Okay." She rose to go.

His hand closed over her wrist like a snake striking. "Sit down," he said softly. She tried to pull her arm away, without replying, but his hand was very strong. "Please." She turned back, cold and angry; then looking down she saw something in his blue eyes that she'd never expected to see—that he was hurt by her anger. It shook her to the heart. "Please, Gil."

She stood apart from him for a moment, drawn back to the length of her arm. His fingers were locked around her wrist as if he feared that if he released her, he might never see her again. *And maybe,* Gil thought, *he'd be right.* She saw again the vision of her delirium: warm, bright images of some other life, another world, friends and the scholarship she had hoped to make her life, distant from her and guarded by some dark, terrible form that might have been the Dark and might have been Ingold; she saw projects, plans, research, and relationships falling into a chasm of absence, beyond her power to repair. Rage filled her like dry, silent heat.

Behind her, Rudy said uneasily, "Months is a long time to play tag with the Dark, man."

"I'm sorry," Ingold said, but his eyes were on Gil.

Trembling with the effort, she let go of the rage. Without it to sustain her, all the tension left her body. Ingold drew her gently to sit on the bed beside him. She did not resist.

"I should have spoken to you before the council," Ingold said quietly. "I was afraid that this would happen."

Gil still could say nothing, but Rudy ventured, "You said something about that yesterday morning, when you were taking off for Gae with the Guards. About how, if the Dark showed up, we maybe couldn't get back."

"I did," Ingold said. "I feared this all along. I told you once before, Gil, that our worlds lie very close. Close enough for a dreamer to step inadvertently across the line, as you did. Close enough for me to step quickly from one world to the next, like a man stepping behind the folds of a curtain. In time this closeness will become less, as the conjunction between worlds comes to its end. At that time, Dark or no Dark, it will be safe enough for me to send you back through.

"I am aware of the Void, always and subliminally, as I am aware of the weather. The first time I crossed it, to speak to you in your apartment, I was aware of a weakening all through its fabric in the vicinity of the gate that I had made. Even then, I began to fear. The Dark Ones do not understand the Void, but I think then they were first aware that it exists. And after that, they watched. The second time I crossed, escaping the battle in the Palace at Gae, I felt the single Dark One follow me across. The opening that I made caused a whole series of breaks in the Void. Most of them would not have admitted a human, but the Dark, with their different material being, were able to use at least one. That was why I tried to get you away from the cabin, Gil. But naturally, you were both too stubborn to go."

"*I* was stubborn?" Gil began indignantly. "You were the one who was stubborn . . ."

"Hey, if you'd told me the truth, man . . ."

"I did tell you the truth," the wizard said to Rudy. "You simply didn't believe me."

"Yeah, well . . ." His grumbles trailed off into silence.

Ingold went on. "I felt that sending you back yesterday would be marginally safe, with the Dark Ones fifteen miles off in Gae. But now it's out of the question. The single Dark One who crossed with me increased their awareness of the Void. And they know, now, that humans exist in the world on the other side."

"How do you figure that?" The barrel staves creaked as Rudy changed position, bringing his feet up to sit cross-legged, leaning acid-stained elbows on his knees. "The one that followed you got fried on the other side. He never made it back to report."

"He didn't have to." Ingold turned to Gil. "You saw last night how the Dark Ones fight, the speed with which their bodies maneuver and change position. How the communication between them works I'm not sure, but what

140

one learns, I believe, they all then know. If we weaken the fabric of the Void, so that several of them pass through behind you and Rudy—if, as I suspect it may be, their knowledge of events is simultaneous rather than cumulative—it would be only a matter of time before they learned to operate the gates through the Void themselves.

"As Guardian of the Void, I am responsible. At this time, I cannot endanger your world by sending you back."

In the silence that followed his words, the drift of Janus' voice from the court below was faintly audible, along with the clear metallic tap of hooves on cobbles. Somewhere a dog barked. The light in the room faded as twilight drew down on the stricken town.

Rudy asked, "So what can we do?"

"Wait," Ingold said. "Wait until the turn of the winter, when our worlds will have drawn apart far enough to permit safe crossing. Or wait until I can speak with the Archmage Lohiro."

Gil looked up. "You've talked about him before."

The wizard nodded. "He is the Master of the Council of Quo, the leader of all the world's wizardry. His understanding is different from mine and his power greater. If anyone can help us, he can.

"Before the Dark Ones broke forth at Gae, before the night I spoke with you, Gil, I spoke with Lohiro. He told me that the Council of Wizards, and indeed all the mages of the West of the World, were coming together at Quo. Wizardry is knowledge. Piecing together all wizardry, all knowledge, all power, we might come to a way to defeat the Dark. And until that time, he said, 'I shall ring Quo in the walls of air, and make of it a fortress that no darkness can pierce. Here we shall be safe, and from this fortress, my friend, we shall come in light.' " As he quoted these words, Ingold's eyes lost some of their sharpness, and his voice shifted, picking up the inflection and tone of another man's voice.

"And since that time, my children, I have heard nothing. I have sought . . ." He touched the crystal that lay on the sill next to his elbow, and its facets flashed dimly in the light. "At times I think I can make out the shape of the hills above the town, or the outlines of Forn's Tower rising through the mists. But I have had no word, not from Lohiro nor from any of the wizards. They are surrounded in spells, ringed in illusion. And so they must be sought—and only a wizard can seek them."

Gil said softly, "Then you'll be leaving us?"

Ingold's eyes flickered back to her, growing brighter and more present again. "Not at once," he said. "But we will be leaving Karst. At dawn tomorrow, Alwir is leading the people south to the old Keep of Dare at Renweth on Sarda Pass. You may have heard us speak of it in council—it was the old fortress-hold built against the Dark by the men of the Old Realms, many thousands of years ago, at the time of the Dark's first rising. It will be a long trek, and a hard one. But at Renweth you will be safe, as safe as you would be anywhere in this world.

"I shall be going with the train to Renweth. Though I am no longer considered a member of the Regents, I am still held to the vow I made Eldor before his death. I promised to see Prince Tir to a place of safety and that I will and must do, whether Alwir wishes me to or not. I am afraid, my children, that you have leagued yourselves with an outcast."

"Alwir can go to hell," Gil said shortly.

Ingold shook his head. "The man has his uses," he said. "But he finds me—unbiddable. On the road to Renweth, Tir will be in constant danger from the Dark. I cannot leave him. But Renweth will be, for me, only a stopping place, the first stage of a greater journey."

"Well, look," Rudy said after a moment's thought. "If we went with you to Quo, couldn't you send us back from there? If it's so safe, it would be the one place where the Dark Ones couldn't get through."

"True," Ingold agreed. "If you made it to Quo. I wouldn't recommend the trip. In the height of the Realm's power, few people would venture to cross the plain and the desert in winter. It's close to two thousand miles, through desolate lands. In addition to the Dark, we would be in danger from the White Raiders, the barbarian tribesmen who have waged bloody war on the outposts of the Realm for centuries."

"But you're going," Rudy pointed out.

Ingold's blunt, scarred fingers toyed with the crystal on the windowsill. "And you might be safe, traveling with me. But believe me, your chances of seeing your own world again are far greater if you remain in the Keep of Dare."

Gil was silent, her bony hands folded on her knee, staring into the murky gloom of the gatehouse. She tried to picture that fortress among the mountains, tried to picture weeks and months there alone, knowing no one, isolated as she had always been isolated. Her jaw tightened. "You will come back for us, though, won't you?"

"I brought you into this world against your will," Ingold said quietly. He laid his hands over hers, the warmth of his touch going through her, warming her, as it always did, by its vitality. "If for no other reason than that, I am responsible for you. Lohiro may have a better answer than I can give you. It may even be that he will be able to return with me to the Keep."

"Yeah," Rudy said dubiously. "But what if you can't find the wizards? What if they're locked up so tight even you can't get in? What if— Suppose the Archmage is dead?" He hadn't wanted to say it, since Ingold seemed to be operating on the assumption that Lohiro was alive, but Ingold's frown was one of consideration rather than of anxiety or annoyance.

"It's a possibility," Ingold said slowly. "I had thought of it, yes, but—I would know if Lohiro were dead." The last of the twilight glinted on his bristling white eyebrows as they drew down over his nose. "The spells that surround Quo might mask it—but I think I would know. I know I would."

"How?" Rudy asked curiously.

"I just would. Because he is the Archmage, and I am a wizard."

"Is that why Alwir kicked you out of the council?" Gil asked, remembering the cold eyes of the Bishop and the way Alwir had spoken of Ingold at the gate below. "Because you're a wizard?"

Ingold smiled and shook his head. "No," he said. "Alwir and I are enemies of long standing. He never approved of my friendship with Eldor. And I fear he will never forgive me for being right about the dangers of coming to Karst. Alwir, as you may have guessed, has never thought much of the idea of retreating to the Keeps. The Keeps are fortresses, safe for the most part from the Dark, but limited in scope. To retreat into them will fracture the Realm beyond hope of repair and destroy thousands of years of human civilization. Such a fate is inevitable, in an isolated so-

143

ciety, where transportation and communication are limited to the duration of the daylight; culture will wane, narrow-mindedness set in; the human outlook will shrink from urbane tolerance of all human needs to a kind of petty parochialism that cannot see beyond the bounds of its own fields. As you know from your own studies, Gil, private law begets a host of its own abuses. Decentralized, the Church will degenerate, its priests and theologians degraded into sanctified scribes and passers-out of the sacraments to a squabbling, superstitious peasantry. I fear that wizardry, too, will suffer, becoming more and more polluted with little magics, losing sight of the mainstream of its teachings. Anything that requires an organized body of knowledge will vanish—the universities, medicine, training in any form of the arts.

"Eldor was a scholar, and saw this; he knew what had happened before, through his own memories of the long years of superstition and darkness and the mean-minded fears of men to whom the unknown was always threatening. Alwir and Govannin see it coming, and know that once they let their hold on centralized power slip, nothing can get it back.

"And so, Quo could be our only hope."

Rudy cocked his head curiously. "Didn't Alwir talk about some plan—about getting allies to invade the Nests of the Dark? Is that still coming off?"

"It is," Ingold said thinly. "He has sent south, to the great Empire of Alketch, for help in this endeavor, and I do not doubt he shall get it."

The flat, repressive note in his voice startled Rudy, who looked up from idly turning the crystal in his fingers, angling it to what remained of the waning light. "Sounds like not a bad idea," he admitted.

Ingold shrugged. "It would not be," he said, "but for two things. The first is that, deny it though we might, our civilization is all but broken. Even if we drive back the Dark, to what new world of Light will we come? I have seen in the crystal, and by other means, that the depredations of the Dark are far lighter in the south than they are here. The Empire of Alketch is a strong realm still. They can help us in Alwir's invasion; and then, when the remains of the forces of the Realm have taken the brunt of the casualties, they will be on the spot, ready to take the land left depopulated and defenseless in the aftermath. Alwir will have exchanged death for slavery—and there are varying opinions on which is the worse fate."

The blue eyes glittered under the heavy brows. "I know Alketch, you see," the wizard went on quietly. "The southern Empire has long coveted these northern lands. I know Alketch—and I know the Dark.

"Alwir finds a great deal to say about the number of things for which mine is the only word. He is right. About the Dark, mine *is* the only word, now that Eldor is gone and the sole male heir of the House of Dare is too young to speak. And I know that an invasionary force to the Nests will surely fail.

"I have been to a Nest. I have seen the Dark in their cities beneath the ground."

The wizard leaned back against the wall behind him. The room was sinking in shadow all around. His voice was quiet, distant, leading his listeners to another place and time.

"A long time ago I was the local spell-weaver for a village, oh, way over in Gettlesand. It was a good-sized village, but not so large that the Lord of Gettlesand would think to look for me there. I was, in fact, hiding out, but that is part of another tale.

"The dooic run wild in tribes in that part of the country. They prefer the empty plains, but they do hide in the hills, and they have sometimes been known to carry off small children. One of the children of the mayor of my village had vanished, and I tracked her and her tribe of kidnappers for a night and a day, back into the hills. It was in a cave, in a ridge of foothills beneath a desert mountain range, that I first saw one of the Dark Ones. It was night. The creature dropped from the ceiling of the cave where it had been clinging and devoured an old male dooic which had taken shelter there. It was not aware of my presence.

"Now I had learned about Dark Ones in old books that I had read, and from the ancient legends handed down to me, like this jewel, from my master Rath. I realized this must be a surviving Dark One, and it occurred to me that isolated groups of these creatures, which had once overwhelmed mankind and then vanished from the face of the earth, might still be hiding in the fastnesses of mountain and desert. And because I am, and always have been, in-

145

curably inquisitive, I followed it back through the darkness, down tunnels so steep I had to cling to the walls and floor to keep myself from sliding headlong into the blackness. I remember thinking to myself at the time that the numbers of the Dark Ones had shrunk so badly that they lived thus for their own protection; a wretched remnant of a force that had once dominated the face of the world and changed the courses of civilization.

"I followed the little Dark One—for it was crawling along the floor, and only about so big—" He gestured with his hands. "—deeper and deeper into the heart of the earth, crawling and climbing and scrambling to keep up with it. And do you know, at that point I was almost sorry for the vanished Dark Ones in what I supposed to be their exile. Then I saw the tunnel widen ahead of me and I looked out into their—city."

The quality of the old man's voice was hypnotic, and his eyes had the faraway look of seeing nothing in that small twilit room. "It was completely dark, of course," he went on. "I do see clearly in the dark. The cavern below me must have run on for almost a mile, stretching downward and back and farther down into the earth. The tunnel in which I lay overlooked it, and I could scarcely see the other end of the cave, lost as it was in shadows. The stalactites of the ceiling, as far back as I could see, were crawling with the Dark, covered with them, black with their bodies; the rattle of their claws on the limestone was like the sound of hail. And down the wall to my right, at floor level, there was an entrance to another passageway, about as high as a man could walk through. There was a stream of them, coming and going from deeper underground. I knew that under that cavern there was another one, as large or larger; and below that, possibly another. That was only one city, situated miles from anywhere, in the midst of the deserts, probably not even their largest city." Memory of the horror deepened the lines that age and hard living had scrawled in his face; he looked like some Old Testament prophet, gifted with the sure knowledge of civilization's downfall and helpless to prevent it. Rudy knew that he saw, not them, not this room, but the endless cavern of darkness, and felt afresh the impact of that first realization that unguessably vast hordes of the Dark Ones still lived beneath the surface of the earth—not in exile, not out of necessity, but because it was their chosen habitat. And there was nothing to prevent them from rising, as they had risen once before.

Rudy's voice broke the quiet that had followed the wizard's account. "You say they were all across the ceiling of the place," he said. "What was on the floor?"

Ingold's eyes met his, darkened with the memory and almost angry that Rudy should have asked—angry that he'd already half-guessed. "They have their—flocks and herds," he said unwillingly, and would have left it at that, but the young man's eyes challenged him to say it. "Mutated, adapted, inbred after countless generations of living in the dark. I knew then, you see, that human beings were their natural prey."

"That's why the stairways," Rudy said thoughtfully. "The Dark don't need stairs—they haven't got any feet. They could drive dooic . . ."

"These weren't dooic," Ingold said. "They were human —of a sort." He shuddered, repelled by the memory. "But you see, my children, all the armies in the world would be hardly enough for what Alwir proposes. All that an invasion will do is cripple the existing fighting force of the Realm and leave too few men to guard the doors of their homes against the Empire of Alketch—or against the Dark.

"The alternative, retreating to the Keeps and letting civilization die around us in the hopes that one day the Dark will pass, is hardly a more appealing proposition; but at this point I literally cannot see a third course. Even Alwir has been forced to recognize that we cannot simply flee them, and it is not likely that the Dark Ones will spontaneously become vegetarians.

"So you see," he concluded quietly, "I must find Lohiro and find him quickly. If I do not, we are faced with a choice of disasters. Wizardry has long garnered its knowledge in an isolated tower on the shores of the Western Ocean, apart from the world, teaching, experimenting, balancing itself in the still center of the moving cosmos— power working for the perfection of power, knowledge for the perfection of knowledge. Nothing is fortuitous—there are no random events. It may be that the whole history of wizardry from Forn on was for this end only: to save us from the Dark."

147

"If it can," Rudy said softly, and handed him back his jewel.

"If it can," Ingold agreed.

Darkness had fallen. Thin gray rain slanted down on the wreckage of the town of Karst, flurrying the dark slickness of the puddles in the soupy mud of the court, staining the timber and thatch of the lean-to sheds. Bitter winds blew down off the mountains, whipping Gil's wet cloak around her ankles as she and Rudy crossed the court.

"Three months," Rudy murmured, raising his head under the downpour to survey the ruin of the town, the ruin of the civilization that had built it. "Christ, if the Dark don't get us, we'll freeze to death in that time."

Distant thunder boomed, like far-off artillery. Gil sought shelter from the rain in the darkness of the lean-to barracks, watching Rudy as he crossed the court to where the glow of a sheltered fire marked the common pot. Guards were moving around it, dark ghostly shapes, the brotherhood of the sword, their stained black tunics marked with the white quatrefoil emblem of their company. The sounds of men talking drifted through the sodden drumming of the rain.

Strong hands slipped over her shoulders from behind. A colorless voice purred, *"Gil-shalos?"* She glanced at the hands, close by her cheek; long and thin, the fingers calloused and knotted from the discipline of the sword. Past the black shape of a tunic and the tasseled ends of white braids, she saw a thin face and cool, disinterested eyes. In a flanking maneuver, two other forms appeared and made themselves at home on either side of her.

The swordmaster Gnift took her hand and pressed it to his breast in a good imitation of passion. "O Pearl of my Heart," he greeted her, and she laughed and pulled her hand away. She had never spoken to the instructor, and indeed had been rather awed, watching him coach the Guards. But his teasing took away her shyness and eased the bitterness in her heart. On her other side, Seya was silent, but the woman's thin, lined face smiled. She was evidently long familiar with Gnift's mock flirtations.

"What do you want?" Gil asked, still grinning, shy with them and yet feeling strangely at home. In the brief time she had known them, Seya and the Icefalcon—and now, evidently, Gnift as well—had accepted her for what she was. She had rarely felt so comfortable, even among the other scholars at the university.

Distant firelight reddened the smooth dome of Gnift's head—his baldness was like a tonsure, the hair around the sides growing thickly down almost to his collar. Under the overhanging jut of his brows, his brown eyes were bright, quick, very alive. He said quietly in answer, "You."

And with a flourish he produced the bundle he'd been half-hiding at his side. Unwrapping it, Gil found a faded black tunic, homespun shirt and breeches, a surcoat, and a belt with a dagger. All were marked with the white quatre-foil sign of the Guards.

CHAPTER NINE

Though members of the various military companies mounted guard in the town throughout the night, no sound battered the outer walls but the steady drumming of rain. After a rationed supper of porridge and cheese, Gil took her position with the Guards of the first watch in the Town Hall. The refugees huddled in the shelter of that great, half-empty cavern bowed to her in respect, as they did to all the Guards.

Rudy saw the change in her when he himself strolled into the smoky dimness of the hall later; it puzzled him, for his experience with women, though extensive, had been within a very narrow range. "Talk about hiding out on the front lines," he remarked.

Gil grinned. She was finding that Rudy's opinion of her mattered much less than it had earlier. "We're all on the front lines," she replied equably. "If I'm out there, at least it will be with a weapon in my hands."

"Have you seen the way they train?" He shuddered delicately.

"The insurance is cheap at the price."

But they both knew that this was not the reason she had accepted Gnift's offer of inclusion in that elite corps, though neither Gil nor Rudy was quite clear about the true reason.

In the early part of the evening the great hall was wakeful, though without the boisterous quarrelsomeness that had characterized the previous days. The massacre at Karst had broken the spirits of those who had survived it, had brought home to them, as well as to their rulers, that there was no escape and nowhere to hide.

Still, Rudy was surprised to see how many had survived. Some of them he even recognized: that was the fat man with the garden rake of last night, and the pair of tough old broads he'd talked to in the woods yesterday; over in the corner he could see the little gang of tow-headed kids, keeping watch over the sleeping woman they seemed to have taken for their guardian. Stragglers who had hidden in the woods all day came into the hall by ones and twos, as well as people lost from their families who had taken refuge in other buildings in the town. From Gil's post by the doors, Gil and Rudy saw them enter the hall, all ages, from young teen-agers to creeping oldsters; they would enter and move slowly through the little groups engaged in bundling up their miserable belongings, searching the faces of the people. Sometimes, rarely, the searcher would find the one he sought, and there would be tears and anxious words, some questions and usually more tears. More often the seeker would leave again. One stout man in his forties, in the muddy remains of a respectable black broadcloth tunic and hose, hunted through the hall for the better part of two hours, then sat on one of the piles of smashed and discarded utensils and rags by the door and cried as if his heart would break.

Rudy was thoroughly cold and depressed by the time the gray-haired Guard, Seya, came over to them from the shadows of the great stairway, her face drawn and grim. "Do either of you know where Ingold might be found?" she asked them quietly. "There's a man sick upstairs—we need his advice."

"He should still be at the gatehouse," Gil surmised.

Rudy said, "I'll see." He crossed the main square where the torchlight fitfully gilded the rain-pocked mud. The old fountain brimmed with water, slopping in ebony wavelets over its leeward edge. Icy wind bit into his legs below the wet, flapping hem of the cloak he'd scrounged. Not even the Dark Ones, he decided, would be abroad in a downpour like this.

A gleam of gold led him toward the gate into the Guards' Court. Someone sheltering in the old stables was playing a stringed instrument and singing:

"My love is like a morn in spring,
    A falcon fleet when he takes to wing;
And I, a dove, behind will fly,
    To ride the roads of the summer sky . . ."

It was a simple love song, with words of hope and bright-ness, but the tune was filled with melancholy and an aching grief, the singer's voice all but drowned in the pounding of the rain. Rudy entered the dark slit of the doorway and groped his way up the treacherous stair, guided by the faint light that came down from above. He found Ingold alone in the narrow room. A dim, bluish glow of ball lightning hung over his head, touching the angles of brow and nose and flattened triangular cheekbone with light, and plunging all the rest into shadow. Before him the crystal lay on the windowsill, its colored refractions encircling it in a ring of fire.

Silence and peace coalesced in that room. For a moment Rudy hesitated on the threshold, unwilling to break into Ingold's meditations. He saw the wizard's eyes and knew that the old man saw something in the heart of the crystal, bright and clear as tiny flame; he knew that his own voice, his own intrusion, would shatter the deep, welling silence that made that concentration possible. So he waited, and the silence of the room seeped into his heart, like the deep peace of sleep.

After a time Ingold raised his head. "Did you want me?" The light above his face grew stronger, brightening to silver the shaggy hair and the beard where it surged over the angle of his jutting chin; it broadened to take in the obscure shapes of sacks and firkins, of scattered rushes and sawdust on the floor, and the random pattern of the stone ceiling's cracks and shadows, like incomprehensible runes overhead.

Rudy nodded, releasing the room's silence with regret. "There's sickness over at the hall," he said quietly. "Bad, I think."

Ingold sighed and rose, shaking his voluminous robes out around him. "I feared that," he said. He collected the crystal and stowed it somewhere about his person, shrugged into his dark mantle, drew the hood up over his head, and started for the door, the light drifting after him.

"Ingold?"

The wizard raised his brows inquiringly.

Rudy hesitated, feeling the question to be foolish, but driven nevertheless to ask it. "How do you do that?" He gestured toward the slim feather of light. "How do you call light?"

The old man held out his open hand; slowly the glow of light grew up from his palm. "You know what it is, and summon it," he replied, his voice low and clear and scratchy in the room. The brightness in his hand intensified, white and pure, stronger and stronger, until Rudy could no longer look at it and had to turn his eyes away. Even then he saw his own shadow cast huge and black against the stonework of the wall. "You know its true name and what it is," the wizard went on, "and by its true name you call it. It is as simple as picking a flower that grows on the other side of a fence." Against the white brilliance, shadows shifted, and Rudy looked back, to see the old man's strong fingers close over the light. For an instant its beams stabbed out from between his knuckles; then the brightness of it dimmed and was gone.

The vagrant glowworm of the witchlight that had been over Ingold's head wandered before them down the inky stairwell, to illuminate their feet. "No dice with Quo?" Rudy asked after a moment.

Ingold smiled at his words. "As you say, no dice."

Rudy, looking back at the sturdy, white-haired old wizard, remembered that it was this man who had worked that subtle enchantment of the languages; he saw Ingold again going against the Dark in the vaults, unarmed but for the noonday blaze of his power. "Are they all like you?" he asked suddenly. "The wizards? Other wizards?"

Ingold looked like an overage imp when he smiled like that. "No, thank God. No. Wizards are really very individualistic crew. We are formed by what we are, like warriors or bards or farmers—but we're hardly alike."

"What's Lohiro like?" The Archmage, Master of the Council of Quo—Rudy found it difficult to picture a man whom Ingold would call master. He wondered just how this tough old maverick got along with the leader of the world's wizardry.

"Ah." Ingold smiled. "That's a good question. No two people who have known him have the same answer. They say he is like a dragon, in that he is the boldest and most guileful, the bravest and the most calculating—and that,

153

like a dragon, he seems to those who meet him to be made of light and fire. I hope one day that you will have the opportunity to judge for yourself."

They paused in the doorway. Beyond them lay the court of the Guards, drowned under the drenching rain; to their left, the shadow of the gateway, and the broken street beyond. The gutter down its center was roaring like a mill-race. The ground in the square would be nothing but sucking ooze. Rudy asked, "Do you like him?"

"I would trust him with my life," Ingold said quietly. "I love him as if he were my son." Then he turned away and vanished into the shadows of the street, a stooped, weary form in his hooded robe. Rudy watched him disappear into the sodden darkness, and it occurred to him that this was the first time Ingold had come out with a straight answer about his personal feelings. Shining wetness picked out the peak of the old man's hood as he passed under the glow of a lighted window far down the lane. The light was dim, the soft glow of a single candle or a shaded lamp. Rudy's eyes were drawn to the window, and he saw a wavering shadow pass across the mullioned panes within.

He knew that window.

After a moment he thought, *What the hell? Why not?*

He stepped from the shelter of the gate and hurried down the black lane in the rain.

Alde looked up, startled, as he tapped at her open chamber door. Then she recognized him, and her violet eyes darkened with pleasure. "Hello."

"Hi." He stepped hesitantly into the room, made uneasy by the dead stillness of the house below. The room itself was in wild disorder, curtained in shadow; bed, chairs, and floor were strewn with clothes, books, and miscellaneous equipment; dusky blood-rubies glittered on a pair of combs in the shadow, and white gauntlets lay nearby, like wrinkled upturned hands. Minalde herself was wearing the white gown in which he'd first met her; it was evidently a favorite, like an old pair of jeans. Her black hair, unbraided, lay in great crinkled swatches over her slim shoulders. "I came to see if you might like a hand with your packing."

"That was kind of you." She smiled. "I don't need a hand so much as an extra brain, I'm afraid. This—

154

chaos . . ." She gestured eloquently at the confusion all around her.

There was a clicking tap of hard-heeled shoes in the hall behind him, and the short, stout woman Rudy remembered from the terrace—*Christ, was that only yesterday evening?*—came bustling in, dragging a small chest behind her and carrying a pile of empty sacks thrown over her arm. She bestowed a glance of withering contempt upon him, but didn't deign to speak. To Alde she said,, "This was all I could find, your Majesty, and bless me if I don't think it's all we'll have room for in the cart. That and the great chest of my lord Alwir's."

"That's fine, Medda." Alde smiled, taking the sacks from her. "It's a miracle you could come up with this, in all this confusion. Thank you."

The older woman looked mollified. "Well, it's truth that the house is like a shambles, and I could barely find this. What you're coming to, your Majesty, I don't know—forced to ride in a cart, and hardly the clothes on your back and all. How we'll reach Renweth alive I'm sure I can't think."

"We'll make it," the girl said. "Alwir will get us there."

Without a word or a second glance for Rudy, Medda scurried to the corner of the room, where she began folding blankets and sheets, packing them firmly into one of the sacks. Alde returned to her own packing, folding the great mass of flame-cut crimson velvet that Rudy recognized as the cloak Alwir had worn that afternoon. "Most of this is Alwir's," she said to Rudy, nodding to the tumble of cloaks, tunics, and robes that half-covered the big bed. "He asked me to sort his things for him. It's hard to know what to take and what to leave behind." She packed away the cloak and picked up a quilt of star-embroidered silk, the colors of it changing and rippling as it moved. Rudy came over to give her a hand with it, being well-versed in the ways of laundromats, and she smiled her thanks.

"Well, packing was an easy one for me," he said. "All I've got is a blanket and a spoon and what I've got on. For a Queen, you're traveling awfully light."

She smiled at him and shook back the dark hair from her face. "Have you seen the cart I'm going to be riding in? It's about the size of that bed. I'm not usually this unencumbered; anywhere I go I always seem to end up taking

155

carts and carts of things, books and clothes and spare
cloaks and tennis rackets and a chess game. My maid
takes—" Her voice caught suddenly on the words, as if
she had physically stumbled in a swift run. It was thin and
shaky when she finished the sentence. "My maid used to
take more than this." Then, with a forced lightness, she
continued. "On longer trips I'd have furniture and bedding
and dinner service and windows . . ."

"Windows?"

"Of course." She looked at him in genuine surprise, for-
getting momentarily, as the Icefalcon forgot when speaking
to Gil, that he was an outworlder and a stranger in the
land. "Have you any idea how much glass costs? Even we
quality folks have to bring our own windows with us when
we travel. One could never afford to glaze all the windows
in all of one's houses." She smiled at his expression of
dawning comprehension. A little ruefully, she went on.
"But I don't think we'll need the windows in the Keep of
Dare."

"What's it like?" Rudy asked. "The Keep, I mean."

She shook her head. "I really don't know. I've never
been there. The Kings of the Realm abandoned Renweth
so long ago; there was never even a hunting lodge there.
Until—Eldor—" Again there was that hesitation, almost
an unwillingness to speak his name. "Until the King went
there some years ago, to have it regarrisoned, I don't think
a King of Darwath had visited it in generations. But he
remembered it. My grandfather remembered it, too."

"Your grandfather?"

"Oh, yes. Our House, the House of Bes, is descended
from Dare of Renweth, a side descent. Now and then the
memories show up in our people, sometimes hundreds of
years apart. Grandfather said he remembered mostly the
darkness inside the Keep and the smoke and the smell. He
said he had memories of twisting passageways lit by grease
lamps, and rickety old makeshift stairways going up and
down into darkness. He remembered himself—or Dare, or
some ancestor—walking through the corridors of the Keep
and not knowing whether it was day or night, summer or
winter, because it was always lamplight there. When he'd
speak of it," she went on, her hands pausing, still and white
against the colors of the gown she was holding, "I could
almost see it, it was so close to him. I could see the stairs,

going up like scaffolding, and the fitful gleam of the lamps on the stone. I could smell it, damp and murky like old blankets and dirty clothes, and could feel the darkness surrounding me. It will be hard to live always by torchlight."

"Always is a long time," Rudy said, and Minalde looked away.

They talked a while longer of the Keep, of the Palace at Gae, of the small doings that had made up the life of the Queen of the Realm of Darwath. The fire sank in the open brazier that warmed the room, the flames playing in a small, steady amber glow over writhing scarlet coals; the soft smells of camphorwood and lemon sachet drifted from the folded clothes. "A lot of this will have to be left, I'm afraid," Alde sighed. "We have only three carts, and one of those has to be for the records, the archives of the Realm." She was sitting on the floor now, turning over in her hands book after book from the small pile beside her. The firelight sparkled off their jeweled bindings and spread gold, like a warm suntan, on the soft flesh of her chin and throat. "I'd wanted to take all of these, but some of them are terribly frivolous. Books are so heavy, and the ones we take really ought to be serious, philosophy and theology. These may very well be the only books they'll have in the Keep for years."

Behind the gentle run of her voice Rudy heard the echo of another voice, Gil's voice, saying, *Do you realize how many of the great works of ancient literature didn't survive? All because some Christian monk didn't think they were important enough to preserve?* He'd forgotten the context and the conversation, but the words came back to him, and he ventured, "Probably a lot of people are going to hang onto the philosophy and theology." *And, God knows, I wouldn't want to be shut up for years with nothing to read but the Bible.*

"That's true," she mused, weighing the two books in her hands, as if measuring pleasure and emotional truths against fine-spun scholastic hairsplitting. Then she turned her head, the dark sheet of her hair brushing his knee where he sat on the edge of the bed behind her. "Medda?"

The stout servant, who all this time had worked in silent disapproval in the darker corners of the room, came forward now, and her manner softened imperceptibly. "Yes, my lady?"

"Could you go up to the box room and see if you can locate another trunk? A small one?"

The woman bobbed a curtsy. "Yes, my lady." Her heavy tread with its clicking heels diminished down the dark hall. Rudy thought to himself, *Score one for Gil and ancient lit.*

Alde smiled at him across the gemmed fire-glint of the gilded bindings. "She doesn't approve of you. Or of anybody, really, who isn't sufficiently impressed by my being Queen. She was my nurse when I was small and she puts a lot of store in being the Queen's Nurse. She isn't like that when we're alone. Don't let her worry you."

Rudy grinned back at her. "I know. The first time I saw the two of you together, I thought you were some kind of junior servant, the way she bossed you around."

The fine, dark eyebrows raised, and there was a teasing light in her eyes. "If you'd known I was the Queen of Darwath, would you have spoken to me?"

"Sure. Well, I mean——" Rudy hesitated, wondering. "Uh ——I don't know. If somebody had said, 'Look, that's the Queen,' maybe I wouldn't even have seen you, wouldn't really have looked at you." He shrugged. "We don't have kings and queens where I come from."

"Truly?" She frowned, puzzled at the incomprehensible thought. "Who rules you, then? Whom can your people love and honor? And who will love and guard the honor of your people?"

To Rudy, this question was equally incomprehensible, and since his major area of success in school had been evasion of classes, he had only a sketchy notion of how the United States Government worked. But he gave her his perceptions of it, perhaps more informative than political theory, and Alde listened gravely, her arms wrapped around her drawn-up knees. Finally she said, "I don't think I could stand it. Not because I'm Queen—but it all sounds so impersonal. And I'm not really a Queen anymore."

She leaned her back against the carved post of the bed frame, her head close by his knee. Profiled against the amber glow of the fire, her face seemed very young, though worn and fragile and tired. "Oh—they honor me, they bow to me. It's all in my name. And Tir's. But—it's all gone. There's nothing of it left." Her voice was small and tight suddenly, as if struggling to be calm against some sup-

158

pressed emotion. He saw the quick shine of tears in her violet eyes.

"And it all happened so suddenly. It's not the honor, Rudy, not having servants who wait on me. It's the people. I don't care about having to pack my own things, when all my life servants have done it for me. But those servants, the household at the Palace—they'd been around me for years. Some of them were from our House, from when I was a girl; they'd been with me since I was born. People like the Guards who stood outside my bedroom door—I didn't know them well, but they were like part of my life, a part I never really thought about. And they're all dead now."

Her voice flinched from it, then steadied. "You know, there was one old dooic slave who scrubbed the floors in the hall at the Palace. Probably he'd done so for his whole life, and he must have been twenty years old, which is very old for them. He knew me. He'd grunt and sort of smile at me when I went past. In the last battle in the Throne Hall at Gae, he grabbed up a torch and went with it against the Dark Ones, swinging it like the men swinging their swords. I saw him die. I saw so many people I knew die." One tear slid down the curve of her cheek, those lobelia-dark eyes turning to meet his, seeking in them some comfort, some bulwark against the fear and grief she'd locked in.

"It wasn't being Queen or not being Queen," she went on, wiping at her cheek with fingers that shook. "It's the whole life, everything. Tir is all I have left. And in the last fight, I left him, too. We locked him in a little room behind the throne, my maid and I. They needed every sword in the hall, though neither of us had ever handled one before. It was like a nightmare, some—some insane dream, all fire and darkness. I think I must have been half-crazy. I thought I was going to die, and that didn't matter, really, but I was terrified they'd get Tir. And I left him alone." She repeated the words in a kind of despairing wonder. "I left him alone. I—I told Ingold I'd kill him if he didn't take Tir and go. He was going to stay and fight to the last. I had a sword. I told him I'd kill him . . ." For a moment her eyes seemed to see nothing of the shadowy golden warmth of the curtained chamber, reflecting only relived horror.

Rudy said gently, "Well, he probably didn't believe you,"

and was rewarded to his joy with a tiny smile of self-mockery and the return to the present of those haunted eyes. "And anyhow, I don't think you could have hurt him."

"No." She laughed softly, shakily, as people do when they remember any desperate passion which has lost its importance. "But how embarrassing to meet him afterward." And whether, as Ingold had said, it was the sentiments or the social gaffe that made her smile, it was enough to break the grip of the horror and let its raw memory fade.

The rain had almost ceased, its persistent drumming dimmed to a soft pattering rustle on the heavy glass of the window. Coals settled in the brazier, the glow of them like the last heart of a dying sunset. Minalde stood and moved through the dimness of the room to kindle a taper from the embers and transfer the flame to the trio of candles in the silver holder on the table. She blew out the touchlight, and smoke folded around her face as she laid it aside.

"That was what I couldn't endure," she went on, her voice quiet, as if she spoke now of someone other than herself. "That I'd left my child to die. Until Ingold came to me, the night before last—until he brought Tir back to me —I never even knew if they'd survived or not. All the rest of it, the Dark Ones surging down on us over the torches, the—the touch of it, the grip of it, like an iron rope—the Icefalcon's face when he picked me up off the floor of the vaults—it doesn't even seem real. Only that I'd left my child, the one person, the one thing that remained out of everything else in my life . . ."

Her hands and her voice had begun to shake again. Rudy came over to her in the halo of the candles, took her hands to still them, and felt the fragile bones in his own rough grip. His touch seemed to bring her back, for she smiled, half-apologetically, and looked down, away from his face.

"Alwir tells me I was delirious with shock," she said softly. "I'm glad I don't remember leaving Gae. They tell me the city was ruined. Now I'll always remember it in its beauty." She looked up at him again, that soft little smile of self-mockery reappearing in one corner of her sensitive mouth. "That's why most of the things here are Alwir's and not mine. They're not the things I would have brought with me if I'd left Gae under my own power."

"Don't worry about it."

"But last night," Alde went on, "I think I would have killed you if you'd tried to stop me from going back for Tir. I wasn't going to leave him again. I'll always thank you for going with me, for staying with me through the vaults, for keeping us both safe. But I think I would have gone alone."

"I still think you were crazy," Rudy said gently.

She smiled. "I never said I wasn't."

Outside, the rain had ceased entirely. Beside them the smooth, waxy glow of the candles lengthened into slim columns of yellow and white, the light growing stronger in the still deep silence. For a time the peace of the room surrounded them, bringing them a curious, isolated moment of happiness in the confusion and wreckage of all the world. Rudy was conscious, as he had seldom been so acutely conscious of anything in his life, of her fingers resting lightly in his. The smell of her hair came to him, a scent of sweetgrass and bay, and with it the soft tallow smell of the candles and the richness of cedar and lavender. Enclosed in the heart of a jewel-box of time they were alone and at rest with each other, her eyes gazing up at him, almost black in the shadows. Looking into them, Rudy knew—and knew then that she knew—what was inevitably going to be. The knowledge went through him like a bolt of lightning, but it was without any real surprise. It was as if he had always known.

They stood thus for an endless single moment of time, consumed by that shared knowledge. The only sound in the room was the soft swiftness of their breath. Then an opening door downstairs stirred the air, and the flame of the candles dipped, making the shadows bow and tremble. On that incoming cold draft, Alwir's voice echoed mellowly in the unnaturally servantless hall. ". . . ponies around to the courtyard. It will take most of the night to load them. Your things will go in the third cart." And though no words were audible, they heard Bektis' light voice replying, a querulous interrogation from Medda, and the sharp, sudden jingle of sword belt and mail.

Alde made a move to go, and Rudy caught at her hands. Their eyes met again, puzzled, seeking some answer to why what had been between them had happened. The liking between them had changed—everything had changed and was colored by what had passed. In her face Rudy saw

161

desire, fear of this terrible newfound intimacy, and the reflection of his own bewilderment at a feeling he had never known himself capable of possessing. Then her cheeks flamed suddenly pink in the candlelight, and she pulled her hands away, stammering, "I—I can't—" She turned to flee.

"Alde." He called her softly back, and at the sound of his voice she stopped, her breath quick and uneven, as if she had run a long way. "I'll see you on the road tomorrow."

She whispered, "All right," and turned her eyes away. A moment later he heard her footsteps flying lightly down the hall.

CHAPTER TEN

A long time ago and perhaps in a previous incarnation, Rudy recalled seeing a movie called *The Ten Commandments* which, among other things, had contained a memorable scene of the Children of Israel getting their butts out of the Land of Egypt. Charlton Heston had lifted up his staff and they'd all been organized and ready to go, and the whole clear-out had taken about three minutes of screen time, goats and granddaddies and all, leaving not so much as a crumpled bread wrapper or a pile of dog droppings on the tidy streets of Thebes.

Karst had been stirring since several hours before dawn. Rudy, standing by the cart in which the rations earmarked for the Guards would be hauled, had a good view of most of the square, and it didn't look to him as if anybody would be going anywhere until damn near noon, if then. It had begun to rain again, and the ground was like porridge. The cart wheels bogged in it; people running back and forth on aimless errands churned it to ever-deeper ooze. Mud and rain covered everything, soaked Rudy's cloak and his clothing underneath, and plastered the clumped, dirty agglomerations of depressed-looking refugees who stood or sat around that scene of sodden chaos. Even Alwir, storming his elegant way among them, was beginning to look shopworn and dirty.

By midmorning, the square was a total confusion of people, goods, and makeshift transport. Children wandered from their parents and got lost. Escaping pigs had to be chased through the standing carts, pack beasts, and little

163

mounds of personal belongings, upsetting everything in their flying path. The larger families and groups, and the households of minor nobles, were engaged in last-minute problem-solving sessions, among much cursing and the waving of arms, arguing whether to go north to the Keep of the landchief Harl Kinghead, south to Renweth in the mountains, following Alwir and the Council of Regents, or beyond that, over Sarda Pass, to Gettlesand, to risk the threat of the White Raiders in the minor Keeps of the landchief Tomec Tirkenson. Rudy could see Tirkenson, big, scarred, and ugly, cursing his followers into line with a vocabulary that would have curled a bullwhacker's hair.

Rudy himself could have left town at a moment's notice. From the leavings of the dead, he'd collected himself an outfit of warm clothes—a brown tunic, shirt, breeches, and boots, a hooded cloak that was too large, and a pair of gauntlet gloves stitched with gold and emeralds. His California clothes he carried in his pack, along with shaving things scrounged, like everything else, from those who had not survived the coming of the Dark to Karst, his American-made buck-knife, a horn spoon, and his big blue plastic comb. The unfamiliar weight of a sword dragged at his hip.

Leaning his shoulders against the tall wheel of the cart, shivering in the wind that drove the rain and tossed the dark trees that were visible above the black, gabled roofs, he surveyed the milling chaos before him. Mud-slathered people negotiated for space in two carts, tied dirty little bundles onto muleback or into crude wheelbarrows or travois, and argued about what to take and what to leave. Watching them, his face stinging in the icy wind, he remembered California as if his whole life there had been something that had happened to someone else.

"There," the cool, husky voice of the Icefalcon said at his elbow. He turned to see the tall captain pointing out to Gil the small train of wagons drawn up outside the Bishop's palace, adjacent to the Church on the opposite side of the square. Red-robed monks were loading two of them with chests that were obviously filled with something heavy, under the arrogant direction of the Bishop herself. "I find that typical," the Guard went on. "They claim to work for the salvation of souls, but from all I've seen, they only collect the tithe, and keep records of how much is owed

164

and what souls have been born and baptized and confessed and died, like a miser counting gold. Fleeing for their lives, they will carry paper rather than food."

"*They?*" Gil echoed curiously, and glanced up at the tall young man with the incongruous pale braids lying rain-slicked over his dark shoulders. "You're not of the Faith?"

A disdainful sniff was all the answer she got.

Past the Church wagons, Alwir's household and the remnants of the government of the Realm were holding what appeared to be a Chinese fire drill on the steps of the Town Hall. Rudy saw Alde seated in the front of one of the carts there, muffled in black fur, her eyes peeking from the shadows of her streaming hood. On her lap she cradled a great bundle of dark, trailing blankets, in which no round pink baby face was visible; but once he saw the blankets squirm. That would be Tir. Medda, her round face swollen with weeping, clambered up to take her place at the Queen's side. Alde turned her head, her gaze searching the crowd. Across the milling confusion she met Rudy's eyes, then quickly looked away, as if ashamed to be caught seeking sight of him. Beyond her, Bektis was climbing into another wagon, his narrow face framed in a great collar of expensive marten fur, looking down his elegant nose at the bedraggled mob in the square.

Then someone was calling out orders, Commander Janus' harsh, braying battle voice rising above the sluicing drum of the rain and the clamor of argument and preparation. Alwir appeared from around the corner of the Town Hall, mounted on a slim-legged sorrel mare. His great cloak flapped in the wind as he bent from the saddle to exchange last-minute instructions with someone on the ground. The Guards moved into line, a ragged double file on either side of the Chancellor's wagons. Like a kettleful of oatmeal coming at last to a boil, the people in the square, alone or by couples, families, or clans, caught up their few possessions and jostled for a place within that doubled line, or, failing that, as close to its protection as they could get. Those who weren't ready to go yet redoubled their preparations, hastening in the hope of catching up on the road. Whatever their ultimate goal, the north or Gettlesand or Renweth, sticking with an armed convoy was far preferable to taking that long road alone.

Rudy was a little surprised at what a mob there was,

once they got out on the road. They moved almost without order, a vast confusion of provision wagons, transport carts for the furniture of Alwir's household and the records of the government of the Realm, small herds of cattle and sheep, here and there coveys of spare horses for those fortunate enough to be riding to Renweth, the shambling rabble of household servants, and the few remaining dooic slaves that an occasional wealthy family had brought out of the ruin of their world. Families straggled behind and around the main body of the royal wagons, with their crated chickens and barking dogs, their pigs and their milk goats; it was astonishing how many families had actually succeeded in holding together through the chaos of the last few weeks, though many of them, Rudy knew, were missing members. Fathers and mothers were carrying the bulk of the load, older children carrying those too young to walk, others leading or driving such livestock as they'd been able to save or acquire. There were not a few grannies and grandpas of startlingly venerable years, too— Rudy wondered how some of those old people had managed to run fast enough to escape the Dark. But they were there, leaning on walking sticks or on the shoulders of their grandchildren or great-grandchildren, chirping to one another with the equable calm of those who have long since ceased being surprised by fate. And as they departed from Karst, that great straggling mob passed an infinitely greater number of half-assembled households, still loading the last of their belongings onto donkey back or dog travois, or trying to sort out the least essential essentials, arguing and watching with apprehensive eyes as the convoy slopped past in the driving gray rain. By the looks of it, Rudy calculated, people would be drifting out of Karst all day.

A mud-spattered old man with a shabby bundle and a stout walking stick fell into step with Rudy as they passed the last outskirts of the town. The path dipped steeply in a treacherous slide of black muck. Rudy's feet slithered on it, and a strong hand grasped his elbow. "Cut yourself a staff from the woods," a familiar scratchy voice advised. "The roads aren't going to get any easier, once we reach the mountains around Renweth."

"We're leaving the mountains, though," Rudy said, picking his way more carefully in the wizard's tracks. "Are these the same mountains we're heading for, or different?"

"Different," Ingold said. "We're picking up the Great South Road outside Gae and following it down the valley of the Brown River, which runs through the heartlands of the Realm. The road up to Sarda Pass crosses it, and we'll take that up into the Big Snowies, the great wall of mountains that cuts the Realm, the lands of the Wath, in two, dividing the river valleys from the plains and the desert of Gettlesand. Renweth stands above Sarda Pass. Watch the ground."

Rudy scrambled over slippery autumn-yellow grasses around a noxious patch of black quicksand. The road from Gae up to Karst had been graded and cut so as to be easily negotiable in good weather, but the constant coming and going of the refugees, combined with the rains and the steady departures that had been taking place from the town since dawn, had reduced the way to a treacherous river of slop. Those refugees who waited until the afternoon to quit Karst would have to wade all the way to the plain. Rudy looked around at the darkness of the misty gray woods and pictured what the land would be like for those who got bogged in the road when night began to fall. He shivered.

"How far is it?" he asked suddenly. "How many nights are we going to have to spend in the open?"

"Close to a hundred and seventy miles," Ingold replied, making his way through the wet brush on the firmer ground at the edge of the roadbed. "Eight or ten nights, if the weather stays good and the Arrow River isn't too high to cross when we get there."

"You call this good?" Rudy grumbled. "I've been freezing my tail off since I came here. I don't think I'll ever dry out."

Ingold held out his hand, and the rain collected, a tiny lake, in his calloused palm. "It could be far worse," he said mildly. "We've had harsh winters these last ten years, with killing snows on the plains beyond the mountains driving the White Raiders, the barbarians of the plains, to attack the settlements out of pure famine. This winter promises to be the worst yet—"

"Fantastic."

"—but it has been noticed that the Dark Ones seem to attack less in foul weather. High winds, heavy rains, or

167

snow seem to keep them underground. Few blessings or disasters come unmixed."

"Great," Rudy said, without enthusiasm. "So we've got a choice of the Dark Ones or pneumonia."

The old man raised his eyebrows, amused. "So which would you prefer?"

They turned a corner of the road, as Gil had done two days before, and the rusty woods seemed to part, revealing below them the dim, tawny plain and, half-hidden in the pearl of the river mist, the ruined city of Gae. Used to the megalopolis of Los Angeles, Rudy found the city very small, but there had been a grandeur to it, a walled unity with which the sprawling, featureless towns of his own experience could not compare. In his mind he pieced it together to put roofs on the burned walls of the close-set, half-timbered houses and leaves on the gray lace of bare branches. He remembered Minalde's low, gentle voice saying wistfully, "Now I'll always remember it in its beauty . . ."

That thought brought others, and he stood for some time, looking out over the pastel vista of ochre and silver-gray, until a dimming of the noise behind him alerted him to the passing of the convoy, and he thrashed back to the road and hurried to catch them up, plowing his way through torn black mud in which white chicken-feathers were caught like flakes of fallen snow.

Still more refugees joined them on the plain by the walls of Gae. The Karst–Gae road crossed the Great South Road a few miles from the multiple turrets of the city gates, in a great trampled circle amid the withered grass. Just north of the crossroads loomed Trad's Hill, named for some hero of ancient wars, the only prominence on that flat plate of land, and from that hill a lichenous cross of carved stone bestowed its arcane sanction on the joining of the ways. There they were met by a motley horde of fugitives from Gae itself, braver, or more foolish, or more conservative souls who had hung on in the looted ruin of the capital, hoping that the danger would somehow miraculously pass. They were far better provisioned and more heavily burdened than those who had fled to Karst earlier in the week; better clothed, leading carts and mules and horses, driving milk cows and pigs and chickens, carrying great satchels of books, money, spare bedding, and the family silver.

"Where'd they get the cows?" Rudy demanded of Gil, who happened to be walking close by him at the time. "They didn't keep all them animals in the city, for God's sake."

Gil said, "People in New York, Boston, and Chicago kept cows and pigs clear up to the 1890s. How do you think you got milk if you lived in town?"

As the two parties converged, he heard the buzz of talk pass down the length of the swelling caravan. "Is that really her Majesty? Is her Majesty really well and safe? And his Little Majesty?" People crossed themselves thankfully and craned their necks to see. As an American, and not a particularly well-informed one at that, Rudy had expected the subjects of a monarchy to fear and resent those who had such absolute power over them, and it surprised him to see the reverence in which they held Alde and Tir. He remembered what she had said last night, about love and honor—that people needed a ruler they could love, as well as a law they could follow. Offhand, he couldn't think of any member of his own government he even respected, let alone one for whose survival he'd offer up prayers of joy. It caused him to look with new eyes at the tall, hide-topped cart with its drooping standards of black and red and to think about the dark-haired girl inside.

The day wore on, and they followed the Great South Road through the drenched green farmlands along the river. In contrast to the muddy track down the mountain, the road was wide and well-drained, with deep, weed-grown ditches on both sides and a pavement of worn, close-fitted hexagonal blocks of some kind of pale gray stone. As the centers of the blocks were more worn than the edges, they caught the rain in each separate hollow and turned the road into a shining scarf of fish-scale silver, stretching away into misty distance. The caravan left the wide sweep of the plain of Gae behind them and crossed a bridge beneath frowning, empty towers, to enter into the fertile bottom lands where the road sought its lazy way between meadow and farm and woods.

No countryman, Rudy was nevertheless impressed by the solid appearance of prosperity that lay over the land. The farmhouses were well-built, most of them boasting more than one room, with separate quarters for the animals —not always the rule in nonindustrial societies, Gil re-

169

marked cynically. But the emptiness of the land was chilling. They saw very few people—only the eyeless stare of vacant houses, the abandoned cattle, and mile after mile of half-harvested corn, rotting in the rain. Those people they did meet were the farm families, or the remnants of them, who came out to the road with all their worldly goods—plow, seed, and poultry—and the youngest baby of the household piled haphazardly into ox carts, to swell the ranks of the moving army of refugees, with children and servants and herd dogs driving little bunches of sheep and cows in their wake. As they passed through those desolate farmlands, the Guards, or the Red Monks, or men and women acting on their own left the train to forage in the ruined fields and the oddly crushed, deserted barns for what they could find, though Rudy noticed they seldom went into the houses that they passed. Sometimes they came back with wagonloads of seed and grain, or livestock, pigs, and bleating sheep, or the small cobby farm horses— beasts whose masters would take no further interest in husbandry.

And still it rained. The convoy had grown to an army, plodding along the silver road in the downpour. Rudy thought of the sheer number of miles involved—*Hell, that's like walking from Los Angeles to Bakersfield*—and wondered what the hell he was doing there. Above the dull overcast and slanting rain, the gray day was sickening toward twilight.

He shaded his eyes and squinted out across the wet landscape; he saw, as he had seen several times that day, a person—man or woman, he couldn't always tell—wandering aimlessly in the distance, driven by the cutting wind. He wondered about those people, for none of them had made any sign that they saw the passing convoy, and none of the company on the road spoke or waved to them. Sometimes alone, sometimes two or three together, they moved like zombies, stood staring listlessly at nothing, or lay on the ground in the fields, looking blankly into the hollow sky.

He grew more and more curious about these outcasts. Toward evening, when he saw a man and two young women standing at the bottom of the drainage ditch on the side of the road, gazing vacantly into space, he left the pavement and went scrambling down the side of the culvert, slithering through weeds and mud, and waded over to where they stood.

The man wore a loose white cotton shift, plastered to his soft, paunchy flesh by the rain. His hands and mouth were nearly blue with cold, but he seemed to take no notice of the ankle-deep ice water in which he stood. The girls wore dripping silk rags, wilted flowers and colored ribbons braided into their wet, snarled hair. Their lobotomized eyes followed his motions, but none of the three made a sound.

Rudy passed his hand cautiously across the man's line of vision. The eyes tracked, but registered no understanding of what they saw. The girls were the same—beautiful girls, dainty and sweet as lilies of the valley. Rudy would cheerfully have taken either or both of them to bed with him, except for the creeping horror of that empty stare.

"This," Ingold's voice said behind him, "is the other thing that the Dark Ones do."

Rudy swung around, startled; he hadn't heard the wizard approach, even through four inches of water. The old man's face looked taut and sick, barely visible in the shadows of his drawn-up hood. "We didn't see much of it at Karst; probably because the victims were trampled by those seeking safety, or lost in the woods around the town. But I know this from Gae. I daresay most people know it."

"What's wrong with them?" Rudy looked from the wizard to the three shivering, empty-eyed automatons and felt a creeping of his flesh that, for once, had little to do with the cold.

"I think I spoke of it earlier," Ingold said quietly. "The Dark Ones devour the mind as well as the flesh—which is why, I suspect, they prey upon human beings and not upon beasts. As well as human flesh and human blood, the Dark Ones devour the psychic energy, the intelligence— the mind, if you will. Perhaps to them that is the most important of the three."

Reaching out, Ingold shut the eyes of the man with his thumb and forefinger and, closing his own eyes, meditated for a moment in silence. The man's knees buckled abruptly, and Ingold stepped lightly back from him as he splashed noisily into the rain-thrashed water and lay face down. Rudy was still staring, aghast, at the corpse when Ingold touched each of the girls in turn. They fell and lay with

171

their flowered hair floating around them in the dirty water of the ditch. The wizard turned away and, leaning on his staff, clambered up the bank again. Rudy followed him, water dripping soggily from the hem of his mantle, cold and shivering and shocked at what he was pretty sure Ingold had done.

They did not speak for some time, but trudged down the road in silence. Then Rudy asked, "They don't get over it, do they?"

"No." The wizard's voice came disembodied from the shadows of his hood. *A harmless old man*, Rudy thought. *A charming old lunatic. No wonder people are afraid of him.*

"No," Ingold went on. "If they are indoors they generally starve. If they are outdoors they die of exposure."

"Uh—anybody ever take care of one, to see if his mind might come back?"

Ingold shrugged. "Not easy when you're fleeing the Dark yourself. Up in Twegged in the north, at the start of all this trouble, it was tried. The victim lasted two months."

"What happened after two months?"

"Her caretakers killed her." The wizard added, in a tone of explanation, "They were the victim's husband and daughter, you see."

Rudy looked back over his shoulder. The evening mists were coming down heavily, shadow and darkness covering the land. Still, he thought he could see in the distance the curve of the road, the ditch, and the whitish blur against the darker ground.

The night fell, and for miles up and down the Great South Road the refugees sought what sleep they could. Watch fires threaded the darkness like a glittering necklace on both sides of the road, and all who could bear arms took their turn at them. In the low ground, the puddled rain turned to ice.

Alde came to Rudy's watch fire in the night, with Medda escorting her like a stout, disapproving shadow. She was shy with him, and they did not speak of what had passed between them at Karst, but Rudy felt a joy in her presence he had never known with any other human being. As they sat together with their backs to the fire, not touching, talking of Tir or of the small doings of the road, the intimacy between them was as close and warm as if they shared a cloak.

The morning dawned clear and freezing cold. The wind had broken the overcast and piled the clouds in the south, like the immeasurable slopes of achingly white mountains against the soaring blue of the morning sky. Word came down the line that wolves had attacked the horse herd belonging to the Church and had been driven off by the Red Monks; four night guards had been found dead by their watch fires, bloodless victims of the Dark. Nevertheless, Bishop Govannin gave a cart-tail service of thanksgiving, and those who had survived the night thanked their God that it had been no worse.

They came into a rolling country now, the great road looping through the gray-green hills. To their right, the distant heads of the western mountains were sometimes glimpsed, plum and blue and gray, or covered in the lour of clouds. It was a land of streams, ice-rimed in the morning, that flowed down toward the green, lush bottom lands in the east. These streams were sometimes crossed by narrow stone bridges, but often the road simply led to shallow fords, so that everyone was perpetually half-wet and shivering. Rudy, stiff and aching in every joint, took Ingold's advice and cut a straight sapling from the next grove of trees they passed, to trim into a walking stick. He had never been much good at botany, but the Icefalcon told him the wood was ash.

Toward noon they crossed a broad saddle of land that lay between two hills, and from it a vista spread before them of all the countryside down to the river, the long grass rippling palely in the wan light of a heatless sun. The red-clothed trooper leading the mules of Minalde's cart paused there to breathe them, and Rudy came up close at her side. Many people stood there, having stopped to rest in the neck of that miniature pass and look down on the lands below. Alde turned to him and smiled. "How are you?" she asked quietly, a little shy at speaking to him in the light of day.

"Sore as hell." Rudy leaned on his staff, not caring if it made him look like an old man. "How in God's name do you people stand it? I feel like I'm fixing to die."

"So do most of these people," Alde said. "So would I, if I didn't have a cart to ride in because I'm the Queen.

We've been passing women all day, with children as young as Tir. Carrying them. They'll carry them clear to Renweth, unless they die on the road." She tucked the blankets closer around the child she held propped at her side. Tir made a little noise of protest and a determined effort to divest himself of the blankets and, Rudy guessed, to roll off the seat. The kid was going to be a real pest when he started to walk.

"Die?" he said uneasily. He remembered things people had said about those who straggled from the caravan . . .

"Of cold," Alde said. "Or hunger. We're doing all right for food now, but when we get out of the farm country, there won't be nearly enough. Not for the children or for the old people or for those who are sick—"

She broke off, startled, lifting her head to stare off across the hills, and Rudy followed her gaze down the smooth, falling curves of the gray-green land. Far off he could see huge brown forms stalking the distant pastures, swaying like monstrous animated haystacks—impossibly large, monsters in the icy distance.

"What are they?" he asked, shading his eyes. Then he glanced back at Alde and saw the worry on her face. "Are they . . ."

"Mammoths," Alde said, and her tone was puzzled and surprised. "Mammoths this side of the mountains . . ."

"Mammoths?"

She glanced down at him, hearing but misinterpreting the shock in his voice. "Woolly elephants," she explained. "They're common on the northern plains, of course, but they haven't been seen in the river valleys since—oh, for hundreds of years. And never this far south. They must have come over the passes of the mountains for some reason."

But mammoths were not the only things to come over the passes of the mountains.

That night, as he and Alde sat talking quietly under Medda's disapproving chaperonage by the watch fire, Rudy thought he heard the distant thunder of hooves, an unlikely sound in the convoy where horses were few and precious, guarded more carefully than a miser guards his hoard. After a time, the night wind brought him the faint, damp drift of smoke and a sound that reminded him of the howling of wolves, although there was a difference to this sound. In the morning he rode out with Ingold and the slim handful of Guards whom the convoy could afford to mount to look for the source of the sound.

They found it long before the sun had managed to burn off the thick, white river mist. The charred hulk of a gutted farmhouse loomed in the opal fog, haunted by the gliding black shapes of spectral crows and the smell of roasted flesh. They found some of the farm family a little ways from the house. At first Rudy didn't register that the body staked to the ground was human; when he did, he came as close to fainting as he ever had in his life. He looked away, his face clammy with sweat and the taste of vomit in his mouth. He heard Janus' boots squishing in the mushy grass and the faint, restless jingling of bridle-bits as the horses tossed their heads in alarm. He heard Janus say, "Not the Dark," and Ingold, skirting on foot the trampled weeds beyond him, reply, "No."

Faintly, another Guard's voice drifted to him. "Dooic? Gone feral or—or mad?"

Another responded. "On horses? Be serious."

Ingold returned, materializing like a specter from the mist, holding in his hand a strip of rawhide trimmed with chips of colored glass, from which a long feather dangled, its end tipped in blood. "No," he said, his voice calm in spite of the butchered horror lying in the grass nearby. "No, I fear this is the work of the White Raiders."

"On this side of the mountains?" Janus asked nervously, looking around him.

Ingold nodded and held out to him the rawhide, the spinning feather brushing his wrist and marking the flesh with blood. "Lava Hills People," he identified briefly, and gestured toward the grisly evidence, scattered over several square yards of grass. "It's a sacrifice, a—propitiation. An offering to something they fear."

"The Dark?" the Commandehr asked. He took and examined the rawhide tag.

"Doubtless," Ingold said slowly, and looked around him at the burned trees, the scorched remains of the outbuildings, and the fallen house surrounded by a hideously suggestive cloud of screeching carrion-birds. "Doubtless. Though if the Dark were their principal fear—why did they cross the mountains? The danger of the Dark is thickest in the valleys of the river."

175

"Possibly they didn't know."

"Possibly." The wizard's tone was still dubious, and he moved restlessly along the trampled verge of the grass, scanning the flat opaque whiteness of a countryside turned two-dimensional with fog, as if sniffing the wind for the scent of unknown danger. "In any case, it puts us in a bad position. You see, the hoof-tracks here are shod, which means they're already short of horses, stealing what they can find from the valley farms. My guess is that they're too few to protect their herds from wolves. They'll be turning on the convoy soon."

"Would they?" Janus asked doubtfully.

"If they thought they could get away with it, yes." Ingold came back to him, brushing the dew from his sleeves. He walked, Rudy noticed, with an instinctive cat-footed care that left hardly a mark in the sodden grass. "The combined force of the Guards, Alwir's troops, the Church troops, and the remains of the Army, plus Tirkenson's men, outnumber the Raiders at least twenty to one. But the convoy is nearly seven miles long on the march; four miles, bunched up to camp. They could strike us like a spearhead at any point."

The Guards were mounting to go. Only Janus and Ingold remained afoot, talking in low voices, the red-haired Commander of the Guards towering over the smaller form of the wizard. From his uneasy perch on the restless horse, Rudy looked down at the pair of them, wondering about the friendship that was so evident, despite the Church strictures against wizards. It occurred to him that, apart from himself and Gil, Janus seemed to be the only friend Ingold had in the convoy. People, ordinary people following the road to the myth of refuge in the south, treated the old man with a combination of awe, distrust, and outright fear, as something completely uncanny; even Minalde, whose life and child he had saved from certain doom, was timid and silent in his presence. Rudy wondered what the bond was between the wizard and the Guards.

"And how much danger are we in, from the Dark?"

In the diffuse light Ingold's face was thoughtful, his gaze going past the Commander to scan the landscape that was slowly revealing itself as the mists dissolved into pale and heatless daylight. Far off, a dark sense of movement along the bases of the round hills marked the road, with its endless chain of pilgrims; closer, crows hunched in the bare black trees and watched the Guards with bright, inquiring eyes. All around them, north and south and west, lay a desolation of sun-silvered grass. Rudy felt he had never seen a land so empty.

"More than we think," the wizard said quietly. "We had a good moon last night, but I could sense them, far off, masses of them. There was a Nest of them at one time, blocked long ago. at the foot of the mountains. The road will run quite close to it."

Janus' glance cut sharply back to him, but Ingold did not elaborate. He only said, "Right now, speed is our ally, and the weather. We must reach the Keep and quickly; every day on the road heightens our danger. It may be that, when we reach it, we will have to hold the Keep against more than the Dark."

CHAPTER ELEVEN

A fever of uneasiness seemed to spread down the convoy. The unseen presence of the White Raiders dogged them by day, as the threat of the Dark dogged them by night, and all that day and the next Rudy felt it, following the endless road. He heard it in the snatches of conversation he caught and picked it up, unsaid, from the people he talked to during the days; he saw it in the movements of the refugees who still clung, a vast tattered horde, to the nucleus of what had been the government of the greatest Realm in the West of the World. Little groups and families would accelerate past him, a man pushing an impossibly piled wheelbarrow, cursing an exhausted woman with a child in her arms and a goat on a frayed rope behind her to hurry, hurry, get a little farther down the road before something—the Dark, the wolves, the invisible Raiders—got them. Later Rudy would pass them, sitting in a tired huddle on a worn milestone, the child wailing hungrily while the man and woman looked over their shoulders at the empty lands beyond. Tempers shortened. At the crossing of the Mabigee River, its bridge flooded out by unseasonable storms in the mountains, Alwir and Bishop Govannin came to bitter words over the cartloads of ecclesiastical records that the Bishop had brought from Gae. The records could be left behind—the carts were needed for the sick, the injured, the very old and very young whose strength was failing them due to poor food and exhaustion.

The Bishop bit back at him, "Yes, and then all record of precedent, which puts the dominion of God above the commands of man, may be left behind, too, when we reach the Keep."

"Don't be a fool, woman!" Alwir snarled. "God would rather have souls than a load of moldy paper!"

"He has their souls," the Bishop snapped, "or should. If it's souls that concern you, my lord Chancellor, turn out your tame mirror of Satan, your pet conjurer, and let your precious sick ride in his place. A man who takes the advice of wizards should be the last to talk of souls."

The river crossing left the refugees soaked and exhausted, and no one traveled more than a few miles onward after that. The main body of the convoy halted in an abandoned village and took shelter in the stone houses that were half-falling into ruin, scorched by the fires their defenders had lit against the attacking Dark, or caved in by the power of the Dark themselves. Those parties that could not fit into the houses spread out like water across a flood plain all around, making a great tangled city of tents and makeshift shelters, ringed in the far-flung watch fires of its bright perimeter against the coming of the night.

Rudy's campfire was built in a little dip in the ground a hundred yards from the building farthest from the road. He'd found a tiny dugout cabin nested into the side of a hill that, in better days, had been used for a wood store and still contained ample sticks for his fire. The hill itself, facing away from the road and the camp, made a fair windbreak against the bitter, searching winds from the west.

All that day the mountains had been visible, growing perceptibly in the west and south. Now, in the last of the sunset, they hung like a black wall against the cloud-heaped sky of evening, their heads wreathed in storms and, when the wind cleared the cover a little, white with the mantle of winter. He had been told that Sarda Pass lay high in those mountains. Rudy thought of snow and shivered. He had grown used to being wolf-hungry all the time, and, to his surprise, his body seemed to be adapting to days of walking and the weariness of night guard. But since his coming to the Realm of Darwath, he had always been conscious of being cold. He wondered if he would ever get warm again.

When the night was fully dark, Alde and Medda appeared, bringing him some mulled wine. Rudy sipped it thankfully, reflecting to himself that he'd rather have had

179

about six cups of the foulest black truck-driver coffee and a handful of caffeine tablets. Still, he reasoned, looking across the gold rim of the cup at the girl's dark eyes, it proved she cared, or at least felt something for him. *Alde, Minalde,* he thought despairingly, *you're the goddam Queen of Darwath and I'm a bum passing through, and why does this have to happen to me?* His desire for her was palpable, urgent, but they could not so much as touch hands. Medda sat, a stout bundle of silent disapproval, on the other side of his fire, far enough away so as not to overhear their conversation, if they kept their voices low. For the rest, her mere presence lent them a respectability without which Alde would not have been able to see him at all.

"Would Alwir be mad if he knew you were coming out like this?" Rudy asked, without taking his eyes from the darkness. It was a soldier's trick the Icefalcon had taught him, not to look at the campfire. It blinded the eyes to the movements of the night.

"Oh—" Her voice was unwilling. "Probably. He half-knows. Alwir worries about me."

"If you were my sister, I'd want to keep an eye on you, too."

"Not that way, silly." She smiled at him. "He's concerned about my 'state.' So is Medda, for that matter."

Rudy glanced briefly across the fire and met the fat woman's disdainful eyes. She'd given him dirty looks whenever their paths had crossed these last five days, and tonight he sensed the silence between Alde and Medda that spoke louder than any words. He guessed she'd said something to her charge, the beautiful young woman who had once been her little girl, about going out alone at night to see a man, a mere Guard and an outworlder at that. He could feel in that frosty silence how that conversation had gone; he knew that Medda had reminded Alde of her station in life and had had the words thrown back in her face.

"If it will make you trouble . . ." he began.

She shook her head, the great cloudy mass of her unbound hair sliding on the fur collar of her cloak. "I'd only lie awake, nights," she said. And her eyes met his, knowledge passing between them.

So they were quiet for a time, sitting side by side, not too close, not touching, only comfortable in each other's presence. He watched the darkness beyond the ring of the firelight and judged, with his ears, the noises of the night. In the distance he saw a dark shape walking back toward the camp along the line of the wide-spaced fires and knew it was Ingold, Ingold who seldom slept now, but divided his nights between a solitary, silent patrol and long hours of watching, staring into the heart of his enchanted crystal, in the cold time before dawn.

Wind moved the clouds down from the west, obscuring the brightness of the moon. The camp was far enough away, behind the sheltering hill, to give them a greater illusion of privacy than they had ever had before, while the moon gave enough light between the clouds for Rudy to be sure nothing was sneaking up on them. He was less afraid of the Dark Ones than of the White Raiders or the wolves, though in all that dim world he saw nothing move, nor heard any howling nearer than the far-off river. So they drank the spiced wine Alde had brought and spoke of everything and nothing, of their childhoods and their past lives, trading memories like a couple of children trading marbles. More clouds gathered, and the darkness surrounding them deepened, the firelight warming and bright on their faces.

The brief downpour, when it rushed without warning from the sky, took them completely unawares. Hand in hand, they ran for the dugout cabin, with Medda grumbling behind and stopping to pick up the discarded wine cup and a stick from the fire. They fell, laughing, through the door. From inside, they could just barely see Medda, leaning over the torch to protect it from the rain and stumping grumpily through the long grass. But for the moment they were alone in the damp, earth-smelling dimness of the little house.

The realization that this was the first time they had been alone together out of anyone's sight came to both of them, and their laughter faded. In the darkness of the shack, he could hear Alde's breathing and he sensed that she was afraid of something she had never felt before, something to which she was not yet ready to give herself. She did not move when he put his hand up to push aside her unbound hair. Her cheek was cold under his touch. He could feel her trembling, feel her breath grow quick and uneven against his face. She put her hands against his chest, resisting as he pulled her to him, and the cloak slid from her shoulders and fell with a soft thud around their feet. He took her mouth, forcing it open with his own. Though she made a small noise of denial in her throat, she did not pull away from him. She went limp against him, shaking as his hands molded her body under the soft texture of the gown, her arms sliding up around his shoulders, his neck, uncertain at first and then clinging tighter and tighter, as if she would never let him go. Through the burning urgency of his own desire, his common sense told him that Medda would be there soon—that the old nurse could probably see them already and would be clucking her shocked disapproval of them.

Releasing Alde's searching mouth from his, he raised his head and looked out. The rain was easing to a gentle shower, and a sliver of moon had broken through a hole in the clouds. By its light, he saw Medda.

She stood less than four feet away. She wasn't looking at them. Though her eyes were open and staring, she wasn't looking at anything. The wine cup dangled forgotten from one nerveless hand, and the torch had gone out in a puddle at her feet. All this Rudy saw across Alde's shoulder in a split second of time, and he felt a chill, directionless wind ruffle across his face from somewhere in the darkness.

With a violence born of the pure reflex of terror, he slung Alde into the back of the dugout and jerked the door shut with a slam like a gunshot. She fell against the wall, catching at it for balance, her eyes dilated with fear and, he suspected, misinterpretation of the situation. "Get me one of those sticks," he commanded roughly. Warned by something in his voice, she obeyed immediately. He used it to bolt the door and found another to use as a wedge for good measure, his hands shaking with shock.

"There's a Dark One out there," he told her quietly. She said nothing, but in the dim light of the cabin's single window, he could see her eyes get wider. "It—got Medda."

"Oh!" she whispered.

"Do you have anything to make a fire with?"

She shook her head, a tiny gesture, stunned. Then suddenly she turned, looking around the almost lightless interior of the room. "There's wood all along the back here," she said, her voice low and tense. "Your fire outside . . ."

"It's a long way to my fire," Rudy said shortly, "and

182

the rain probably put it out. I wouldn't leave you alone here, anyway." The ceiling of the tiny place was barely high enough for him to stand. He waited, drawn sword in hand, before the door, trying desperately to think what to do next. Behind him Alde gathered sticks together and made a competent little arrangement of them, with dead leaves and twigs for tinder, working swiftly, without display of the fear that must have been screaming inside her.

Still tensed to spring, Rudy knelt down and fingered the wood. Soft and splintery. Did one need a special kind of wood, to make fire by rubbing two sticks together? Anyhow for sure, this trash wouldn't work. He examined the hilt of his sword. *Steel. Flint and steel.* Was it worth it to try to get a spark from the steel blade of the sword, at the risk of ruining the thing for fighting purposes? Anyhow, the walls of the dugout were made of wattle-and-daub, not stone, let alone flint.

The rain now drummed lightly and steadily on the front wall. The moon must be hidden again, since he could see almost nothing in the darkness. But he felt suddenly that same chill wind creeping around the edges of the door. It stirred in the tinder, made a thin, dry whispering among the leaves, and closed off the breath in his throat with the strangling grip of fear.

Flint, he thought through his panic. *We've got to strike a spark somehow.*

"Are you wearing any jewelry? Any stones at all?"

She shook her head, her eyes wide.

What the hell, I probably wouldn't know what to do with flint if it jumped out and bit me . . . "Well, after this you're going to have a gold ring made with a hunk of flint as big as a walnut set in it, and you're going to wear it all the time, you understand?"

"All right," she whispered breathlessly.

What the hell am I talking about? There's not going to be anything after this.

Alde crouched back, keeping out of his way so as not to encumber his sword arm, though her terror cried for the comfort of his touch. High up, near the top of the door, Rudy heard a soft bumping noise, like a testing finger tapping, and then a faint scratching on the heavy glass of the window. His heart slamming sickeningly against his ribs, Rudy thought, *All I can do is take a swing straight down at whatever comes through that door. What's stone? What's flint? What will make a spark? I wish to Christ Ingold were here. He could make a fire just by looking at the wood.*

Wonder if I could do that?

Ingold's words came back to him, spoken in the darkness of the gatehouse, the light glowing up from his empty palm. *You know what it is . . . by its true name you call it . . .* Rudy looked at the tiny pile of wood, the dried leaves and tinder scattered beneath. That would catch, he knew it would. *Its true name . . .* Maybe there was some kind of a magic name for fire. But whatever you called it, fire was fire. The smell of it was the same, the brightness. He thought how it would smell as it caught off those twigs, sort of sweet and sharp. It would give off snappy, sputtery little gold sparks, little crackly sounds . . . He called them to mind, the shape and smell and brightness, straining eyes and mind to see the tinder in the deepening darkness. He saw only that the room was fading; even his consciousness of Alde kneeling beside him and his chilled fear of the death that waited outside the door began growing less important than the fire, the fire purely for its own sake. He could see it, hear it, smell it; he knew how it would splutter out of that tinder.

The dry leaves fluttered a little in the wind. From far off, he could see Alde press her knuckles to white lips, all the while without a sound. Detachedly, he saw the fire in his mind, in the first instant of its sparking, and knew exactly how it would be. He could see it, just couldn't touch it yet. He felt his mind and body relax, withdrawing to some great distance, his perspective on the world altering, narrowing to only the dry shapes of leaf and twig and wood that he could see, quite clearly, in the utter darkness. The wood, the dry little heap of leaves, the tiny gold sparks like stars . . . Without moving, he reached his mind across from where he was to where the fire was, as easily as picking a flower that grew on the other side of a fence.

There was a sudden, bright crackle of little gold sparks, and the sharp, sweet smell of dry leaves catching. Rudy bent forward, still detached from himself, calm, half-wondering if it could be a hallucination, but calmly certain that it was not, and fed one twig and then another to the fire, real fire where no fire had been before. The light spread quickly into the room, threw gleeful shadows across his face, and danced flickering, crazy jigs of triumph that reflected in tiny points of light in Alde's eyes as she brought up more and bigger sticks without a word.

And then it hit him, like a blow from a club. *I did that,* he thought. *I did that.* The warmth scorched his trembling fingers and seeped into the cold flesh of his palms and face. The wind that had rustled so evilly at the door faltered, then waned and ceased, and all outside the dugout became terribly still, except for the faint drizzling of the last of the rain.

Rudy's mind echoed like a thunderclap with the shock, and rocked wildly with surging triumph. One part of him, it seemed, was screaming, *I did it! I did it! I called the fire, and the fire came,* and another was saying, *I shouldn't have been able to do that.* But more real than either, deeper, within his true heart, there was only a calm knowledge, clear and small like a little light—the memory of that first crackle of flame in the dry leaves and the knowing that he could do this.

Then he looked up and met Alde's terrified eyes. They were wild with fear, a fear tinged with hysteria and relief and superstitious terror, fear of the Dark, of the fire, of him. He saw that newfound power reflected in her eyes, saw it as others would see it, alien and terrible and uncanny. She couldn't speak the wild question in her eyes, nor could he have answered, and for a moment they could only stare at each other in the firelight, as once before they had stared in the shocked, shared knowledge of their desire. Then, with a sob that seemed to rip her soul from her body, she threw herself into his arms, weeping wildly, holding onto him as if he were her last hope of life itself. Magic and terror and death released him, the tension breaking with an almost physical shock, and he clutched the slender girl in his arms with a grip that seemed to drive her bones into his and buried his face in her dark hair. Desperately they took one another beneath their shared cloaks on the floor, while the fire threw its shadow dance across the low rafters.

Afterward Alde slept, terror exhausted in passion, and Rudy lay awake, sword close to his hand, watching the fire and letting his thoughts of past and future have their way with him, until the rain outside stopped, and dawn came.

"You think that's fighting?" Gnift roared in a voice that cut like the steel of his grip-worn sword. "Get him! *Get him!*" The Icefalcon, armed with an eighteen-inch wooden stick, feinted warily at his opponent, a massive Guard wielding three feet of split bamboo that could draw blood like metal. The young captain was marked with it, face and hands; Rudy, sitting on the sidelines, shuddered. Gil, he noticed, watched beside him with an alert interest. She looked as if she'd already had her turn at this game, and gotten the worst of it.

Stubborn broad, he thought. *They'll have to kill her before she'll give it up.*

Gnift yelled, "Attack him, you puling coward! Don't make love to him!"

The big man swung, and the Icefalcon shifted back out of range. Exasperated, Gnift stepped forward under the arc of the wooden blade, grabbed the back of the captain's black tunic, and shoved him into the fray. The result was bloody, painful, and exhausting for both combatants.

Rudy said thoughtfully, "One of these days somebody's gonna take a poke at that little bastard."

"Gnift?" Gil raised her split eyebrow in amused surprise. "Not bloody likely." Rudy remembered seeing Gnift sparring with Tomec Tirkenson, the big landchief of Gettlesand, yesterday evening about this time, in the last of the daylight after the long march. Maybe Gil was right.

They watched for a time more, sitting side by side on the square of groundcloth just off the makeshift training floor. Around them, the camp was settling itself down for the night once again. It would soon be time to collect their meager rations and make for the watchfires. Rudy noticed that Gil looked drawn and exhausted, a thin, almost sexless shadow with a great straggling mane of black hair. He knew that in addition to marching and guard duty she was training this way nightly, on starvation rations, with the mess of her half-healed arm wound, as if deliberately driving herself to collapse.

Wind sneered down off the mountains and washed over the camp like incoming tide. The mountains loomed above them now, hugely close, blacking the western sky, a sheer wall, like the Rockies. That morning they had passed the crossroads, which were watched over by a crumbling stone cross, and set their feet on the great road that ran up to Sarda Pass. It was colder here in the shadows of the foothills and desolate of all habitation.

In the wan twilight before them, the Icefalcon was holding his own, retreating before the great swinging strokes of his opponent's sword. Sweat bathed his face, white in the frame of ivory hair, and his pale eyes were desperate with exhaustion. Cursing, reviling, Gnift circled the fighters, finally stepping lightly up behind the captain and hooking his feet out from under him with a deft sweep of one leg. The Icefalcon went down, his opponent dropping on him like grim death from above. There was a confused blur of movement. The younger man came up under the arc of the longer sword with a clean slash across the big Guard's belly and turned the end of the movement into a circle-throw that hurled his attacker over his head and flat on the Guard's back in the mud. He got both swords and scrambled to his feet, gasping. The bigger man lay on the ground, puffing and cursing. Gnift yelled, "When you get your man down, do something, don't just take his sword and stand there like a fool. If you did that . . ."

Rudy, who'd been tremendously impressed with this last maneuver, whispered, "Do all warriors have to do that? I mean, Alwir's Guards and the Church troops?"

"The method is much the same," Ingold's mild voice remarked behind them. "Gnift is stricter than most, and the Guards have the reputation of having the best instruction in the West of the World. Methods differ in different modes of combat, of course. In Alketch, for instance, they train their famous cavalry by chaining a slave by one wrist to an iron post in the middle of the exercise hall, putting a sword in his free hand, and having the cavalry trainees practice their saber-charges on horseback against him."

"What's their budget for replacements?" Rudy wanted to know. "Somebody remind me never to visit Alketch."

Gil glanced sideways, from the old shackle gall on the wizard's wrist to his serene face, and said, "Somebody told me once that you used to be a slave in Alketch."

"Did they?" Ingold's eyes twinkled. "Well, I have been and done many things in the course of my misspent life.

Rudy, if you could spare me a moment, I would like to talk with you in private." He rose and led the way through the orange-lit confusion of the settling camp with Rudy tagging at his heels. At a distance they passed Alwir's wagons, and Rudy recognized the sable standards of the House of Dare and knew that Minalde was there with her son.

He had hardly spoken to Alde during the day. She had turned away from him, silent and more shy than before, as if withdrawing herself after the shattering intimacy of last night. Rudy was puzzled but not surprised; they had taken each other in the passion that followed tension and terror; such things could change drastically come morning. It could be grief at Medda's death, though she must have known, after the Guards led the poor, stumbling zombie who had been her oldest companion out of the camp, that there was no way to bring her along with the train. It could be shame, either at the act of sex itself or at its implicit betrayal of her dead King. Rudy wondered about that. Alde seldom spoke of Eldor and shied almost visibly at the mention of his name. It might be shame that she'd lain with a commoner—though from remarks about history that Gil had dropped in passing, that wasn't something that seemed to bother female royalty much—or, more likely, fear and a kind of revulsion that she'd lain with a wizard. Alde was a good daughter of the Church. Rudy remembered the look in her eyes, awe and a wild kind of horror, staring into his across the new brightness of the flames.

But whatever her reasons, he sensed in her no anger toward him, only a terrible emotional confusion. And he knew, looking back at the square gray silhouette of the wagon top against the fading salmon of the sky, that he must bide his time. Rudy had been around enough to know that sleeping with someone once could happen to and with literally anybody. It was the second time, and those after, that had meaning. Impatient as he was to be with her again, he was aware that to rush her would be fatal. He knew Alde and knew that behind her deceptive gentleness lay a core of steel. For all her quiet diffidence, she was not a woman who could be bullied into bed.

And that would be fine, he thought, as his breathing suddenly constricted, *if she were the only one involved.*

He forced himself to turn his eyes away.

"Now." Ingold halted on the grassy open ground that lay between the edge of the camp proper and the guard line where the watch fires were being kindled. Here they were alone, camp and lines both fading into the featureless gray of the evening. The wind blew the cold rain-smell down around them, surging through the grass and over the bare patches of stony ground beneath their feet. "You told me this morning how you called fire at need last night. Show me what you did."

Rudy gathered a few sticks together that had been dropped from the making of the watch fires and found a patch of dry ground. With his thumbnail he peeled enough dry bark to make a little tinder and sat cross-legged beside that small pinch of wood, his cloak wrapped about him. He relaxed his body and mind, shutting out the smells of the camp, the smoke and scent of wet grass, and the lowing of the cattle. He saw only the twigs and the bark, and how the stuff would catch. *Smokier than last night's leaves,* he thought. *A little spot, like one made with a magnifying glass in the sun . . . a different smell from the leaves . . .*

The fire came much more quickly than it had come before.

There was a hint of triumph mixed with anxiety in the glance Rudy gave Ingold. The older wizard watched the new flames impassively for a moment, then without moving put them out. He produced the stump of a candle from somewhere about his person and held it a few feet from Rudy's eyes.

"Light the candle," he instructed.

Rudy did.

Ingold blew it out thoughtfully and regarded him for a moment in silence through the whitish drift of the smoke. Then he set it aside. From a pouch in his belt he fished a piece of string with a dangling bit of lead on it like a fishing-sinker. He held the string before him and steadied the suspended weight to stillness with his free hand.

"Make it move."

It was like starting the fire, only different.

"Hmm." Ingold gathered the plumb weight into his hand again and put it away without speaking.

A little ripple of evening wind stirred the grasses beside them. Rudy fidgeted, his mind shying from the implications

189

of what he had done. "What is it?" he asked nervously. "I mean—how can I do this?"

The wizard straightened his sleeves. "You know that," he said. "Better than I do." Their eyes met and held. Between them passed the understanding of something known only to those who had felt what it was. There were not even words for it among those who did not know already. "The question is the answer, Rudy. The question is always the answer. But as to your Power, I'd say you were born with it, as we all are."

We, Rudy thought. *We*. He stammered, knowing Ingold must be right, his mind fighting the nets of the impossible. "But—I mean—I never could do this before."

"In your own world you couldn't," Ingold said. "Or possibly you could—did you ever try?"

Rudy shook his head mutely, helpless. It had never occurred to him past his childhood. But unbidden images invaded his mind, images of dreams he had had as a very small child, before he started school. Things he was not sure whether he had done or only dreamed of doing. The memory of the need in him struck like an arrow, a need deeper than his love for Alde, a wordless yearning so deeply buried he had never sensed its loss in all his aimless life. The need for something they had taken away from him when he was far too young to fight back. And, like the child he had been, he felt the tears choke him.

"Never?" Ingold whispered, and his eye was like a dragon's that holds and reflects, a mirror that swallows the soul. In it Rudy saw his own memory of the spark leaping from the dried leaves, the dark, terrified gaze of deep blue eyes into his. He saw the scattered pictures from childhood dreams, and felt the utter grief he had felt when he had first learned that they were impossible. Ingold's voice held him like a velvet chain. "You have talent, Power. But even your little power is dangerous. Do you understand that?"

Rudy nodded, hardly able to breathe. "Will I—can I—" Was there some kind of etiquette about it, some way of asking? "Will the Power grow, if I learn how to use it right?"

The old man made a slight movement of assent, sky-blue eyes remote and cool as water.

"Will you teach me?"

The voice was now very soft. "Why do you want to learn, Rudy?"

He felt then for the first time the terrifying extent of the old man's power. The blue gaze pinned his brain like a spear, so that he could neither answer nor deny. He saw his own thoughts, stripped before that watching power, a mushy jumble of half-formed longings and a selfish, disproportionate indulgence of his own passing emotions, pettiness, indolence, sensuality, a thousand sloppy, stupid errors past and present, murky shadows he had turned his back on, probed by glass-edged light. "I don't know," he whispered.

"That's no answer."

Rudy tried desperately to think, to express more to himself than to the old man that terrible need. This, he understood suddenly, was what Gnift did to your courage, your spirit, your body, making you understand your own truth before you could manifest it to another. He understood then why Gil trained with the Guards, understood the bond of commitment and understanding that lay between Ingold and the Commander. And he knew he had to answer and answer right, or Ingold would never consent to be his teacher.

But there is no right answer! the other half of his mind cried. *It's nothing—it's only that calm. It's only knowing that it's right, and I have to do it. It's only that I wasn't surprised when I could call the fire. But it's different for everyone, everything.*

And suddenly Rudy knew, understood, as if something had been turned within him and the truth of his own soul had focused. *Tell the truth,* he told himself. *Even if it's stupid, it is the truth.* He whispered, "If I don't, nothing will mean anything. If I don't learn—about that—there won't be any center. It's the center of everything, only I didn't know it."

The words made sense to him, though they were probably utter Greek to the wizard. He felt as if some other person were speaking through him, drawn out of his immobilized mind by the hypnotic power of that depthless gaze.

"What's the center?" Ingold pressed him, quiet and inescapable as death.

"Knowing—not knowing *something*, but just knowing. Knowing the center is the center; having a key, one thing that makes sense, is sense. Everything has its own key, and knowing that is my key."

"Ah."

Being released from that power was like waking up, but waking up into a different world. Rudy found he was sweating, as if from a physical shock or some great exertion. He wondered how he could ever have thought Ingold harmless, how he could ever have not been half-afraid, awed, loving the old man.

Dryly amused fondness briefly crossed the old man's face, and with slow illumination, Rudy came to realize the vast extent of Ingold's wizardry, seeing its reflection in the potential of his own. "You understand what it is," the wizard said after a moment. "Do you understand what it means?"

Rudy shook his head. "Only that I'll do whatever I have to. I have to do it, Ingold."

At that, Ingold smiled to himself, as if remembering another very earnest and extremely young mage. "And that means doing whatever I tell you to," he said. "Without question, without argument, to the best of your ability. And only you know what that best is. You will have to memorize thousands of things that seem to have no meaning, foolish things, names and riddles and rhymes."

"I'm not very good at memorizing stuff," Rudy admitted shamefacedly.

"Then I suggest that you get good, and quickly." The eyes turned cold again, distant, and in the clipped, decisive tone Rudy could feel once more the flash of that terrible power. "I am not a kindergarten teacher; I have my own work. If you wish to learn, Rudy, you will learn as and how and when I choose to teach you. Is that clear?"

For a split second, Rudy wondered what would happen if he said, *What if I can't?* But if the question was the answer, the answer would surely be, *Then you can't.* It was entirely his choice. And though he would be as friendly as before, Ingold would never mention the subject again.

Rudy saw his own future, made suddenly clear, and what the commitment would mean: a change, enormous, all-encompassing, irrevocable, and terrifying, in everything

192

he was, everything he would do or be. The choice was being thrust violently into his shaky, unprepared hands, a decision that he must make, could never back out of, and would never, ever be able to make again.

How come stuff like this always happens to me?

The question was the answer. *Because you want it.*

He swallowed hard and found his throat aching with strain. "Okay," he said weakly. "I'll do it. I'll do the best I can, I mean."

Night had fallen around them. Ingold folded his arms, a dim, cloaked shadow against the distant glitter of the camp lights. Thin, translucent ground mist had risen, and the sounds and smells of the camp were obscure behind them; Rudy had the sense of being isolated in a wet, cold world of nothingness, as if he had been kneeling there in the damp grass for hours, wrestling with some terrible angel.

And he had won. His soul felt light and empty, without triumph or anxiety, as if he could drift upon the wind.

Then Ingold smiled and was nothing but a shabby little man in a stained and rusty brown robe. "That," he said pleasantly, "is what I shall expect of you at all times. Even when you are bored, and tired, and hungry; when you're afraid of what I tell you to do; when you think it's dangerous, or impossible, or both; when you're angry with me for prying into what you consider your trivial personal life. You will always do the best you can; for only you understand what it is. God help you!" He stood up, shaking the damp grass and stray twigs from his rough robe. "Now get back to camp," he said, not unkindly. "You still have your shift of watch to stand."

Cold wind keened down the foothills, whining in the canyons surrounding the refugee camp that lay strung out along the road. It flattened Rudy's little fire to thin yellow streamers that paralleled the ground and sent chill fingers through cloak and tunic and flesh, searching out his bones. The first hard, mealy, little flakes of snow had begun to fall.

Alde had not come.

Rudy knew why and was sorry. What had happened last night had changed things between them. That, too, was irrevocable; if she was not his lover, she could no longer

193

be his friend, either. And, good daughter of the Church that she was, she would be no wizard's woman.

He would miss Minalde. His body hurt for her, but the longing was deeper than that, a loneliness, a need for her company, for the sound of her soft voice. It brought home to him with a painful little stab that he was now an outsider, as he would be an outsider for the rest of his life. In this world, or in his own, he had cut himself off from all hope of communication with those who did not understand. It would be worse when he went home—that much he knew already. But having seen the center, the focus, the key of his own life, he knew there was no way he could not pursue it. Even when he left the peril-fraught world of the Dark and returned to the electric jungles of Southern California, he knew he would be driven to seek it there. And he knew that somehow, some way, seeking, he would find.

The wind stung his face, carrying with the snow the mourning of the wolves. Behind him he sensed the camp slipping into its dark sleep, and the endless road behind him, down the foothills and out onto the plains, marked on both sides by a broken chain of watch fires.

He cast his mind back to his interview with Ingold earlier in the evening, trying to recall that reflected glimpse he'd had of his own mind, or soul, or the center of his own being. The memory was hazy, like the memory of intense pain. He could recall seeing it, but could not call back clearly what it had been—only the grip, the cold, of Ingold's thought on his, and the clear certainty, for the first time in his life, of knowing what he was.

He hadn't known then that it would cost him Minalde. He hadn't known it would cost him everything that he was, for that was what it amounted to. *But if the question is the answer, it wouldn't have mattered if I knew or not.* He only knew that if he had turned away, he would always have been sure that he'd had it within his grip and let it go. He knew that he couldn't have let it be taken from him a second time.

The fire crackled, the wood sighing as it broke and fell. Rudy took a stout branch and rearranged it. The shower of ascending sparks glittered like fireworks among the spitting snow. He huddled deeper into his cloak, then glanced back in the direction of the camp. By the renewed light of the fire he could see a dark figure walking toward him, wrapped from head to heel in fur. Her black cloud of hair blew about her in the wind, and the firelight, when she drew near him, laid blue and golden shadows across her violet eyes.

CHAPTER TWELVE

"Be still. Let your mind be silent. See nothing but the flames." The hypnotic smoothness of Ingold's voice filled Rudy's mind as he stared at the brightness of the Guards' campfire by which he sat. He tried to push aside his own chasing thoughts, his fatigue and need for sleep, and his wondering about the White Raiders he thought he'd glimpsed, dogging the line of march. He tried to think of nothing but the fire, to see nothing but the little cluster of sticks, transfigured by the flames and heat. He found that the less he tried to think of something, the stronger it crowded back.

"Relax," Ingold said softly. "Don't worry about anything for the time being. Only look at the fire and breathe."

The wizard turned away to speak to a middle-aged woman who'd appeared on the edge of the Guards' encampment with a sickly-looking young boy in tow.

Doggedly, Rudy tried to obey his last instructions. The cold, overcast daylight was fading out of the sky again, the eighth day from Karst. Voices bickered distantly along the line of the road as thin rations were handed out. Far off he heard the castanet-click of wooden practice swords and the harsh bark of Gnift's sarcasm blistering his exhausted students. Somewhere he heard Alde singing and Tir's little crowing voice joining in, making baby sounds of joy. A feeling went through him such as he'd never known before, a desperate tangle of yearning and relief and affection, and it distracted him hopelessly from the matter at hand.

He glanced up. Ingold was sitting on his heels, looking gravely into the sick youngster's dutifully opened mouth, then into his eyes and ears. The mother wore that harried, angry look so common in the refugee train now. She was looking away, pretending she hadn't brought her son to an old excommunicate wizard; but her eyes slid back to the child, anxious and afraid. There were doctors in the West of the World who were not wizards, but few of them had survived the coming of the Dark. Those few who moved south with the convoy had their hands full, between sickness and exposure, fatigue and starvation; people were not as fastidious about going to a wizard for help as they had once been.

Ingold stood up and spoke briefly to the woman, his hand resting on the boy's dark, ruffled hair. When they had gone, he turned back to Rudy and raised his eyebrows inquiringly.

Rudy shrugged helplessly. "What am I supposed to be looking for?" he asked.

Ingold's eyes narrowed. "Nothing. Just look at the fire. See how it shapes itself."

"I have looked," Rudy protested. "And all I see is fire."

"And what," Ingold asked tartly, "did you expect to see?"

"Uh—I mean—" Rudy was conscious of having missed the boat somewhere but wasn't sure where. "I see you watch the fire every night and I know for sure you aren't just watching wood burn."

"No," the wizard said. "And when you've been a wizard for fifty years, maybe you'll see more than that, also. You must love things wholly for their own sake, Rudy, before they will give themselves to you."

"Sometimes I just don't understand," Rudy said much later to Alde, when she'd slipped away from her wagon to sit in the warmth of their shared cloak. "I feel that I should understand all this stuff, but I don't. I don't even know what I don't know—I feel as if I've been dumped in the ocean and I'm trying to swim, but it's a million miles deep. I don't even know how deep it is." He shook his head. "It's crazy. A month ago—" He broke off, unable to explain to this girl, who had grown up knowing kings and mages, that a month ago he would have laughed at anyone claiming to possess such powers.

Her body moved closer to him, her breath a little white mist in the air. Due to the narrowness of the canyons through which the road now wound, the lines of watch fires lay only a dozen paces from the edges of the sleeping convoy, hemmed in by the shoulders of the mountains whose heads were hidden behind towering promontories of granite, furred over with the black of the pine forest. Now and then that day, Rudy had been able to catch glimpses of the higher peaks of the Rampart Range of the Big Snowies gouging the clouds like broken teeth. But mostly he was conscious of the forerunners of that looming range, and the way they overlooked the turnings of the road and hid what lay beyond.

Alde's voice was comforting. "If the water's a million miles deep or only six feet, all you have to do is to keep your head above it," she said. "For an outlander, you're doing well." And her arm tightened around his waist.

He grinned at her and returned the pressure gently. "For an outlander, I'm doing fantastic," he said. He shifted his arm around her shoulders to look at the tattoo on his wrist.

Alde noticed the movement and looked, too. "What's that for?" she asked.

He chuckled. "Just thinking. A girl I knew used to tease me about my tattoo. That's my name on the banner there across the torch. She used to say I got it so I could remember who I was, if I ever forgot."

"And do you need to be reminded?"

He looked out for a moment into the bitter stillness of the alien night, then up to the great, burning stars. His ears caught the distant howling of wolves. All the scents of the looming mountains came to him, shrub and pine, rock and water. The long hilt of the killing sword lying close by his right hand reflected the dim sheen of firelight, as did the braided hair of the woman curled, warm and fragile as a captive bird, in the circle of his other arm. He remembered, as if in an old legend, a sunburned California youth in a garish pachuco jacket, painting vans in a body shop. About the only thing they had in common, he reflected, was the tattoo.

"Yeah," he said softly. "Yeah, sometimes I do."

"I know what you feel," she murmured. "Sometimes I think I need reminding myself."

"What was it like," he asked, "to be Queen?"

She was so long silent that he was afraid he had hurt her by asking. But looking over at her face, profiled against the dim rose-amber of the fire, he saw in her eyes instead a kind of dreamy nostalgia, of memories whose beauty overrode their pain.

"It was very beautiful," she said at last. "I remember— dancing, and the hall all lit with candles, the way the flames would all ripple in unison with the movement of the ladies' dresses. The smell of the warm nights, lemon- flowers and spice perfumes, coming up-river on the royal barge and the water stairs of the Palace all lit like a jewel- box, golden in the darkness. Having my own household, my own gardens, the freedom to do what I wanted." She rested her head against his shoulder, the looped braids that bound her hair as smooth as satin under his jaw and gleaming like ebony. "Maybe it would have been the same, no matter whom I married," she went on softly. "Maybe it wasn't so much being Queen as having my own place to be." Her voice was wistful. "I'm really a very happy person, you know. All I want is to take life as it comes, to be at peace, with small things, small joys. I'm not really a stub- born, bloodthirsty hellion . . ."

"Oh, yes, you are," he teased her, holding her close. She raised her eyes to his reproachfully. "And I love you anyway. Maybe I love you because of it. I don't know. Sometimes I don't think there is any *why* in love. I just do."

Her arms tightened convulsively around his ribs, and she turned her face away, burying it in his shoulder. After a moment he realized that she was crying.

"Hey . . ." He turned under the weight of the cloak and stroked her shivering shoulders tenderly. "Hey, you can't cry on guard duty." The cloak slithered down as he raised his hands and caressed her bowed head with its gleaming, twisted braids. "Hey, what is it, Alde?"

"It's nothing," she whispered, and began wiping futilely at her eyes with the back of her hand. "It's just that nobody ever said that to me before. I'm sorry, I won't be stupid like this again." She fumbled at the fallen cloak, her face averted and wet with tears.

Rudy caught her firmly under the chin, forced her head up, and kissed her gently on the mouth. Her lips tasted of salt. "I can't believe that," he murmured.

She sniffled and swiped at her eyes with her arm in a child's gesture. "It's true."

Rudy's voice was soft. "What about Eldor?"

At that her eyes filled again, the tears making them seem fever-brilliant in the soft, glowing light of the watch fire. For a moment she could only gaze helplessly at him, unable to speak.

"I'm sorry," Rudy said. So much had happened, he had forgotten how short a time it had been.

She sighed and relaxed in his hold, as if something had gone out of her, a tension whose very pain had kept her strong. "No," she said softly. "No, it's all right. I loved Eldor. I loved him from the time I was a little girl. He had a magic that drew people, a vitality, a splendor. You noticed even the simplest things he did, as if they had a kind of significance that no one else could match. He became King when I was ten." She bowed her head, as if under the weight of memories impossible either to accept or to withstand. Wordlessly, Rudy took her back into the circle of his arm and drew the cloak up over her shoulders to cut out the icy air of the night. In those black cliffs above the road, the wolves were howling again, the full-throated chorus of the pack at the kill, distant and faint in the darkness.

"I remember standing on the balcony of our townhouse in Gae, the day he rode to his coronation." The murmur of her voice was hardly louder than the soughing of the pines above the road and the crackle of the fire. She was a dreamer reliving a dream. "He'd been in exile—he was always in and out of favor with his father. It was a hot day in full summer, and the cheering in the streets was so loud you could barely hear the music of the procession. He was like a god, like a shining knight out of a legend, a royal prince of flame and darkness. Later he came to our house to go hunting with Alwir or to see him on some matters of the Realm, and I was so afraid of him I could barely speak. I think I would have died for him, if he had asked."

Rudy saw her, a shy, skinny little girl, all dark-blue eyes and black pigtails, in the crimson gown of a daughter of the House of Bes, hiding behind the curtains in the hall to watch her tall, suave brother and that dark, brilliant King walk by. He was barely aware that he spoke aloud. "So you always loved him."

That same small smile of self-mockery folded into the corner of her mouth. "Oh, I was always falling in and out of love in those days. For six months I had a terrible crush on Janus of Weg. But this was—different. Yes, I always loved him. But when Alwir finally arranged the marriage, I found out that—that loving someone desperately doesn't always mean that he'll love you back."

And Rudy said again, "I'm sorry." He meant it, though he saw now that the dead King's ghost would always be his rival. She had loved so much, it was monstrous that she should be hurt by not having that love returned.

Silently the pressure of her hand in his thanked him. "He was so—distant," she said after a time, when she had regained control of her voice. "So cold. After we were married, I seldom saw him—not because he hated me, I think, but because—for weeks at a time I don't think he even remembered he was married. Looking back, I suppose I should have seen that that brilliance of his was so impersonal, but—it was too late, anyway." She shrugged, the gesture belied by the quaver in her voice, and she wiped her eyes again. "And the worst of it is that I still love him."

To that there was no possible reply. There was only physical tenderness, the closeness of another human being, and the reassurance that he was there and would not leave her. Against him, he felt her struggle to control her sobs and eventually grow still, forcing living grief back into its proper sphere of memory. He asked, "So Alwir arranged your marriage, too?"

"Oh, yes," she replied, in a small but perfectly steady voice. "Alwir knew I loved him, but I don't think that was the reason. He wanted the House of Bes allied to the Royal House; he wanted his nephew to be High King. I don't think he'd have forced me into it if there had been someone else, but since there wasn't—Alwir is like that; he's very calculating. He knew he would be made Chancellor after we were married. He's always doing things with two intentions."

You're telling me, sweetheart.

"But for all that," she went on, "he's been very, very good to me. Underneath that gleaming edifice of sartorial

201

splendor," she declaimed, half-jestingly, "there really does lurk a great deal of love."

Oh, yeah? Love of what?

He had realized that in Alwir's case, there was no such thing as *Love of whom.*

From her watch fire in the darkness, Gil saw Alde stand up, wrap the soft bulk of her black fur cloak tighter around her, and make her way cautiously down the stony ridge of land back toward the dark silhouette of her wagon against the lighted camp. Gil was apprehensive, for the night seemed to her to prickle with evil, and she wondered how the silly girl could ever have left her child, even with the camp guards there, to go play pattyfingers in the dark with Rudy Solis. Gil was a woman who did not love, and her feelings toward those who did were a mixture of sympathy, curiosity, and occasionally a longing that she would not admit to. Ordinarily she would not have cared whether Rudy and the widowed Queen held hands and talked or engaged in *al fresco* orgies. But tonight was different—tonight she felt the presence of the Dark, that watchful malice she had felt lurking in the stygian mazes of the vaults at Gae, that chaotic, abhuman intelligence, so close to her that, despite the fire at her back, she was always turning her head to see if it were standing at her elbow.

At midnight one of Alwir's troopers relieved her, a big, solid young man in a red uniform much patched and stained. She saw Rudy turn his post over to one of the Red Monks and descend the ridge toward the camp. From the darkness where she stood, halfway between camp and ridge, Gil watched him double back through the shadows of the wagons and slip quietly over the tailboard of the one that bore the banners of the House of Dare.

Gil sighed and started back for the campfire of the Guards. But, like a dog, she scented wrongness in the wind-shifting darkness. She kept looking out into the night that lay beyond the amber glow of the camp lights, feeling, like a cold and heavy hand, the threat of impending doom.

Most of the Guards were already asleep when she returned to their camp, rolled in their blankets and lost in the swift, hard sleep of physical exhaustion. Only one man was awake, sitting by the small glow of the fire like a weathered rock, somehow giving the impression that he had been there from the beginning of time. She'd seen him sitting thus night after night, when he wasn't patrolling the perimeters of the camp. She could not remember when she had last seen him sleep.

Gil hunkered quietly down at his side. "What do you see?"

The wizard shifted his eyes from the blaze, light catching in the shadowy seams of his face as he smiled. "Nothing of any moment." The small motion of his fingers took in the louring silence of the night. "Nothing to explain—this."

"You feel it, too," she said softly, and he nodded.

"We should reach the Keep in as little as three days," he said. "Last night I felt this, dimly and far off. Tonight it's much worse. Yet for three nights now there has been no report of the Dark anywhere along the line of march."

Gil locked her hands around her drawn-up knees and looked at the muted light flickering over her bruised and swollen fingers, reddened with cold. "Is there a Nest in this part of the mountains?" she asked.

"Only the one I spoke of once to Janus. It's an old Nest, long ago blocked. Night after night, I've sought it in the fire and seen no sign that it has ever been touched. Yet night after night I look again." He nodded toward the small fire. "I can see it now. It lies in a broad, shallow-sided valley, maybe twenty miles from here. I can see the foundation lying at the very back of the vale, slanting upward against the cliffs; the valley itself is crowded with foliage; filled with heat and darkness." A log broke in the fire and the scattering embers threaded his face with light.

"The place lies always under a kind of shadow. No reflection of sky or stars touches that polished stone. And in the middle of that darkness, like the mouth of a tomb, there is the deeper darkness of the entrance itself. But I can see that it is blocked, and the heaped earth and rock there are covered over with straggling weeds."

Staring into the fire, Gil could see nothing—only the play of colors, topaz and rose and citrine, and the curling heat shivering over the rocks that enclosed the pit, revealing, like frost-traceries, the ghostly patterns of fossil ferns printed in the fabric of the rock. But his rusty voice put the images in her mind, the way the darkness clotted in those too-thickly twined trees, the stirring in the shadows of the mountain that no wind could account for. The sense of eldritch horror was latent in the whispering night.

"I don't like it," Gil said softly.

"Neither do I," Ingold replied. "I don't trust that vision, Gil. We are three days from the Keep. The Dark must make their attempt, and make it soon."

"Can we go there?"

He raised his head and looked around him at the silent, sleeping camp. Clouds were building above the mountains, killing the stars; it seemed as if deeper darkness were settling over the land. "I don't see," he said, "that we have any choice."

The Dark were all around them. Gil could feel them, sense their presence in the still, sour miasma that overlay the daylight. She stopped on the edge of one of the innumerable tangled woods that snarled the valley like the thick-grown webs of monstrous spiders, looking northward on the rising slant of that unholy land, and found herself firmly repeating in her heart that it was broad daylight and she was with Ingold.

But she knew they were there.

The climb had been an easy one. *Too easy*, she caught herself thinking—an odd thing to think. The broad, round, shallow-walled valley through which Ingold had led her most of the morning was smooth-floored, with an easy grade that would have made considerably better walking than the road below, were it not so badly overgrown. The wind that had tormented them on the long miles down from Karst was cut off here. The walls of the canyon, cliffs marching steadily back toward a tumbled pile of talus slopes and the sudden, dark ramparts of sky-gouging peaks, protected the place. In their shelter the air was warmer than she had encountered anywhere in the West of the World. But, though she was warm now for the first time in days, Gil found that the valley disconcerted her. The woods were too thick to be healthy, the air was too heavy, and the ground was too even underfoot. The clumps of dark, sullen trees that scattered the broad length of the valley seemed to hem her in with a labyrinth of shadow, guarding beneath their entangling boughs thin shreds of a night that never lifted.

"They're here," she whispered. "I know they are."

204

Beside her, all but invisible in the shadows of the trees, Ingold nodded. Though it was not long after noon, the air in this valley seemed to play tricks with the sunlight. The thickness of the atmosphere dragged on Gil's lungs and, she had thought once or twice, on her mind as well.

"Can they be a danger to us even by daylight?"

"We know very little about the Dark, my dear," Ingold replied quietly. "All power has its limits, and we have seen that the power of the Dark grows with their numbers. We walk on a layer of ice that covers the depths of Hell. Tread carefully." Drawing his hood over his face, he moved forward, a wraith in the vaporous, leaden air.

As they climbed the valley, this sense that they were tampering in evil far beyond human ken grew upon her. There was something hellishly symmetrical about the valley, some persistent wrongness in the geology of the crowding, stratified rock of the cliffs that whispered warnings to Gil's mind. The land under their feet smoothed its way up over a great fault that cut the valley in half, with wild grape and a particularly tough-fibered species of ivy tangling over the break and the natural causeway that bridged it. Fossils Gil had seen on the stones of last night's campfire repeated themselves, peeking from broken rock—huge ferns, long-fingered marine weed, and the crawling things of times long past, trilobite and brachiopod, imprinted forever in the stamp of the slate. The ground seemed leveled by the passing feet of millions, hard as an ancient roadbed among its pathless labyrinth of crowding trees.

Ingold paused and turned to check their backtrail for what seemed like the hundredth time that day. Gil rubbed her aching eyes; she had snatched a few hours of sleep before setting out from the camp before dawn, but the lack of it was beginning to tell. Not, she reflected wryly, that she had gotten whole bunches of that particular commodity since this trail drive started. Some anomaly in the lay of the ground caught her attention, a stream bed that did not lie as it ought, a formation of rocks . . .

Looking back, she found she was alone. Momentary panic seized her. Even a few weeks ago she would have thrown caution to the winds and yelled for Ingold, even on the very doormat of the Dark. But living like a winter wolf and associating with the Icefalcon had altered her reactions, and she stood perfectly still, scanning the too-regular landscape.

A hand touched her shoulder and she swung around. Ingold caught her wrist as her sword was half out of its scabbard. "Where did you go?" she whispered.

The wizard frowned. "I didn't go anywhere." His hand still on her wrist, he looked around them doubtfully.

"You sure as hell weren't here a minute ago."

"Hmm." He scratched thoughtfully at his scrubby beard. "Wait here," he said finally, "and watch me." With these words he released Gil's arm and walked away, his feet making barely a sound in the knee-deep jungles of under-growth. Gil tried her best to watch him. Tired as she was with the weariness that seemed to have settled around her bones, she was certain she hadn't moved or shut her eyes. But somehow she lost sight of the wizard, in open ground, in the sunlight, without an inch of cover in yards.

She blinked and rubbed her eyes again. There was something, she thought, in the air of this place, some foul-ness, an invisible game of blindman's bluff. Then she looked back and saw Ingold standing about twenty feet off at the end of the track of flattened ivy, as if he had al-ways been there. As he came back to her, she had no trouble following his movements.

Gil shook her head. "I don't understand." She hitched her cloak up on her shoulder, a gesture that was quickly becoming automatic, like straightening her sword belt. Always before, the cloak had never provided quite enough protection from the cold, but in this place, with its stifling air, it seemed hot and heavy. She was acutely aware of the wrongness of this place. "Do you know what's going on?"

"I'm afraid I do," Ingold said slowly. "The power of the Dark is strong here, very strong. It seems to be interfering with the cloaking spell I've had over both of us, which is a pity, because that probably means I'll have to dispense with it."

"You mean," Gil said in surprise, "we've been under a spell all along?"

"Oh, yes." He smiled at her startled face. "I've been keeping a number of spells on the convoy all the way down from Karst. Mostly ward and guard, aversion and

206

protection. They wouldn't hold back a concerted attack, but they have served to deflect random misfortune."

She flushed, annoyed at herself. "I never knew that."

"Of course not. It's the mark of a good mage that he's never seen doing anything at all." She glanced suspiciously at him to see if he were teasing her, but he seemed perfectly serious—as serious as Ingold ever looked.

"But would a—a cloaking spell protect us from the Dark in the first place?"

"Probably not here in their own valley," Ingold replied casually. "But the White Raiders have been following us since we left the road. If the cloaking spell is unreliable, we're going to have a devil of a time getting back."

They reached the place in midafternoon. Gil felt it from afar, horror coalescing in her veins. She knew without being told that this was the place that Ingold had seen reflected in the depths of the fire. The ground was unnaturally even, tipped at a steep angle, with a great slanting slab of basalt jammed into the foundations of the mountain behind it, its farther end rising like the hull of a heeled wreck; one corner was buried in the valley floor as if driven there by some unspeakable cataclysm lost in the abysses of time. The slanted angle showed how deep the slab was founded; though it had been displaced upward a good thirty feet, there was no sign of bottom. And in the midst of it gaped the black hole of its stairway, the plunging road down into the chasm of the Dark.

The stairway was open. Little trace of the earth and rock Ingold had seen in the shadow image of the fire remained anywhere near that hideous gulf. A great scattering of stones, like the fan-trail of a volcanic spew, littered the slope below, but Gil could see from the way the clutching, ubiquitous weeds grew over them that the stones had been blown from that hole many years since. Still she picked one up. On its side, she could see the dry ghost of a lush, obscene orchid, frozen in some primeval swamp a million years ago and fragmented by the violence of that ancient blast. Ingold, too, was examining the wide-flung pattern of the stones, working his way methodically toward the crazily tilted pavement and the hole that yawned like a silent scream at the day.

He paused at the place where the rank, overgrown

ground ended and the black pavement began. Gil saw him stoop to pick up a stone and stand in thought for a moment, turning it over in his hands. Then he stepped cautiously onto the slick, canted surface of the stone and began his careful climb toward the stairway itself.

Though her whole being shrank from it, as it had on that other pavement in the vaults at Gae, Gil followed him. She struggled through the foliage that clung with such perverted persistence to her feet, scrambled up after the wizard onto the tilted pavement, and saw, ahead of her, Ingold pause to wait, his shadow lying small and leaden around his feet. Seen under the light of day, naked to the sky, the sheer size of the pavement awed her; from the corner buried in the weed-choked earth to the corner tilted upward and buried in the out-thrust knee of the mountain, it must have measured close to seven hundred feet. In its midst Ingold seemed very small and exposed. It was a tricky scramble up the smooth incline; when she reached his side, Gil was panting in the gluey, breathless air.

"So we were right," Ingold said softly. "The vision was a lie."

Below them stretched the stairway, open to the winds. A cool drift of damp air seemed to rise from it, making Gil's sweat-matted hair prickle on the back of her neck. There was nothing now between them and the Dark except the presence of the sun, and she glanced at the sky quickly, as if fearing to see the gathering of clouds.

"So what can we do?"

"Rejoin the convoy as quickly as possible. We do not yet know what they plan, but at least we know the direction of the attack. And in any case, it may be possible to thwart them and cover Tir's retreat to the Keep."

Gil glanced across at him. "How?"

"Something Rudy said once. If we—"

He broke off and caught her by the wrist. Gil followed the direction of his eyes along the smooth, tangled floor of the vale and spotted a stirring in the dark woods near one of those queer formations of black stone that dotted the valley. A movement was quickly lost to sight, but Gil knew what it was. There was only one thing that it could be.

She asked, "Have they seen us?"

"Doubtless. Though I should be surprised if they came

any closer." Balancing himself carefully with his staff, Ingold began his cautious descent from the ramplike pavement, with Gil edging gingerly behind. When they reached the ground, Ingold scanned the valley again, but could see nothing further. "Which doesn't mean anything, of course," he said, turning to walk along the rising edge of the pavement. "Just because you don't see White Raiders doesn't mean they aren't there."

"So what are we going to do?"

Ingold pointed with his staff toward the narrowing maze of crevices and hanging valleys at the end of the vale of the Dark, a great ruinous confusion of old avalanche scars, split and faulted from the rock. "There should be a way up there," he said calmly, pausing in the vine-entangled shadows of the seamless black wall.

"You're kidding," Gil said, aghast.

"I never kid, my dear." He started off up the talus slope.

Gil stayed where she was for a time, watching him disappear up the curve of the land. The ground rose and buckled oddly around the featureless wall of the black foundation, but whatever upheaval had disrupted it had been so long ago that the geology of the valley had settled around it. That in itself bothered Gil—the thing was so old, so incredibly old. Eons had rolled by since some arcane power had founded it here, so that the very shape of the lands and seas had changed. More fossils caught her eyes. *My God,* she thought, *this place was a tropical swamp when this was wrought. How long have the Dark Ones inhabited the earth, anyway?*

Who could ever tell, since they didn't have a bone in their floating plasmoid bodies? And yet they had intelligence, the intelligence to sink shafts, to build these dark pavements at their heads and have them endure for millennia with very little appearance of decay. They were intelligent enough to work their own kind of magic, different from the nature of human magic, ungraspable by any human brain. They were intelligent enough to keep tabs on the convoy, to know where Tir was, and to know why he had to be put out of the way.

Arms folded, Gil stood for a while in the lengthening shadows and meditated on the Dark.

After a time she looked up and saw Ingold again, appearing and disappearing among the twisted confusion of boulders and huddled trees at the end of the valley. Some primordial cataclysm had broken the side of one of the guardian peaks of the valley, leaving a wilderness of split granite and bottomless chasms, and time had overlaid the ruin with plant life grown far too large for the vertical rocks. The result reminded her vaguely of a Chinese painting, with full-size trees sprouting unconcernedly from the sides of cliffs. But this was messier, fouler, darker; here dead trunks had fallen to rot in gullies bristling with dead white spikes below the crumbly footing above. She could see Ingold's brown mantle shifting along impossibly narrow rock ledges high on the faces of those cliffs.

Ingold saw her looking and paused, flattened to the rock behind him. "Come up," he called down to her, his voice echoing faintly among the rocks. "There's a trail."

What the hell. Gil sighed. *You only die once.*

Gil had never liked heights. Scrambling over the treacherous footing, she envied the wizard his six-foot staff, for in places the ledges narrowed to inches, and in others cascades of vines sprawled over the trail and masked any hint of the footing underneath. She found herself backtracking a dozen times, scrupulously avoiding looking up or down or anywhere but at her own scratched hands when a promising ledge petered out or a slit between two huge rock faces became too narrow to be passed, or too choked with rotting foliage that could house any number of creatures less Lovecraftian, but certainly as deadly, as the Dark. She wondered if there were rattlesnakes in this world—or, for that matter, poisonous snakes without rattles.

She finally caught up with him in the mouth of a dark slit in the rocks, after a precipitous scramble around the convex face of a boulder on a ledge over a nightmare maw of tangled thorn and broken stone. She was sweating and gasping in the afternoon heat and fighting for balance on the sandy, crumbling ground. The shift of the sun over the backbone of the Rampart Range had thrown the chasm into deep shadow. Ingold was barely visible but for the pale blur of face and beard and the bright glitter of his eyes.

"Very good, my dear," he greeted her mildly. "We shall make a mountain climber of you yet."

"The hell you will," she gasped, and looked back down behind her. If there was any kind of trail she'd come up, she was damned if she could see it now.

"We should be able to follow this chasm up toward the top of that ridge there," he went on, pointing. "Once over the ridge, we should be nearly to the snow line and, I believe, out of reach of the Dark for the time being. With luck, we should be able to pick up another trail on the other side that will lead us down to the Vale of Renweth, and hence to the Keep of Dare."

Gil calculated the distance as well as she could in the deceptive clarity of the mountain air. They seemed to have climbed above the drifting haze of the valley; things seemed blindingly clear up here, and the slanting shadows altered the apparent positions of peak and ridge. "I don't think we'll make it by dark," she stated doubtfully.

"Oh, I don't either," Ingold agreed. "But we can hardly spend the night in the valley."

Gil sighed resignedly. "You have a point there."

The wizard jabbed his staff cautiously at the loose rock hiding the foot of the trail, and a boulder curtsied perilously, sending a little stream of gravel and sand down across their feet and over the edge of the trail. Muttering to himself about the advisability of taking along a rope next time, coupled with imprecations against the unseen Raiders in the valley below, he began to scout cautiously for an alternate route. While he did so, Gil turned to look back over the cliff, appalled anew at the suicidal ascent she'd just made. Her gaze wandered to the valley below them and was held there by a queer, cold feeling of shock.

"Ingold," she called quietly. "Come and look at this."

Something in the note of her voice brought him scrambling and sliding to her side. "What is it?"

She pointed. "Look. Look out there. What do you see?"

Viewed from above and behind, the land wore a different aspect, the angle of the sunlight westering on the mountains changing the perspective of that darkness-haunted place. From here the symmetry was obvious, the nuclei of the long-overgrown woods lying in some kind of pattern whose geometry was just beyond the range of human comprehension, the stream beds following courses that held the echoes of perverted regularity. The clinging mats of the ubiquitous vines took on a curious appearance from

211

this angle, the shifts in their color and thickness disquiet-
ingly suggestive. Almost directly below them the great
rectangle of pavement lay, and its position relative to the
anomalous mounds of black stone that thrust through the
foliage became suddenly, shockingly, clear to a woman
trained in the rudiments of archaeology.

Ingold frowned, staring down at the distorted counter-
pane beneath them. "It's almost—almost as if there were
a city here at one time. But there never was, not in human
history." His eye and finger traced the mathematical ob-
scenity of a curved shadow in the weeds, the queerly
obtuse angles faintly visible in the half-hinted relationships
between stream and stone. "What causes that? It's as if
the vines grow thinner in places . . ."

"Buried foundations," Gil softly replied. "From the looks
of it, foundations so deeply buried that they leave barely
a trace. The trees are more stunted on that line because
their roots cannot go so deep. Look, see the line of that
stream? And yet—" She paused, confused. "It looks so
planned, so regular, but it's not like any city I've ever
seen. There's a layout—you can see that in the angle of the
sunlight—but the layout's all wrong."

"Of course," the wizard said mildly. "There are no
streets."

Their eyes met. The meaning of this came to her slowly,
like a whisper from incomprehensble gulfs of time.

"Come," Ingold said. "This is no place for us to remain
once the sun has gone in."

CHAPTER THIRTEEN

Once they were out of the valley, the winds began, searingly cold, ripping at their grip on the precarious handholds with active malice. At times they were far over the timberline, scrambling perilously over goat trails slippery with old snow, at others working their way through knots of vegetation, or clinging for support to the wind-flayed roots of twisted acrobat trees, trusting to their strength over a sightless abyss. Gil and Ingold moved through a world whose only elements were cold, rock, wind, and the distant roaring of water, where they could not have stopped if they had wanted to, for there was nowhere to rest. Without the threads of witchlight Ingold had thrown to outline the ledges, Gil was certain they would not have survived the climb; even so, looking back on it later, she felt only a kind of dull astonishment that she had done it at all.

They slept, finally, in the crevices of the bare rock slopes, locked together for warmth; it was the first sleep Gil had had in close to forty hours. In the deeps of the night she felt the weather change and, in her dreams, smelled the far-off threat of snow.

In the morning the going was easier, not much worse than a rough backpacking trip. By noon Ingold found the ghost of a trail-head and followed it down the sheer, tree-covered western face of the Rampart Range, to reach, by midafternoon, the cold, winding Vale of Renweth.

Gil shaded her eyes and squinted into the long, bright distance. "What the hell?" The cold winds that snaked down the valley tore her breath away in rags and rippled in patterns like swift-pouring water over the knee-deep fjord of colorless grass. "What *is* it?"

"It's the Keep of Dare." Ingold smiled, folding his arms to keep warm and shivering slightly in spite of it. "What did you expect?"

Gil wasn't sure what she'd expected. Something smaller, anyway. Something more medieval. Not that trapezoidal monolith of black stone that rose, bone of the mountain's bone, on the great knoll at the foot of those distant dark-browed cliffs. Its roof was taller than the pine trees that grew on the ridge behind. Thin, powdery snow blew in clouds from the Keep's flat roof, but none lodged anywhere on its sides, which were as bare and smooth as unflawed glass.

"Who the hell built that thing?" Gil whispered, awed. "How big is it?" She could believe, now, that in it human-kind had withstood the Dark. The might of the Dark Ones, which could shatter stone and iron, would find this fortress impregnable. With a sense of surprise, she realized that there was, after all, a place of refuge in this dark and cold and terrible world into which she had been unwillingly cast.

"Dare of Renweth built it," Ingold's voice said at her side, "using the last of the technology and power of the ancient Realms, power which is far beyond our means to-day. In it he sheltered those of his people who survived the first onslaught of the Dark, and from it he and his line ruled this valley and Sarda Pass and all that was left of an empire whose name, bounds, and nature have been utterly lost to human memory. As to how big it is—" He gazed into the distance, surveying the black monolith that guarded the twisting expanses of the valley beyond. "It is small. It can hold some eight thousand souls in some sort of comfort, and the valley can be cultivated to support almost twice that many. The records no longer exist, if they ever existed, as to how many it has actually sheltered at any one time."

As they waded toward it through the champagne grass of the Vale, the thing seemed to grow in size, shadowless in the cold overcast of the day. Gil looked around her at the Vale as well, a walled series of upland meadows scattered with stands of aspen, birch, and cottonwood, their leaves glittering restlessly in the winds that whined down from the peaks above. There was a hard, bright beauty to the place, first heartland of the Realm and last, cradle and grave. Her bones ached, even muscles trained to the endurance of swordsmanship burning with the lingering effects of that tortuous climb.

As a place to be cooped up in for years on end, she thought, *it isn't bad.* Still, familiar as she had been with petty neighborhood bitchery, she had recognized its seeds already in the gossip that even a twenty-four-hour state of crisis hadn't eliminated from the refugee train, and she saw where it would lead—a small town, cramped in an impenetrable fort with the same people, bound together year in and year out, and nowhere to go.

"The Keep has stood a long time," Ingold said as they came at last to the roadway that led up past the Keep toward Sarda Pass, the same road where, miles below, Alwir led his people along in their quest for semimythical safety. "Yet the Runes of Power are still on the Keep doors, marked there by the wizards who helped in the building of the place—Yad on the left, and Pern on the right, the Runes of Guarding and Law. Only a wizard can see them, like a gleaming tracery of silver in the shadows. But after all this time, the spells of the builders still hold power."

Gil turned her eyes from the towering masses of the mountains that rose, wall on wall of black, tree-enshrouded gorges cut with the distinct, shallow notch of Sarda Pass, to view again the looming shadow of the Keep. She could see nothing of the Runes, only great panels of iron, hinged and strapped in steel, and untouched for centuries.

The great gates stood open. Waiting in their shade were the assembled members of the small garrison Eldor had sent down years before to ready the place as an eventual refuge, when Ingold had first spoken of the possibility of the rising of the Dark. The captain of the garrison, a petite blonde woman with the meanest eyes Gil had ever seen, greeted Ingold with deference and seemed unsurprised at the news that Gae had fallen and its refugees were but a few days off.

"I feared it," she said, looking up at the wizard, her gloved fingers idling on the hilt of her sword. "We've had no messages from anywhere in over a week, and my boys report seeing the Dark Ones drifting along the head of the valley almost every night." She pursed her lips into a wry expression. "I'm only glad so many as you say got clear. I remember, when I was in Gae, people were laughing at you in the streets about your warnings, calling you an alarmist crackpot and making up little songs."

Gil made a noise of indignation in her throat, but Ingold laughed. "I remember that. All my life I wanted to be immortalized in ballads, but the poetry of the things was so bad that they were completely unmemorable."

"And," the captain said cynically, "most of the people who made them up are dead."

Ingold sighed. "I'd rather they were still alive to go on singing about what a fool I am, every day of my life," he said. "We'll be here the night. Can you feed us?"

The captain shrugged. "Sure. We have stock . . ." She gestured to mazes of cottonwood-pole corrals that stretched out beyond the knoll, where a gaggle of horses and half a dozen milk cows stood rubbing their chins on the top rail of the fences, staring at the strangers with mild, stupid eyes. "We even have a still over in the grove there; some of the boys brew Blue Ruin out of gaddin bark and potatoes."

Ingold shuddered delicately. "'At times I see Alwir's point about the horrors of uncivilized existence." And he followed her up the worn steps to the gates.

"By the way," the captain said as the other warriors of the garrison grouped up behind them, "we have Keep Law here."

Ingold nodded. "I understand."

They entered the Keep of Dare, and Gil was struck silent with awe.

Outside, the Keep had been intimidating enough. Inside, it was crushing, frightening, dark, monstrous, and unbelievably huge; the footfalls of the Guards echoed in its giant sounding-chamber like the far-off drip of distant water, the torches they bore dwindling to fireflies. The monstrous architecture with its blending of naked planes had nothing to do with the gothic liveliness of Karst— nothing to do with human scale at all. The technology that had wrought this place out of stone and air was clearly far beyond anything else in this world or, Gil guessed, in her own. She gazed down the length of that endless central cavern, where the small bobbing candles of torchlight were reflected in the smooth black of the water channels in the floor, and shivered at the cold, the size, and the emptiness.

"How was this place built?" she whispered, and the chamber picked up her voice and sighed her words to every corner of that towering hall. "What a shame it couldn't have been the chief architect's memory that got passed on, as well as the Kings'."

"It is," Ingold said, his voice, too, ringing faintly in the unseen vaults of the ceiling. "But heritable memory is not governed by choice—indeed, we have no idea what *does* govern it." He moved like a shadow at Gil's side, following the diminishing torches. Gazing around her, Gil could see, as far as the torchlight reached, that the towering walls of the central hall were honeycombed with dark little doorways, rank on rank of them, joined sometimes by stone balconies, sometimes by rickety catwalks that threaded the wall like the webs of drunken or insane spiders. Those dark little doors admitted onto a maze of cells, stairways, and corridors, whose haphazard windings were as dark as the labyrinths below the earth.

"As to how it was built—Lohiro of Quo, the Master of the Council of Wizards, has made a study of the skill of that time from such records that survived, and he says that the walls were wrought and raised by magic and machinery both. The men of those days had skills far beyond our own; we could never create something like this."

They crossed a narrow bridge over one of the many straight channels that led water from pool to pool down the length of the echoing hall. Gil paused for a moment on the railless span, looking down into the swift, black current below. "Was that why he made such a study?" she asked softly. "Because he knew the skill might be needed again?"

Ingold shook his head. "Oh, no, that was years ago. Like all wizards, Lohiro seeks understanding for its own sake—for his own amusement, as it were. Sometimes I think that is all wizardry is—the lust for knowledge, the need to understand. All the rest—illusion, shape-craft, the balance of the minds and elements around us, the ability to save or change or destroy the world—are mere incidentals, and come after that central need."

* * *

"The trouble with this," Ingold grumbled much later, after they had shared the meager supper of the Guards and been shown to a tiny cell next to those of the garrison, "is that I can only look for what I know. It's absolutely useless for what I don't know." He glanced across at Gil, the pinlight-sparkle of triangular lights thrown by his scrying crystal scattering like stars across the roughness of his scarred face. They had kindled a small fire on the tiny hearth to take the chill off the cell. To Gil's surprise, no smoke came into the room itself—the place must be ventilated like a high-rise. Her respect for its builders increased.

Ingold had sat watching the crystal for some time now. Gil, fortified with porridge and warmth, was sitting with her back to the corner, meticulously sharpening her dagger in the manner the Icefalcon had shown her, sleepy and content in the wizard's presence. From the first, she had felt that she had always known him. Now it was impossible to conceive of a time when she had not. She held the blade up critically to the light and tested it with an inexperienced thumb. For all the terror she had undergone, for all the burden of constant physical weariness and the unending pain in her half-healed left arm, for all her exile from the only world she had known and the only thing she had ever truly wanted to do, she realized that there were compensations. She never felt the weight of her exile when she was with him.

And soon he'd be gone. She'd be here for endless weeks while he pursued his solitary quest across the plains to Quo, in search of the wizards, his friends, the only group of people who really understood him. She wondered what he would find there. She wondered, with a chill, if he'd even return.

He will, she told herself, looking across at the old man's still profile and calm, intent eyes. *He's tough as an old boot and slippery as a snake. He'll make it back all right, and the other wizards with him.*

She shifted the ball of her wadded-up cloak a little more comfortably behind her aching shoulders and blinked out at the room. After last night's trek over the bare backbone of the world, even a watch fire by the road would have looked good; this nine-by-seven cell in which she could hardly stand was a little corner of Paradise.

The place, viewed by more critical eyes, would have been called dingy: the warm gold of the firelight probing into the cracks of the rough-plastered walls and flagged floor cruelly revealed the unevenness, the shoddy workmanship, the patina of stains and soot-blackening, and the dents and scratches of hundreds of generations of continuous habitation and a thousand years of neglect. The cell would be awfully crowded for a family, Gil reflected. Unbidden to her mind leaped Rudy's picture of his own boyhood home, shrill with the bickering of acrimonious female voices. She grinned as she wondered what the incidence of sibling murder had been in the Keep's heyday.

The shadows by the fire shifted as Ingold put aside his crystal and lay down across the other end of the room, drawing his mantle over him as a blanket. Gil prepared to do likewise, asking him as she did so, "Could you see the convoy?"

"Oh, yes. They're settling in for the night, under double guard. I don't see any sign of the Dark. Incidentally, the crystal shows the Nest in the valley of the Dark as being still blocked."

"They like that, don't they?" Gil drew her cloak over her, watching the changing patterns of flame and shadow playing across the rickety wall that had long ago partitioned this cell off from a larger one. Her thoughts idled over the world enclosed within those narrow walls, over the great black monolith of the Keep, guarding its darkness, its silence, its secrets—secrets that had been forgotten even by Ingold, even by Lohiro, Archmage of all the wizards in the world. Those dark, heavy walls held only darkness within.

She rolled over onto her side and propped her head on her arm. "You know," she said dreamily, "this whole place—it's like your description of the Nests of the Dark."

Ingold opened his eyes. "Very like," he agreed.

"Is that what we've come to?" she asked. "To living like them, to be safe from them?"

"Possibly," the wizard assented sleepily. "But one might then ask why the Dark Ones live as they do. And when all else is considered, here we are, safe; and so we shall remain, as long as the gates are kept shut at night." He rolled over. "Go to sleep, Gil."

Gil blinked up at the reflection of the fire, thinking

about that for a moment. It occurred to her that if once the Dark came into this place, the safety here would turn to redoubled peril. In the walls of the Keep was lodged eternal darkness, like the mazes of night at the center of the earth, which no sunrise could ever touch. She said uneasily, "Ingold?"

"Yes?" There was a hint of weariness in his voice.

"What was the Keep Law that the captain talked about? What did that have to do with our spending the night here?"

Ingold sighed and turned his head toward her, the dying firelight doing curious things to the lines and scars of his face. "Keep Law," he told her, "states that the integrity of the Keep is the ultimate priority; above life, above honor, above the lives of family or loved ones. Anything that does not require the presence of human beings after dark is left outside the gates, and when the gates are shut at night, it is, and always must be, the ruling of the Keep that no one will pass them until sunrise. In ancient days the penalty for opening the doors—on any excuse whatsoever—between the setting and the rising of the sun was to be chained between the pillars that used to surmount the little hill that faces the doors across the road, to be left there at night for the Dark. Now go to sleep."

This time he must have laid a spell on the words, for Gil fell asleep at once, and the wizard's words followed her down into the darkness of her dreams.

The Dark hunted. She could feel them, sense them, sense the dark shifting of movement through spinning, primordial blackness, the vague stirrings in unspeakable chasms that light had never touched. Groggily, through a leaden fog of sleep, Gil tried to remember where she was— the Keep, Dare's Keep. Fleeting, tangled images came to her of slipping through nighted corridors and converging on a chosen prey. She could sense that eyeless, waiting malevolence, smell, as they smelled, the hot pulse of blood, and sense, through the thick gloom of vibrating, purple darkness, the glow of the prey, the centerpoint of a whirling vortex of lust and hate . . . But it wasn't the closeness of the Keep at all that surrounded her, but wind, utter bone-piercing cold, the roaring of water among pillars of stone, the white surge and fleck of spray, and the

220

freezing touch of the air above the flood. Greedy power gnawed at stone, greedy minds counted out glowing beads on a four-mile chain of tangled sleep and laughed with a gloating laughter that never emerged to sound.

Her eyes snapped open, and sweat drenched her face at the memory of that gloating laughter. She whispered, "Ingold . . ." almost afraid to make a sound, for fear they might hear.

The wizard was already awake, his white hair tousled with sleep, his eyes alert, as if he listened for some distant sound that Gil could not hear. A dim blue ball of witchlight hung above his head; the fire in the cell had long grown cold. "What is it?" he asked her gently. "What did you dream?"

She drew a deep breath, grasping at the fast-fading rags of sensation, of things she'd heard and smelled. "The Dark . . ."

"I know," he said softly. "I felt it, too. What? And where?"

She sat up, drawing her cloak around her shoulders, as if that would still her shivering. "I don't know where it was," she said, a little more calmly. "There was water rushing, and—stone—hewn stone, I think, pillars. They were tearing pieces of stone out of pillars, throwing them into rushing water—and—and laughing. They know where Tir is, Ingold," she added, her voice low and urgent.

He came across the room to her and put an arm around her shoulders for comfort, though for her the worst was past. His voice was grim as he said, "So do I. He's with his mother, half a day's journey below the stone bridge that crosses the gorge of the Arrow River."

Somewhere above the inky overcast, the sky might have been lightening, preparatory to the breaking of day; but if so, Rudy Solis could see little indication of it. The canyon through which the road at this point wound was like a black wind tunnel, the smell of the wind strong and somehow earthy, its sound like the roar of the sea in the pines above the road. He prowled restlessly through the rousing camp, unable to account for his uneasiness, threading through little knots of bundled-up fugitives huddled around their breakfast fires, making his way almost subconsciously back to the wagons he had stealthily quitted before the camp was astir.

The fires there had been built up and threw an uneasy flickering glow over the camp. Alde was awake, feeding Tir on bread soaked in milk in the little island of shelter at the back of her wagon. On the other side of the fire, a handful of troopers of the House of Bes were wolfing down their meager rations in silence. Farther out among the wagons, another woman, a servant of the household, was ordering two small children about as she fed a baby smaller than Tir, while her husband fed the ox teams in sullen silence. Overhead, the banners cracked like bull-whips in the icy stream of the wind.

Rudy shook his head and grinned down at Alde, leaning his shoulder against the uprights that supported the wagon's roof. "You know, what amazes me about this trip is how many kids have survived. You see them all over the camp. Look at that one there. He looks as if the first stiff wind would blow him away."

"It's a she," Alde replied calmly, watching the child in question playing tag with herself under the feet of the wagon teams. The little girl's mother saw what she was doing and called her back to the fire with a screech like a parrot's, and the child, with the sublime unconcern of those who have only recently learned to walk, came running happily back out of danger, arms open, a treasury of broken straws in her hands.

Rudy reached out to stroke Tir's downy hair absent-mindedly. *He'll grow up like that,* he found himself thinking. *Learning to run in the dark labyrinth of the Keep of Dare, learning swordsmanship from the Guards ...* Strange to think of Alde and Tir going on living for years in that fortress Rudy had never seen, long after he was gone.

If they make it there. And he shivered, not entirely from the cold.

"And it isn't so unusual," Minalde went on, a glimmer of timid mischief in her blue eyes. "If you've noticed, it isn't the women and children who sit down by the roadside and die. If a wagon breaks down, the man will moan and despair—the woman will start pushing. Watch sometime."

"Oh, yeah?" he said, suspicious that she was baiting him.

She gave him a sidelong, teasing glance. "Seriously,

Rudy. Women are tougher. They have to be, to protect the children."

He remembered the wind-stirred gallery at Karst, the flutter of the white dress of a girl who was running down the hall in darkness. "Aaah—" he conceded ungraciously, and she laughed.

More children eddied into the circle of the fire, the gaggle of camp orphans with the slim young girl they'd taken as their guardian carrying the youngest in her arms. The girl and the servant woman stopped to speak. Seeing them together, Rudy was reminded of the way he'd seen Alde and Medda that first day on the terrace of the villa at Karst.

A new thought crossed his mind, and he frowned suddenly. "Alde?" She looked up quickly, getting milk all over her fingers. "How do the Dark Ones know who Tir is?"

Slim brows drew together in thought. "I don't know," she said, startled by the question. "Do they?"

"Yeah. They went after him at Karst, anyway, and at Gae. There were beaucoup kids in the villa at Karst. As far as they should have known, he could have been any one of them. But they were right on the spot outside his nursery."

She shook her head, puzzled, the cloak of her unbound hair slipping across her shoulders. "Bektis!" she called out, seeing the tall figure crossing the camp to his own wagons.

He came forward and gave her a gracious bow. "My lady pleases?"

The Sorcerer of the Realm didn't look any the worse for two weeks in the open; like Alwir, he was fastidious to the point of foppishness, and there wasn't so much as an untoward wrinkle in his billowing gray robe.

Rudy broke in. "How do the Dark Ones know where to find Tir? I mean, they haven't got eyes, they can't tell he looks different or anything. Why do they know to come after him?"

The sorcerer hesitated, giving the matter weighty consideration—probably, Rudy guessed, to cover the fact that he was stumped. At length he said, "The Dark Ones have a knowledge that is beyond human ken." *He is stumped.* "Perhaps my lord Ingold could have told you, had he not chosen this time to disappear. The sources of the knowledge of the Dark—"

Rudy cut him off. "What I'm getting at is this. Do the Dark Ones really know it's Tir, or are they just going after any kid in a gilded cradle? If Alde went on foot with the kid in her arms, like every other woman in this train, wouldn't she be safer than being stuck in the wagon?"

Bektis looked down his long nose at this grimy upstart outlander who, he had been informed, had presumed to show signs of being mageborn. "Perhaps," he said loftily, "were we presently in any danger from the Dark. Yet it has been noted that no alarm of their presence has occurred since we reached the high ground . . ."

"Oh, come on! You saw how well that high ground stuff worked at Karst!"

". . . *and*," the sorcerer grated, with an edge to his high, rather light voice, "I have seen in an enchanted crystal the only Nest of the Dark known in these mountains, and I assure you that it is blocked, as it has been blocked for centuries. Naturally my lady may do as she pleases, but for reasons of her own comfort and health, and on account of her state and prestige, I doubt that my lord Alwir will permit my lady to walk in the back of the train like a common peasant woman." Turning on his heel, the old man stalked back toward his wagon, his fur cape swirling behind him like a thundercloud.

Minalde sat in unhappy silence for a time, rocking her child against her breast as if to protect him from unseen peril. Distantly, the sounds of the camp's breaking came to them, the braying of mules and the creak of harnesses, the splash and hiss of doused fires. Somewhere quite close, voices raised in anger, Alwir's controlled and cutting as a lash, and after, the dry, vituperative hiss of Bishop Govannin's.

Alde sighed. "They're at it again." She kissed Tir's round little forehead, following up the mark of affection with a businesslike check of the state of his diaper, and proceeded to tuck him up in his multiple blankets again; the morning seemed to be growing colder instead of warmer. "They say we should reach the Keep tonight," she went on in a low voice, excluding from hearing any but the man who stood beside her in the shadows of the wagon. "Sometimes it has seemed that we'd travel forever and never reach the place. So Bektis is probably right."

Rudy leaned his elbow on the wagon-tail. "You think so?"

She didn't reply. Beyond, there was the clatter of trace-chains and the sound of troopers talking casually among themselves as they harnessed the oxen. "Will we reach the Keep in daylight, or will we have to push on after sundown?"

Her hands paused in their restless readying of the wagon for travel. In a low voice she said, "After sundown, I think."

Ingold slumped back exhaustedly against a boulder and rested his elbows on his drawn-up knees. "I am very much afraid, my dear," he said tiredly, "that we are not going to make it."

Gil, who for the last several hours had been aware of very little beyond the form of the wizard, who had always seemed to be walking farther and farther ahead of her, could only nod. The little bay among the rocks above the road where they had taken shelter offered no protection from the increasing cold, but at least they were out of the wind. They had fought the wind all day, and, like a wolf, it had torn at their cloaks and mauled their exposed faces with savage violence. Gil could sense on it now the smell of the storm moving down from the glaciers on the high peaks. Even in this comparative shelter, hard bits of mealy snow had begun to fly. It was now late afternoon; there was no chance, she knew, of reaching the Arrow Gorge before the convoy did. Whatever the Dark Ones had done to the bridge there, it was beyond her power or Ingold's to warn the people of it.

After a little time she recovered enough to disengage the flask she wore at her belt, draw the stopper, and take a tentative sip—the stuff made white lightning taste like lemonade. "The captain at the Keep gave me this," she explained, passing it over.

He took a drink without turning a hair. "I knew there was an ultimate reason in the cosmic scheme of things for you to accompany me," he said, and smiled through the ice in his beard. "Now that makes twice you've saved my life."

Over their heads in the rocks, the roaring of the wind increased to a kind of cold, keening shriek, and a great gust of snow blew down on them. Gil drew herself closer to Ingold's side. "About how far above the Arrow are we now?"

"Two or three miles. We would be able to see it, but for the winding of the road. That's what worries me, Gil; if they had passed the bridge in safety, we would have met them before this."

"Might the storm have slowed them down?"

"Possibly. But it won't really hit until about sundown. It would be suicide for them to stop now."

"Can't you do anything about the storm?" she asked him suddenly. "Didn't you say once that wizards can call and dismiss storms?"

He nodded. "And so we can," he replied, "if that is what we wish to do." As he spoke she noticed that, instead of gloves, he was wearing mittens—old and frayed now, like everything about him, but, by the intricacy of their design, clearly knitted for him by someone who cared very much for the old man. "We can send storms elsewhere, or call them to serve us—all except the ice storms of the plains, which strike without warning and make this—" He gestured at the whirling snow flurries. "—resemble a balmy spring breeze. But I think I pointed out to Rudy once, and I may have mentioned to you as well, that the Dark will not attack under a storm. So it may be that in doing nothing about the storm, we will be choosing the lesser of two evils."

He rose to go, wrapping his muffler tighter around his neck and drawing his hood down to protect his face. He was helping Gil to her feet when they heard on the road below them the muffled clop of hooves and the jingling of bits, echoes thrown into the sheltered pocket of boulders and dried grass that a moment ago had hidden all sound of the troop's coming. Beyond the boulders, Gil saw them come into view, a weary straggle of refugees. She recognized, in the lead, the big, scarred man on a brown horse whose head drooped with exhaustion. She and Ingold exchanged one quick, startled glance. Then the wizard was off, scrambling down the rocks to the road, calling, "Tirkenson! Tomec Tirkenson!" The landchief straightened in his saddle and threw out his hand as a signal to halt.

Gil followed Ingold with more haste than seemliness down to the road. The landchief of Gettlesand towered over them in the leaden twilight, looking like a big, gaunt bandit at the head of his ragged troop of retainers. Glancing down the road, Gil could see that his followers—a great gaggle of families, a substantial herd of bony sheep and cattle, a gang of tough-looking hard-cases riding point-guard—were hardly a sixth of the main convoy.

"Ingold," the landchief greeted them. He had a voice like a rock slide in a gravel pit and a face to match. "We were wondering if we'd run into you, *Gil-shalos*," he greeted her with a nod.

"Where did you leave the rest of the convoy?"

Tirkenson grunted angrily, his light, saddle-colored eyes turning harsh. "Down by the bridge," he grumbled. "They're making camp, like fools."

"Making camp?" The wizard was aghast. "That's madness!"

"Yes, well, who said they were sane?" the landchief growled. "I told them, get the people across and to hell with the wagons and the luggage, we can send back for that . . ."

Ingold's voice was suddenly quiet. "What happened?"

"Holy Hell, Ingold." The landchief rubbed a big hand over his face wearily. "What hasn't happened? The bridge came down. The main pylons went under the weight of those carts of Alwir's, took the whole kit and caboodle down with them—"

"And the Queen?"

"No." Tirkenson frowned, puzzling over it. "She was afoot, for some reason, up at the head of the train. Walking with the Prince slung on her back, like any other woman. I don't know why—but I do know if she'd been in a cart, there would've been no saving her. So what's Alwir do but start salvaging operations, hauling the stuff up out of the gorge, and rigging rope pontoons across the river down below. Then the Bishop says she won't abandon her wagons, and they start breaking them down to carry them across in pieces, and half the people are cut off on one side of the river and half on the other, and squabbling about getting baggage and animals across, and before you know it, everybody's saying they'll settle there for the night.

"I tried to tell them they'd be froze blue by morning, sure as the ice comes in the north, but that pet conjurer of

227

Alwir's, that Bektis, says he can hold off the storm, and by the time Alwir and the Bishop got done slanging one another, they said it was too late to go on anyway. So there they sit." He gestured disgustedly and leaned back into the cantle of his saddle.

Ingold and Gil exchanged a quick look. "So you left?"

"Oh—Hell," Tirkenson rumbled. "Maybe I should have stayed. But Alwir tried to commandeer that big wagon of the Bishop's, the one she's dragging the Church records in, and you never heard such jabber in your life. She threatened to excommunicate Alwir, and Alwir said he'd slap her in irons—you know how she is about these damn papers of hers—and people were taking sides, and Alwir's boys and the Red Monks were just about pulling steel over the argument. I told them they were crazy, with the camp split and the storm and the Raiders and the Dark all around them, and they got into it again about that, and I'd had enough. I got my people and whoever else wanted to come with us to Gettlesand and we pulled out. It might not have been the right thing to do, but staying another night in the open sure as hell looked like the wrong thing to do. We figure we can make the Keep before midnight."

Ingold glanced briefly at the sky, as if able to read the time by the angle of an unseen sun above the roof of clouds. The sky was no longer gray but a kind of vile yellowish brown, and the snow smell was unmistakable. "I think you did right," he said at last. "We're going on down, and I'll try to talk them into moving on. You'll have to fight the weather before you reach the Vale, but if you can, get them to open the gates and build bonfires on both sides of them, frame them in fire, and guard them with every man in the train. With luck, we'll be there sometime tonight."

"You'll need luck," the landchief grumbled. "I'll see you at the Keep." He raised his hand in the signal to go on. The train began to move like some great beast dragging itself along in the last stages of exhaustion. Tirkenson reined away from where Ingold and Gil stood, clicking encouragement to his tired horse. Then he paused and turned back, looking down on the two pilgrims in the frozen road.

"One more thing," he said. "Just for your information. Watch out for the Bishop. She's got it around that you and Bektis are leagued with the Devil—and Alwir, too, just

228

coincidentally by association, you understand—and she's got Hell's own support in the train. I never held with it—wizards trading their souls for the Power—but people are scared. They see Alwir's helpless. You might say the powers of this world are helpless. So if they're gonna die anyway, they're gonna die on the right side of the line. Stands to reason. But scared people will do just about anything."

"Ah, but so will wizards." Ingold smiled. "Thank you for your warning. Good riding and a smooth road to you all."

The landchief turned away, cursing his exhausted mount and threatening to rowel him to dogmeat if he didn't get a move on. Gil glanced from the big man's wicked, star-shaped spurs to the untouched flanks of the tired horse and knew, without quite knowing how, that Ingold's parting blessing had contained in it spells to avert random misfortune, to shake straight the tangled chains of circumstance, and to aid the landchief of Gettlesand and those under his loud-voiced and blasphemous care.

CHAPTER FOURTEEN

It was snowing in earnest when Gil and Ingold came within sight of the camp on the near bank of the Arrow. In the swirling grayness they could make out huddled shapes bunched around the feeble yellow flickers of campfires, the dark milling of small herds of animals, the restless activity on the bank of the gorge, and the shadowy comings and goings around the broken bridge. Across the gorge more activity was visible, lights moving here and there around the farther camp, and the distant threnody of bleating goats and a child's wailing cries drifting on the intermittent veering of the wind. Between the two camps lay the gorge, a sheer-cut chasm of darkness, filled with the greedy roaring of the river. On either bank of the gorge, great tongues of broken stone thrust out over the void.

"How deep is the gorge at that point?" Gil asked, squinting through the blurring gusts of snow.

"About forty feet. It's a difficult climb down the side and up again, but the water itself isn't very deep. As you can see, they've swum most of the stock." Ingold pointed to where three men were driving a small herd of pigs up the trail. "From what you told me of your dream, it would seem that the Dark weakened the central pillars of the bridge, so that they gave way under the weight of the wagons—as pretty an attempt at murder as you're likely to see. And even though the attempt failed, Prince Tir is stranded in camp on the banks of the river tonight, cut off from most of the convoy, with the camp in confusion.

Either way, the Dark could hardly have missed." Leaning on his staff, he started down the steep slope toward the fires.

Rudy met them on the outskirts of camp. "What did you find?" he asked them.

As they made their way through the dark chaos toward Alwir's massive tent, Gil filled him in on the valley of the Dark, Renweth, the Keep, and what Tomec Tirkenson had said. In the end, she asked, "Why wasn't Alde in her wagon?"

"I talked her out of it," Rudy said. "I had a bad feeling they'd try something tonight, but I never thought about anything happening by daylight. We were only a couple feet in front of the section of the bridge that went."

"And you still believe in coincidence," Ingold chided reprovingly. "I'm surprised at you."

"Well," Rudy admitted, "not as much as I used to."

Alwir's was one of the few tents left in the train. It was pitched in the lee of some trees, out of the wind; in the darkening of the late afternoon, yellow lights could already be seen glowing within. Gil could make out a confusion of voices coming from it, Bishop Govannin's harsh half-whisper, and now and then Bektis' light, mellifluous tenor.

". . . full ferocity of the storm is by no means upon us," the sorcerer was saying sententiously. "Nor will it be, for I will turn its force aside and keep it over the mountains to the north until such time as we can come to the Keep."

"Turn it aside?" Govannin rasped. "Have you been to the camp across the river, my lord wizard? They are half-buried in the snow there and freezing."

"Yet we cannot go on tonight," Alwir said and added, with smooth malice, "We have too few carts and horses to make good speed. What must be carried, must be carried on the backs of men. And if they will not rid themselves of what is useless . . ."

"Useless!" the Bishop spat. "Useless to those who would dispose of all precedents for the legal position of the Church, perhaps. Mere technicalities to those who would rather forget their existence."

Alwir protested, as sanctimonious as a preacher, "God's Church is more than a pile of mildewed paper, my lady. It lies in the hearts of men."

"And in the hearts of the faithful it will always remain,"

she agreed dryly. "But memory does not lie in the heart, nor does law. Men and women have fought and died for the rights of the Church, and the only record of those rights, the only fruit of those spent lives, is in those wagons. I will not leave that to perish in the snow at the mere word of a baby King's running-dog."

Ingold pushed aside the flap of the tent. Beyond him, Gil saw Alwir's face change and stiffen into a mask of silver, barred and streaked with ugly shadow, the mouth made of iron. The Chancellor lurched to his feet, his head brushing the bottom of the single hanging lamp, towering over the slight scarlet figure of the Bishop with clenched fist; for a moment it seemed that he might strike her where she sat. But she only looked up at him with flat black eyes, emotionless as a shark's, and waited in triumph for the blow to fall.

"My lord Alwir!" Hoarse and unmistakable, the voice cut like a referee's whistle between them, breaking the tension with an almost audible snap. They both turned, and Ingold inclined his head respectfully. "My lady Bishop," he finished his greeting.

Just perceptibly, the Bishop's taut body settled back into her chair. Alwir placed his fist upon his hip, rather than visibly unclench it at another man's word. "So you decided to come back," the Chancellor said.

"Why did you make camp?" Ingold asked without preamble.

"My dear Ingold," the Chancellor soothed, "as you can see, it has begun to grow dark . . ."

"That," Ingold said acidly, "is what I mean. You could have pushed on, to reach the Keep sometime tonight, or gone back across the river, to be with the main body of the convoy. Isolated on this side of the river, you're nothing but bait."

Patiently, Alwir said, "We have, as you may have noticed, a temporary bridge, across which we are slowly bringing the rest of the convoy, as well as sufficient troops to deal with any emergency that may arise in the night."

"You think the Dark couldn't deal with that as easily as they deal with solid oak doors? As easily as they dealt with the stone pillars of the original bridge?"

"The Dark had nothing to do with that," Alwir said rather sharply.

"You think not?"

Bektis' long fingers toyed with a huge solitaire cat's-eye he wore on his left hand. "You cannot pretend it anymore," he said rather pettishly. "You are not the only mage in the train, my lord Ingold, and I, too, have cast my powers of far-seeing here and there in the mountains. The only Nest that was ever in these parts was blocked with stone long ago, and you yourself know that we have felt no threat of the Dark since we have come to the high country." He raised heavy white lids and stared from under them at Ingold, defiance, resentment, and spite mingling in his dark, burning eyes.

"So they have made it appear," Ingold replied slowly. "But I have come from that Nest and I tell you that it lies open."

"And is this another of those things," the Bishop asked dryly, folding her fingers before her on the table, like a little pile of ivory spindles, "for which yours is the only word?"

Lamplight glittered in the melting snow on his shoulders as he turned toward her. "It is. But there are things, like the commandments of God, which we must all take upon trust, my lady. Surely you yourself know that we have only one man's word on the true means of salvation and that those means are not what a reasonable man would logically conclude. For now mine—and, incidentally, Gil's—must be the only word you have that the Dark are in that valley, that they have held back from the train deliberately, and that they have broken the bridge in order to kill the Prince or isolate him on this side of the river."

Govannin opened her mouth to speak, then shut it again thoughtfully.

Ingold went on. "They will never allow Tir, with what he could become and the secrets he may hold, to reach the Keep. The storm has given us our chance, and I suggest that we take it and push on now, tonight, under its cover to the Keep."

"Cover?" Alwir swung around to face him, his voice jeering. "Shroud, you mean. We'll freeze to death . . ."

"You'll freeze just as quickly here," Ingold pointed out.

Piqued, Bektis announced primly, "I am quite capable of holding off such a storm as this . . ."

"And the Dark as well?" Ingold retorted.

The sorcerer stared at him for a moment, hatred in his narrow face, and a watery flush of red crept up under his white cheeks.

Without waiting for his reply, Ingold said, "Nor could I. There are limits to all power."

"And to all endurance," the Bishop said imperturbably. "And I for one will not be stampeded by fear, like a sheep into the shambles. We can weather this storm and push on in the daylight."

"And if the storm does not break until this time tomorrow?"

Alwir leaned a kid-gloved hand on the back of his carved chair. "Don't you think you're putting too much importance on this storm? I am agreeable to whatever may be voted, provided I can find cartage for the effects of the government . . ."

Govannin's eyes blazed. "Not at the cost of—"

"Don't be a pair of fools." The words were spoken quietly as the white embroidery of the tent-curtains rippled, and a girl stood framed in gleaming silk against the shadows of the room beyond. Minalde's face was very white against the raven blackness of her unbound hair. She was wrapped for warmth in a star-decorated quilt, holding Tir against her under its folds. The child's eyes, wide and wandering in fascination over the lamplit interior of the tent, were a jewel-blue echo of his mother's and of Alwir's own.

"You are both acting like fools," she went on in a low voice. "The tide is rising, and you are arguing about who will be the first one into the boat."

Alwir's aristocratic nostrils flared in annoyance, but he only said, "Minalde, go back to your room."

"I will not," she replied in that same quiet voice.

"This is none of your affair." His was the voice of a man to a recalcitrant child.

"It *is* my affair." She kept her words soft, but Alwir and Rudy both stared at her, more astonished than if she had burst forth into colorful profanity. All the breath went out of Alwir as if she'd kicked him; he had obviously never even considered that his gentle and acquiescent little sister would defy him. Rudy, who remembered how she'd shoved a torch into his face on the haunted stairs at Karst, was less surprised.

234

"Tir is my son," she continued. "Your stubbornness could get him killed."

The Chancellor's impassive face flushed; he looked ready to tell her to mind her tongue before her elders and betters. But she was, after all, Queen of Darwath.

"*If* what my lord Ingold says is true," he said.

"I believe him," she said. "And I trust him. And I will go on with him to the Keep tonight, if I go alone."

From where she stood in Ingold's shadow by the corner of the tent, Gil could see that this girl, wrapped in stars and darkness, was trembling. It couldn't have been easy to defy a man who, by all accounts, had run her life for years; Gil's respect for Minalde, who had been up to this moment merely a name and a silhouette in the darkness, increased.

"Thank you for your trust, my lady," Ingold said quietly, and their eyes met for a moment. Gil knew from experience that the wizard's gaze could strip the spirit bare and defenseless; but whatever Alde saw in his eyes, it must have reassured her, for she turned away with a straight back and an air of resolution.

Alwir caught her arm, drew her to him, and said something that none of them could catch, but his face was intent and angry. Alde pulled her arm from his grip and went inside without a word. It was just as well that she did, for she did not see her brother's face, transformed by cold rage into the mask Gil had seen when first she'd entered the tent, a mask all the more inhuman because it was so impersonal. But when he turned back to them, his smile was deprecating. "It appears," he said, "that we are moving on tonight after all."

It was clear that this was the opening line to something else, but the Bishop cut him off so smoothly that the interruption had every appearance of being accidental. "If that is so," she said in her slow, dry voice, "I must go and make ready the wagons of the Church." And she was gone, far more quickly than anyone would have believed possible, before he could speak any command.

It was almost fully dark by the time the camp broke. Snow was coming down harder now, the wind whirling little flurries of grainy flakes into the ashes of the stamped-out fires and coating the churned mud in a thin layer of

235

white. Word had been carried across the river over the makeshift bridge, and families were crossing slowly, men and women balancing precariously on the shaky spiderweb of rope and cottonwood poles, with their bundles on their shoulders. Oddly enough, when Rudy walked down to the jerry-built bridgehead with Ingold and Gil to see about the single wagon Alwir had negotiated from one of his merchant friends, he found that a spirit of optimism seemed to have seized the train, grossly at odds with the circumstances. The grumbling wasn't any less prevalent, and the curses were just as loud and vivid. Men and women packed up their few belongings, rubbing chapped hands in the flaying cold, snapping, bickering, and fighting among themselves—but something had changed. The bitter desperation of the early part of the march was gone. An aliveness crackled through the blinding air that had not been felt before—a hope. This was the last march, if they could make it. They were within striking distance of the Keep.

"That should do," Ingold remarked, watching Guards and Alwir's private troops dragging the half-disassembled wagon box up the crooked trail. "Granted, it should make Minalde and Tir a target, but in this case that's better than risking losing them in the snow. As for you two . . ." He turned to them and laid a hand on each of their shoulders. "Whatever you do, stay close to that wagon; it's your best hope of reaching the Keep alive. I'm going to be up and down the train; I may not see you. I realize none of this is any of your business—that you were hauled into it against your will, and neither of you owes me anything. But please, see that Alde and the child reach the Keep in safety."

"Won't you be there?" Gil asked uneasily.

"I don't know where I'll be," the wizard said. Snow lodged in his beard and on his cloak. In the failing light Gil thought he looked worn out. Not surprising, she thought. She herself was operating on nervous energy alone. "Take care of yourselves, my children. I'll get you safely out of this yet."

He turned and was gone, the stray ends of his muffler whipping like banners in the wind.

"He looks bad," Rudy said quietly, leaning on his staff as the snowy twilight swallowed the old man. "You guys must have had one hell of a trip."

Gil chuckled dryly. "Never doubt he's a wizard, Rudy.

He has to be, to get people to follow him on crazy stunts like that."

Rudy gave her a sidelong, thoughtful glance. "Well, you know, even back in California I thought the setup was crazy, but I just about believed *him*. You do. You have to."

And Gil understood. Ingold had a way of making anything seem possible, even feasible—that an aimless motorcycle drifter could call forth fire from darkness, or that a mild-mannered and acrophobic Ph.D. candidate would follow him over the perilous roof of creation to do battle with bodiless, unspeakable foes.

Or that a ragged train of fugitives, split by dissensions, frozen half to death and at the end of their strength, could make a fifteen-mile forced march through storm and darkness to find at last a refuge they had never seen.

She sighed and hitched her too-large cloak over her narrow shoulders. The wind still bit through, as it had torn at her all day. She felt tired to the bones. The night, she knew, would be terrible beyond thinking. She started to move off, seeking the Guards, then paused in her steps. "Hey, Rudy?"

"Yeah?"

"Take care of Minalde. She's a good lady."

Rudy stared at her in surprise, for he had not thought she had known, much less that she would understand. Rudy still had much to learn about coldhearted women with pale schoolmarm eyes. "Thanks," he said, unaccountably touched by her concern. "You ain't so bad yourself. For a spook," he added with a grin, which she returned wickedly.

"Well, it beats me why she'd hang out with a punk airbrush-jockey, but that's her business. I'll see you at the Keep."

Rudy found Alde where the few remaining servants of the House of Bes were packing the single wagon. She herself was loading bedrolls into it; Medda, if she had still been alive, would have expired from indignation at the sight. He kissed her gently in greeting. "Hey, you were dynamite."

"Dynamite?"

"You were great," he amended. "Really. I didn't think Alwir would go along with it."

She turned back, blushing suddenly in the diffuse glow of the torchlight. "I didn't care whether he went along, as you say, or not. But I ought not to have called them fools. Not Alwir, and certainly not my lady Bishop. It was— rude."

"So do penance for it at confession." He drew her to him again. "You got your point across."

She stared in silence for a moment into his eyes. "He's right, isn't he?" she whispered intently. "The Dark are in the mountains."

"That's what Gil tells me," he replied softly. "He's right. They're nearer than we think."

She stood for a moment, her hands clasped behind his neck, staring up into his face with wide, desperate eyes, as if unwilling to end this moment because of all that must come after. But a noise from the cart made her break away and scramble over the tailboard to replace her wandering son in his little nest among the blankets. He heard her whisper, "You lie down." A moment later she reappeared around the curtains.

"You're gonna need a leash for that kid once he starts crawling," Rudy commented.

Alde shuddered. "Don't remind me." And she disappeared inside.

The convoy began to move. The wind increased in violence, howling down the canyons to fall on the pilgrims with iron claws. Rudy stumbled along beside the wagon, blinded by the snow, his fingers growing numb through his gloves. The road here was disused, but better than the road from Karst had been, with pavement down the center where it had not been broken up by tree-roots or buried by neglect. Still, the drifting snow made treacherous footing, and Rudy knew that those at the tail of the convoy would be sliding their way through a river of slush. Wind and darkness cut visibility to almost nothing. The shapes of the Guards surrounding the wagon grew dim and chaotic, like half-guessed shadows in a frightful dream.

Remembering Ingold's teachings, Rudy tried to call light to him. He managed to throw a big, sloppy ball of it about three feet in front of him to light his steps. But the effort took most of his concentration and, as he slipped in the snow or staggered under the brutal flail of the wind, the light dimmed and scattered. The snow thickened in the air, like swirling gray meal all around him, except where it passed, unmelting, through the witchlight, which transformed it into a tiny roaring storm of diamonds that made his eyes ache. His cloak and boots dragged wetly on his limbs, and his hands passed quickly from insensibility to pain. Once, when the wind slacked like the slacking of a rope, he heard Minalde's voice from the wagon, singing softly to her child:

> "Hush, little baby, don't say a word,
> Papa's gonna buy you a mockingbird . . ."

He wondered numbly how that song had ever leaked its way into the tongue of the Wathe.

He lost all track of time. How long he'd been struggling through the blinding wilderness he had no way of knowing, could not even guess. He felt as if it had been hours since they'd broken camp, the ground always rising under his slipping feet, the wind worrying at him like a beast at its prey. He hung onto the wagon grimly with one hand and onto his staff with the other; at times it seemed as if those were the only things keeping him on his feet. He knew by then that if he went down, he would die.

At one point, Gil came up beside him, so thin and ragged he wondered dully why she didn't blow away. She yelled at him over the gale. "You okay?"

He nodded. *A lady and a scholar,* he thought. *And tough as they come.*

Others passed them, or were passed by them, fighting the wind with desperate persistence. He saw the old man from Karst with his crates of chickens still piled on his bowed back, wrapped up in blankets and laden with pounds of trapped snow. The struggling band of camp orphans were roped together like goslings behind their chief. A stout woman leading a goat passed them; a little farther on he saw her lying face down in the snow, the goat standing wretchedly over her body.

And still they pushed on. Rudy stumbled and fell, his body so numb he was scarcely aware of hitting the ground. Someone bent over him, hauled him to his feet, and shook him out of his stupor with a violence that surprised him— a ghostly, dark shape in a blowing mantle, with a blue-white light burning on the end of his staff. Rudy staggered wordlessly back to the wagon, catching the cover ropes for support, and the shape melted into the dark. In the lightless chaos he could see other shapes moving, dragging stragglers to their feet, urging them on with words or pleas, curses or blows. He clung to the ropes grimly, reminding himself he'd promised to get Alde to the Keep, reminding himself that there was a goal, somewhere in this black universe of unending cold. He had learned already that, under certain circumstances, death could be very sweet indeed.

Time had become very deceptive; every movement was ponderously slow, an incredible effort barely worth the trouble, like that old Greek guy who had to push the stone up the hill, knowing full well it was just going to roll to the bottom again. The night was far gone. He could tell by the changing note of the wind that they were coming clear of the deep gorges, coming into a more open space. Feebly, mind and will drowning in a blind darkness that was within him as well as without, he tried to call back a little of the witchlight, but raised not even a glimmer.

Just keep putting one foot in front of the other, he told himself grimly. *You'll get there.* The wind struck him like a club; he went down and this time decided not to get up. They could make it to the Keep without him. He was going to sleep for a while.

He drifted for a time in memories, chiefly of the warm hills of California, the rippling gold of the sunbaked grass, and the way the sun had felt on his bare arms as he hauled down Highway 15 on his chopper in the late evening, the wind streaming through his hair. He wondered if he'd ever get to do that again. *Probably not,* he decided. But even that didn't matter much. *Who'd have figured that leaving on a beer run would end up with me freezing to death in a range of mountains that never even existed?*

Life is weird.

A seven-foot giant with a kick like a mule loomed suddenly in the darkness and booted him in the ribs. Cold returned, and a thin leakage of pain spread into every muscle and joint. He mumbled, "Hey," protestingly, and the giant kicked him again.

"Get up, you sniveler." *Why did a seven-foot giant have Gil's voice?*

Arrogant egghead bitch. "No."

240

Even a few weeks of swordmastery training had given her a grip like a claw. Surprising, too, that somebody wasted down to ninety-eight pounds of brittle bone could have the strength to drag him to his feet and throw him with such violence against the side of the moving wagon, so that he had to catch hold of it.

"Now keep moving," she ordered.

Stupid of her not to understand. "I can't," he explained groggily.

"The hell with you!" she yelled at him, suddenly furious. "You may be a goddam wizard, but you're a coward and a quitter, and I'll be damned if I'll have you let everybody down by up and dying on the road. You die when you get to the Keep if you want to so bad. We're only a couple miles from it."

"Hunh?" Rudy tried to keep a grip on the rope with his fingers, but they were too numb. He thrust his whole arm through the space between the rope and the flapping cover. "What did you say?"

But as if in answer to his words, he felt a sudden change in the air. The titanic winds veered, and the relentless hammering force of them slackened, making him stagger, as if for a support suddenly lost. The snow, instead of peppering his body like bullets from a Tommy gun, fell straight for a few moments, then ceased. He could hear the roaring of the wind in the pines above the road and its shrieking whine in the rocks, but the air around him, though freezing cold, was still.

The wagon team halted, one ox managing a plaintive low. Boots scrunched in the squeaking snow all about him; somewhere leather creaked. He could hear his own breath and that of the woman beside him.

"What is it?" he whispered. "Has the storm let up?"

"Not like that, it wouldn't. Besides, you can still hear it overhead."

He blinked against the darkness and raised a shaking hand to scrape ice crystals from his eyes. "Then what . . ." Then he realized what must have happened. Shock and fear sent a jolt of adrenalin into his veins that cleared his groggy mind. "Oh, Christ," he whispered. "Ingold."

"He stopped the storm, didn't he?" Gil said softly. "They must have been losing too many people . . ."

"But you know what that means?" Rudy said urgently.

"It means the Dark will be coming now." He took an experimental step away from the wagon and found he could stand after a fashion by leaning on his staff. "We gotta get moving."

The Guards were closing in around them, some thirty strong; he could pick out their voices in the darkness. God only knew where the rest of the train was. They'd gotten so badly strung out in the storm, it was every man for himself. He flexed his right hand stiffly, trying to convince himself it was still really his; he heard Gil's voice speaking softly to the Guards around them and, brief and cold, the Icefalcon's breathless laugh. Gil came back to him. "Can you call up some light?" she asked. "The land flattens out from here on; we could lose the road completely. Look."

There was, in fact, only one thing to look at: a tiny square of orange light, distant and sharp in the wastelands of cold.

"Tomec Tirkenson's up at the Keep. That's the fire around the doors."

"Okay," Rudy said. "We can make for that, if nothing else." He tried several times to call light, but his fatigue-drugged consciousness was unequal to the task. They were moving again, heading steadily toward that tiny orange star, the going impossibily rough over the steep, uneven ground. From the wagon behind him, he heard Tir's thin, protesting wails and Alde's voice, softly shushing him. He trod on something hard that rolled sickeningly underfoot, stumbled, and put his hand on it in falling. It was an iron cook pot. Despite the cold and danger, he grinned—others had made it this far. The whole Vale was probably littered with discarded household goods, flung away in a last, desperate effort to keep on going. Well, if they could do it, he could do it.

And then he felt it—a breath of wind in the stillness, a wind not like the might of the storm, but a thin, directionless whisper that spoke of stone and damp, warm darkness, a faint stirring of air from above and behind and all sides. Turning, he saw the Dark.

How he saw them he wasn't sure—perhaps by some wizard-sense, grown from the exercise of his powers. They flowed over the snow toward the wagon, scarcely distinguishable one from the other or from the shifting river of illusion in which they swam. Whiplike tails steered and

242

propelled, and they moved with a sinuous glide, the jointed legs tucked in folds like bamboo armor under the soft, dripping tentacles of the slobbering mouths. For a moment he stood hypnotized, fascinated by the changing shapes, now visible, now only wavering ghosts. He wondered in what sense they could be said to be material at all. What atoms and molecules made up those sleek, pulsing bodies? What brain, or brains, had conceived the stairways that led down to the blackness under the earth?

Then one of the oxen gave a great bellow of terror and tried to leap forward; it fell, pulling down its teammate in a tangle of harness and splintering the wagon tongue under its threshing weight.

"The Dark!" Rudy yelled in desperate warning, and tried to summon light, any light, for aid against the unseen foes. He heard Alde scream. Then from behind him a shattering blaze of witchlight pierced the darkness like a strobe, and that pouring river of shadow and illusion broke against it and swirled away like a great ring of smoke. Ingold came striding out of the unnatural stillness, his shadow thrown hard and blue onto the glittering snow at his feet.

"Cut that ox loose, get my lady out of the wagon, and get moving," he ordered briefly. By the burning light, the Guards came running to them, faces haggard under the crusting of frost. "Janus, do you think you can make it as far as the Keep?"

The Commander, barely recognizable under the ice that scaled his hair and cloak, squinted at the light in the distance, against which the tiny figures of men were now clearly visible. "I think so," he panted. "Again, you've saved us."

Ingold retorted, "It's about a mile and a half too soon to say that. My lady . . ."

He turned back to the wagon. The Icefalcon had cut the team loose, but the wagon was clearly beyond further use. From the curtains at the front, a white face looked out, framed in the darkness of a black fur hood and a cascade of crow-black hair.

Rudy stepped quickly over to the wagon. "We've got to run for it, babe," he said softly, and she nodded, turning unquestioningly back into the shadows of the cart to fetch Tir. She reappeared a moment later with the heavily muffled infant in her arms, her face pale in the light of Ingold's staff, her eyes wide with apprehension. Gil held out her arms and received the child awkwardly, while Rudy helped Minalde down over the broken wagon tongue. Even through two pairs of gloves and the burning numbness of his fingers, he was conscious of the touch of her hand.

"How far?" she whispered.

Gil nodded toward the distant orange gleam of the Keep doors. "About two miles."

Alde took the baby back, feeling as she did so the chill, prickly sensation she had known before, the subconscious awareness of the presence of the Dark. The Dark Ones had not been defeated by the advent of the light. They had merely drawn off to wait.

The wind still howled overhead, but near them the air was uncannily still. From all around them in the Vale they could hear voices, distorted by cold and distance, voices of fear, hope, despair. Refugees throughout the dark mountains were making for the lights of the Keep, unseen forms fighting their way through stillness and deep snow; but within the circle of light cast by Ingold's staff, the little group of Guards around the fallen wagon were alone. Coated with frost, they seemed to be some kind of fantastic ice-creatures, beaded with diamonds and breathing crystal smoke. And beyond them, invisible in the blue-black ocean of the night, that sense of restless motion stirred just out of the range of vision.

Ingold came over to the little group by the wagon tongue, his light harsh on their drawn, haggard faces. He was a man who imparted his own strength to others; Gil found she drew warmth from his presence, as from a fire, and saw that Rudy and Alde looked a little less deathly as well. He put a hand briefly to Alde's cheek and gazed sharply into her face. "Can you make it?"

"I have to," she said simply.

"Good girl. Rudy . . ."

Rudy stepped forward hesitantly.

"Channel your Power through your staff; that's what it's there for, not just to keep you from stubbing your toes."

Rudy looked in surprise at the six-foot walking stick he'd cut for himself miles up the road. "Uh—you mean,

244

that's all? You don't have to do anything special to make a staff magic?"

Ingold appeared to pray briefly for patience. "All things are inherently magic," he said patiently. "Now . . ."

Tentatively, Rudy called light again, feeling the power of it through his hand, through the wood that had become smoothed to his grip by its use, through the air. Light began to burn smokily from the end of the staff, growing brighter and throwing doubled shadows, blue and black, on the spokes of the wagon wheels, on the thin, frightened faces of the two girls, on the dilapidated cart, and on the deep-set hollows of Ingold's eyes.

Softly, the wizard said, "Don't leave them, Rudy." Rudy had the sudden, uncomfortable feeling that the old man knew about his giving up, his lying down to die and leaving the others to their own devices. He felt himself flush.

"I'm sorry," he mumbled.

Wind stirred around his feet. He swung about, scanning the darkness beyond. He felt a counterspell, like the cold touch of an alien hand, slipping into his mind from the darkness. He felt the light dimming, looked up, and saw that Ingold's staff, too, had begun to flicker unsteadily. At the same time he smelled the cold, bitter, acid stink of the Dark. Steel whined as Gil drew her sword; all around them was the muted flashing of blades as the Guards closed in an outward-facing ring.

What instinct warned him he never knew, but he ducked, drew and turned, and slashed in one movement, almost before he was aware of the thing that fell suddenly on him out of the night. He heard Alde scream and got a confused glimpse of Gil, with a face of stone and a blade of fire, cleaving darkness in a long side-on cut that seemed to cover them all in an explosion of blood and slime. The witchlight dimmed to gray, and the Guards pressed back, defending as best they could against the slimy onslaught. The counterspell sucked at him, draining his power as if from a cut artery, and for a time he saw nothing, knew nothing but that he must keep between the Dark and the woman at his back.

Then, without warning, they were gone, and the strength of the witchlight was renewed. Somebody yelled, "Come on!" and Rudy found himself grasping Alde's right arm while Gil held her left, hurrying over the slime-spattered muck of the snow, the light of his staff brightening over the mess of mud and bloody bones, with the Guards closing around them in a tight flying wedge. Ingold strode ahead, white breath smoking in the light that showed the snow all around them trampled by stampedes of fleeing feet and strewn with the discarded bundles of the refugees. Groggily, Rudy tried to keep up with him, leaden with cold and fatigue and stumbling in the drifted mess, trying to keep his eyes on the brilliant square of orange light in the distance that marked the end of this nightmare road. He could make out movement there clearly now, small shapes in those great doors. He could sense the Dark massing above them like storm clouds and felt the touch of their spells again, drawing and sapping at his strength.

Then the soft, sinister shadows dropped like vultures from above, a half-seen cloudy death that filled the night. Rudy's sword seemed to be weighted with lead, his arm shot full of Novocain. He knew that if he hadn't been in the center of the pack, he would have been killed at once. Seeing Gil slash and dodge in the gray darkness and step in under the whining arc of a spined whip half again as long as she was, he understood why Gnift flayed the bodies and souls of his Guard students and why Gil and the others trained the way they did, doggedly, through injuries, cold, and fatigue. It was only their training that saved them now.

Thin winds ruffled mockingly around them, and the Dark were gone. Rudy, gasping for breath, hung onto his staff for support, holding the half-fainting Alde with his other arm and wondering if he'd have the strength to drag her as far as the Keep. Though they were less than a mile off, the roaring glow of the gate-fires could barely be seen through the massed, cloaking shadows that filled the night.

The Guards closed up again.

"Now," Ingold said quietly. "Go. Go quickly."

Horrified, Janus protested, "They're all around us, they'll never let us through."

The wizard was panting with exertion, and the pallid light showed his hands cut and noisome with slime. "They will if you go now. Hurry, or—"

"You're not staying!" the Commander cried.

"But—" Rudy began, stupefied.

"Do as I say!" the wizard thundered, and Rudy stepped

246

back a pace, shocked. Ingold drew his sword in a single gleaming movement, the blade flashing in the dark. *"Go!"*

Janus looked at him for a long moment, as if he might, at the last, disobey. Then abruptly he turned and strode off through snow and darkness; after a momentary, uncertain pause, Rudy and the others followed, he and Gil half-dragging Minalde between them. He could feel the spells of the Dark shifting aside from the light he bore and could sense their malice concentrated elsewhere. Glancing back over his shoulder, he saw Ingold standing where they had left him, a dark form in the burning aureole of the light, his head cocked to listen to the sounds of the night, blood dripping from his gashed knuckles to stain the snow at his feet.

The wizard waited until the little party of Guards had gone almost two hundred yards from him. Then Rudy, turning again to look back, saw him throw down his staff in the snow. The light went out. The sword blade swung in a searing, phosphorescent arc. Rudy knew that the Dark had closed in on the old man.

They ran on. Tir had begun to wail, his cries thin and muffled with exhaustion, within the shelter of his mother's cloak. There was no other sound; but looking across Alde once, Rudy got a glimpse of Gil's face, a pale-eyed mask of pain. The blazing gates seemed to get no nearer, though he could now clearly distinguish the shapes grouped on the steps in the glare of the bonfires, with the Runes of Guarding and Law looming behind them, reflected in the bloody light. One dark shape he knew must be Tomec Tirkenson; another, he thought, was Govannin. There seemed to be something wrong with his perception of distance. The air was still, without movement or scent or breath, without even the sensation of the nearness of the Dark—though he knew he had to be wrong about that; it must be only the effect of his senses slipping gradually away. The Dark had to be following, waiting the moment to strike. Twice he looked back over his shoulder and saw the firefly movement of Ingold's blade in the darkness. He wondered dizzily why the wizard had sent them on and wondered, with all the strength left in him to wonder, if they'd make it as far as the gates before the Dark finally fell on them from above. The ground steepened; he seemed to be moving through a knee-deep sea of slush, struggling to keep to his feet.

Then from above them, the wind streamed down—not the winds of the Dark, but the storm winds, swirling snow down on them as they fled toward the blazing Hell-mouth of the gates. The howl of the rising gale was like the keening of wolves on the kill. The storm winds that hit them with a force that made Rudy stagger were blinding, freezing, raging over them with wild, malicious glee. He struggled on, seeing before him the towering darkness of some vast, somber cliff, the storm winds driving the flames into thirty-foot maypoles of fire. He tripped on something in the darkness and fell, Alde's arm sliding from his grasp. Looking up, he saw before him the blazing gates; he had fallen on the steps. He could see Gil dragging Alde up the steps, framed in a wild coruscation of snow and fire, the wind mixing their dark hair into a single streaming cloud.

Someone came down to him and hauled him up and into that red inferno. Sick and half-fainting, he could see only that the hand that gripped his arm was covered by a black velvet glove glittering with rubies, like droplets of new-shed blood.

When his eyes cleared, he was lying on the floor just within the gates, half-covered in blowing snow. Men and women were coming inside, staggering with cold and exhaustion—children, too, he saw, and realized Gil had been right. His surrender to fate back in the snowy darkness had been an act of cowardice that an eight-year-old could have bettered. Beyond them, silhouetted against the ruddy light, he saw Govannin, a skull with live coals in the eye sockets, a sword in her skeleton hand. Alwir was a dark tower, his sister leaning on the strength of his mighty arms, her child sobbing exhaustedly at her breast. Alwir's eyes were not on either of them, but looking beyond, into the dark cave of the Keep itself, calculating the dimensions of his new kingdom. And past them was Gil, her coarse, witchy hair fluttering in the backwash of the storm as she stood at the gates, looking out into the darkness. But in all that waste of ice and bitter wind, Rudy could see no trace of any moving light.

CHAPTER FIFTEEN

"Where is he?" Rudy asked.

"With the Guards." Gil adjusted her sword belt without meeting his eyes. He could see that she had been crying.

Rudy rolled over and found he had to use the wall to climb painfully to his feet. His body ached, and little electric flashes of pain were stabbing every muscle and joint as he tried to move. Lassitude gripped not only his bones but his spirit as well, so that nothing—not last night's flight, nor the news Gil had wakened him with this afternoon—brought him either sorrow or joy. He recognized this as a symptom of extreme fatigue.

When I get back to California, he vowed tiredly, *I am never, ever going to gripe about anything again. I will always know for a sure fact that things could be loads worse.*

If I get back to California, he amended, and followed Gil out of the cell.

The cell was one of a warren of partitioned-off cubicles that stretched haphazardly beyond a door to the right of the gate. To get out, he had to pick his way through ill-lit huddles of those who still slept, lying where they'd fallen in blind exhaustion, and step over and around the pitiful little bundles of pots and blankets heaped in the corners of the tiny rooms. Next to a small hearth, a porcelain-headed doll slumped like a dead child against a pair of broken boots. The place stank of unwashed clothes and a child's neglected diaper. Blinking in the dim light, Rudy stepped out into the central hall of the Keep.

Looking around him at the dark fastnesses of that fortress,

he could only wonder at the human powers of recuperation and the human tendency to make oneself at home. Here, in this awesome fortress of stone and steel, after they'd fought their way through peril and death and darkness, people were settling themselves in cozily for the winter. Children —Minalde was right, children were tough little survivors— ran madly up and down that great, echoing hall, their shrill, piercing yells ringing off the unseen vaults. He heard women's voices, sweet and high, and a man's genuine laugh of pleasure. Down at one end of that monstrous space, a rectangle of blinding light marked the doors—daylight, filtered with clouds and snow. At the other end of the hall, a couple of monks in patched red robes were putting up a bronze crucifix over a cell doorway otherwise indistinguishable from a hundred small black doorways exactly like it to establish the domain of the Church—Renweth Cathedral and the administrative offices of Bishop Govannin. She was evidently wasting no time. On the narrow catwalk above, he saw Alwir, like Lucifer in his velvet cloak, quietly surveying his dominion.

The Guards had a complex of cells to the immediate right of the great Keep doors. Gil led Rudy through a narrow entrance. By the smoldering light of grease lamps, he saw Janus arguing with a couple of indignant-looking burghers who had the air of having been men of property before the Dark had made hash of wealth and land and prestige.

Janus was saying patiently, "Cell assignments aren't the province of the Guards, they're the responsibility of the Lord of the Keep, so I suggest . . ." But neither of the men looked as if he were listening.

The room was heaped with provisions and mail, weaponry and kindling. Guards were sleeping in the chaos, with their slack, pinched faces showing the last stages of weariness. In the room beyond, the confusion was worse, for most of the Guards there were sitting around, eating a scratch dinner of bread and cheese, sharpening their swords, and mending their uniforms. The Icefalcon, his white hair unbraided and hanging in a sheet of liquid platinum past his waist, was keeping a pot of water from boiling by watching it impatiently. People looked up and called greetings, cheerful and noisy, which Rudy returned with what bloodless enthusiasm he could conjure. The place stank of filth and grease and smoke. What the hell was it going to be like in a year? Or two years? Or twenty? The thought was nauseating.

A grubby curtain partitioned off a sort of closet, where the Guards had stored their spare provisions in wildest disorder. Stepping through the grimy divider, Rudy blinked at the dimness, for barely any of the greasy yellow illumination managed to leak through from the room beyond; he had the impression of heaped sacks, scarred firkins, a floor mucky with mud and old hay, and an overwhelming smell of dusty cheese and onions. Across the back of that narrow cell somebody had excavated a makeshift bed on the fodder-sacks. On the bed, looking like a dead hobo, lay Ingold.

"You're crazy, do you know that?" Rudy said.

The blue eyes opened, drugged and dreamy with fatigue. Then the familiar smile lightened the whole face, stripping the age from it and turning it impish and curiously young.

"You could have got killed."

"You have an overwhelming capacity for the obvious," Ingold said slowly, but his voice was teasing, and he was obviously pleased to see Gil and Rudy alive and well. The wizard's hands were bandaged in rags and his face welted and snow-burned, but on the whole, Rudy thought, he looked as if he'd live. He went on. "Thank you for your concern, though the danger was less than it appeared. I was fairly certain I could keep the Dark Ones at bay until I released the spells over the storm. I knew I could escape them under cover of the storm, you see."

"Yeah?" Rudy asked, sitting down at the foot of the bed. "And just how the hell did you plan to escape the storm?"

"A mere technicality." Ingold dismissed the subject. "Is it still snowing?"

"It's coming down pretty heavy," Gil said, drawing her knees up like a skinny grasshopper and settling herself beside the head of the bed. "But the wind's stopped. Tomec Tirkenson says this is the coldest it's been in forty years. The Icefalcon said he's never seen the snow pile up in the canyons like this so early in winter. You're gonna have one chilly trek over the Pass." Barely visible in the smoky darkness, her face looked thin and haggard, but at peace.

"I'll wait until it actually stops snowing," Ingold said

251

comfortably, and folded his bandaged hands before him on the moth-eaten wool of the coverlet. Half-hidden in the gloom, he looked white and ill. Rudy didn't like the dreamy weakness of his voice, nor the way he lay without moving, propped on the sacks of grain. Whatever he said, the old boy had had one hell of a close call.

"I can't delay much longer than that," the wizard continued. "Things have happened about which it has become imperative that I consult Lohiro, quite apart from the fact that, so far as I know, Alwir still proposes to assemble his Army here, for the invasion of the Nests of the Dark."

"Look," Rudy began. "About your going to Quo . . ."

But before he could finish, the muted voices outside rose to a quick babble, followed by the hasty scuffle of too many people all trying at once to get respectfully to their feet in too small a space. The ragged curtain was thrust aside, and a towering shadow blotted the infalling light. Alwir, Lord of the Keep of Dare, stepped through. At his side, dark and slender as a young apple tree newly come to blossom, was the Lady Minalde.

The Chancellor stood silent for a moment, gravely regarding the old man lying on his bed of sacks. When he spoke, his melodious voice was quiet. "They told me that you were dead."

"Not much of an exaggeration," Ingold said pleasantly, "but not strictly accurate, as you see."

"You could have been," the Chancellor said. "Without you, we might all have been, back by the river. I have come—" The words seemed to stick in his throat like dry bread. "I have come to say that I have wronged you, and to offer you my hand in friendship again." He held out his hand, the jewels of his many rings flaming in the shadows.

Ingold stretched out a grubby, bandaged hand to accept, a king's gesture to an equal. "I only did as I promised Eldor I would," he said. "I have taken his son and seen him to safety. My promise is fulfilled. As soon as the weather permits, I shall be leaving to seek the Hidden City of Quo."

"Do you think, then, that it can be found?" Alwir's frown was one of troubled concern, but his eyes were calculating.

"I can't know that until I seek it. But the aid of the Council of Wizards is imperative: to your invasion, to the Keep, to all of humankind. Lohiro's silence troubles me.

252

It has been over a month, without word from him or from any member of the Council. Yet it is impossible that they cannot know what has happened."

"But you still think Lohiro isn't dead?"

Ingold shook his head decisively. "I would know it," he said. "I would feel it. Even with the spells that surround the city like a ring of fire, I would know."

Minalde spoke for the first time, her eyes dark with concern. "What do you think has happened, then?"

Ingold shook his head and said simply, "I don't know."

She looked down at him for a moment, hearing, as no one else in the room did, the undercurrent in his voice of helplessness and fear—not fear for the world's wizardry, but for his friends in Quo, the only people in the world to whom the old man truly belonged. She had seen him before only in his strength and command, and sudden sympathy clouded her face. She said, "You would have sought them weeks ago, but for your promise. I'm sorry."

Ingold smiled at her. "The promise had nothing to do with it, my child."

She stepped quickly forward and bent to kiss the top of his rough, silvery hair. "God be with you," she whispered. She turned and fled the room, leaving lover and brother staring after her in bemused surprise.

"You seem to have made a conquest," Alwir chuckled, though, Rudy thought, he didn't sound a hundred percent pleased about it. "But she is justified. Your service to the Realm goes beyond any payment we can possibly make." He looked around him at the grimy, low-ceilinged room with its dirty walls, the smells and steam from the guardroom outside drifting in, along with Gnift's cracked, tuneless voice singing of love in cornfields. "It certainly deserves better than a back room in the barracks. The Royal Household is a regular warren—we can put you up there in the comfort that befits your state, my lord."

The wizard smiled and shook his head. "Others could use the space there better than I," he excused himself. "And in any case, I shall be departing soon. As long as there is a spare bunk in the Guards' quarters, I shall have a home."

The Chancellor studied him curiously for a long moment. "You're an odd bird," he said finally, without resentment. "But have it as you will. And if you ever get tired of your gypsy existence, the offer will always stand. The quarrel between us has wasted your talents, my lord. I can only ask your leave to make restitution."

"There is no leave," Ingold said, "nor restitution. The quarrel is forgotten."

Chancellor Alwir, Regent of the Realm and Lord of the Keep of Dare, bowed himself from the room.

A moment later the Icefalcon slipped in to give Ingold a cup of the tea he had been brewing. The steam had a curious smell, but it was supposed to prevent colds. It occurred obliquely to Rudy that, although he'd been frozen, wet, half-starved, and nearly dead of exhaustion, at no time had he felt even mildly ill. *Probably there was no time for it,* he decided. *And what I've been through would scare any self-respecting bacteria into extinction.*

"Ingold," Gil said quietly after the Guard had left. "About your going to Quo . . ."

"Yes," the wizard said. "Yes, we shall have to talk about that."

Rudy shifted his position at the foot of the bed. "I don't think you should go alone."

"No?"

"You say it's dangerous as hell—okay. But I think you should take me, or Gil, or one of the Guards, or somebody."

The old man folded his arms and asked detachedly, "You don't believe I can look after myself?"

"After that stunt you pulled last night?"

"Are you volunteering?"

Rudy stopped short, with a quick intake of breath. "You mean—you'd take me?" He couldn't keep the eagerness out of his voice or, to judge by Ingold's expression, off his face. The prospect of going with the old man, no matter what the dangers—of learning from him even the rudiments of wizardry—overshadowed and indeed momentarily obliterated everything he had ever heard or feared regarding White Raiders, ice storms, and the perils of the plains in winter. "You mean I can go with you?"

"I had already considered asking you," Ingold said. "Partly because you are my student and partly due to . . . other considerations. Gil is a Guard—" He reached out to touch her hair in a wordless gesture of affection. "—and the Keep can ill spare any Guard in the months ahead.

254

But you see, Rudy, at the moment you are the only other wizard whom I can trust. Only a wizard can find his way into Quo. If, for some reason, I do not make it as far as Quo, it will be up to you."

Rudy hesitated, shocked. "You mean—I may end up having to find the Archmage?"

"There is that possibility," Ingold admitted. "Especially after what I learned last night."

"But—" He stammered, suddenly awed by that responsibility. The responsibility, he realized, was part of the privilege of being a mage; but still . . . "Look," he said quietly. "I do want to go, Ingold, really. But Gil's right. I am a coward and I am a quitter and if I didn't screw you up or get you into trouble on the way—if I had to find the Council by myself, I might blow it."

Ingold smiled pleasantly. "Not as badly as I would already have blown it by getting myself killed. Don't worry, Rudy. We all do what we must." He took a sip of his tea. "I take it that's settled, then. We shall be leaving as soon as the weather breaks, probably within three days."

Three days, Rudy thought, caught between qualms and excitement. And then, to his horror, he realized that, faced with the chance of continuing his education as a wizard, he had forgotten almost entirely about Minalde.

I can't leave her! he thought, aghast. *Not for the five or six weeks the journey will take!* And yet he knew that there had never been any consciousness of a choice. To go with Ingold, to study wizardry under the old man, was what he wanted—in some ways the only thing he wanted. He had known, far down the road when he had first brought fire to his bidding, that it might lose him the woman he loved; even then he had known that there was no possibility of an alternative course. And yet—how could he explain?

Long ago and in another life, he remembered driving through the night with a scholar in a red Volkswagen, speaking of the only thing that someone wanted to have or be or do. He looked across at her now, at the thin, scarred face with pale schoolmarm eyes, the witchlike straggle of sloppily braided hair. It had been hard for her to leave something she disliked for something she loved. Harder still, he thought, was it to leave something you loved for something you loved more.

Sorely trouble in his mind, he returned his thoughts to

255

what Gil was saying. "So you'll be bunking here until then?"

"I don't take up much room," Ingold remarked, "and I far prefer the company. Besides," he added, picking up his teacup again, "I never have found out who ordered my arrest in Karst. While I don't believe Alwir would put me out of the way as long as he had a use for me, there are cells deep in the bowels of this Keep that are woven with a magic far deeper and stronger and far, far older than my own, cells that I could never escape. The Rune of the Chain is still somewhere in this Keep—in whose possession I cannot tell. As long as I remain in the Keep of Dare, I would really prefer to sleep among my friends."

Rudy's fingers traced idly at the moldy nap of the blanket. "You think it's like that?"

"I don't know," the wizard admitted equably. "And I should hate to find out. The wise man defends himself by never being attacked."

"You call that business last night not being attacked?"

Ingold smiled ruefully. "That was an exception," he apologized, "and unavoidable. I knew that I could draw the Dark away from Tir and hold them off long enough to let you get close to the gates. There weren't very many of them left by that time, too few to split up and still have enough power among themselves to work counterspells against me."

"I don't understand," Gil said, tossing the end of her braid back over her shoulder. "I know there weren't a lot of them—but why did they let us go? They've been following Tir clear the hell down from Karst. They know what the Keep is and they knew last night was their last chance to get at him. But they turned back and went after you. Why?"

He didn't answer at once. He lay watching the curl of the steam rising from the cup in his bandaged hands, his face in repose suddenly old and tired. Then his dark-circled eyes shifted to meet hers. "Do you remember," he said slowly, "when I almost became—lost—in the vaults at Gae? When you called me back from the stairways of the Dark?"

Gil nodded soundlessly; it had been the first day, she remembered, that she had held a sword in her hand. The darkness came back to her, the stealthy sense of lurking fear, the old man standing alone on the steps far below her, listening to a sound that she could not hear, the white radiance of his staff illuminating the shadows all around him. It had been the last day she had been a scholar, an outworlder, the person she had once been. The memory of that distant girl, alone and armed with a borrowed sword and a guttering torch against all the armies of the Dark, brought a lump to her throat that she thought would choke her.

He went on. "I guessed, then, what I know now—that Prince Tir is not their first target. Oh, they'll take him if they can get him—but, given a choice, as I gave them a choice last night, it isn't Tir they want."

"It's me."

"You?" Rudy gasped.

"Yes." The wizard sipped his tea, then set it aside. From beyond the curtain, Gnift's voice bitingly informed someone that he had less stance than a wooden-legged ice skater. "I can evidently be of more ultimate harm to them than Tir can. I suspected it before, and after last night there can be no other explanation."

"But how—I mean—your magic can't touch them," Rudy said uneasily. "To them you're just another guy with a sword. You don't know any more about the Time of the Dark than anybody else. I mean, Tir's the one who'll remember."

"I've wondered about that myself," Ingold said calmly. "And I can only conclude that I know something that I'm not yet aware that I know—some clue that hasn't fallen into place. They know what it is, and they're concerned lest I remember."

Rudy shuddered wholeheartedly. "So what are you going to do?"

The wizard shrugged. "What can I do? Take elementary precautions. But it might be well for you to reconsider your offer to accompany me to Quo."

"To hell with that," Rudy reconsidered. "You're the one who should reconsider."

"Who else can go?" Ingold reasoned. "And if I were afraid of getting myself killed, I should never have taken up this business in the first place. I should have staved in Gettlesand and grown roses and cast horoscopes. No—all that I can do now is stay a few steps ahead of them and

257

hope that I realize what the answer is before they catch me."

"You're crazy," Rudy stated unequivocally.

Ingold smiled. "Really, Rudy, I thought we'd long settled the question of my sanity."

"You're all crazy!" Rudy insisted. "You and Gil and Alde and the Guards . . . How the hell come I always end up completely surrounded by lunatics?"

The old man settled comfortably back among the blankets and picked up his tea again, the steam wreathing his face like smoke from the altar of a battered idol. "The question is the answer, Rudy—always provided you want an answer that badly."

Considering it in that light, Rudy was not entirely sure that he did.

Alde was waiting for him in the outer room. Most of the Guards had gone. Beyond the black, narrow arch of the doorway, Janus' voice could be heard in the next room, still arguing with the same merchants. In a corner, the Icefalcon had fallen asleep, relaxed and self-absorbed as a cat. But for him, they were alone.

"Alde . . ." Rudy began, and she stood up from the bunk where she had been sitting and put a finger to his lips.

"I heard," she said softly.

"Listen . . ." he tried to explain.

Again she shushed him. "Of course you should go with him." Her fingers closed, cool and light, over his. "Was there any question of your not going?"

He laughed softly, remembering his own apprehensions. "I guess—not to me. But I sure didn't think you'd understand." They stood together, as close as they had on the road when they'd been accustomed to share a cloak on watch at night. The ebbing yellow glow of the fire masked them in dim, pulsing shadow, and he could smell the sweetgrass braided into her hair. "I didn't think anybody would understand or could understand. Because I sure as hell don't."

She chuckled with soft laughter. "He's your master, Rudy," she said. "And your need is to learn. Even if I wanted to, I could never stop you from it." But she moved closer to him in the shadows, belying her own words.

We all have our priorities, Rudy thought, and brushed

aside the dark silk of her hair to kiss her lips. *If it came to a choice between me and Tir, I know damn well who'd get left out in the cold.* She, too, had her choices between loves.

The embers in the hearth whispered a little and collapsed in on themselves, sending up a spurt of yellow flame and almost immediately cloaking them both in deeper shadow. From outside the room, the constant murmur of voices from the hall beyond came to them like the mingling of a stream. Rudy was finding already that he had grown used to the Keep, the noises, the shadows, the smells. He could feel the weight of that mountain of stone pressing down around them, as it had pressed for thousands of years. But as he kissed her again, holding her slenderness tight against him, he reflected that there was a great deal to be said for stillness and silence and love without fear.

Her breath a whisper against his lips, she murmured, "I understand, Rudy—but I will miss you."

His arm tightened convulsively about her shoulders. Scraps of conversations drifted back to his memory, things said in Karst and in the night camps all down that perilous road. She had lost the world she had known and everyone in it she had loved, except her son. And now he, Rudy, was leaving her, too. Yet she hadn't said, *Don't go.*

What kind of love, he wondered, understood that need and tried to make easier the separation it would cause?

None that he'd ever run into.

Alde, you're a lady in a million. I wish to hell you weren't the Queen. I almost wish I weren't going back, or that I could take you and Tir back with me when I go.

But either course was impossible.

As she slipped away from him, gathering her cloak about her shoulders as she vanished through the darkness of the far doorway, it occurred to him that she hadn't even asked him that other thing—*Will you miss me, too?*

Against the blurred gleam that backed the grimy door curtain, Gil watched the shadows of man and woman embrace, meld, and separate. In the stillness of the room, she heard Ingold sigh. "Poor child," he said softly. "Poor child."

She glanced across at him, invisible but for the glitter

259

of his eyes in the darkness and his bandaged hands folded on his breast. "Ingold?"

"Yes, my dear?"

"Do you really believe there's no such thing as coincidence?"

The question didn't seem to surprise him, but then, few things did. Gil had known people—her mother, for one—who would have replied, "What a question to ask at a time like this!" But it was a question that could be asked only at such times, when all the daylight trivialities had been put aside, and there was only the understanding of people who knew one another well.

Ingold gave it some thought, and said at last, "Yes. I believe that nothing happens randomly, that there is no such thing as chance. How could there be?" There was a faint squeaking rustle as he settled himself back against the sacks of fodder. "Why do you ask?"

"Well, " Gil said uncertainly. "I think I understand that Rudy came here to—to be a wizard, to find that for himself—because he was born one. But I wasn't. And if there are no such things as random events, why am I here? Why me and not somebody else? Why was I taken away, why did I lose everything I had—scholarship and friends and —and life, really, the life I had? I don't understand."

Ingold's voice was grave in the darkness, and she saw the faint touch of light on his cheekbone as he turned his head. "You once accused me of dealing, magelike, in double talk. But truly, Gil, I do not know. I do not understand any more than you do. But I believe there is a purpose to your being here. Believe me, Gil. Please believe me."

She shrugged, embarrassed as she always was by anyone's concern. "It's not important," she lied, and she knew Ingold heard the lie. "You know, I resented it like hell when you told me Rudy would be a wizard. Not because I wanted to be one, but—it's as if he's gained everything and lost nothing, because he really had nothing that he cared about to lose. But I lost everything . . ." She broke off, the silence coming between them like the ocean between a swimmer and the shore.

"And gained nothing?" To that she could not reply. "It may be that it is not Rudy's purposes that are being served at all by his coming here. Rudy is a mage, and the Realm, the world, is suddenly in desperate need of mages. And it may be that in the months to come, the Keep will have as great a need for a woman with the courage of a lion, trained in the use of a sword."

"Maybe." Gil rested her chin on her drawn-up knees and stared through the darkness at the dim reflections of the embers on the wall, like a streak of false dawn in the night of the Keep. "But I'm not a warrior, Ingold. I'm a scholar. It's all I ever have been and all I've ever wanted to be."

"Who can say what you are, my child?" Ingold asked softly. "Or what you may be eventually? Come," he said, as the voices outside rose in volume. "The Guards are back. Let us go out."

The Guards were trooping back into the room when Gil and Ingold came quietly through the curtain, the wizard leaning heavily on her shoulder. The Guards greeted him with boisterous delight, Janus all but dragging him off his feet, hauling him into the circle of the new firelight. The rose and topaz hearth-glow picked out the shabbiness of the wizard's patched robe and the lines and hollows of strain in his face. It flickered in a warm amber radiance over scarred faces, frayed black surcoats with their white quatrefoil emblem, and seedy old blankets making shift as cloaks. The finest fighting corps in the West of this world, she thought, huddling around a scratch fire like tramps in a boxcar. Her brothers in arms. People a month ago she hadn't even known.

Yet their faces were so familiar. Janus' blunt, square mug she'd seen, nameless, for the first time by the cold light of a quarter moon in a frightful dream whose memory was clearer to her than the memory of many college parties she'd attended. And those white braids draped over a sleeper's anonymous shoulders—she remembered them, briefly, from that same dream, remembered wondering if their owner was the foreigner he looked to be. They had been nothing to her then—extras in a drama whose significance she had not grasped. Yet she knew them now better than she had known any of her otherworld lovers—better, with one exception, than she had ever known anyone in her life.

Ingold was sitting near the hearth at the head of the Icefalcon's bed, the Guards around him, his gestures expansive, relating some story that made Janus throw back his head with laughter.

A voice spoke at Gil's elbow. "Well, he's alive, anyway."

She looked over and saw Rudy leaning against the wall on the other side of the curtained arch. His long hair was tied back, and that and the firelight made his rather aquiline face more hawklike than ever in the dim orange light. He had changed, she thought, since that night he had called the fire. Older, maybe. And not so much different as more like himself than he had been before.

"I'm worried about him, Rudy."

"He's tough," Rudy said, though his tone was uneasy. "He'll be okay. Hell, he'll probably outlive thee and me." But he knew that this was not what she meant.

"What if he gets killed, Rudy?" Gil asked softly. "What happens to us then?"

He had turned his mind away from that thought time and time again, since the night in Karst when Ingold had disappeared, imprisoned by order of the council. He whispered, "Hell, I don't know."

"That's what bothers me," Gil went on, hooking her bony hands with their nicks and scars and practice-blisters through the beat-up leather of her sword belt. "That's what's bothered me all the way along. That maybe there's no going back."

The question is the answer, Rudy thought. *The question is always the answer.* "But there's no going back from anything we do," he said. "Not from anything we are. It changes us, good and bad. What it is, we become. If we're stuck, we're stuck. Would that be so bad? I've found my power here, Gil, what I've always been looking for. And a lady in ten million. And you . . ."

"A home," Gil said simply, realizing the truth. "What I've always been looking for."

And suddenly, unexpectedly, Gil began to laugh. Not hysterically, or nervously, but with a soft, wholehearted chuckle of genuine amusement. Rudy could not remember ever seeing her laugh. It darkened her frost-gray eyes to blue and softened the bony hardness of her white face.

"And my advisor will love it." She grinned up at him. "What a Ph.D. thesis! 'Effects of Subterranean Incursions on Preindustrial Culture.'"

"I'm not kidding," Rudy protested, still astonished at

262

how changed she was, how beautiful, scars and swords and all.

"Neither am I." And she laughed again.

Rudy shook his head, amazed at the difference in her. "So tell me truthfully," he said. "Would you go back from this? If it was a choice between the other world and what you have and where you are now, and if this had all never been—would you go back?"

Gil looked at him consideringly for a moment. Then she turned her eyes back to the hearth, to Ingold, his warm, rasping voice holding his listeners enspelled, to the firelight on the faces of the Guards and the blackness of the shadows beyond, and, past that, to the dark weight of the Keep, the night it held within its walls, and the shifting, wind-stirred night that waited outside. "No," she said finally. "I think I must be crazy to say so, but no, I wouldn't."

"Lady." Rudy grinned, touching the emblem of the Guards she bore on her shoulder. "If you weren't crazy, you wouldn't be wearng that."

Gil looked him speculatively up and down. "You know, for a punk you have a lot of class."

"For a spook," Rudy said gravely, "it's real perceptive of you to notice."

The two of them went to join Ingold by the fire.

About the Author

At various times in her life, Barbara Hambly has been a high-school teacher, a model, a waitress, a technical editor, a professional graduate student, an all-night clerk at a liquor store, and a karate instructor. Born in San Diego, she grew up in Southern California, with the exception of one high-school semester spent in New South Wales, Australia. Her interest in fantasy began with reading *The Wizard of Oz* at an early age and has continued ever since.

She attended the University of California, Riverside, specializing in medieval history. In connection with this, she spent a year at the University of Bordeaux in the south of France and worked as a teaching and research assistant at UC Riverside, eventually earning a Master's Degree in the subject. At the university, she also became involved in karate, making Black Belt in 1978 and competing in several national-level tournaments. She now lives in Los Angeles, California.